P9-DSZ-341

SEPTEMBER

STRIKE

SEPTEMBER STRIKE

Ward Tanneberg

VICTOR BOOKS

A DIVISION OF SCRIPTURE PRESS PUBLICATIONS INC.
USA CANADA ENGLAND

Copyediting: Carole Streeter; Barbara Williams
Design: Paul Higdon
Cover Illustration: Tom Galasinski

Library of Congress Cataloging-in-Publication Data
Tanneberg, Ward M.
    September strike / by Ward Tanneberg.
        p.   cm.
    ISBN 1-56476-339-0
    1. Marriage—United States—Fiction. 2. Clergy—United
    States—Fiction. 3. Terrorism—Israel—Fiction. I. Title.
PS3570.A535S45   1994
813'.54—dc20   94-4346
                                                                    CIP

© 1994 by Victor Books/Scripture Press, Inc. All rights reserved.
Printed in the United States of America.

   2   3   4   5   6   7   8   9   10   Printing/Year   98   97   96   95   94

This book is a work of fiction. Names, characters, places, and incidents are either the product of the author's imagination or are
used fictitiously. Any resemblance to actual events or locales or
persons, living or dead, is entirely coincidental.

No part of this book may be reproduced without written permis-
sion, except for brief quotations and critical reviews.
For information, write Victor Books, 1825 College Avenue,
Wheaton, Illinois 60187.

This One
Is Dedicated
to
Dixie

Acknowledgments

There are several people to whom I am indebted. My friend and fellow writer, Ken Jones, who encouraged me at the beginning of this project. Ken Moore, private investigator and nationally known airport and industrial security expert, shared insights that were most helpful. Then there were the television news personnel who helped to uncover the mysteries of the media process.

Carole Streeter has given liberally of her professional expertise in editing. Greg Clouse, editorial director of Victor Books, has been a faithful encourager and advocate. I am grateful to them both. My friend and able assistant, Linda Lenz, helped in so many ways that only another person involved in manuscript preparation can truly appreciate her contribution.

There are others who remain nameless. Among them, the many members and friends in the church that I serve. They are special people.

Finally, my gratitude to the one whose role as wife and best friend keeps her in the unenviable position of putting up with the many plots and preoccupations that she finds stacked in all the corners of our lives.

WT

Cast of Key Characters

In Canada and California

- Carl Deeker, ranger at Goat's Head Ranger Station, Montana
- Akmed el Hussein, leader of Terrorist Team 1
- Aziza, terrorist
- Ihab Akazzam, terrorist
- Mousa Ekrori, terrorist
- Mamdouh Ekrori, terrorist

In New England

- Jim "Grandpa" Brainard, innkeeper
- Marwan Dosha, leader of Terrorist Team 2
- Mohammed Ali Atta (alias Robert Jibril), member of Terrorist Team 2
- Safwat Najjir, terrorist
- Yusif Shenuda, terrorist
- Rosa Posadas, housemaid

In California

- Esther Cain, senior pastor's wife
- Jeremy Cain, the Cains' seventeen-year-old son
- Jody Ansel, KFOR assistant news director

- Tom Bernstein, KFOR news anchor
- Connie Farrer, KFOR news reporter
- Philip and Sherri Heiden, church members
- Sidney Orwell, the doctor
- Helen Orwell, the doctor's wife
- Allison Orwell, their daughter
- Ken Ralsten, local attorney & church board member
- Elizabeth Ralsten, the attorney's wife
- Geoff Ralsten, their son
- Sarah, Geoff's girlfriend
- Joe Randle, lieutenant, Baytown Police Department
- Duane Webber, Special Agent-in-Charge, FBI

In California & Israel

- John Cain, senior pastor, Calvary Church in Baytown
- Jessica Cain, the Cains' twelve-year-old daughter
- Edgar Anderson, tour group member
- Gisele Eiderman, tour group member
- Bob Thomas, tour group member
- Yazib Dudori, leader of Terrorist Team 3
- Fathi Adahlah, terrorist
- Pasha Bashera, terrorist
- Imad Safti, terrorist
- Islamic Jihad, a radical Palestine restoration organization

▼▼▼

We didn't make the alcohol, but our highways have drunk drivers. We don't sell drugs, but our neighborhoods have those who do. We didn't create international tension, but we have to fear the terrorists. We didn't train the thieves, but each of us is a potential victim of their greed. We are tiptoeing through a minefield which we didn't create.

— *Max Lucado,* And the Angels Were Silent
(Multnomah, © 1992 by Max Lucado)

I have told you these things, so that in Me you may have peace. In this world you will have trouble. But take heart! I have overcome the world.

— The Bible, *John 16:33*

▲▲▲

Prologue

....

Hafez Tabatai leaned back in his chair and scratched his ample belly. He squinted at the other two through smoke curling up from a homemade cigarette that dangled from wet lips. The room was cold, but he seemed oblivious to the lack of heat as well as to the ashes that threatened to drop from the cigarette onto his lap.

The three sat around a table covered with randomly scattered papers and the remains of an earlier meal. A single light bulb, covered with dust, hung down on a long cord over the table, producing what light there was in their dismal meeting place. From the far side of the room, a mangy orange and black cat padded slowly across the ancient stone floor. Tabatai kicked at it with his foot. The cat meowed and quickly retreated to a dark corner.

No one spoke. Smoke swirled in the dim light.

Suddenly, Tabatai leaned forward, cursed, and sent the papers flying off the table with an angry sweep of his arm.

"What are you doing?" exclaimed Mahmoud Assad, leaping forward in a vain attempt to catch the papers before they dropped on the filthy stone floor.

There is nothing here!" Tabatai emphasized his disdain by spitting through tobacco-stained teeth at the papers. "These plans are good for nothing. They are the dreams of incompetent women! Blow up this building. . . . Kidnap that person. The world has become jaded by these inept operations. The New York Trade Center. A miserable fiasco carried off by fools! They deserved to be caught! The only thing it accomplished was to tighten U.S. security and make it more difficult than ever for the rest of us. Then Arafat tears out the souls of our people by his secret agreements with the Jews. He thinks that he speaks for the Palestinians. Instead, he betrays us! He speaks only for himself!"

He shifted his bulk in the chair. "Such tactics are no longer adequate. Routine terrorism is not enough. We must do something so astonishing, so unusual, so attention-getting, that the media will fall over themselves to declare our desires to the world. The American infidels are the key. They must be pushed to the edge. Only they can bring the Jews to heel. Until that happens, we have nothing. All we have are children's games. There has to be something we can do that will wake up the world!"

"You are right, of course." Assad sighed, getting up from his chair. "What we need is an atom bomb. Unfortunately, we are no closer to possessing one than we were ten years ago. Maybe we should kill Arafat. That would remind the world that we are still here!"

The third man had been silent through Tabatai's outburst, his face partly hidden in the shadows. Now he leaned forward until his features could be seen in the light. A handsome face. Dark hair. Piercing brown eyes. His beard did not entirely cover the knife scar running from cheek to ear, a reminder of hand-to-hand fighting with three cellmates almost five years earlier. Women found his looks appealing in a dangerous sort of way. They were drawn to him and fearful at the same time.

Marwan Dosha, the most wanted terrorist in the world, folded his hands on the table and looked first at Assad, then at Tabatai.

"I have a plan," he said quietly. He stared into each man's eyes for a long, silent moment. "If we are successful, it will be much better than dropping an atom bomb. And we will not have to kill Arafat. Others will do it for us when we have finished!"

I

▼▼▼

Our battle with the Jews is long and dangerous, requiring all dedicated efforts. It is a phase which must be followed by succeeding phases, a battalion which must be supported by battalion after battalion of the divided Arab and Islamic world until the enemy is overcome, and the victory of Allah descends.

— *from the Introduction to the* Charter of Hamas

Nay, we hurl the truth against falsehood, and it knocks out its brain, and behold, falsehood doth perish!

— The Holy Quran, *Sura 21: Anbiya ':18*

The angel of the Lord also said to [Hagar]:

"You are now with child and you will have a son. You shall name him Ishmael, for the Lord has heard of your misery. He will be a wild donkey of a man; his hand will be against everyone and everyone's hand against him, and he will live in hostility toward all his brothers."

— The Bible, *Genesis 16:11-12*

▲▲▲

ONE

It was dusk when the blue minivan came to a stop alongside the tiny, olive-colored shelter. Park Ranger George McClintock glanced up in time to see the driver's side window slide downward, revealing the dark, handsome face of the person behind the steering wheel. McClintock's memory stored the man's features in an instant, a skill of which he was very proud, the result of years at this kind of work. His eyes darted across the van's interior, taking in the passenger, a striking woman, hair pulled back, eyes hidden behind dark glasses, high cheekbones, silk blouse, and jeans.

In her early twenties, McClintock guessed, returning her smile. *Some looker she is too. What a great way to end the day.*

"Hello. Welcome to Waterton International Park. Hope you've had a pleasant day of travel."

"It's been very nice," the driver answered with a smile.

"Where are you folks from?"

"We're from Toronto, but today we've come from Lethbridge," the man replied.

"Enjoying your vacation?"

"Yes. But, actually, it isn't a vacation. We're on our honeymoon. We were married two weeks ago."

"Well, wonderful. Congratulations to you both."

Wouldn't you know it. The beautiful ones are always taken.

"Staying long in the park?"

"Three or four days," the man answered. "We want to do some rafting. Maybe a little hiking. Nothing too strenuous."

McClintock smiled to himself as he gathered brochures together for these end-of-the-shift visitors to his park. Glancing up again at the attractive couple, his eyes rested for a moment on the woman.

She really is beautiful!

"Okay, this is a map of the area," McClintock said, passing the small handful of printed matter through the shelter window. "That'll be six dollars for the park pass. See here? Camping sites are marked with a tent symbol. Plenty of great hiking trails in every direction. Downtown Waterton is small, but you can get supplies there. Everything you need, really. Good restaurants too. Some motels, but rooms are scarce. At this hour of the day a room may be hard to come by, unless you already have a reservation. I expect you'll see a few wild goats and deer in town too. Leave them alone, though. Don't ruin your honeymoon by getting too friendly with the animals."

The man handed McClintock the exact amount.

As the vehicle pulled away, McClintock observed camping gear stacked behind the driver's seat. He made a mental note of the inflated raft tied to the van rooftop and the vehicle's Province of Ontario license plate. Actually, not much ever missed McClintock's keen eye. He took pride in the fact that his powers of recall regularly impressed his fellow rangers.

Today, however, he missed something important. He did

not see the four men who lay motionless on their backs beneath the pile of camping gear. Nor did he see the four automatic weapons tucked between them, barrels pointing directly at the shelter in which he was standing.

THE VAN CONTINUED UP THE ROAD leading past the Prince of Wales Hotel. The venerable old inn stood on its high hill as it had for so many years, a solitary wooden monarch, reigning over the tiny village and lake below. High mountain peaks, still capped with last season's snow, embraced the lake in surrealistic beauty. Rays from the late afternoon sun ricocheted off the towering slopes, bursting in fiery dances of daylight against the hotel's immense lobby windows.

Couples strolling across the grassy knoll in front of the hotel now and then brushed at pesky mosquitoes. Children laughed with delight as gray squirrels raced along their well-traveled miniature highways. At the bottom of the hill, encased in this bowl of majestic mountains, Waterton Lake was turning from green to dark blue.

Akmed el Hussein drove slowly until they reached the bottom of the hill, then turned left onto a narrow, paved road that passed several camping sites. He had visited the area in July, so the twists and turns of the road were familiar, as he guided the van along the lakeshore. They drove in silence for several miles, keeping an eye on the side mirrors. There did not appear to be any other vehicles on the road. During his July visit, Akmed had carefully researched the habits of the locals and their summer guests along this particular stretch. He'd observed that most people were in the main camping sites by this time of day. That was perfect.

Eventually, they came to a small parking area situated at the water's edge. They had met no other autos along the way and this parking site was empty. It was nearly dark as they came to a stop.

Things are as they should be, he thought. *They could not be better. Allah is with us!*

The woman was the first out of the van. Quickly, she opened the sliding side door.

"It's clear," she declared to the pile of camping gear.

Movement. Feet, then legs, and finally, a full-body roll as each man made his exit from the van, standing upright with weapons in hand. They stretched stiff, sore muscles, their backsides aching from lack of exercise and the merciless road-pounding absorbed while lying so long a time in the same position. Still, adrenaline was pumping as they peered into the shroud of semidarkness closing in around them.

"This is the place?" asked one of the men.

"Yes," replied Akmed. "It's the end of the road. From here we take the boat. Now, hurry. We must leave before someone discovers we are here and starts asking questions."

Silently, the men loosened the raft from the van's roof-top, carried it to the shore, and dropped it onto the dark, watery surface. With well-choreographed movements disclosing no wasted motion, they moved quickly to complete their assignments.

Mousa Ekrori grasped the rope attached to the raft and wrapped it securely around a large rock to keep it from drifting away. His younger brother, Mamdouh, put the outboard motor in place while Ihab Akazzam attached the fuel tank. Two sets of canoe paddles. Five sleeping bags. A single canvas tarp tightly rolled. Knapsacks filled with enough food for several days' journey. Canteens. Rope. Five automatic weapons. A first-aid kit. Ammunition. Small shovels. Two canvas bags filled with grenades. Five ponchos. Three bags filled with plastic explosives and timing devices. A single copy of the *Quran.*

By the time they finished, total darkness covered every movement. Forming a line, they stepped forward to embrace the fourth man who had earlier hidden beneath the gear stacked inside the van.

"Allah u Akbar, Ali Shabagh," Akmed declared solemnly. "God is greater. May he give you and us a safe journey."

Ali turned and walked slowly toward the van, gravel crunching beneath his boots. Opening the door, he pulled himself up into the driver's seat. For a brief moment, the dome light illuminated his face, once again reminding the others of how easily he could be mistaken for Akmed el Hussein. That, of course, was the whole idea. They had thought of everything, even the possibility that if the van and driver were observed leaving the park, no one would give it a second thought. People drove out and returned every day.

"I wish that I was going with you," Ali said wistfully.

"I know," replied Akmed.

Ali started the engine. The others watched in silence as the van backed away from the water's edge and turned toward the road over which they had traveled less than an hour before.

"May Allah go with you," Ali called out softly, signaling farewell to his friends with a wave of his hand. The van rolled away, slowly at first. Then, gathering speed, it soon disappeared.

It was quiet . . . the awesome quiet of the wilderness at night.

They stood staring into the darkness, each person dealing with a sudden unexpected feeling of abandonment. For the past several hours, their close proximity in the van had given them a sense of security. Now that feeling, however false it had been, was gone. The only human sound to be heard was their own breathing, together with the noise of the van retreating in the distance.

Then gradually, their ears tuned to other sounds. Nearby crickets played nature's nightly symphony and frogs croaked their throaty applause. A cool breeze pushed wavelets against the shore. Finally, someone's feet shuffled in the gravel, breaking their momentary reverie.

"Get in," Akmed commanded, turning his attention to their task. One by one, the men stepped into the raft, followed by the woman. Akmed removed the rope from around the stone anchor. With one smooth motion, he pushed the raft free and jumped aboard. For a few moments they drifted, straining to hear any sounds that would denote danger. Fifty feet. A hundred feet away from the lake's edge. Mamdouh huddled over the engine, double-checking to be sure its clamps were secure. Akmed raised a clenched fist, making a silent, forward motion. With a practiced turn, Mamdouh manipulated the starter. It instantly sprang into life, pushing the craft forward on the next leg of their journey.

The boat moved steadily now as Akmed's gaze followed the darkened outline of the mountains surrounding the lake. He recalled the soul-subduing awe he had felt during his July scouting visit. The regal combination of water and mountain and sky had overwhelmed his senses. On the day he boarded one of the several tourist vessels that regularly traversed the lake each summer, he had been apprehensive. It was crowded with people he did not know. He felt vulnerable standing shoulder to shoulder with all these strangers. Soon, however, he forgot himself and his concerns. There was nothing like this in his homeland. Frigid, ice-blue mountain water. Tall, stately evergreens. Azure blue skies. Even Switzerland did not offer a more majestic panorama than this.

"Somewhere out there, a swath is cut through the forest," he announced to his disciples, above the steady drone of the engine. Pointing to his left, he continued, "It comes straight down that mountain to the water's edge, disappears, then rises on the opposite side of the lake, continuing to the west. If we were traveling in the daylight, we would easily see it."

Each member of the group followed his gaze into the

darkness, trying to imagine this unnatural phenomenon. To-night, however, the swath was invisible to the "honeymoon couple" and their three companions.

Invisible, but nonetheless real.

The line, cut through tall forests of douglas fir and birch, is a benchmark of international accomplishment. It identi-fies a long stretch of unguarded border between two of the world's great nations, Canada and the United States. On one side is the Province of Alberta. On the other, the state of Montana. But for Akmed and his companions, its signifi-cance was hard to measure. For them it was the beginning of the final step toward bringing an unbelieving, unheeding, unholy world to its knees!

ALI SHABAGH SMILED TO HIMSELF as he drove the blue minivan up the road leading past the Prince of Wales Hotel. The old rustic building was well lighted now, its one hundred rooms filled with happy tourists. Before long, he saw the outline of the ranger's shelter at the park entrance. He touched the brakes, slowing down until he observed the headlights of two oncoming cars. As they stopped at the ranger's window, the blue van passed unnoticed, heading in the opposite direction.

It wouldn't have made any difference anyway. Park Ranger George McClintock had been off duty for more than two hours. He was sitting by himself in a small village res-taurant, eating pizza and drinking beer, thinking about the honeymoon couple who had entered the park near the end of his shift. They were undoubtedly enjoying each other in a nearby motel room by this time. Or maybe in a tent at one of the camping sites. He took another sip of his beer as the memory of the man's striking companion flashed across his mind.

Yessir. That's one lucky guy.

THEY WERE MORE THAN A MILE from Goat's Head when they cut the motor. A strong north wind whipped at their backs as Akmed handed a paddle to each of the other three men.

"It's another sign that Allah is with us," Akmed commented as the woman shifted to the front, giving the others room to work. She turned to face them as Akmed continued. "If this wind were coming from the opposite direction, we would have much difficulty. God has provided a wind at our backs tonight. Now it is time to see how well we row together. Aziza, do it the same as we practiced. Count for us to give us the rhythm. And be our eyes to guide us to our destination."

"ONE, two, three, four, ONE, two, three, four, ONE . . . " Aziza called out in a low, clear voice, watching as the men struggled to fit their movements with her cadence. Soon each paddle sliced through the water on the rhythmic count of ONE, propelling their small rubber craft onward with surprising speed.

A full summer moon rose above the mountain peaks. Glancing up now and then, the men could see Aziza's face in the soft moonglow. Her eyes were cool and regal. High cheekbones and a finely shaped nose presented the look of strong beauty. Her lips were full, promising warmth and a touch of the exotic. Reaching back, Aziza untied her hair, letting the movement of the raft and the wind against her face cause it to swirl in constant motion, at once covering and then unveiling her eyes. All the while, she continued calling softly, "ONE, two, three, four . . . " The men kept their eyes on her and their thoughts to themselves.

PARK RANGER CARL DEEKER lay quietly, staring at ceiling shadows broken by a narrow shaft of moonlight leaking through the unwashed window above the bed.

Listening.

Deeker was a sound sleeper. After dinner he had read a while before going to bed. Then, in the middle of the night, he was suddenly wide awake. He'd heard something. What? Then it came to him again. The unmistakable sound of an outboard motor.

What's going on? he muttered to himself. *No one travels on the lake this late at night.*

He continued staring up into the darkened rafters of his cabin.

Could be a lost fisherman, I suppose. Hard to say. But someone's out there, that's for sure. He rolled over, reached for his wristwatch and held it up until he could make out the time in the moonlight.

One-twenty.

Deeker sat up, rubbing his eyes, continuing to listen for unusual sounds. Getting to his feet, he pulled on his pants, grabbed his jacket from the hook by the bed, opened the cabin door, and walked outside.

Now he watched and waited.

The day had been unusually warm for September, filled with tourists who came to him stuffed onto passenger boats. Nothing unusual. Maybe more visitors than normal for this late in the season, but otherwise just another summer's day at Goat's Head. People disembarking, spending anywhere from a few minutes to a few hours on shore, then returning to the vessels and back to "civilization."

Ranger Deeker lectured each group regarding the flora and fauna of the forest, encouraging them to take lots of pictures, answering silly questions, and sending them on their way with a friendly wave. Visitors always took pictures of one another in front of the large Rotary Club emblem that honored members of this worldwide service organization from both Canada and the United States. And they asked the inevitable question: Why a Rotary emblem way out here in the wilderness? The visitors' center and the emblem had been placed there through private donations, Deeker told them, as a symbol of goodwill and peace between the two nations.

The stiff breeze clawed at the collar of his uniform jacket, reminding him that he was still in the north woods and not in sunny Arizona, where he liked to spend the winter.

He kept his attention on the lake.

Nothing. No sound of a motor. Nothing moving either.

Deeker reached back through the door for his boots. Balancing against the porch railing, he pulled on first one, then the other. Moving to the edge of the porch, he stepped off, starting down the path leading to the passenger boat dock, about two hundred yards away.

He stopped again.

Listen.

Deeker strained to pick up an abnormal sound.

Thought I heard something.

He took another step forward, then stopped abruptly.

He saw it now, coming out of the darkness, moving rapidly toward the shore in the direction of the dock.

A raft . . . Must have had some engine trouble. Or maybe they ran out of gas. Can't make out how many there are, but there's at least two of them rowing.

He started down the trail, then hesitated, remembering that he'd left his flashlight on the lamp stand by his bed.

The moon is out, he reasoned, resuming his stroll. *I won't need a flashlight tonight.*

Deeker was still a hundred yards from the dock when the raft ran onto the gravel beach at Goat's Head.

AZIZA LEAPED TO SHORE, rope in hand, holding the raft steady until the men could get out. They went to work quickly, without a word. Akmed helped Aziza pull the raft farther up on the beach. Just as they had rehearsed many times before, each individual became responsible for specific parts of the equipment. Knapsacks, rope, sleeping bags. Automatic weapons, bags of grenades, and plastics. All five worked swiftly, perspiration running in tiny rivulets down their faces.

"What's going on here?"

Whirling about, they saw a dark form standing slightly above them in a clearing where the pebbly beach gave way to the forest.

"Who are you?" the stranger called out again.

Dark shadows from the tall boat-dock timbers partially hid the raft from his view. Akmed saw a man walking toward them, trying to get a better look. His mind raced as he tried to decide what to do.

We must have awakened a ranger. Does he have any idea what we are doing?

He looked around quickly.

The guns were out of the ranger's line of vision, on rocks near one of the pilings. Everything else looked innocent enough.

"We were headed up the lake to go camping and fishing when our motor stopped," Akmed called out. "We tried to get it going again, but haven't succeeded. We aren't sure what's the matter. Plenty of gas. But something's wrong. Where are we, anyway?"

"Goat's Head Ranger Station," Deeker answered, now well out onto the beach and walking straight toward the men. "I'm Ranger Carl Deeker. Glad to meet you."

As Deeker came toward him, Akmed tensed.

Then, in back of the ranger, a dark figure stepped from beneath the boat dock.

"Ranger Deeker?"

Deeker slipped on the gravel as he turned, startled at hearing his name called from behind him, and doubly surprised that it was not a man's voice.

She walked toward him slowly. His eyes widened as her face became visible in the moonlight.

She's beautiful!

"Ranger Deeker, my name is Aziza."

He remained spellbound as she smiled, continuing forward until she stood near him. As he stared into her eyes, a sudden twinge of danger flashed across his mind. They were as cold as they were beautiful. She returned his stare and took one final step. He felt her body press against him.

No.

Not against him.

Into him!

Her smile faded, lips parting slightly. Her face was only inches from his own, her eyes still locked with his, as the long, thin blade slipped under Deeker's rib cage, slicing cleanly into the left ventricle of his heart. Before he could react, the woman pulled the knife from its wound. With her free hand, she pushed him off balance onto his knees. Slowly, he pitched over on his right shoulder.

"Why?" he asked, coughing first, then a long groan, as sensors everywhere in his body began darting madly about, quickly reaching an unbearable crescendo of pain. Rolling in fetal fashion, he looked up at the woman.

"What are you doing here?"

Blood spread between his fingers now, staining his jacket a reddish brown. The darkness of death enveloped him slowly, like a cold blanket.

No one spoke.

His final question remained unanswered, carried away on the night sounds of still another cricket symphony, lost in the noisy applause of frogs.

Then there was nothing.

Carl Deeker, veteran park ranger, would not be going to Arizona this winter.

FOR A LONG MOMENT, NO ONE MOVED. Each person stared silently at the body in front of them. Then Akmed walked over to where he lay. Reaching down, he felt for the man's pulse.

"He's dead."

Ihab shuffled, letting out a sigh of relief.

"Come on," Akmed commanded, his voice filled with urgency. "Help me wrap him in the tent canvas. Quickly, before his blood stains the beach. And quietly! There may be another ranger around. He can't be left here or we'll be followed. We must take his body with us. We'll dispose of it somewhere along the trail."

Listening to Akmed, Aziza was suddenly struck with an absurd awareness of dissimilar pronouns. *How quickly we change our thinking from "him" to "it,"* she mused, forcing some distasteful bile to return to her stomach.

Akmed and Ihab spread the canvas, intended for use later as shelter if they encountered bad weather. They placed Deeker on it, then wrapped it around his still form.

"There's blood on these rocks," said Aziza, now on her knees with a flashlight, carefully examining the killing area.

"Get some lake water and take care of it," responded Akmed. "There must be no trace of us having been here tonight. We've wasted precious time as it is. Let's gather our things and be off."

The five set about shouldering their gear. Each knew exactly what to carry. The two brothers, Mousa and Mamdouh, punctured the raft in several places, releasing the air. They then folded the bulky remains as best they could between them in order to carry it into the forest. Nothing must be left behind to indicate their presence here.

Akmed and Ihab picked up the canvas-wrapped body. They walked from the beach up the steps leading past the Rotary International Peace Park Memorial. From there, they spotted the trail leading inland.

Aziza paused in front of the famous Rotary wheel, adjusting the straps on her heavy pack. There was enough moonlight to enable her to read the motto printed alongside the wheel:

Is it the TRUTH? Is it FAIR to all concerned?
Will it build GOOD WILL and BETTER RELATIONSHIPS?
Will it be BENEFICIAL to all concerned?

"You did what you had to do, Aziza," comforted Akmed, observing the downcast look frozen on her face. He had seen such looks before on faces in Gaza and in the Old City. "Our brothers at home will be proud when they hear of your heroism."

Heroism?

She reached for her thermos, opened it and drank two short swallows of water to help settle her stomach.

I was prepared from the start to kill on this mission. Even to be killed. But not tonight. Not the minute we crossed into America. This is not a good omen. Besides, how much heroism is there in taking out an unarmed man?

Aziza sighed.

There will be more killing before we're done. We ourselves will likely be among those falling in death.

With a final look around, she joined the others as they walked into some of America's most difficult terrain, the rugged mountains of Montana's Glacier National Park.

The remainder of the night passed uneventfully. They were all in superb condition, having spent the summer working out at various health clubs in Toronto. Long, daily jogs through that city's many beautiful parks had honed their stamina and hardened their bodies. Still, given the unexpected encounter with the ranger and the steepness of the trail, progress was slow. On several occasions, they stopped to rest and regain their strength. There was little conversation. Talking required energy and every ounce of energy was needed for the task.

Early in the morning, as dawn's first light began to penetrate the forest, the team veered about a hundred yards off the trail. Deep in tall evergreens and thick foliage, they covered the boat's remains with tree limbs and underbrush. A shallow grave was prepared. Mousa and Mamdouh removed the ranger's body from its canvas blanket. With callous insensitivity, they dropped it near what would be the final resting place for a human being who had come in unsuspecting friendship to his enemies. The men stopped to catch their breath.

Aziza felt a hollow sadness as Akmed pushed the remains of their mission's first American casualty into the grave. Troubled by her feelings, she turned away as the others threw dirt on the lifeless form. Rocks and dead branches were placed over the red dirt. Standing a few feet away, she overheard them agreeing among themselves that no one would ever see it.

Suddenly Akmed was beside her, reading her thoughts as he touched her shoulder. He spoke softly, but firmly.

"There will be more, Aziza. Many more. This one is only the first. But you knew this when you volunteered."

Aziza stared at the ground, moving the dirt with her toe in a circular fashion.

Yes. But that was a long time ago. A different time and far away.

"Allah has honored you with first blood. I am proud of you," Akmed continued reassuringly, watching her carefully.

Actually, he had questioned the wisdom of bringing an untested woman on a mission of such great importance. His superiors, however, had insisted. A woman was essential. And she must be beautiful. Americans were easily won over by feminine beauty. It would seem that their wisdom had been confirmed. Aziza was, indeed, temptingly beautiful.

And she had acted swiftly and skillfully in order to save them.

They made their way back to the trail, careful to leave no trace. Free of the extra burden, they reorganized their packs while devouring small loaves of bread and cheese, purchased fresh the morning before in Lethbridge. At about seven forty-five, they started out. A steady pace was going to be necessary if they were to reach their American rendezvous on schedule.

FORTY-EIGHT HOURS LATER, dense clouds covered Glacier National Park's high mountain country. Visitors remained inside Many Glacier Lodge, huddled around the great fireplace, warming their hands with steaming cups of coffee and hot chocolate. Some wandered through the souvenir center, examining Indian jewelry or thumbing idly through last month's magazine selections. They sadly agreed with each other that the season was nearing an end. Winter did not seem far off today; it was cold and too wet for hiking any of the trails. Through the large windows, the guests watched as raindrops splashed into Swiftcurrent Lake with increasing intensity. Even in this downpour, the September travelers grudgingly agreed that this was still one of the world's most beautiful sights.

Outside in the public parking area, a man wandered slowly among scores of vehicles sporting license plates from several states and provinces. He was dressed in hiking boots, pants that obviously needed to visit a laundromat, and a water-repellent parka. He slouched to keep the rain out of his face, at the same time carefully noting each plate as he walked past.

He turned his face away as a charter bus passed, its driver downshifting and braking while preparing to turn right at the highway entrance.

That's when he saw the vehicle.

Glancing around and seeing no one nearby, the man stepped over a chuckhole filled with water and made his way to a 1991 Chevy van. He looked around again, then reached under the rear bumper, carefully running his fingers along the surface until he felt the keys. Peeling back the tape, he retrieved them from their hiding place. There were two. Quickly, he unlocked the door, opened it, and dropped wearily onto the seat. He inserted the remaining key in the ignition and turned it. The motor started instantly, the gas gauge showing nearly full. Slowly he backed out of the parking stall and drove away in the same direction as the charter bus.

Three miles east, the driver turned off the highway onto a road that was little more than tire tracks through tall grass. When he pulled to a stop, four similarly rain-soaked persons moved out of the brush, surrounding the vehicle. Wearily, they pushed their equipment through the side-door opening. The driver and two of the men crawled in underneath the gear and the tarp and lay on their backs. The remaining man climbed behind the wheel while the woman closed the side door, then pulled herself up and into the passenger seat. They watched both rearview mirrors while backing the van through the undergrowth and out onto the highway. According to the information they had been given, a few miles down the road was another ranger station, this one part of Montana's Glacier Park system.

Sure enough, in about fifteen minutes, they saw it ahead. The van rolled to a stop in front of the small hut in which a female ranger sat reading a paperback novel. The driver acknowledged her with a smile as he held up the Glacier Park tourist pass he had earlier found on the seat. She smiled and waved them through, not wanting to get wet for the sake of a trivial examination of their ticket's date validity. Few people ever tried to cheat the system anyway. The young couple in the van looked honest enough, she reasoned to herself, quickly resuming her novel.

If she had been Waterton Park Ranger George McClintock, she would have recognized the couple as being of Arabic descent. And she would have noticed that the van had California license plates. Even at that, there was no way that she could have understood the implications of this, as the vehicle passed safely through her checkpoint.

Nothing outwardly signaled what was now a stark reality.

Team One was in America!

TWO

John Cain sat in one of the patio chairs, staring listlessly at the object on the bottom of the swimming pool as it completed its aimless meandering. A few minutes later, the hum of the filtering system stopped as well. Complete silence prevailed, broken only by the cooing of a dove perched high overhead in the black pine tree.

The pool sweep is only a machine.

John's rational mind knew that. Yet each time he saw it, its image degenerated into the familiar apparition that constantly lurked in the closets of his imagination. For more than a year now, it had haunted him.

His beloved ghost . . .

. . . "BALL?"

Her eighteen-month-old eyes sparkled at the sight of the ball, all pink and blue and white. It was her favorite. And it was outside on the patio, beyond the screen door.

She looked at it for a while, her face pressed against the

screen. Finally, she stood on her tiptoes, placing a pudgy hand against the metal frame for balance. With the other hand, she reached as high as she could, feeling her fingers touch the shiny brass, half-moon latch. She had watched her mother do it before. Many times. It looked easy. It was easy. She pulled down, the latch released, and the pressure of her hand against the door frame pushed it back.

As she waddled through the opening, bright sunlight caressed her face with a warm welcome. Smiling, she lifted both hands in a child's salute to the sky and walked across the patio toward her ball. Bending over, her outstretched hands almost captured the prize, until her foot accidently pushed it forward out of reach. She paused, watching it roll away.

As quickly as her unreliable feet would take her, she ambled toward the ball, bending once more to pick it up. But the feet she tried so hard to control betrayed her again. This time the ball rolled to the edge of the pool where it fell onto the thermal cover that floated on the water's surface. The cover acted as a water heater on sunlit days and kept the pool from cooling too rapidly during the nights. It was usually in place unless someone decided to go swimming. There were no family plans for swimming today.

She stopped at the water's edge, gazing at the ball. Carefully, she bent forward . . . slowly . . . slowly . . . until she touched it.

"Ball."

She teetered there, bare toes curling around the tile coping along the side of the pool. A happy, innocent smile spread across her face.

"Ball?"

ESTHER LOOKED UP from her casserole preparations for the evening meal. Had she heard something? The stereo played soothingly in the background. A piano concerto by

Mozart. It was the music she loved the best. She hoped that filling their home with beautiful sounds would stimulate Jennifer's taste for good music. Esther had even played Mozart while she was pregnant. Her doctor told her that an unborn child is quite aware of voices and sounds. She wanted this child to love the very best of everything.

"Jenny?"

Esther listened for an answer.

"Jenny?" she called again.

There was no response.

Esther put the mixing spoon down. It was only a moment ago that Jenny had pattered past, outstretched hands brushing against her mother's skirt, heading in the direction of her room. Esther walked through the living room and turned down the hall. The door to Jenny's room was open and her toys were scattered about, a teddy bear turned upside down on its head.

"Jenny, where are you?"

From somewhere deep within, a sudden spasm of fear knifed its way to the surface, alerting all her senses.

Something is wrong!

Esther turned abruptly and began running down the hall.

Through the living room.

Past the kitchen.

Into the family room.

A doll lay twisted in pretzel fashion near John's chair. Her initial fear became a steel sword in her stomach as she looked across the family room. The screen was partially open. She ran to the door, pulled it all the way open, and stepped through.

A quick look.

Oh, thank God. She's not out here either.

Esther let out a sigh of relief.

"Jenny!"

No response.

Then Esther noticed something on the pool cover near the deep end. It was Jenny's ball. In the same instant, she saw fresh water formed on top of the cover. Near the ball. With a cry, she ran to the pool's edge and lifted the cover.

The terrible reality of what she saw slammed all breath from her body.

Esther's peaceful, happy world came crashing down!

Frantically kicking off her shoes, she pulled back the cover and dove in. With one arm she gathered up Jenny's still form. From the floor of the pool, Esther pushed desperately, clawing her way to the surface. Gasping for air, she lifted the child from the water and ran toward the screen door.

"O Jenny, no! Please, God, no! Jenny. Jenny. Jenny!"

With her free hand, Esther flung open the door and rushed inside, placing Jenny's dripping body on the carpeted floor. For a moment she nearly despaired beyond being able to function. With hands trembling, she dialed 911, hysterically giving the operator their address. Then, bending over Jennifer's lifeless body she breathed into her mouth, trying to remember the CPR technique she had learned several years earlier at a clinic sponsored by the local fire department. She felt awkward, inadequate, as she worked desperately to resuscitate the tiny form beneath her. A growing sense of hopelessness crowded its way into her mind until she wanted to scream.

Am I doing the right thing? Come on, Jenny. O, God, help me, please! Please . . . Jenny . . .

The rescue team found them there, Esther's tears bathing Jenny's pale, silent face. Gently, but firmly, they pulled her away.

JOHN LIFTED HIS FOOT from the accelerator, touching the brake, and adjusting the turn signal as he prepared to turn left onto Jefferson Drive.

I'm fifteen minutes late already for dinner. And the leader-ship training meeting begins at seven.

He would have barely an hour to eat, talk with Esther, play with Jennifer, and say hello to Jessica and Jeremy before returning to the church conference room.

I hate days like this. Too little time for the family. None for myself.

Rounding the corner, he saw the flashing lights of the rescue unit. In the next instant, he realized that it was parked in front of his house.

There was a brief hesitation while John's brain reshuffled from preoccupation with the training meeting to the scene before him. Then, pushing the accelerator to the floor, he raced the rest of the way down Jefferson Drive and skidded to a stop in his driveway. John threw open the car door and ran toward the house. His heart sank when he saw that the front door was open wide.

"Esther!"

He rushed through the entrance.

"Esther! Are you all right? What is happening here?"

As he turned toward the family room, John saw Esther slumped on the couch, a vacant stare on her drawn, pale face. His eyes took in two men in blue uniforms kneeling on the floor. Oxygen equipment. A medical bag. The patio screen door ajar. Then he saw her little feet, bare, protruding out from beneath one of the men in blue.

"O Lord, no. Not Jenny. Not our beautiful little Jenny!"

Invisible hands tore at his stomach, then hammered his body beyond feeling. The room swayed as one of the men rose, a look of sadness in his eyes.

"I'm sorry," he said. "The little girl is gone."

John Cain heard a low moan coming from the couch. It increased in volume into an elongated, piercing wail. He looked at Esther. Then at Jennifer.

"My dear God," he said again, his voice stricken with disbelief and pain. "What has happened here?"

THE MEMORIAL SERVICE for Jennifer Gloria Cain was conducted the following Saturday at one o'clock. It was held outside, in the sunlight and fresh air that she had loved with such innocent exuberance. They estimated that about seven hundred people were present. A large crowd for such a little girl. But this was the Cains' daughter, and so everyone who could be there was there.

John and Esther sat huddled together in front of the tiny, white coffin. Sixteen-year-old Jeremy and eleven-year-old Jessica stood behind them, hands on their parents' shoulders. Terri White, the children's minister John had called to the church a little more than a year before, was speaking.

"Jennifer has been like a flower to us all. Her innocence, her love of living was blossoming before our very eyes. There were never any strangers in her world. I remember seeing her walk down the hallway last Sunday, hanging onto Esther's finger." Her voice broke as she brushed tears from her eyes with a small, white handkerchief. "I said, 'Hi, Jennifer, honey, what do you say today?' She broke away from her mother and ran the rest of the way to me. 'Jesus loves me' was her answer as she threw herself into my arms."

Sniffles could be heard throughout the gathering of people. Men as well as women were wiping their eyes and staring off into the distance.

"All of us today know just how true that is," Terri continued. "Little Jennifer has discovered the One who loves her more than we can ever know. She is looking down upon us, in this moment of our grief, safe in the loving arms of Jesus."

Terri continued talking a few minutes more, giving words of solace to the little children who were there, watching and listening, clutched in the arms of parents. Mothers and fathers silently, even guiltily, thanked God that this funeral was not for their children. John Cain stared at a spot just beyond the box with its precious treasure. In the grass, a tiny frog croaked and hopped on its erratic journey toward the tall grass a short distance away.

Jennifer would be glad you came. She'd call you "fog" and take you home in her pocket.

John drew back from his reverie in time to hear Terri speaking directly to his family.

"This is a period of sadness for us all, but especially for John and Esther, Jeremy and Jessica. None of us can truly say that we understand your sorrow. Nor can we ever hope to answer all the 'why' questions that must lurk in the recesses of your hearts. But be assured of our love for each one of you. Our prayers are with you. Even if we don't do it well at times, be certain of this—we care and we'll be here for you!"

Turning to the large, silent crowd, she asked them to join her in praying the Lord's Prayer. And words that have brought comfort and hope to millions of Christian believers in every sort of crisis and circumstance were uttered in unison once again.

Our Father in heaven,
hallowed be Your name,
Your kingdom come,
Your will be done
on earth as it is in heaven.
Give us today our daily bread.
Forgive us our debts,
as we also have forgiven
our debtors.
And lead us not into temptation,
but deliver us from the evil one.

For Yours is the kingdom
and the power
and the glory
forever.
Amen.

Hugs and kisses. Awkward condolences. More tears. All received with pasted-on smiles and expressions of thanks designed to make the comforters feel comforted by their pastor and his family, assured by the feeling that somehow their spiritual leader was different in grief than normal people, sustained by some special kind of "super faith" in God...

...JOHN CAIN CONTINUED STARING at the object resting on the bottom of the swimming pool. The dove flew from the tree and was gone.

How often must I relive this? Will life ever be sane again?

Anger churned in his belly. Bitterness. Tongue and lips shaped words that were foreign to their master. Unspoken curses rolled silently down the dark side of pain. Fists at his side clenched tightly, opening, then closing again. Tears filled his eyes and spilled down his cheeks.

Turning away from his beloved ghost, the Reverend John Cain, Creative Dispenser of Divine Inspiration, Tireless Shepherd of God's Flock, Unending Provider of Faith for Today and Hope for Tomorrow, shuffled toward the screen door.

Numb.

Weary.

Broken.

THREE

Mohammed Ali Atta cast off the last line and jumped on board. He made his way quickly to the wheel of the twenty-four-foot cabin cruiser. Both large outboard motors gurgled to life at the first press of the ignition button. With a practiced eye, he guided the boat away from the dock where larger vessels were moored on either side. A handsome man, graying at the temples, was tying down a sailboat a few feet away. Mohammed waved to the young, barefoot girl in shorts and a windbreaker, standing near the boat's single mast. She smiled and waved back.

Where do young families get the money for a boat like that?

Mohammed watched as the man he guessed to be the girl's father deftly looped a rope around the piling. Then, moving the throttle slowly forward, he turned his attention to the task of getting safely beyond the last of the small boats anchored around him. Most sailors were off the sea for the day. The only other vessel going out was the Bay Lady, carrying a load of tourists hoping to catch the sunset and see the seals playing off the tiny island that divided the center of the bay.

Good. The fewer boats around, the better.

Eventually, he cleared the last of the boats anchored nearby. Mohammed opened the throttle, feeling the powerful engines churn as the boat shot across the darkening surface of the water. The steady beat of choppy seas vibrated through his feet and ankles. Clutching the wheel firmly, he bent his knees against the shock of the bigger waves. Hundreds of colorful lobster markers bobbed up and down on whitecapped waves as the evening breeze began to intensify. The sun disappeared behind the trees lining the far shore, causing the early evening air to take on a cold bite.

Pulling his jacket tightly around his neck, Mohammed reached for the fur-lined gloves stashed in the cubby to his left. Balancing the wheel with his knee, he slipped the right one on first, then the left. Leaning back against the captain's chair, his eyes moved swiftly, scanning the seascape all around. No other vessels were visible. The red beacon from the lighthouse on the point gave off its intermittent warning. Mohammed felt his pulse quicken with a first twinge of excitement. He headed straight out to sea.

THE ACHILLE LARISSA, "Larissa's Warrior," took its name from a city of one hundred thousand citizens, located in the eastern Thessalonican region of Greece. For the last several days, the rusty old freighter had plowed through heavy, North Atlantic seas on its way to New York Harbor. The captain and his small crew were tired. Rough weather made long crossings seem even longer. Only one crew member was on duty in the engine room; the others were in their bunks, sleeping. On the bridge, Captain Nicholas Rotis checked the instruments and peered out into the night. Stars were no longer visible. A fog bank had settled on the water, making long-range sightings impossible.

"Drop her to half speed," Rotis ordered the ship's first mate.

"Half speed, cap'n," was the hoarse, deep-throated reply.

Rotis was always amused by his first mate's voice. It reminded him of the sound a rope makes when a ship pulls against it while tied to the dock.

They could feel the freighter settling deeper into the ocean swells. For a full five minutes no one said a word. Both men kept an eye first on the instruments, then on the blackness of the night that enveloped them.

"Quarter speed," Rotis said abruptly. "We have to be close now."

"Quarter speed, cap'n," the first mate answered.

"Slow her till we're almost dead in the water, then hold her steady while I go below," Rotis called out.

No one was fooling first mate George Theophilous. He'd known about the three mysterious passengers ever since they came on board. He was curious, but knew better than to ask.

The last night the *Larissa* was docked in Piraeus, nearby Athens' seedy port city, he was standing in the shadows on the upper deck, having a cigarette when they arrived. They drove up together in a dark automobile. It had barely come to a stop when the three jumped out, opened the trunk, and began removing baggage. There was a minute or two of undistinguishable conversation with the driver, who remained in the car. Then the driver backed away and disappeared into the night, leaving the three men standing alone on the dock.

They turned and began making their way up the gangplank leading onto the main deck, each carrying a large waterproof duffel bag. The bags appeared to be heavy. Theophilous was certain they must contain more than just a change of clothing. As he watched from the shadows, he wondered who these men were and what was in those bags. He was about to call out to them when Captain Rotis suddenly materialized from the darkness. *Interesting.* Theophilous stayed back out of sight. Rotis carried on a brief conversation with the men, then moved aside as they passed and disappeared below.

Twice since then, Theophilous had seen the men, both times in the late evening. They stood together near the starboard rail, smoking and talking quietly. He had never been able to make out their conversation, but was sure they were not Greeks. The few words he had heard were not his native tongue. Another language. Arabic perhaps. He did not know.

The *Achille Larissa* rolled slowly as Theophilous kept her turned into the cold wind. Dampness from the fog beaded up, trailing across the cabin windows. He reached over to switch on the wipers.

Just then, a dark object fell away from the vessel on the starboard side.

"What the . . ." Theophilous exclaimed, leaning forward. "A raft. They've dropped a raft." He peered past the window wipers, trying to get a better look. For a moment, the upper part of a man's torso was visible, then disappeared.

"One thing for sure," he said to no one in particular. "Whoever these guys are, if they try getting off the ship in these seas they've got to be crazy or dangerous. Or both."

He glanced at the chart in front of him. Eleven miles off the coast. Theophilous shook his head. "It's a long way to row your boat, gents."

BELOW DECK, the starboard cargo door remained partially open. The wind seemed even stronger here as the three men stood in the opening, making last-minute checks of each other's gear. The raft was a dark blob on the surface below, straining and bouncing against its tether like some wild denizen of the deep. A rope ladder was dropped over the side. The distance was only twelve to fifteen feet from deck to sea and easily traversable under normal circumstances. But the wind and choppy seas made it much more difficult tonight.

Captain Rotis stepped forward. Each man shook his hand solemnly. The last man passed him an envelope which he stuffed inside his jacket. Then, padding to the doorway on swim fins, the first man attached a length of safety line to the tether rope, grasped the ladder tightly, and began his descent toward the raft.

Looking down, he tried to gauge his position in relation to the bouncing raft. At about three feet to go, and directly above it, he turned loose of the ladder and dropped. In that same instant, the raft slammed against the ship and twisted away. The man fell against the side of the raft and disappeared into the sea.

Rotis leaned forward, straining to see what was happening. Out of the corner of his eye, he saw the others standing silently in the doorway. Neither of them made a sound. They were completely stoic, without visible emotion as they watched their companion resurface and struggle to reach the raft. His hand came out of the water, grasping for the rope that was threaded through rings around its slippery sides. With a huge effort, he pulled himself up and over, falling into the raft face first. He lay there several seconds, gasping for breath. Then he rolled over and looked up. The others were already starting down the ladder. As the raft banged against the ship again, he reached up and slipped a rope through the ladder's last rung, holding it steady, while the others dropped into the raft without incident. Then he let go.

Looking up, they beckoned to Captain Rotis. At their signal, he attached three water-sealed duffel bags to the tether line and watched as, one by one, they dropped toward the raft. Quickly, the men gathered them in.

Looking up again, they waved as one of them produced a knife from his belt and cut the tether rope. Captain Rotis pulled the rope in quickly, dropping it in a puddle of seawater on the cargo deck. Next, he dragged the soggy rope ladder back through the opening and pressed the button that powered the door. As the door closed, a final glance outside revealed the nothingness of the sea. All traces of his passengers were gone.

All except what counts, Rotis thought, as he touched the envelope tucked away inside his jacket.

"LET'S GET UNDERWAY," Rotis said, as he stepped on the ship's bridge.

"Aye, cap'n," Theophilous answered hoarsely.

In a short while, the old freighter's huge engines were throbbing, thrusting the ship through the trackless ocean on an invisible path that would lead them to New York Harbor by late morning. Right on schedule.

Captain Rotis lit his pipe, drawing deeply on its worn stem.

MOHAMMED ALI ATTA kept his eye on the compass, occasionally glancing at the navigational chart clipped to the board in front of him. The cold was bitter now and he wished that he could dig out an extra sweater. He had put one on board, but he could not leave the wheel long enough to get it. The fog had dropped visibility to nearly zero. Every bit of his attention was focused on the task. In spite of the cold, a damp sweat was forming on his brow.

This is like looking for a small rock in the desert. Let's hope their signal device is working.

He flipped the small switch to an emergency radio channel. And waited.

I should be near them.

Nothing.

He kept her pointed seaward, at half speed now. Waves ran high and the fog was low here, but not all the way to the surface. Mohammed could see a hundred yards or so ahead and to either side. He stared intently into the dark night.

Then he heard it.

A steady *beep . . . beep . . . beep* on the radio channel. He answered with three clicks on his microphone and waited. Silence. *Beep . . . beep*. Then more silence. They had heard. Mohammed knew they would not risk further transmission. They wanted to be discovered, but not by the Coast Guard. Five minutes later, he saw a light flash low against the sea, disappear, then reappear once more. It was at the two-o'clock starboard position. The cruiser churned through the swells toward where the light had last been seen.

There it is again!

Mohammed smiled, partly from elation, partly from relief. *Allah be praised! This is a good sign.*

He flashed a signal in return.

Minutes later he moved the throttle to idle and tossed a line toward the bobbing raft. The increased rolling motion threw him off balance. He missed, cursing as he fell to one knee. Retrieving the rope, now soaked with seawater, he coiled it and heaved it once again. This time it flew accurately, falling directly across the center of the raft. Cold hands grabbed quickly at the line, tying it to the anchor rope eye.

Mohammed turned the cruiser into the wind, powering forward as slowly as possible. Hand over hand, the three in the raft pulled themselves closer. It felt to Mohammed as though it was taking an uncomfortably long time for them to come alongside. They were being careful not to bang into the cruiser's outboard motors. No one wanted to capsize at the last minute.

Finally, one man reached over the side of the cruiser and pulled himself on board. Without a word, he turned to aid the others. The second man balanced himself as best he could, while passing the duffel bags to his teammate. Then, with quick, unwasted motion, all three were on the cruiser. Two of them leaned over the side and slashed at the rubber raft with knives. Satisfied that their task was complete, they cut the rope. The sinking raft disappeared from sight.

They sat in puddles of water, shivering with cold and gasping for breath, as Mohammed turned the craft about and headed for shore.

"Welcome, my friends," he said with a smile, looking back over his shoulder. "And congratulations. You have done well. Leave the bags where they are. They will be fine. Go below and you'll find towels to dry with and a fresh set of clothes for each of you. There are sleeping bags as well. If you are tired or simply wish to get warm again, use them. Go quickly. You've earned a comfortable journey to your next destination."

FROM HIS SITTING-ROOM WINDOW, Grandpa Brainard watched the light move steadily along the water's surface.

On nights when he couldn't sleep, the old man often slipped out of bed, put on his robe and slippers, and shuffled into the next room. From here on top of McKnown Hill, overlooking Booth Bay's harbor, he had the best of all worlds. Hill House was his pride and joy.

After working thirty-three years as a civil engineer for the City of Philadelphia, he and Middie had packed their things and moved "down east." They had no children and both of their parents had long since passed away. However, Jim and Middie Brainard both looked and acted the part of grandparents. Through the years, their snowy hair and warm smiles caused many children to think of them as the grandparents they had never known. So much so, in fact, that "Grandpa" and "Grandma" became terms of affection that followed the Brainards into retirement. In addition, they had each other and continued to share the rare, special gift of mutual love and respect that had carried them through all the years.

After looking several weeks for just the right spot, they invested their life savings in Hill House. It was a decision that turned out handsomely. Middie decorated the guest rooms in a colonial motif, each with a different color scheme and thematic touch. Grandpa made certain that the heating, lighting, and plumbing were functional and that all the bills were paid.

Many new friends from the community had come to the grand opening of Hill House, partly out of curiosity and partly because it was the only thing happening in Booth Bay on that last weekend in April. Champagne and New England cheeses were plentiful, along with ample amounts of punch and coffee. Walking through the well-appointed rooms, or sitting in the spacious parlor of the bed and breakfast, everyone agreed that they liked what had been done to the old place. Before the Brainards came, it had fallen into major disrepair and was looked upon as an eyesore in an otherwise quaintly attractive seaside town. What they saw at the open house was something in which the whole community could take pride. And they did.

It was not long before Hill House was full, with a waiting list of people who wanted to stay there while on vacation. That first summer and fall, Hill House guests fell in love with their hosts. Interestingly, so did the locals, which is not the sort of thing Mainers normally do right away. But there was a genuinely winsome quality about this happy couple. They had not moved here to take so much as to give. "So what is there not to love?" people asked. That's why it was hard, three years later, when they heard the news.

Middie was diagnosed with cancer. Surgery followed, then radiation. But the prognosis was not good. A year, the doctor said. Maybe two. It turned out not even to be that. Nine months later, Grandpa, with his customary tenderness and dignity, laid Middie to rest in the community cemetery. He shed no public tears, shared no expressions of hollow grief. He stood by Middie's flower-bedecked coffin for a solitary minute, a slightly quizzical look crossing his face. He shook his head sadly, turned and walked away. He had purchased this plot and the one next to it only two days earlier. It was the one thing they had not previously taken care of. That was because they had come to Booth Bay to live, not to die.

In the weeks following Middie's death, Grandpa gradually became more reclusive. At first no one noticed. Eventually, however, it became apparent. Grandpa was not the same without Middie.

When friends realized what was happening, the reserve for which Mainers have acquired a reputation caused most to hesitate before "butting in." Privacy is a gift, they said. A privilege. It should not be broken into indiscriminately by outsiders. They postulated that grief is a murky circumstance at best. Those who grew to love and appreciate Grandpa and Middie when they were healthy and happy had not been sure how to respond to their sickness and sorrow. It made them uncomfortable. Now it was easier to just not think about Grandpa struggling in the depths of his loneliness and loss.

Middie had made certain they were in church every Sunday. Grandpa growled about it now and then, but actually, he enjoyed going with her. The drive from their hill to Our Lady Queen of Peace took about ten or twelve minutes in the old car. A few times, during the spring and summer, they had even walked to church, down the hill to Commercial Street, onto the wooden footbridge crossing over a narrow stretch of the bay, and then out Atlantic Avenue. It was a beautiful old building, awash in light at night, thanks to a special gift from the Kennedy family. And it was situated on the side of the harbor directly opposite their beloved Hill House.

Following a service, they would stand around talking to friends they had not seen since the Sunday before. This is what Grandpa liked best. When weather permitted fellowship to take place outside the church, he could small-talk about whatever and, at the same time, look over his fellow parishioners' heads and admire their house on the hill, straight across the bay. It gave him a warm feeling of belonging. All this beauty also made less painful the hard oak pews and the monotonous drone of the priest's voice during Mass. But after Middie died, Grandpa became noticeably absent from regular Sunday Mass.

Grandpa and Middie always ate an early evening Sunday dinner at the Harbor Inn. They never drove, regardless of the weather. In good weather they sometimes extended their return walks from church by sitting at the Fisherman's Memorial, watching boats come and go on the Bay. Occasionally, they spent the afternoon wandering through the small village shops in which tourists liked to browse. In any event, the Harbor Inn was only a ten-minute walk from Hill House.

They sat at the same table each Sunday, chuckling as seagulls glided past on spring's fresh breezes, listening to vacation stories from boaters in summer shorts and tourists in skimpy swimsuits, engrossed in fall's fascinating color changes that decorated the surrounding hillsides, silently enjoying the cold grayness of winter together.

After Middie died, Grandpa was seen only now and then at the Inn. He always ate alone, with a book or newspaper on the table by his plate. He was polite. He smiled. He spoke when spoken to. But no one remembered hearing him laugh after Middie was gone. Not even once.

During daylight hours, the view from the Hill House sitting room was nothing short of spectacular. Grandpa watched boats and people come and go around the docks, at the bottom of the hill. His favorite window commanded a clear, unobstructed view of the bay, all the way to the open sea. During the summer, fresh breezes blew through the screened opening, stroking his face with loving, seductive caresses that reminded him of youth and the touch of Middie's hand on his cheek. Then, when early autumn's crisp brush strokes promised to emblazon Booth Bay's natural canvas with hews of red, yellow, bronze, and green, Grandpa Brainard closed the window and took up his daily vigil in front of it. He was contented, in a sad sort of way. It's just that all of this was meant to be shared.

If only Middie were here.

At night, the magnificent bay became a black hole, befitting Grandpa's feelings of loss and emptiness. The nights he could not sleep, he spent staring into the darkness. He tried to read. Newspapers. Magazines. Books. Anything. His mind wandered. The small television located in the corner near the ice machine remained dark. Eventually, he always returned to the black hole. The abyss. The wearisome wait for dawn...

...The light on the bay came closer.

Grandpa Brainard was able to make out the boat's dark outline as it maneuvered through the jumble of other pleasure craft and two larger sailing vessels. He listened as the sound of the outboard motors diminished and the boat slid silently into its place at the dock.

It's that Arab fella, Grandpa thought, peering through the window as a man jumped from the boat onto the dock, reaching back as someone handed him a rope. *It must be him. He said he'd be late, but I thought he surely meant before midnight.*

He looked at the grandfather clock across the room. It read two-twenty...

... WHEN HE FIRST MET THE ARAB, the grandfather clock was busy striking the noon hour, its chimes ringing true and clear. The seven-foot rosewood-encased timepiece stood statuesquely in the corner by the staircase. It was the one grand purchase he and Middie had made on their only trip to Europe. Two exciting days had been spent wandering along the sidewalks of Triberg, Germany, a paradise for clockmakers and shoppers, located in the heart of the Black Forest. The result was this clock, a gift to themselves, its beautiful sound a fond reminder of their European adventure together.

The Arab walked up the wooden steps and opened the front door. Wind chimes, attached to the door, added their cacophony of sound to that of the clock, signaling his presence.

Grandpa looked up from the cherry wood desk that served as a comfortable place to register guests and pay bills.

The man was small-framed, dark-skinned, and obviously Arabic. Grandpa had not worked in the City all those years without becoming somewhat of an ethnic expert. His clothes looked expensive, but comfortable. Light tan slacks. Knit shirt, open at the collar. Dark blazer. Expensive-looking shoes.

"Hello. What can I do for you today?"

"Have you two rooms available for one week?" the man asked.

"A week, eh?" Grandpa began turning the pages of the registration book. "Well, actually, you are in luck. I had a cancellation come in the mail yesterday. Two rooms reserved for a family from Boston. Last minute thing, I guess. One of the family members is ill so they can't get away."

"How much?" asked the Arab, sitting down in the high-backed leather chair directly opposite Grandpa.

"These rooms normally run $85 each this time of the

year. But, if it's cash and for seven days, I'll let you have them for $65. They have great views out their windows. Quiet too, if you don't mind the stairs. Both rooms are two flights up and just across the hall from each other."

"Fair enough. I'll take them both," said the Arab pleasantly.

"Let's see now," Grandpa said, pressing the numbers into a small pocket-size calculator that lay open on the desktop. "Altogether, that'll be $910 plus the room tax to pay off the government. Is your family waiting in the car?" asked Grandpa.

"No, I am alone. And this is not for my family. I have three friends who are joining me for a few days of rest and recreation. In fact, I've rented a boat for us to do some fishing while we're here. My friends are across the harbor visiting relatives today. I'll pick them up later this evening. I may even take the boat to go after them."

"Sounds like a good plan. Beautiful day for being out in a boat. Here you go. Fill this out, please," Grandpa said, pushing the registration card toward him. "Your friends can take care of theirs tomorrow if that's more convenient. I need your auto license too. Where are you from?"

"I live near Boston," the Arab replied. "I am a production manager for a small research company. By the way, my name is Robert Jibril. And yours?"

"Brainard. Jim. But everyone calls me Grandpa, so you might as well too."

"Grandpa," the Arab repeated. "And do you have many grandchildren?"

"No."

The Arab noted an immediate change, a sadness reflected in the old man's face.

"No, Middie and I were not able to have children. Now, she is gone . . ."

Grandpa busied himself with the registration book. The

Arab smiled as he pulled a money clip from his jacket and counted out eleven $100 bills.

"I believe this will do for our week's stay," he said, handing the money over. "Please keep the change until we are ready to leave. It is possible that we will need something extra before then. And thank you. I'm sure we will enjoy our stay in your lovely home."

Grandpa gave him the keys to both rooms. The man went outside. A few minutes later, he returned with a small leather case and a garment bag in hand. He thanked Grandpa again and made his way up the stairs.

Seems like a pretty nice fella.

He counted the bills again, then placed them in the small floor safe under the desk...

... JUST AS GRANDPA STARTED to turn away, his eye caught further movement. He looked back again at the boat. There were other people on board. One. There's another. And a third man. Three all together, plus the Arab. They were standing on the dock now, passing something between them. Ah, yes, cigarettes. Turning their backs to the breeze and away from Hill House, they remained in the diffused light coming from a nearby street lamp.

As he watched, the men picked up what appeared to be three large duffel bags and walked to a nearby car. A Cadillac. *Must be the Arab's rental car.* The four got in, lights came on, and the car slowly pulled away from the dock, starting up the incline toward Hill House.

Turning away from the window, Grandpa Brainard shuffled wearily back to his room and closed the door, unaware of the implications of what he had just witnessed.

Team Two had landed in America!

FOUR

Jeremy was six when his family moved to Baytown.

They came to their new home in late November, over Thanksgiving weekend. Normally, this holiday was spent with one set of grandparents and Christmas with the other. Gramma and Papa Stevens lived across state, about a five-hour drive. Gramma and Papa Cain lived across town. It didn't matter much which grandparent they visited on either of these special days. His cousins would be there too, and they always had fun together.

But this Thanksgiving was not fun.

Each year previously, the family had sat around the dinner table holding hands, listening to Papa with his deep, bass voice thank the Lord for His many blessings. Then they dug into all that turkey, dressing, mashed potatoes, brown gravy, yams, apple salad with walnuts mixed in, hot rolls, and, of course, a big slice of pumpkin pie with whipped cream on top. But not this year.

This year, six-year-old Jeremy missed all of that.

Last Thanksgiving, he had carried his new baby sister up

to Papa and Gramma Stevens' front door for the first time. He was so proud. He held her up to Gramma and she took Jessica in her arms. Papa looked over her shoulder, beaming with proud delight. It was their first time to see little Jessica and, somehow, Jeremy felt that he was a big part of it all. He was included. Secure. Important. He felt like Jessica's big brother ought to feel.

"Four weeks old today, you are," Gramma whispered huskily, moving the blanket away from Jessica's little face. "O baby, you are beautiful. So beautiful. And Jeremy, you are such a good brother. I can see you really love your new sister. You take such good care of her."

Jeremy took a deep breath, squared his shoulders back, and tried standing a little taller, feeling very important as Gramma looked down at him. Yes, he loved Jessica. He loved his mother and dad. He loved his gramma and papa. He loved life!

So what had happened between six and seventeen? Baytown had happened, that's what.

Their arrival in Baytown had felt strange and hostile to Jeremy. His parents had already been here to visit the little church, while he stayed with Papa and Gramma Cain. When John told him they were moving to a new city so that they could pastor a church there, Jeremy looked into his father's eyes for a long, silent moment.

"What about my school and my teacher, Mrs. Seymour?"

"You'll get a new classroom with a new teacher and you'll make some new friends," John replied ever so gently.

"Will Papa and Gramma Cain come with us?"

"No, they can't come. They'll stay here."

"And Papa and Gramma Stevens?"

"They will stay in their home too. But we can still visit them."

More silence. At that moment, as if she sensed Jeremy's world was starting to crack, Muffin jumped out of her basket by the fireplace, padded over and pressed her cold nose into Jeremy's hand. He put his arms around her and looked at his father.

"And Muffin? What about her? Will she come with us?"

"Yes, Jeremy," his father smiled. "Muffin will come with us."

Another silent pause. Then Jeremy looked up at his father with wide eyes and smiled.

"Okay. Can I go out and play now?"

"Yes, son, but be back in an hour. Dinner will be early tonight."

Jeremy ran out the door. Behind him, his parents breathed a sigh of relief. They kissed each other with congratulations on the completion of a task they had dreaded. It had not gone as badly as they thought it might. In fact, he had taken it quite well, all things considered.

Jeremy stood in the front yard, thinking, hugging himself with both arms. The air was nippy as autumn breezes took turns knocking leaves from the red maple tree by the garden gate. He watched them fall. He was frightened, but didn't want to show the panic he felt.

I don't want to go to California. I like it here at home. My friends at our church, what will happen to them? Why do we have to do this? I don't want to move!

A single tear spilled over. He wiped it away.

It's too cold to play.

Jeremy watched as another leaf dropped from the tree. He turned, went back to the house, upstairs to his room, and closed the door.

During the first week that followed their move to Baytown, Jeremy stayed close to his father. The church was small, but there were other children his age and he began to get acquainted. California wasn't all that bad. In fact, in some ways it was even enjoyable. He missed his grandparents and cousins a lot. They had come to visit during the

Cain family's first year in Baytown. His parents had taken him and Jessica up north on a return visit the next year. After that, though, visits were fewer, shorter and spread farther apart. His dad was busy growing the little church into a bigger one.

One thing he never got over was being made fun of as the "preacher's kid." Allison, the doctor's daughter, was never teased. Geoff, the lawyer's son, escaped being ribbed as well. Why was he the butt of everyone's teasing and jokes? He wasn't exactly sure, but he didn't like it. His father was strict too. Even when he turned sixteen and got his own driver's license, Jeremy had to be in by ten on a school night and before midnight on Friday and Saturday. His friends appeared to have much more relaxed schedules. They sometimes stayed out until all hours.

He guessed that being a preacher's kid was not a total disaster, but it was close. The good news was that it provided an instant identity with everyone in the church, and he secretly enjoyed that spotlight. Still, Jeremy wondered how much attention he might get if his last name wasn't Cain and his father wasn't the senior pastor.

Later, as the church grew, three other pastors joined his father's staff. Two of them had children near his age. That helped. Misery loves company, although he had to grudgingly admit that the other staff kids didn't seem to have as much trouble with self-image as he did. Even that bugged him. He decided maybe it was the result of being the oldest preacher's kid in the church. A kind of elder brother, like the one in the Prodigal Son story. He had to pioneer the "p.k." pathway, while the others had the luxury of following.

As he grew older, his best friends were in the church youth group or at MacArthur High. By his seventeenth birthday, Jeremy stood at six feet, two inches, and worked out on weights every day. As a result, he weighed in at one hundred seventy-eight pounds of lean, hard muscle. Every summer the California sun shaded his body a dark tan and bleached his blond hair even lighter.

As his senior year got underway, however, life was not going as smoothly as Jeremy John Cain wished. It was difficult, and becoming more so every day. He was looking good on the outside, but inside things were happening. Bad things. And Jeremy did not know what to do about them.

He and Aletha had broken up during the summer. That was an unexpected blow. Aletha was last year's homecoming queen. She was bright, beautiful, and popular, and being seen with her really meant something. It meant status. Acceptance. Students he hardly knew before were calling him by his first name and acting as though they were lifelong friends. To make a bad thing even worse, *she* had dumped *him*. So did his instant new friends. It was a real downer, one he had not gotten over.

Now she was going with Bernie Weltham, MacArthur High's all-conference quarterback. Jeremy hated walking down the hall and running into them every morning after first period. He even tried timing his moves between first and second period so that he could avoid them, but it hardly ever worked. Every morning, there she was on Bernie's arm. It made him sick.

As if that wasn't enough, his position as starting point guard on MacArthur's basketball team looked more like a question mark than an exclamation point. It should have been secure in his senior year. After all, he had worked hard to make the team the last two years, turning in excellent performances. Coach Riley had said so. But Jim Burnett, a junior transfer from a big school in Fresno, was making a bid for the same spot this year. And he was good. Very good.

Pressure. Jeremy felt a lot of it. Actually, he could not remember a time when it wasn't there. Life was filled with pressure. Demands. Responsibilities. Deadlines. Up to now, he had been able to stuff it. He wasn't sure just how or where. Maybe in some inner room. His dad talked about the importance of keeping the "inner rooms" of one's life clear and clean. Maybe that's where you stuff things. Only this time, he could not find a room to put things in. They were all full. Finding a way to release that pressure had become critical!

Jeremy tried beer when he was a freshman. It tasted pretty bad. It had been done on a dare anyway, so there wasn't much to it. The next time was during his sophomore year when he was out at the lake with a bunch of the guys. That day he downed a couple of bottles. It left him with a weird sort of high that he had not experienced before.

Once he smoked a joint with a buddy. Again, the feeling of not being in total control caused him to be apprehensive. Both his parents and his school teachers had, throughout his young life, strongly discouraged experimenting with drugs. He wasn't sure about all the bad effects of drugs, but he did possess a healthy fear of their addictive power.

There were plenty of opportunities for drug experimentation, but Jeremy steered clear of them. And as far as smoking was concerned, that seemed stupid to Jeremy. Period. He was very outspoken on the subject and had a real thing about keeping his heart and lungs free from its ill effects. He resented it when others smoked around him and was quick to tell them so.

But, when things had come to a head this past summer, Jeremy determined that he had to do something with the pressure he felt. He was tense a good deal of the time. Anxious. Most of all, he was angry. With Aletha. With Jim Burnett. With Coach Riley. With his father. With ... well ... who knows who else? But mostly he was angry with himself. It burned inside him like a furnace and was increasingly difficult to control.

After he and Aletha stopped seeing each other, he chose what appeared to be the quickest, cheapest, safest release.

The one offering the fastest results. Jeremy started drinking with some friends.

At first, not being in control bothered him. Then one night he got totally blitzed. Fortunately for him, he was at his friend Geoff's home, so his parents did not see him in this condition. He made his first marijuana buy in July. It didn't take long before he was using regularly. By the time school opened in September, Jeremy was well into a downhill slide.

His grades had been okay last year. He was not a great student, but no dummy either. He thought he was college material. Maybe there would be a basketball scholarship, if he had a really good season. The way things were going, however, he didn't much care. A sinkhole had opened inside him. He felt empty. Lonely. Distant. He couldn't talk about it with anyone. Input was impossible. The more he tried to fill the emptiness, the bigger the hole grew.

Jeremy could feel himself slipping and he knew he needed help. But where does a preacher's son go for help? His father was too busy with other people to be concerned about him. Besides, he was part of the problem. Jeremy had tested the water a couple of times, but his dad had been too preoccupied. In fact, since Jenny had drowned, both of his parents were really out of it. They hardly talked to each other, much less to him or Jessica.

Jenny's death. That was another thing...

If the other pastors' kids knew what was going on inside Jeremy, they would tell their parents and that would be that. His coach would kick him off the team if he confided in him. If he went to the principal, he would probably be expelled from school. There was nowhere to go for help. So the slide continued, undetected by those closest to him.

Undetected, that is, until the morning he drove into the driveway, bounced the front left wheel off the pavement and onto the grass, breaking off a sprinkler head in the process.

He squinted at his watch under the dome light. One-fifteen.

Jeremy heaved a sigh, filled with spent emotion. He rested his head on the steering wheel, letting his thoughts drift along on the currents of the evening's events...

...JEREMY HAD DATED ALLISON once after Aletha had broken up with him. Allison's father, Dr. Sidney Orwell, was the best-known orthopedic surgeon in Baytown, and until recently he served as a deacon at Calvary Church. He had just stepped down after two terms, due to the heavy schedule he faced in his medical practice. Allison's mother sang in the choir.

Jeremy had enjoyed their first date. Actually, it wasn't a real date. They had gone with some church kids to McDonalds for burgers and Cokes. Afterward, everyone went to The Castle to play miniature golf. Jeremy asked Allison if she would like to be his partner. They putted around the course, laughed a lot, and genuinely had fun. Of course, they were not strangers, having grown up in the same church. Still, that night at The Castle had been different. Jeremy thought that Allison had noticed it too.

So he called her and asked her out to a movie the next Friday.

He felt good when she said yes.

Would it be okay to have Geoff and Sarah come along? Great.

Geoff was fast becoming one of Jeremy's best friends. He didn't like Geoff's father very much. Jeremy thought he was too egotistical. Hardly ever smiled. Maybe that's the way attorneys are. Besides, he was overweight and Jeremy hated "overweight," though he wasn't exactly sure why. Geoff's dad was also a member of the church board.

No thanks to Geoff.

"Church is for losers," Geoff said one day. "I know your

dad is in the church business and all and he's nice, but I'm sorry. I mean, hey, get a life. There's just too much to do, too many things to experience, and too short a time to do it in. Loosen up, Jeremy. You and I can have some really good times if we want to."

Jeremy did want to.

And tonight was the night.

He was dressed in a blue polo shirt, jeans, and sandals when he knocked on the door at Allison's house. It was nearly seven o'clock "Hi, Jeremy." Mrs. Orwell smiled. "Come in. Just a minute. I'll get her for you. She's out back feeding the dog."

"Thank you, Mrs. Orwell."

He stood in the entry while she went to find Allison. It was an impressive house. From where he stood, he could see lots of wood paneling. Jeremy liked wood paneling. A mahogany hall table stood against the wall by the door. A small mirror in a mahogany frame with gold-leaf detailing hung just above it. It looked expensive. His eyes wandered along the hallway. One wall was lined with pictures of boots and shoes. He had never seen anything like it. A blue velvet shoe. A brown boot. A purple spangle boot. A pink velvet shoe. These must have been worn by women a hundred years ago, he thought. Why would anyone hang up pictures of old shoes? Strange. Different, for sure.

"Hi, Jeremy."

Allison came around the corner.

"Sorry you had to wait. Tango was hungry."

"I didn't know you had a dog."

"Seven years. A beagle. And she's *so* sweet. I just love her."

Jeremy held the door open. Just then, Mrs. Orwell reappeared.

"Honey, don't forget that your father and I have a fund-raising dinner for the hospital tonight. When that's finished, we've been invited to the Hatfields for a reception. You remember them, don't you? He is the administrator at St. Joseph's Hospital. We won't get in until after midnight. What time do you plan to be home?"

Allison looked at Jeremy.

"We're picking up Geoff and Sarah, Mrs. Orwell. We figured we'd take in a movie and maybe go for something to eat afterward. What time should I have Allison back?"

Mrs. Orwell smiled and put her hand on his shoulder. "I'd like her home around midnight."

"No problem."

"If you are going to be later than that, please call. If we're not home, here is the Hatfields' number. Okay?"

"Okay, Mom, I will." Allison took the number and gave her mother a kiss on the cheek. "Bye."

"Bye, dear. Bye, Jeremy. Have fun."

Jeremy followed Allison through the doorway and down the porch steps. She was wearing denim walking shorts and a white, short-sleeve cotton knit top. Her skin was bronzed from the summer sun. From church youth outings at the beach, Jeremy knew that Allison loved the outdoors and was an excellent swimmer. Her brown hair was thick and long, past her shoulders. He opened the passenger door. As she stepped in, he noticed silver ear hoops with dangling blue drops. Hazel eyes. She is tall too, Jeremy decided, carefully closing the door and walking around to the driver's side. Maybe five-eight? It's funny how you can be in the same youth group all your life and not really notice someone.

"What are we seeing?" Allison asked, as they drove away.

"I don't know. We'll wait to see what's playing."

Three stop signs and a signal light later, they saw Geoff and Sarah sitting on a bus-stop bench at the corner, just south of Sarah's house. Geoff wore bright green cutoffs, sneakers with no socks, and a yellow shirt open part way down the front. Jeremy knew that Sarah had just turned sixteen. He'd been invited to her birthday party. She could pass for eighteen or nineteen, however, and had been known to do so. Her well-developed figure was an item of more than a little locker-room conversation at school. Sarah was dressed in roll-up jean shorts, a light-orange cotton top, buttoned down the front, with long sleeves pushed up to the elbow. She wore her auburn hair in a short pixie cut. Short hair was becoming the "in" thing again, according to Jeremy's little sister. She and Geoff each carried a brown sack.

"Hi, guys," greeted Geoff, sliding into the backseat. "Let's party."

"Hi, Allison," smiled Sarah. "Haven't seen you in a while." She and Allison both attended MacArthur, but were in different classes. And Sarah hadn't darkened the church door in months. Not that there was much encouragement at home. Her parents went on Easter and Christmas, if they went at all.

"What's in the bags?" asked Jeremy, pulling into the street and turning left onto Sonora Drive. It was about a mile to the movie theater.

"What else?" exclaimed Geoff, reaching into the bag and lifting out a six-pack of beer.

"Where did you get it?"

"Never mind. We got it. That's what's important." Geoff took an opener from his pocket. "You can never start a party too early, I always say."

Jeremy heard the cap pop as Geoff opened the first beer. He handed it to Sarah. A second bottle was passed over the seat to Allison.

"No thanks, Geoff. We're almost to the theater."

"Here, Jeremy. Down the hatch." Geoff laughed.

Jeremy suddenly felt awkward. He glanced at Allison. She was watching to see what he would do.

"Not yet, Geoff. There's plenty of time later. Right now we have to pick out a movie. What do you guys want to see?"

They pulled into the cinema parking lot. Geoff and Jeremy put the beer in the trunk of the car. They walked toward the box office, reading the marquee descriptions of movie titles and times for showing.

A PG-rated movie was their stated choice. They purchased four tickets and went inside. The multiplex cinema was showing six films. One G-rated Disney film, a PG, a PG-13, and three R-rated movies.

After the tickets had been torn by the usher, they stood in line for popcorn.

"Let's see *The Torn Edge*," suggested Geoff, as they moved closer to the counter.

"But you bought tickets for *Thornton's Country*," said Allison.

"It doesn't matter. Once you're inside, nobody ever checks. We can take in whatever flick we want to. I want to see *The Torn Edge*. I've heard it's really good."

"Well, I've heard it's got lots of sex and violence in it. Some of it is supposed to be pretty explicit."

"Like I said, Allison, I've heard it's pretty good!"

They were at the counter now. Two large popcorns and two large Cokes. Four straws. Napkins. Jeremy and Geoff carried the popcorn buckets and Cokes as they walked away from the counter. Allison reached over, lifted a handful and offered some to Jeremy. He opened his mouth as she guided the popcorn across his lips with her fingers.

"Jeremy," she whispered, turning away from Geoff and Sarah for the moment.

"Hmmm?" he responded, mouth full of popcorn.

"I really don't want to go to *The Torn Edge*. Can we see *Thornton's Country* instead, like we planned?"

Jeremy looked at Allison. It was obvious that she was

troubled. He could tell by the look on her face.

"No problem. Hey, Geoff, we want to see *Thornton's Country*. If you want to see the other flick, we'll meet you here later."

"Ah, come on, you guys. Come with us."

"There is only a ten-minute difference in starting times, so they'll be over about the same time. All right? Then we can get something to eat."

"Okay. But you're making a bad choice here. I mean, really. This is a four-star flick!"

"We'll see you guys later," said Sarah, taking Geoff by the arm. "Hurry, Geoff. We don't want to miss the beginning."

The couples parted and walked away.

"I'm sorry, Jeremy. I hope you don't mind not going to that other film."

"It's okay. I'm having a good time just being with you."

"It was nice of you to say 'we' just now, instead of 'Allison.' I'm kind of embarrassed. Are you sure you're okay about it?"

"No problem." Jeremy felt good. As luck would have it, he had stumbled into the right pronoun for once in his life.

The lights were dimming as they found their seats.

When the movies were over, the four of them drove to a nearby café. After eating, they began cruising the main streets of Baytown. It was warm, so they drove with windows rolled down. The breeze blowing through their hair felt wonderful. And the beer was in the backseat again. It was proving to be a great way to top off their burgers and fries.

Allison had accepted a bottle from Geoff after they left the cafe. She put it to her lips a couple of times, Jeremy noticed, but it didn't appear that she drank very much. He got the feeling that she was uncomfortable. Most of the beer was still in her bottle by the time the rest were digging into the second six-pack.

After a few turns up and down the main drags, they parked on a dark side street near the MacArthur High School campus.

"Come on, guys," exclaimed Sarah, reaching for the door handle. "Let's go out to the football field."

They scrambled out of the car, reached for the remaining bottles of beer, and began running toward the field. Jeremy felt light-headed, his first telltale reminder of losing control. He knew he shouldn't. The caution light went on in his brain, but he kept on running anyway.

They fell in a heap together at the center of the field, right on the fifty-yard line. Sarah's laugh was a bit louder than normal.

"Shhh," Geoff admonished with a hiss. "Keep it down, Sarah. We don't want to get caught out here. Especially with this beer."

"Then let's drink it up," said Sarah defiantly, already giving evidence of having consumed more than enough. She reached for the opener and held bottles out to the others. "Come on. We're on the fifty-yard line. Think about it. We'll be sitting in those bleachers over there next Friday watching a stupid football game. But we'll be thinking about tonight."

Bottles clinked. Laughter filled the warm night air. Jeremy hesitated for a second, then joined the others. In the back of his mind he noted that Allison was still holding her first bottle. At least he thought it was her first. Better slow down. In no time, however, all that remained were empty bottles.

Lying on the grass, they looked up at the starry night.

"There's the Big Dipper," said Geoff, pointing toward the sky.

"Where's the little one?" Allison asked.

"Who cares?" said Sarah, turning until her arm was across Geoff's chest. Jeremy watched as she brushed her lips over Geoff's.

"You taste like lipstick and beer," Geoff laughed. He put his arms around her and drew her close. They kissed again.

It was silent on the football field. Geoff and Sarah were obviously engrossed in each other. He turned his attention back to Allison. She sat cross-legged, across from him, drawing patterns in the grass with her finger. His eyes struggled to focus clearly. Was she just quiet? Sad? Or what? Maybe she was waiting for him to make a move? He couldn't tell. He reached for her. She hesitated at first, then scooted closer until his arm went around her. He felt light-headed as he bent to kiss her. Their lips touched tentatively. Hers felt cool.

Encouraged, he drew her even closer. His hand dropped to her bare leg.

She pushed his hand back, twisting away at the same time.

"Stop, Jeremy," she whispered. "Please stop."

Stunned, Jeremy sat back, staring at Allison. *What is this? Why the sudden rejection?*

Allison stood, turned, and walked away.

Jeremy looked over at Geoff and Sarah. They were locked in each other's arms, oblivious to anything else that might be happening.

Jeremy pushed himself to his feet, swaying slightly, and followed after Allison. She was standing just across the side-line, in the out-of-bounds area.

That's significant, Jeremy, a little voice inside his head whispered. Jeremy paid the little voice no attention. Actually, he was getting pretty good at paying no attention these days.

"What's wrong?" His words slurred as he came up to her.

She looked up. He saw that she was crying.

"Hey, I'm sorry. I didn't mean to do anything to upset you." Jeremy remembered their kiss. His hand had . . .

"You're drunk."

Pause.

"Pardon me? I'm what?" he asked incredulously.

"You're drunk!"

Allison's blunt accusation sank in slowly.

"Wait a minute. I'm not drunk. I've only had . . . oh, maybe three beers tonight."

"You've had at least five! That I've counted."

"That you've counted? You counted?" he repeated.

"Yes, I counted."

"Who do you think you are?" Jeremy raised his voice angrily. "My father?"

No answer. She brushed at tears with her hand.

"Well?"

"Give me the car keys."

"What?"

"The keys. Give them to me."

"Hey, wait a minute. It's my car. These are my keys. I'm not giving them to you or anybody else for that matter."

"Jeremy, give me the keys or I walk home. I'm not getting in a car with a drunk driver!"

He peered at her in the moonlit shadows. Tears stained her face. But she was not shaking or sobbing. She was not emotionally out of control. What was it in her eyes? A look of . . . disappointment? She extended her hand toward him, palm up. Without a word, he reached into his pocket, pulled out the keys, handed them over to her, turned abruptly and walked back to the others.

Geoff and Sarah were sitting close together now, holding hands.

"You guys ready?" Jeremy asked.

"Sure. Hey, what time is it?"

Jeremy held his watch up close.

"It's past midnight."

Geoff and Sarah stood and started walking away, still holding hands.

"Wait," said Jeremy, feeling very light-headed. "Help me pick up the bottles."

"Oh, right! Like, hey, man, who cares about the bottles? Let some bozo pick them up on Monday."

Jeremy flashed Geoff an angry look, but said nothing. All at once, he didn't like Geoff very much. He was acting too much like his old man. Jeremy bent down and started putting bottles into the bags.

"Chill out, man," Geoff responded gruffly. "Come on, Sarah. Let's give Mr. Clean here a hand."

"Where's Allison?" asked Sarah, wiping at her nose with her forearm.

"Over by the car," answered Jeremy. "Geoff, get those two over there. They're the last ones."

ALLISON DROVE.

Everyone was quiet on the way home.

Geoff and Sarah got out at the corner near where they lived. They dumped the bags of bottles into a garbage can chained to the bus-stop bench. Allison continued driving toward her house. Jeremy leaned against the door, glaring with a sullen stare out the side window. Once in a while, she glanced over at him. He did not look at her.

"Jeremy, why are you so angry?"

Her question startled him. He struggled with his thoughts, trying to find a suitable response.

"I don't know." *Not very original,* he thought to himself. "What makes you think I'm angry?"

No answer.

Allison slowed the car and pulled to a stop in front of her house. She shut off the motor.

They sat in silence.

"Do you want me to drive you home?" she asked.

"No."

"I don't think you should be driving in your condition."

"Stop judging me!" Jeremy snapped.

Silence.

"I'm not judging you, Jeremy. I care about you. A lot. In fact, sometimes I think I care about you more than you do yourself."

More silence.

"What do you mean?"

"I mean, I want to know why you are so angry. I've been around you in the youth group for a long time. What I saw tonight is not the Jeremy that I used to know. You're a different person . . . an angry person. It frightens me. I didn't know you drank like this. I tried being cool tonight but it's not me. I don't even like the stuff. And I hate seeing you drunk. It seems like such a waste."

Pause.

Jeremy did not stir. At first, Allison thought he had fallen asleep. She leaned closer. His eyes suddenly burned straight into hers. Surprise. "I was disappointed earlier too," she continued, speaking quietly, but with conviction. "I mean with Geoff and Sarah. What they did made me . . . sad. First of all, buying tickets for one movie and going to another was dishonest. Also, the booze was illegal because we're all under age. Only a few months, maybe, but still. . . . You know what my dad says? He says, 'We become tomorrow what we feed our minds and bodies today.' I've decided he's right. Don't you think he's right?"

Jeremy sat up straighter in the car seat. "I think you *are* my dad," he muttered.

"Why do you keep saying I'm your dad?"

"Because you sound just like him when you preach," the slightest trace of a grin forming on his face.

"I'm *not* preaching!" Allison laughed, slapping him gently on the shoulder. I'm just concerned about you, that's all. Talk to me, Jeremy. What's making you so uptight that you have to drown it in all this alcohol?"

A long silence.

Why am I so uptight? That's the big question, isn't it? How many answers is she ready for? Because my world is falling apart? Because I don't feel accepted? Because I hate being a preacher's kid? Because I had to leave my family and friends so that Dad could "answer God's call"? Because the church people take everything he has to give and there's nothing left for me? Because my old man doesn't know who I am? Even Mom doesn't care. She just suffers alone for Jenny. Well, I miss her too. Jeremy felt the "inner furnace" flare suddenly at the thought of his tiny sister. *Jenny! How could God ever allow such a thing to happen? Maybe if we hadn't come here in the first place, all this might never have happened!*

He opened his eyes. He hadn't realized that he'd squeezed them shut until that moment. Allison was watching him.

"I guess I'm not ready to talk about it," he said, shifting his legs and reaching across the seat to take her hand. "Not yet, anyway. You know something? You are the first person to ask. No one else ever has. No one. Thanks for asking, but I think that right now the best thing for me is to go home."

Jeremy pressed her hand gently.

"I'd like to ask you out again, though. This time, just you and me. No *Torn Edge* movies. No beer. No Geoff and Sarah. Maybe I'd like to talk then. Give me another chance?"

Allison stared out the window.

Jeremy thought about how he'd handled things these last few months. There wasn't much to be proud of. He hadn't been brought up this way. He felt ashamed. He guessed he was a hypocrite, and that was a word he really hated. He'd let Geoff control the evening. Even Sarah was more in charge than he had been. He felt embarrassed. Humiliated. Weak. And angry. Why was he so angry? Maybe it would help to talk about it. Later.

"Allison, the truth is I don't really know much about anything right now." He hesitated. "I know that I like you."

Both of them laughed at that.

She leaned over, resting her hand on his shoulder, and kissed him on the cheek. He sat perfectly still and looked into her eyes. They glistened, promising more than he could fathom at the moment. He got out of the car, walked around and opened the door for her. They stood close. Then, without a word, she started up the sidewalk.

"Jeremy." She paused, turning toward him. "Be careful driving the rest of the way, okay?"

He waved and grinned.

"And with all the conditions you mentioned a moment ago, the answer is yes. Call me."

She ran up to the door and disappeared into the house.

He thought about Allison the rest of the way home.

And he smiled.

He felt . . . almost peaceful . . .

. . . JEREMY LIFTED HIS HEAD from the steering wheel, removed the key from the ignition, and opened the door. Carefully balancing himself, he got out. The effect of too much alcohol was starting to shut him down now. He was glad to have made it home safely and looked forward to hitting the sack. His stomach was feeling queasy.

He tried closing the car door quietly, but when it shut, it sounded much louder than it should. He walked toward the house, stumbling as he came around the corner of the garage. Catching himself before he fell, he looked up to gauge how much farther it was to the porch.

That's when he saw his dad sitting on the stone bench near the door.

FIVE

The sea lay calm, the night air still warm and muggy.

The full moon serenaded the Sinai desert with its ancient hymn of light, illuminating a landscape as stark and unyielding as the moon itself. It composed a silver symphony improvising its way through rugged hills, dancing across the Gulf of Aqaba, striking a chord of unearthly solitude on its journey toward fabled Petra's desert reminders of a civilization long past. The lights of Jordan's Aqaba city flickered dimly on the far shore. A span of darkness, brief enough to surprise first-time visitors to the area, separated their lackluster specter from the luminescence of Eilat, Israel's southernmost resort community.

Eilat's hotels, ranging from modest to magnificent, illuminated the night. Surrounding them, lesser lights dotted the hillsides, emanating through curtained windows from look-alike cinder-block houses. Even at this late hour, children laughed and played freely in the streets. No one seemed in a hurry to go home. Tonight, everybody felt safe.

In ancient times, this resort city was known as Ezion-geber. Moses and the Children of Israel stopped here, when there was little more than a drinking well and some palm groves. Later, Solomon developed copper and iron mines a few miles to the north. Ezion-geber became the terminal port for Solomon's renowned trading fleet that sailed to and from Ophir and Arabia. It was a center of business, not pleasure. But that was then. This is now.

Tonight, music and dancing was heard coming from the hotel section as lovers and tourists made their way slowly back to their rooms. Eilat's gravelly beach, filled with sunbathers and looking ever so much like the Italian Riviera in the daylight, was empty, the only sound that of boats rubbing against wooden pilings. Nearby, a small group of young people surrounded a table at an outdoor food stand, sitting on wooden benches. Watermelon rind and empty soda cans cluttered the red-and-white checked tablecloth. They were dressed casually, in T-shirts and shorts, except for one young man wearing a soldier's uniform. Their conversation was punctuated by occasional loud bursts of laughter.

It was a beautiful night and Eilat's guests were enjoying a much-needed respite from life's realities. Some were already back in their rooms, planning for tomorrow's cruise on one of the several small passenger vessels that would take them a few miles out to sea, offer a lunch served with Israel's finest homegrown wine, a swim in the Gulf, and a leisurely return to Eilat in the afternoon.

Eilat. Delightful. Captivating. Fun-loving.

And tonight, the doorway to danger!

SEVERAL MILES AWAY, in a top secret defense intelligence center, satellite watchers sat hunched over the data routinely gathered and evaluated on a nightly basis in Israel. Their log would later show that on September 10, the only activity along the coastal road to and from southeastern Israel and the Egyptian Sinai consisted of normal border crossings . . . a few trucks, thirteen cars, six four-wheelers battered from their frequent use on Sinai roads, and three buses loaded with tourists, one group from Japan, the others from the U.S.

These intrepid bus travelers were completing a grueling, daylong, round trip to St. Katarina's Monastery, located at the base of Mt. Sinai. Tradition indicates this to be the place where God met Moses and the Israelites on their wilderness journey, giving them the Ten Commandments, etched by Yahweh's finger on tablets of stone.

Even the occasional camel rider, making his way across the desert in the timeless fashion of his ancestors, is pin-pointed by this silent cylinder high in the heavens. These bedouin wanderers recognize no borders and serve as regular fixtures throughout the Middle East landscape.

On this night, four such tribesmen, together with their camels, were observed by satellite photo establishing a night camp in a deep wadi approximately six kilometers west of Eilat on the Israeli side of the border. This was a common sighting. Nomads traversed their invisible wilderness highways every twenty-four hours. More than likely, they would all be on the move again before dawn. In fact, night travel was often preferred because of the extreme heat during the day.

By early evening, all border crossings had been closed as the nation of Israel drew its curtains and locked its doors for the night.

Border guards, standing at the Taba Crossing that leads into the Egyptian-held Sinai, did not notice the four. They were too far away. The watchman at Eilat's popular Underwater Observatory was much closer, but he did not see them either. He was distracted by his cigarette lighter's refusal to function. Occupants of an army jeep, moving rapidly from the border crossing north on Highway 90 toward the city, did not notice anything unusual. Anyway, they were off duty, anxious to get home and go to bed.

Israeli patrol boats lazily drifted near the dividing line between the portion of the Aqaba belonging to Israel and the remainder claimed by Jordan. There was nothing out of the ordinary to report. Besides, underwater electronic surveillance was fully operational and prepared to signal against any sneak attack. In the morning, new satellite photos would show four camels still tethered in the wadi, west of Eilat. Perhaps the person examining the pictures would wonder where their bedouin owners had gone.

Perhaps, but probably not.

Yes, Eilat's curtains were drawn, her doors locked. The alarm system was turned on.

But, it would not make any difference.

The enemy was already in the house!

YAZIB DUDORI and his three team members knew all about Israel's alarm system. Well, maybe not *all* about it, but enough to believe they could avoid detection if they were willing to work at it. About that willingness, there was no doubt.

For six months, they had trained for this specific assignment. It was the toughest and the most important they and their teammates had ever been given. It was one thing to slip into the United States undetected. That task had been given to others. It was something else again in Israel.

They knew Israel's security to be the finest in the world. This was due in large part to the diminutive size of its land mass, combined with sophisticated, ultramodern, advance-warning equipment and the excellent skills exercised by those whose business it was to guard her borders. The recognition that her neighbors would just as soon bathe her in blood and push her into the sea gave the added motivation.

So, on this night, Yazib swelled with pride at the realization that he had been chosen by the Council to lead a major strike force into enemy territory. Territory that he believed, by every right, belonged to him and his countrymen. The task was full of danger. He understood that this might not only be his greatest adventure, it could also be his last. If so, he was ready. He was totally committed. His acts would be memorable, so as to insure his place among the greatest Freedom Fighters. Of that, he was certain.

MORE THAN TWO YEARS EARLIER, on May 12, Yazib and three others had made a daring early morning escape from the Gaza Central Prison. They were not missed until the duty officer began his routine, six o'clock head count of the nearly seven hundred prisoners crowded into the cells of the huge fortified police station that also serves as the Israel Defense Forces (IDF) headquarters in Gaza.

When the officer reached Cell 1, in the Security Wing that houses the members of terrorist organizations, he noticed something was awry. Four of the twenty-five prisoners were missing. A further check of the cell showed that the bars over the window had been sawed through with files. Yazib and his cohorts had warned their cell mates against trying to join in, so as to keep noise to a minimum. They then climbed through their cell window, jumped into the inner courtyard, cut through the barbed wire covering it, and climbed over the wall right on to the main street of Gaza, which at that early morning hour was already busy with people on their way to work in Israel.

Once the alarm was sounded, the IDF set in motion an immediate and sweeping search. Navy ships stopped fishing boats already out on the water and forbade any others to leave shore. Army troops joined Border Police in combing the local citrus groves. The Shin Bet, Israel's General Security Services, questioned all its sources to no avail, in an effort to discover where the fugitives were headed.

One of the four escapees was captured three days later, but would say nothing about the intentions of the others. As days turned into weeks, the authorities assumed the remaining fugitives would sit tight in their hideouts or try to get to Egypt. In actuality, they had already been smuggled from the area. They had been chosen as the persons best suited for an act of terror designed to crescendo into a worldwide cry of "Enough," forcing the hated Jewish usurpers to their knees and ushering in the long-awaited State of Palestine. It would be their moment of glory.

The three escapees-at-large included Yazib Dudori, Imad Safti, and Fathi Adahlah. They were hard-core members of the Islamic Jihad, a terrorist organization operating in the Palestinian arena. All were under the age of twenty-three and were calloused killers. Acting in the name of their ideals, they had been operating as a band of assassins throughout the Gaza Strip. None of them had formal military training, yet they had undergone arrest and interrogation and had not broken.

Initially, even their Palestinian brothers viewed them as reckless fanatics, motivated by ambition and childish bravura. Then came their daring escape—the stuff of myth and legend—and overnight the Jihad kindled the minds of thousands of Palestinian youngsters with pride and renewed national identity. They were heralded as gallant men by a people seriously lacking in heroes.

Imad Safti and Fathi Adahlah, while students at Gaza's Islamic University, had been deeply involved in a philosophic war waged between the highly activistic religious faction and the less intense, but far more popular, nationalist organization. Israelis had welcomed the rivalry between these two groups as an impediment to the PLO—that is, until the friction got out of hand. Eventually, a lecturer at the University was stabbed and killed. A few weeks later, a member of Safti's family was shot by a PLO supporter. The offense: lighting a cigarette in a taxi cab during the fast of Ramadan.

Then one day Imad and Fathi were worked over by goons from the Islamic Congress—the front organization of the religious faction. Subsequently, they decided to sever relations with the group, reaching the conclusion that the Congress was more interested in settling scores with the PLO than in working against the occupation. Besides, they were angry about their treatment at the hands of the Congress' goon squad. Together with several close friends, they joined forces with a clandestine split away from the Congress, the Islamic Jihad.

Jihad leaders called on the radical, cold-eyed Pasha Bashera to take the place of the captured terrorist as the fourth member of the strike force. Bronzed skin, dark eyes, hair cut short, she was attractive but not beautiful. Her reputation of courage and resourcefulness in the face of danger was growing among her zealous "born-again Muslim" companions. She was wanted by Israeli police for the slaying of two Jewish taxi drivers in Tel Aviv and an Israeli Arab from the village of Abu Ghosh, just west of Jerusalem. In each case, the murder had been committed in cold blood and in broad daylight, with dozens of people nearby. The killer's identity was confirmed by witnesses, and Pasha became the subject of a national all-points bulletin.

Even before turning to terrorism, Pasha had been well known among youth in the area as the daughter of one of the leading Fatah figures in the Gaza Strip. From childhood, she had refused to remain compliant or passive toward Jewish injustice. She joined with older youth in rock-throwing escapades against armed soldiers before she was twelve. When her father was arrested, and their home blown apart with explosives as an example to other Arabs, she vowed never to forget. From that time, she devoted her life to the destruction of the evil occupiers of her homeland. Her father promoted Fatah policy by holding anti-Israeli demonstrations as an act of protest. Pasha, however, believed such demonstrations were a sign of squeamishness and that there was no substitute for violent action. Filled with hatred and schooled in violence, in every way she was prime for this assignment.

The Jihad's ultimate aim was a call to arms against Israel. They had made the fight against the occupation a central doctrine. Israel's defeat was the condition for an Islamic revival and a return to religious values. The Jihad numbered only a few hundred activists, mostly organized into cells of five to seven members. In dissimilar fashion to that of other militant Islamic groups, they went to great lengths to remain anonymous and secretive. Men were ordered not to grow beards and to forgo wearing the jalabiya, a long cotton or linen robe worn by traditionalist Muslims. Of course, this was looked on with disfavor by traditionalists who held such acts to be overt violations of the explicit command of the Prophet Mohammed.

So, while not in the mainstream of Islamic thought and practice, the Jihad represented a kind of new order. It successfully brought together a hard core of angry young fundamentalists, fed by religious fervor and ready to use terrorism as a tool for determining the future of the world.

Now their finest hour was only days away.

Soon the world would kneel.

Soon the challenger would be crowned the champion . . .

. . . THEY HUDDLED TOGETHER TENSELY, listening for some word from their leader.

Yazib ran his tongue over dry lips as he peered around the large boulder about twenty yards from the highway. An army jeep was coming, carrying four soldiers—two in front and two in back. The driver's weapon appeared to be stowed by the gearshift. The others held theirs on their laps. A portable radio in the back, tuned to the Army's popular AM 1000 station, blared pop music accompanying the voice of a female singer.

To his right, Yazib could see the Underwater Observatory. No one seemed to be about. The soldiers in the jeep were well off to the left now, their backs toward him. A glance at the wrong time in the rearview mirror? A chance they would have to take.

Now!

"Run. Don't stop until you reach the sea!"

The four of them raced out from behind the boulder, covering the remaining distance to the road in a matter of seconds. They no longer wore the garb of the bedouin. That had been buried in the desert about a half mile from the camels. Each person had changed to dark boots and black cotton pants and shirt. Black, waterproof shoulder packs carried the rest of their equipment. Masks covered their faces.

Now, however, it felt as though they were naked. Out in the open anything could happen. If someone spotted them, it was over. The echo of their boots as they crossed the pavement seemed like thunder. On they ran, slipping in the gravel and finally falling into the darker shadows of a children's playground slide.

"Quiet," rasped Yazib under his breath.

Chests heaving and hearts pounding from repressed tension, they held their breath, listening to the night sounds. Remaining perfectly still, they watched for a long minute. Then another. Their breathing had nearly returned to normal when Yazib stood to his feet, a grim smile on his face.

"So far, so good. Now, let's get ready for a swim."

They moved a short distance apart and quickly began undressing.

OF ALL THE PROS AND CONS regarding the steps required to make it to the staging area, this one had evoked as much debate as any during planning sessions. They had pored over maps, spending hours in heated discussions regarding all possible options for moving undetected from their hiding place into Eilat and beyond. The way that everyone finally agreed offered the best chance had been suggested by Pasha. She was an excellent swimmer. So was Fathi. Both had grown up diving off rocks into the Mediterranean, then seeing who could swim the farthest out to sea and back. Imad was only a fair swimmer. So was Yazib.

"Let's get to the public beach near the Observatory," she said, pointing to its location on the map. "We'll be well inside any underwater electronic detection systems. From there we simply swim across to the main beach and walk into town."

It represented a long swim for Yazib and Imad, but Pasha and Fathi had gone that distance and beyond many times. A long discussion followed.

The water would be cold, but not so cold as to make it impossible without wet suits. The weight of the suits and oxygen tanks was a major concern and appeared prohibitive, since the last six kilometers of their journey to Eilat would be over rough terrain and on foot. They would not carry weapons with them. Those would be provided later. Still, the added weight of the gear was an issue. But the possibility of being discovered while swimming on the surface was too high. That must not be permitted to happen.

Once again, Pasha came up with the solution. "It doesn't matter how much time we take once we're in the water," she observed. "Just as long as we get there before the sun comes up."

The others laughed, imagining the specter of the four of them suddenly rising from the sea in front of a beach filled with Jewish sunbathers. They were beginning to like this new member of their group, even if she was a woman. Her reputation was admirable. And she seemed able to do anything the men could do.

"We'll take two small tanks and four lightweight wet suits. When we swim, Yazib and Imad can wear the tanks." She looked at them and grinned. "It will give you more confidence under water. Fathi and I will stay close to each of you and breathe off of your systems. It should be easy. We'll carry just enough weight to keep us under. When we get close enough to stand on the bottom, we'll take off the gear. We can either swim out and sink it or put it in our packs, walk up to the beach, get dressed, meet our contact and be on our way."

The men sat listening. Thinking.

"It will be easy," Pasha smiled. "We'll practice with the tank a few times after we get the equipment. I know we can do it. It is the best way. No one will suspect."

In the end, they all agreed. It was the best way.

THEY HUDDLED UNDER THE SLIDE once again, scanning the darkness. Listening for an unusual sound, something that indicated discovery.

Nothing.

Pasha checked Yazib's scuba gear one last time. Then she felt the weights around her waist, glancing at Fathi as she did. He had just finished the same exercise with Imad.

He gave her an OK sign.

She smiled and returned the gesture.

"Are we ready?" Yazib whispered.

All heads nodded affirmatively.

"Then, let's do it."

The moon had moved away from them now, shining more from west to east. Once again, the feeling of exposure gripped each person as they stepped from the dark shadows of the children's slide and made their way into the moonlit waters.

Careful. Careful. Don't splash the water!

They moved slowly into the sea, feeling the chill of the cold water rising against their bodies. A few yards out, Yazib crouched low. The others followed him. They moved forward in their stooped positions, exposing as little of themselves as possible. In the far distance, they heard the faint sound of music.

Then the sea covered them.

Yazib took the lead. Pasha hooked her left hand through his belt. They had practiced this before. It was simple enough. Yazib possessed a strong stroke and a good kick. The fins helped. Pasha moved her right hand in a full stroke and let him do the rest. They did not plan to stop and look back. It was up to Imad and Fathi to keep up.

They swam steadily through the darkness.

After about thirty minutes, Yazib felt his hand brush against seaweed rising from the floor of the bay. He stroked slightly upward. Gradually, the water's color turned from inky black to blue.

Okay, time to go up for a look.

Their heads broke the surface.

Eilat's lights were directly ahead. The beach was only a hundred yards or so away. They looked around. Where were the others? Just then, two dark, round objects broke the surface about twenty feet away. Success.

Yazib saw the docking area in the distance. There were boats. It would be a good place to slip from the sea. Lots of shadows, but possibly some people too. He continued looking for a safer landing spot. Then he saw where they should go. Away from the dock there was an open stretch of beach. In a few more hours, it would be filled with people, but it appeared empty now. Yazib gave the signal.

Slowly, just beneath the surface, they swam for shore. A

few yards away, it became shallow enough to stand on the slippery, rocky bottom. Their heads were the only part of their bodies above the surface. Silently, they removed the scuba gear and their wet suits. They had earlier decided to sink all the gear, keeping only a single waterproof pack in which they had placed their last changes of clothes and two towels. Pasha and Fathi tied the gear and the weights together. Swimming well away from shore, they released their package and watched as it sank into the darkness. Then, diving, they swam silently and unseen toward the beach.

Near the shore, they came up for air. They were close enough to stand on the sea bottom once again. Pasha strained to see where Yazib and Imad had gone. At first, nothing. Then, she saw a hand waving from beneath yet another children's slide in a sandbox play area. She looked over at Fathi, motioning that she had seen the others.

Fortunate for us these Jews and their children like to play.

Quietly, they glided through the water until at last they stepped out of the sea and onto Eilat's public beach.

Yazib and Imad were finished changing when the others ducked under the metal slide. They passed the towels and turned away to watch the beach in either direction. Working swiftly, Pasha and Fathi stripped off their wet underclothing and began drying themselves with the damp towels. Pasha shivered, feeling the effects of the cold water and wishing the towels were not already wet. She was conscious of her nakedness and the nearness of the three men, but she went on with the task, keeping herself covered as best she could. There was a moment when she sensed Yazib was looking at her. Turning away, she lowered her eyes, drying herself as rapidly as possible, and hiding the smile that started to form on her lips. Yazib *was* interested in her. Good.

Dry underthings. Jeans and a tank top. Sandals on her bare feet. She ran the towel through her dark hair again.

The air feels warmer now. My hair will soon be dry. I am about to walk through town, looking like any dark-skinned Jew woman on vacation. Incredible.

Pasha proceeded to stuff the towels and wet underclothing in the remaining backpack, now sticky with wet sand.

"Let's go. Slow and casual," said Yazib, in a low voice, pitched with excitement. Pasha wondered if part of his excitement had to do with her.

Yazib and Pasha walked slowly across the sand, stepping over a low cement divider. They held hands, keeping their heads close, like two young lovers out for a stroll. Imad and Fathi walked across the street, following at a distance. The street was dark and deserted.

They came to an outdoor food stand. There were wooden benches, pushed in at different angles around two tables with red and white table cloths. A nearby garbage bin overflowed with melon rinds and soda cans. Another bin, half full, was situated next to it. No one else was around. The place was closed for the night. Yazib dropped the backpack into the second garbage bin, covering it with overflow from the other receptacle.

"With a little luck, the collectors will throw it away without even noticing it," he said softly, wiping his hands on his jeans.

They moved on up the street. For the first time tonight, Pasha could feel herself beginning to relax.

As they strolled along the boat channel past the King Solomon Hotel, she gaped at its modernistic sandstone contours rising upward from the earth into the night. Outdoor lighting gave the ultramodern facility the look of a sheik's palace.

Yazib glanced at his watch. "It is nearly one-thirty, Pasha. Most of the guests must already have turned in."

"Wouldn't it be nice to spend a night in that hotel? A clean pool, a hot bath, and a soft bed?" Pasha mused, scanning the sweeping hotel entrance and the enormous swimming pool, shimmering under the outdoor lights. "Our enemies do know how to live."

With a long look, Pasha and Yazib gathered in the beauty of the architecture, appreciating what had just been said. Then, Pasha let her thoughts move to their reason for being here.

She had never been to Eilat before. But according to their instructions, the house at which they would meet their contact should be only two or three blocks from here. They had succeeded in crossing the open desert and swimming the Red Sea with none of their avowed enemies the wiser. The most difficult part of getting to the staging site appeared to be over.

The Islamic Jihad's third and final piece to its most sophisticated, daring, and deadly operation to date was in place.

As they stood admiring the scene, Pasha glanced away from the hotel and back to the street.

That was when she saw the police car moving slowly toward them.

She swallowed a sudden impulse to run!

He stopped, startled by the outline of his father on the moonlit porch. For a long moment, they stared at each other. Jeremy's mind raced through a kaleidoscopic pattern jammed with emotional bits and pieces. He desperately wanted to turn and walk away, avoiding the inevitable confrontation. But his feet seemed to melt into the concrete sidewalk. He could not move.

The moon cast eerie shadows on his father. He looked sad, angry, tired, a mix of emotions lining his face. Impossible to sort out. Slowly, he stood.

"You're late, Jeremy," he said quietly, breaking the tense silence between them.

"I know," mumbled Jeremy, dropping his gaze to the sidewalk.

He's going to know I've been drinking if I get any closer. I smell like a brewery.

"I'm sorry. The time just got away from me."

Did I slur my words? Oh, man, what's the best thing to do here?

"Come inside, Jeremy. I'll make us some coffee."

He knows.

Jeremy's tenseness heightened as he put one leaden foot forward, then the other.

Don't weave.

He attempted to focus on the front door, avoiding his father's steady gaze. He blinked several times in an attempt to clear the blurriness from his vision, but it was hard. Jeremy had not been into serious drinking for long, and then only when he became totally depressed. His body was still not used to assimilating great quantities of alcohol. As luck would have it, the amount consumed tonight was near his personal record.

Try to be cool.

Unfortunately, his effort to appear sober was of such a quality that, under other circumstances, it would have landed him in the backseat of a patrol car.

His father's eyes never left him, even when he walked to the door and opened it. Standing back, he waited for Jeremy to enter first. Jeremy grasped the doorjamb for balance as he stepped up and in. He turned to his left and went into the kitchen. With a feeling of relief at having arrived successfully, he sat down at the table and watched his father go to the coffee maker, pour in some freshly ground coffee, add water, and push the on-switch.

John stood hunched over the counter top for a long moment, looking at the coffee maker. Then, turning, he went to the table and sat down.

The long silence between them continued, punctuated by the gurgling sounds of water making its journey from the well, across the heating element, through the coffee beans and into the pot waiting underneath.

How long does it take to make coffee? And how long before he asks me the question?

John shifted in his chair.

"You've been drinking."

Well, so much for timing. And no questions either. Just a matter-of-fact statement.

"Yes, I have," Jeremy answered, in as defiant a tone as he could muster.

A long pause.

"I thought you were going to a movie and then coming home."

"That's what we intended to do."

"We ...?"

"Yeah, Geoff and I."

Pause.

"We went by and picked up Allison. And Sarah too," Jeremy continued, adjusting the facts of his story slightly, in an effort to make them more palatable to his father. "We went to the movie and afterward we had a couple of beers. Then we took the girls home and here I am."

Jeremy looked up, returning his father's quiet gaze.

John rose and went to the counter. He took two mugs from the cupboard above the coffee maker, removed the pot, and poured. Returning to the table with a cup in each hand, he held one out to Jeremy. Jeremy took it, but said nothing. The heat emanating through the ceramic surface warmed his hands. Lifting it to his mouth, he sipped the strong, black liquid.

"Where did you go after the movie?"

"We had something to eat. Then we drove around town for a while."

"The movie must have been over by nine-thirty. That's a long time to just drive around town, don't you think?"

No answer.

"So, I'm asking you again, Jeremy. Where did you go after the movie?"

"What is this, Dad," snarled Jeremy, "the Inquisition or something? Hey, we drove around a while and then stopped by the ball field."

"At your school?"

"Yeah. Then, we dropped the girls off and here I am."

John looked steadily into his son's eyes.

"I didn't know there was a game tonight."

Jeremy locked his eyes with his father's. Then he dropped his gaze to the table, slowly turning the coffee cup in his hands.

"So, I take it that there was no game. Son, what were you doing at the school at this time of night?"

"Look, what do you want me to say?" Jeremy's voice raised in defensiveness. "That we took the girls out on the field, jumped out of our clothes and had sex together? Is that what you want to hear? Well, we didn't. We had a few beers, got back in the car, and everybody went home. That was it. Now I'm tired of this. I just want to go to bed. Okay?"

Jeremy started to stand up. He felt a hand on his shoulder, pushing him back.

"I'm not done talking to you, son," John said, his voice tinged with anger.

"Well, I'm done talking to you, Dad."

Jeremy spit the words out, glaring defiantly at his father as he stood again. This time, John made no attempt to stop him. Jeremy started toward his room.

"Come here and sit down, son."

No answer. His back was to his father as he continued walking away.

"Jeremy!"

He kept moving, feeling as vulnerable as a duelist stepping away from his opponent, all the while wondering if the other person would turn and shoot before they took their allotted paces. His steps quickened as he went down the hall and into his room. The door slammed behind him.

He sat on the edge of the bed, brushing away tears with a clenched fist.

"Damn," he said angrily, flinging a shoe into the corner. It was a word no one ever used in the Cain family household.

"Damn," he said again.

JOHN SAT AT THE KITCHEN TABLE, the cup of coffee between his elbows, untouched and cold. The house was quiet ... only an occasional night sound brought on by changing temperatures. He looked across the family room and through the patio door. The late night moon glistened on the water in the pool.

I guess the only good thing about tonight is that we didn't wake up the girls.

John felt old. Much older than his forty-four years. His thoughts moved from Jeremy to the breakfast meeting scheduled with the church board, only a few hours from now. It was not a meeting he looked forward to. Then there were Sunday's services. He still had some sermon preparation to complete before then. Oh, yes. There was the Hollister and Sanderson wedding too, Saturday afternoon. He'd almost forgotten about that.

Early Monday morning, he would be counting noses at San Francisco International, gathering passports for presentation at the departure counter, as he and twenty-four other passengers boarded United for a short flight to Los Angeles. Then, taking a transfer bus from domestic arrivals to international departures, they would board KLM for a nonstop flight to Amsterdam. There the group would overnight at the Krasnapolsky Hotel on Dam Square. John liked the Krasnapolsky. It was a great hotel in the old European tradition. The following day at noon, it would be back to Schiphol Airport and still another KLM flight, this one to Israel.

He knew the routine well. This would be his sixth trip to Israel, the fifth time to lead a group there. On previous journeys, last-minute preparations just added to the excitement. But not this time.

Esther had decided that she did not want to go. John disliked taking long trips without her. He had tried talking her into it, thinking that the time away might help them both. But she finally grew angry and demanded that he quit manipulating her. She didn't want to go and that was it.

So John had given up. Instead, he decided to take Jessica. She would miss two weeks of school, but she was an excellent student. John talked it over first with Esther, then with Jessica's principal. Both agreed that this would be an experience of a lifetime and very educational.

John had been pleasantly surprised at Esther's willingness to let Jessica miss school and accompany him, but he did not question his good fortune. He looked forward to having Jessica with him.

Still, John felt a gnawing depression. Esther remained locked in her grief and despair over Jenny's death. Oh, everyone had been sympathetic. It was not your fault, they said. It could happen to anyone, they said. You must get on with your life, they said. They meant well. But John could see that the more people pressed their sympathy and concern on her, the more Esther retreated into herself.

He had made arrangements for her to see a psychologist with whom they were both acquainted. She went once. After that, she refused to return. No explanation. Just adamant refusal.

The last time John and Esther made love had been more than five months ago. She had not refused him. But she did not respond either. After the accident, lovemaking had been hard for them both. The last time had been a disaster. They had not attempted it since. As married couples often do, they sensed that their relationship was fragile, clinging to a tiny thread of hope. They both seemed frozen in fear of what might happen if that slender thread was inadvertently broken.

Tonight, John wished that this trip had not been scheduled. He had almost cancelled it a month ago. So many from the church wanted to take the trip, however, that he finally determined to go through with it. Letting Jessica see Israel through her child eyes was added incentive. But now, on top of everything else, there was Jeremy. John had been increasingly concerned with Jeremy's attitude and behavior in recent months. Tonight's episode brought it all to a head.

What's going on, God? Why are so many bad things happening to us? Where did we go wrong?

Getting up from his chair, John walked into the family room and stood at the patio door. Moonlight shimmered incandescently on the surface of the pool. It was one of John's favorite night sights. At least it used to be. He peered through the glass, recalling happier times. Memories leaped and played like phosphorescent dancers on the water.

He thought about the last night he had truly felt happiness.

It seemed so long ago . . .

. . . THE PHONE RANG, interrupting a heated discussion swirling around the boardroom table about Calvary Church's current financial shortfall and what to do about it. John had been listening for the past hour to what seemed more like a symposium on establishing past blame rather than dealing with the present problem.

"Hello."

"Hello, dear. How's the meeting going?"

"Well, I guess you could say that we're moving along," he answered quietly, turning his chair away from the others while, at the same time, smiling at one of the board members who looked at him questioningly. "It's my wife," John mouthed silently in response to the questioning look. The board member frowned and turned back to the discussion.

"When will you be home?"

"Not soon enough."

"When?"

"Before we began, everyone agreed to be out early, not later than ten o'clock. So probably by ten-thirty or eleven."

"Have you eaten?"

"No. Nothing all day. Didn't have a chance. The staff meeting took up this morning. I've had counseling appointments the rest of the day right up to the beginning of the finance committee meeting. Straight from there to the board meeting. I tried catching up on paperwork during the noon hour."

"Hungry?"

"Is the Pope Catholic?"

"Good. I'll have something for you when you get home. Okay?"

"Sure, great. I'll call before I leave."

"Bye."

John smiled as he hung up the phone, took a deep, weary breath, and turned back to the debate.

It was eleven-ten when John walked through the door and dropped his briefcase on the entry floor. The pungent smell of food from the kitchen reminded him of just how hungry he really was. Esther met him with a glass of grapefruit juice in each hand. He took one from her and their glasses clinked.

"Well, what a nice way to be welcomed home."

Their lips touched in greeting.

"My man deserves it after the day he's put in. Come over to the table and sit down. Here, let me have your jacket. And take off your tie. It's time for you to relax."

John loosened the tie and handed it, together with his jacket, to Esther. She disappeared for a moment. He could hear her removing hangers from the closet. When she came back he looked at her again. She was wearing a white, two-piece lounging outfit that he had never seen before. Her brown hair was tied back casually in a ponytail.

"Unless I miss my guess, you've been shopping today, my dear."

"How could you ever tell?" she smiled, pirouetting gracefully, glass in hand. "Do you like?"

"I do like. In fact, my love, you are ravishing tonight. What's the occasion? Did I forget our anniversary?"

"No occasion. Just us. That's occasion enough, isn't it?"

"Absolutely," John replied, downing the remainder of his glass, suddenly not nearly so weary as he had felt an hour earlier. "Are the kids tucked away in bed?"

"We have no kids. Just us."

"Are you serious?"

"Yes. I traded them off for a night alone with you. Bob and Joyce took Jenny and Jessica. Jeremy is spending the night at Geoff's house." Esther moved closer. Her gray-green eyes sparkled. He could smell her perfume. "Is that okay, fella?"

"Fantastic. I just wish I'd been here two hours ago."

"Two hours ago, I wasn't ready for you," she replied, turning to the oven. "Go sit down, John. You've been feeding souls all day. I'll be with you in a minute bearing nourishment for your starving body."

John walked over to the table and started to sit down.

"Not there, love," Esther reprimanded coyly. "In the dining room."

John went into the dining room. The table was ready with two place settings, one at the end and the other close at hand on the right. The only light came from two candles flickering at the center of the table. He was still standing, admiring the ambience, when Esther came in carrying two attractively appointed plates holding baked potatoes, a green vegetable, and generous portions of filet mignon.

It was after midnight when they finished dinner, lingering over small portions of gelato and coffee. They sat talking, holding hands, taking what nourishment they needed just from being together in the flickering candlelight.

"Let's go out by the pool," John suggested. "It's still warm tonight."

They took their coffee cups outside and sat at the pool's edge. Esther was barefoot. John pulled off his socks and they proceeded to dangle their feet in the warm water. Moonlight illuminated the pool's surface.

"You were right. It *is* still warm out."

Esther stood to her feet, setting her cup on the patio table.

"What are you doing?" asked John as he watched.

"I'm going for a swim."

With a deft movement, she stepped out of her clothes and stood poised at the side of the pool. Then, she dove gracefully into the water.

Soon they were swimming together, laughing and splashing like small children without any cares in the world.

And then they were in each other's arms...

...MEMORIES OF LOVE.

But not tonight. Not any night, it seemed.

Life is too hard. Love is too hurtful.

Neither of them had been in the pool since that beautiful night together.

The next afternoon... Jenny died!

Now there was only pain where once lived passion and delight. John stared at the dark outline of the sweep resting at the bottom of the pool, recognizing the familiar apparition.

Jenny.

His beloved ghost.

Slowly, he turned away from the door.

He tiptoed into the bedroom and slipped under the covers. His body ached with weariness. His spirit had fallen into a dark hole. Again. Each time it happened, the hole grew deeper than before. After a while, he sank into a fitful sleep.

HER FACE WAS TURNED TO THE WALL.
She did not move, but she had heard it all.
Loud voices in the kitchen, heavy footsteps, the slamming door, and much later, her husband's entry into their room and their bed.
She heard everything.
But she remained silent.
Her eyes were open and dry.

John set the carton of donuts and basket of fruit on the large, mahogany conference table. He had promised Cary that he would bring something for the fellows to eat. Force of habit caused his gaze to take in the room, verifying its readiness for the meeting. Twelve chairs covered with worn dark leather surrounded the table.

Cary Johnson, the church business administrator, walked behind each chair, placing agenda sheets on the table. He had already retrieved paper plates and napkins from the small counter-sink-storage area at the far side of the room, putting them at the end of the table nearest the door. The sounds and smell of coffee in the making filled John's nostrils. He needed a cup of coffee. Moving over to the wall, he straightened one of the several pictures. There were pictures of former pastors and families, as well as large framed photographs of board members through the years and of people engaged in various church activities.

The picture that was crooked was of Reverend William Jaspers, his wife, Betty, and their two sons, Mike and Cole.

John stepped back for a better look. As he checked it out, he wondered what it would feel like to be framed and photographed as the most recent "former pastor."

Will anyone care if my picture is hanging crooked? Probably not.

He turned toward the door as voices in the hall signaled the arrival of the deacons. A moment later, Jerry North strolled in.

"Hi, pastor." Jerry, a big grin on his face, extended his hand. "How are you this bright, sunny day?"

Jerry was always warm and gregarious. Dressed in an open-collar, multicolored shirt and jeans, he never seemed to change. White tennis shoes finished off the look of comfortableness. It all revealed the inner spirit of a man at peace with himself, his God, and the world. Except this morning, Jerry seemed even more effusive than usual. Almost too much so, John thought.

"I'm fine, Jerry. And you?"

"How could anyone be anything other than terrific on a morning like this? Just look at that day, would you?"

John turned his gaze to the large windows at the other end of the room. Immediately beyond, a drip irrigation system was watering the flowering atrium. Birds had made it their very own sanctuary, fluttering in and out with ease. It was a tranquil picture, providing a calming effect on discussions that often needed scenes of tranquility to help soothe the "savage beast." Or "beasts," as the case might be.

John greeted Harold Cawston next. He was the youngest member of the board. His father, George, had served four terms and was working on the fifth when he became ill with cancer. Harold had been chosen by congregational vote to finish his father's term of office. George still came to worship services as often as he could, but treatments and failing health had made it more difficult the last few months. John was going to miss him when the time came. In many ways, he had been like a second father to John.

Mike Dewbar and Scott Peping were golfing pals, each possessing an under-ten handicap. On any other Saturday, they would be playing by this time, and they appeared a little bent out of shape with the idea of a board meeting. John noted their golfing togs, however, and decided they were not planning to miss their day in the sun. Tee-off would just be later than usual.

Ken Ralsten, one of Baytown's leading attorneys, walked in and went straight for the coffeepot. The circles under his eyes seemed darker than usual this morning. John wondered if he and Geoff might be having problems, similar to those he and Jeremy were encountering. Maybe Ken was up late last night too.

I'd like to ask, but if they are doing fine, it will tip my hand that things are not what they should be at my house. Ken is not my most favorite person in the world anyway.

David Bolling and Dennis Lanier finished out the number expected for the meeting. David owned his own marketing and consulting business and Dennis was Baytown's city manager. David was outgoing, personal, and very likeable, though John sometimes wondered just how deep his commitment was to the church and spiritual things. He always seemed more at ease dealing with business topics than spiritual ones. His work also required him to travel a great deal, which probably did not help.

Dennis was thirty-seven, thoughtful, able to see the big picture instantly. After Sidney Orwell asked to not be considered for another term, Dennis had seemed the logical successor. He and Barbara had enrolled their two children in Calvary Christian School this year. It had been a big decision. They faced a good deal of pressure to place them in public school because of his visibility in the community. But after much prayer and discussion, they made the choice and it appeared to be the right one for their children.

Seven men. The perfect number.

At least that was the idea expressed in biblical numerology. Six was the number of imperfect man, seven the number of divine perfection. Seven men had been chosen to serve the early church in the Book of Acts. So, it stood to reason that seven men should serve the church in Baytown. Or so it seemed to those older and wiser heads of yesteryear who had established Calvary's constitution and bylaws.

For a few minutes, small talk ensued.

"Do you have season tickets for the 49ers this year?"

"Yeah. They play Seattle on Sunday."

"Will it be televised locally?"

"I think Channel 5 has all the games, home and away, this year."

"How about Ken and Elizabeth's Hawaii vacation? Ken never got to the golf course."

"Hey, listen, Ken, if *we* had been there ... "

"Do you think we'll get a break in the drought this winter?"

"I don't know. Have you heard any long-range predictions?"

"When do you leave for Israel, John?"

"Monday? Terrific. Hope you have a good trip."

"Are you looking forward to this one, John? Or does it get old after a while?"

"How many times is this for you?"

"This will make six, but the experience never seems to get old."

Coffee is poured, donuts and fruit distributed. All move toward their usual places. Heads bow for prayer. Harold leads in asking God's blessing on the meeting.

Minutes of previous meeting. Approved.

Financial report. Received.

Minutes of other church committees. Received.

Quarterly calendar of church events.

"There is one correction. The date of our next meeting was changed and both dates are still in the calendar."

"Move to correct."

"Second."

"Received as corrected."

For about twenty minutes, housekeeping matters preoccupied the attention of the group. They were necessary exercises in the parliamentary process, but not anyone's favorite reason for board meetings.

New church members were noted, twenty-three in the most recent class. Also noted were thirteen people transferred to the inactive list. Five had moved from the area to other communities in California. One had been transferred by her company to Ohio. The remaining seven were attending other churches in the area.

For a large church like Calvary, with more than eleven hundred members, this seemed normal enough. It did bother John, though, that seven of Calvary's members were now attending other churches. It was hard not to take such moves personally, feeling somehow that he had failed where these people were concerned. Intellectually, he knew it was unrealistic to believe Calvary Church would be able to meet everyone's needs and desires. He also understood that he was not alone in responsibility for the welfare of the church family. Still, it bothered him.

It also disturbed him that the majority of new members were transfers from other churches and not new converts. It was his feeling that the church merry-go-round did little to grow the kingdom of God and often simply moved people and their problems from one church body to another.

John was not prepared, though, for what was about to follow.

Ken was settled back in his chair, staring seriously at the table. He locked his hands together and slowly twirled his thumbs.

"Pastor," he began. pausing before continuing.

Oh, oh. I hate when this happens, thought John, looking in Ken's direction. *Whenever he calls me pastor instead of John, I know I'm in trouble. And when he twirls his thumbs and gives me his dramatic lawyer pause, I start feeling defensive before he opens his mouth.*

"Pastor," Ken repeated again, clearing his voice. By now, everyone had turned toward him, waiting. "Doesn't it seem a bit ominous to you that seven of our good members are now attending other churches in Baytown? I've checked the member records from the last six months and we have a total of thirty-two Calvary members who have left us for other congregations. When we add these seven, it makes thirty-nine. Now, I understand that some have moved away from Baytown. But most of these folks are still right here. Can you shed some light on what could possibly be behind this?"

John gazed steadily at a neutral point in the center of the table, preparing his response.

Be careful, fella. There's an edge to that man's voice this morning. He's come loaded for bear. And he's probably got a little buckshot reserved in case he misses the first time.

"It always hurts when good people leave to attend another church, Ken. At least, it always hurts me. Some go for good reasons. They're the ones who talk it over with me first. Most of the time it has to do with opportunities to serve that they feel they will never get here. And there are other reasons. Jack and Julie Stevens, for example, have transferred to Faith Church because their son is the new pastor there. We can hardly fault them for wanting to be supportive of their son in his first pastorate, now can we? Unfortunately, some have left because they don't like the style of our worship. And I know two of the families on this list feel the church is getting too big. They want something smaller. We've tried to encourage them into some of the home small groups that meet in their area, but so far, we've not been successful."

"Thirty-nine fine members," Ken said again, as though he had not heard John's response. Then he lifted his gaze and directed it toward John.

"How many more are on the way out, pastor? Do you know?"

It was silent around the conference table. The only sounds were the stirrings of bodies on leather seats. Harold, Mike, and Scott looked at Ken, puzzled at what they were hearing, wondering where he was headed. David and Dennis leaned forward, waiting for John's reaction. Obviously, Ken had discussed this with them beforehand. Jerry glanced nervously at John, then proceeded to stare out the window. Cary sat quietly, waiting. Tension had suddenly gripped the meeting.

"I'm not sure what you are getting at, Ken. It's a little hard to read the minds of each church member. Help me understand where you're going with this."

John remembered a quote he had read recently, *When you swim in the ocean, you get attacked by sharks and guppies. Don't worry about the guppies.*

Like any pastor, through the years John had taken his share of negative criticism. He had learned to field it as well as anyone while it was happening. It was always later, when he was alone, that he would give way to the hurt that tore at the fragile nature of his inner being.

Outwardly, as the group absorbed the stillness enveloping the room, he remained calm and casual, displaying his most confident pastor's smile. Inwardly, the alarm he had learned to recognize was sounding and a voice kept repeating, *Trouble, John . . . shark attack!*

Ken? Shark? He started thinking about all the lawyer-shark jokes he had ever heard. The inner tension subsided momentarily. Then he reminded himself that this was no joke.

"Where I'm going with this, pastor," answered Ken, "is to a conclusion that appears rather obvious to me and to some of the rest of us. Something is amiss here. I've been receiving a lot of complaints recently. Some folk don't like the stuff we're singing on Sunday mornings. Too much with the hymns, not enough upbeat music. I hate to be the bearer of bad news, John . . ."

Yes, I'll bet you do.

" . . . but more than a few complaints have been coming in to some of us about the quality of our pulpit."

John knew that Ken wasn't talking about pulpit furniture. He remained silent, glancing around the table at the others.

Harold was the first to speak.

"Ken, you know that people complain from time to time about everything. They even grouse about us once in a while. I certainly haven't heard anything negative about John's preaching. Personally, I don't think he has ever done a better job than recently. I just can't believe what you are saying is representative input."

Scott and Mike nodded in agreement.

David and Dennis silently kept their eyes on John.

Jerry stirred nervously, now staring down at the table.

"It's out there, I'm telling you," Ken answered. "Not that I believe what is being said is true, you understand. No, I never said that. It is probably not justified."

Probably? thought John.

"But I feel it is my duty as a deacon to call it to everyone's attention in this room," Ken continued. "Including yours, pastor. If people are not happy with the pulpit, attendance drops. When attendance drops, giving drops. When giving drops . . . well, you've seen the financial report. We're headed for trouble if we don't do something."

If it is not justified, why didn't you try to disarm the criticism?

"What do you recommend we do, Ken?" asked John quietly. "Do you have something specific in mind that you want to bring before the board this morning?"

Ken's eyes locked on John. The look was unyielding and intense.

"All I'm saying is what has been said. I know you carry a heavy load, pastor. I know your time is taken up with a lot of things. And I know it has not been easy for you since . . . well, since you and Esther lost Jennifer. I'm sure it has affected the whole family, including Jeremy and Jessica."

How much do you know about what's going on in my family?

"Now, here are you, going off to Israel. You'll be gone for two weeks. This is a critical time for the church, John. I'm not sure you ought to be leaving right now. Who knows what will happen? Maybe you should be staying closer to home. I know a little about the importance of adequate preparation before addressing a jury. Perhaps a little more time in the study would help."

A jury? Our congregation is a jury? What am I supposed to be? The defendant?

"But we've approved these group trips that John makes to Israel," John overheard Scott reply. "They've become a kind of teaching and relationship-building experience that John does with the congregation. Surely you can't be serious, Ken."

Ken shrugged, resuming the slow, circling thumb motion and returning his gaze to the tabletop.

The remainder of the meeting was completed by dodging through the strained feelings that were everywhere present. The threatening implications in Ken's comments had caused a pallor to settle on the group. It was difficult to talk or think about anything else.

Outside, birds sang and the sun shown brightly. Inside the room, a cloud had settled over the conference table.

Deep inside, John did his best to control his feelings. He spoke in soft tones. He did not dare to think about or say what he truly felt. Hurt smouldered, ready to flare instantly if fueled with the anger he was doing his best to contain.

AFTER THE MEETING WAS OVER, John sat alone in his office. Louvered window shades kept most of the daylight outside. In the room's diffused light, his eyes wandered across book-lined walls. Each book was catalogued and accessible through a card reference system that enabled him to quickly locate any volume by subject, title, or author. He had personally hired a professional librarian to set up the system some years ago.

A slight smile crossed his face as he stared at the shelves housing a variety of Bible commentaries. When preparing to preach from a particular section of the Scriptures, John had, over the years, made a habit of perusing catalogues and bookstores. He normally purchased three or four, sometimes up to a dozen of those he felt were the best. They were the tools of his craft, as he prepared to let the Scriptures speak through him to the minds and souls of those who frequented Calvary Church each week.

Once, a woman with little appreciation for books had suggested that the hundreds of volumes on these shelves should be arranged according to the colors of the covers. It would add to the decor of the room, she said, which in her opinion could use a good deal of help. John had politely thanked her for her kind interest and creative idea. When she had gone, he laughed out loud. Then, he went to find Cary to tell him what the woman had said.

Now, John sat staring.

Maybe she was on to something after all.

He swiveled back to the computer table next to his desk, reached behind the machine and pushed the power switch.

It warmed up in minutes, displaying an array of options. John moved the mouse to the *Letters* folder and double-clicked. After requesting a new file, he began writing:

Calvary Church Board of Deacons
Calvary Church Family
4455 21st Avenue N.E.
Baytown, California

Dear Members of Christ's Family,

After much prayer and consideration, I am submitting my resignation as senior pastor of Calvary Church, to be effective at a date to be determined by the board and myself.

It has been my joyful opportunity to serve this wonderful church during the past eleven years. I shall always be grateful, both to God and to you, for this privilege. To the best of my ability, I have been a faithful and honorable shepherd. In that regard let me urge you to *"join with others in following my example, brothers, and take note of those who live according to the pattern we gave you."* —Philippians 3:17

The love Esther and I hold for each and every one of you remains so strong that stepping away is filled with deep emotion. Since we answered God's call to Calvary Church, He has permitted us a long tenure of ministry among you. While much remains to be accomplished, it will be done under the leadership of another. Now, it is time for us to go, in the same spirit of obedience in which we came.

Rest assured that as our Lord entrusts us with new responsibilities in another part of His harvest, no other ministry and no one else can ever take your place in our hearts.

Humbly yours,

John Cain

When it was finished, John read through it again. Then, preparing the computer for shutdown, he reached behind it and pressed the switch. The screen went blank.

That's it. It's time. There's nothing about me that's not burned out. When I get home from Israel, I'll mail a copy to each board member. So much for eleven years of faithful ministry. I guess it's really over.

II

▼▼▼

Therefore, in the shadow of Islam, it is possible for all followers of different religions to live in peace and with security over their person, property, and rights. In the absence of Islam, discord takes form, oppression and destruction are rampant, and wars and battles take place.

—*from the* Hamas Charter, *Article Six*

When faith is lost there is no security nor life for him who does not revive religion;
And whoever is satisfied with life without religion, then he would have let annihilation be his partner.

—*Muhammad Iqbal, Muslim poet*

Peacemakers who sow in peace raise a harvest of righteousness.

—The Bible, *James 3:18*

▲▲▲

EIGHT

"Honey, are you ready? We're going to be late again."

"I'll be there in a minute."

Sherri Heiden stood by the kitchen counter, slowly sipping from her water glass. The refreshing coolness crossed her lips and tongue. Then like a tiny waterfall, it disappeared. She closed her eyes.

Closing her eyes had become a favorite habit in recent weeks. It helped her shut out the growing amount of house clutter. With a hand, Sherri swept her long brown hair across her shoulder. Her other hand moved back and forth over her full form. *Hi, baby.* She smiled, looking down as she felt a small foot pushing inside her. Their baby was awake and kicking.

Philip and Sherri Heiden were expecting in early October. Dr. Carrington had declared the tenth as "B-Day." They had dreamed of this day for six years. It had been that long since repeating their vows in Sherri's home church. Six years!

Is God good or what?

Sherri sipped more water, her mind meandering along the well-traveled trails of past memories...

...PHILIP HAD LIVED IN PORT TOWNSEND, Washington from the time he was ten. His father, a retired Navy officer, and his mother operated a Victorian style bed-and-breakfast situated on a hill overlooking the Strait of Juan de Fuca.

Sherri Copeland also came from a Navy family. Her father, Jim, had spent his entire career attached to submarine service. He arrived at the Bremerton base after spending the last three years in Newport, Rhode Island. Sherri's mother, Suzanne, immediately fell in love with the area. The beautiful Puget Sound looked like the place to put down roots. So they did, in the nearby community of Poulsbo. No more long months at sea for Jim. No more lonely days and nights in base housing units for Suzanne and Sherri. They were determined to be a normal family, with steady jobs and house payments and PTA meetings and crabgrass in their very own yard.

Sherri started her first year in high school the September following their transfer. She never minded the Puget Sound's two hundred sixty overcast days each year. Being a Navy "brat" had given her an extra measure of adaptability. Besides, this little Scandinavian community with its narrow streets, quaint tourist shops, and friendly natives, was the first place she had ever felt really and truly at home. She loved the evergreen trees that dotted the hillsides, rising majestically from the seashore, standing tall as far as the eye could see. Sherri just knew that she would never live anywhere else. This was heaven on earth.

Then, during her senior year in high school, she went to a basketball game with her best friend, Holly. That night, heaven took on a fresh, new dimension in the form of an angelic stranger seated across the way in the visitor's section.

His sweater sported the familiar colors of Port Townsend, one of Poulsbo's rival schools, and the opposing team that night. He appeared to be sixteen or seventeen, medium height, with fair complexion and blond hair. Sherri and Holly sat directly across the playing floor. In typical teenage fashion, they spent most of the first half discussing his looks and that of his two friends. The fellows were definitely into the game, every once in a while punctuating a good shot by jumping to their feet and yelling, "All right! Yes!"

At halftime, the score was 34–32 in favor of the home team. Sherri and Holly watched as "Port Townsend" stood, stretched, and began walking with his friends toward a nearby exit.

"Who *is* he?" asked Sherri, squeezing Holly's arm excitedly as she stared across the floor.

"Easy, girl," Holly winced, shifting to ease Sherri's grip. "A guy who looks like that is probably a womanizer of the first order. I'll bet he's got a girl in every port. Or maybe he's got some social disease or likes guys or something."

"Stop it," giggled Sherri. "He's probably a minister's son and has never been kissed."

"Oh, I'm sure. Anyway, they're gone. So what do you want to do after the game? How about getting a sandwich at the drive-through and going to my house for some late night television? We could stay up and do our nails."

"How terribly exciting. Let's think about it during the next half. Right now, I'd like a Coke. How about you?"

"Let's do it."

They jumped to their feet and bounded down one bleacher seat to another until reaching the playing floor. Then they made their way toward the exit leading to the snack bar. Beyond the doorway, students were milling around, waiting to be served. Sherri glanced down, fumbling through her purse for some dollar bills as they went through the door.

That's when she collided with another customer, sending Coke in one direction and hot dog in the other!

Students jumped back to avoid the sticky liquid spreading across the floor.

"I'm sorry. Oh, I wasn't watching. It's all my fault," Sherri exclaimed, looking down at the mess.

Glancing up, she saw a red and yellow streak of catsup and mustard running from "Port Townsend's" chin almost all the way to his hairline. He stood silently, hot dog pointed at his ear, mustard and catsup dripping crazily between his fingers. Sherri felt her face flush with embarrassment.

Putting her hand to her mouth, she began to giggle.

For a moment, his look was a mix of sternness and surprise. Then, a smile broke across "Port Townsend's" face, turning into a deep chuckle, then to all-out laughter, his eyes all the while remaining on his "attacker." Reaching for the napkin he had earlier jammed into his hip pocket, he wiped off the catsup and mustard as best he could. Holly busied herself cleaning up the mess on the floor. Sherri reached out and touched his arm apologetically.

"I am so embarrassed," she exclaimed nervously. "Did you get any on your clothes?" She stepped back for a quick look at his school sweater and blue jeans. Seeing no major evidence of the crime, she looked up again.

Blue. His eyes are blue.

"There's a little bit of Coke on your pants. Other than that, I guess I'm a lucky girl or you might throw me out of here."

"Hi." His voice had a baritone quality. At the same moment, she noticed a music staff on his sweater.

"Hi," he said again, smiling as they moved away from the doorway.

"Oh, I am sorry. Hi. I've been apologizing so much that I didn't answer."

"No problem. My name is Phil."

"I'm Sherri."

"And I'm Holly," came the voice from the floor. "You guys create the mess and I have to introduce myself."

"I'm sorry, Holly. Oh, there I go again, still apologizing," Sherri said, bending down to help with the cleanup.

Phil gathered the soiled paper napkins and the drink container and dropped them into the trash barrel at the opposite side of the doorway.

"My friends and I saw you girls sitting across from us during the game. We wondered if we might get a chance to meet you. I guess God works in mysterious ways, huh?"

Holly looked up at Phil. "You're not a minister's kid, are you?"

"No," answered Phil. "What makes you ask that?"

Sherri and Holly burst out laughing.

"Listen, I've got to get back to my friends for the second half. Are you sticking around?"

Both girls nodded.

"Then, how about all of us going to Jerry's for a sandwich after the game? That is, if you don't have any better plans."

Sherri and Holly burst into laughter again. They agreed to meet later at the main exit and started back to their seats . . .

. . . SHERRI HEARD HIS VOICE SPEAKING SOFTLY. "I'm ready, sweetheart."

She opened her eyes.

Phil was standing there, grinning from ear to ear.

"Where have you been?" he asked, knowing how she loved to journey off in her mind to some favorite memory. "From the look on your face, it must have been good."

"Never mind. Let's go. I hate going in to church late. Especially looking like the Goodyear Blimp!"

"You don't look like a blimp," Phil said, opening the door to their apartment. "You look like the beautiful mother of our child."

Sherri smiled. "You said the right thing, mister."

They walked single file along the sidewalk to the car. Sherri paused while Phil unlocked the passenger door of their more-than-slightly-used Pontiac. He helped her get in, closed the door firmly, and went around to the driver's side. It was a sunny California day as the Heidens backed out of the carport and drove off in the direction of the church.

CALVARY CHURCH held three services every Sunday morning. The early service was generally the smallest, with about two hundred attending. The nine-thirty service was the largest of the day. Five or six hundred people normally were present, in addition to the choir and musicians. It was also the service that could be seen live on local television. A volunteer crew with a three-camera setup produced this special outreach each week. Then, at eleven, another four to five hundred gathered for the third service of the morning.

From his location on the platform, John had a commanding view of each service's parishioners. This morning, Mike Dewbar and Scott Peping were sitting near each other with their wives, as the second service got underway. John thought these two would be great models for a health club ad. Even their wives were sparkling with end-of-summer tans and sun-bleached hair that represented more than a few hours beside swimming pools and at the beach with their children. Mike saw John looking in their direction and gave him an encouraging wink.

Jerry North was sitting with Teressa, but well toward the back of the sanctuary, far away from their usual seats near the front on the left-hand side. Given the tenor of yesterday's board meeting, John wondered what was running through

Jerry's mind. Normally an outgoing, agreeable person, he had seemed distant and uncomfortable when they passed in the hallway between services. Could that have anything to do with where he and Teressa were sitting this morning? Had Ken's comments gotten to him?

Well, so what? The die is cast. I won't need to worry about all this much longer.

About ten minutes into the service, as the last hymn neared completion, John noticed them. The attractive Arabic-looking couple, the same two he had observed in the early service, were sitting next to the Heidens. John didn't know the Heidens very well. He remembered that they were from up north, either Oregon or Washington. They were new, having started to attend regularly about three months ago.

Her name is Sherri. What is his name? Bill? Or is it Phil? Phil, I think.

They appeared to be a nice young couple who were eager to get involved. She was obviously pregnant. John made a mental note to check on whether or not they had been contacted by Calvary's Young Marrieds' volunteer follow-up staff. He knew how important connecting with others could be in stabilizing people's lives, following their entry into new surroundings.

His gaze returned to the couple seated next to them.

Arabic. I'm sure of it.

John had spent too much time in the Middle East not to see the traits etched in their facial features. Sculptured noses, dark eyes, olive skin.

I wonder what their background is? Christian? Probably. It isn't likely that Muslims would be here for one service, much less two. Maybe they are products of a Christian mission. What do you suppose prompted them to attend service again?

John's attention returned to the final words of the hymn.

He drew his thoughts together, momentarily forgetting the pair that had piqued his curiosity. The last phrase was sung, and sounds of the organ filled the church. The television camera zoomed in on his face as John stepped forward to lead in the pastoral prayer.

The prayer was followed with a worship chorus sung by the congregation and choir together. Next, an announcement concerning Calvary's annual men's retreat. It was scheduled to get under way with a golf tournament the day following Pastor Cain's return from Israel. Visitors were acknowledged and given the usual information folder by the ushers. Everyone was encouraged to stand, greet each other, and welcome new friends to the church.

TURNING, THEY SPOKE to the couple beside them.

"Hi. I'm Phil. This is my wife, Sherri."

"Good morning," the handsome strangers responded with a smile. They shook hands.

"My name is Akmed and this is Aziza, my wife."

"We're pleased to meet you."

"Have you been here a long time in this church?" Akmed inquired as people around them chatted noisily.

"Not long. What's it been now, Sherri?"

"Nearly three months. We're pretty new. I haven't noticed you before. Is this your first visit?"

"Yes. We are from Canada. Actually, we're on our honeymoon."

"Congratulations," Sherri whispered, squeezing Aziza's hand as they sat down. She turned her attention back to the platform where the soloist stood ready as the introductory strains of a taped music background poured through the sound system. A few minutes later, Pastor Cain was preaching. The Heidens quickly became absorbed in the message. They loved the teaching emphasis and admired the skill with which Pastor Cain was able to relate Bible passages to present-day living.

JOHN FELT THE WEARINESS OF THE DAY inching along his body as the third service got under way. He had long since discovered that the further into the morning he went, the harder it was to stay focused. Energy faded. His mind wandered. He flashed back briefly to the kitchen incident with Jeremy early yesterday. It seemed longer than just hours ago. They had not seen one another to talk since then. Jeremy was still sleeping when John left for yesterday's breakfast meeting with the board. By the time he returned, Jeremy was gone. Their paths had not crossed all day. A painful heaviness stirred in John as thoughts of his son crowded into his mind.

This is such a crucial time in his life. What is going to become of him? And Esther. I can't imagine what hurts and bitterness are still hidden inside her. What is all of this doing to us?

After Jenny's funeral, Esther had continued functioning each day in robotlike fashion. Cleaning house. Doing laundry. Spending hours alone by the window, a faraway look in her eyes. Reading occasionally. Mostly staring. It was the quiet between them that got to John. It was not the spiritual quiet that exists comfortably between two contented lovers. This quiet was abnormal. Dangerous. They didn't seem able to share anything deeper than surface talk anymore.

His eyes skimmed across the third congregation of the day. There she was, sitting near the back, with Jessica by her side. Jeremy had not been at either of the first two services. A quick scan confirmed that he was not in this one either. John's heart sank further.

Then his eyes fell on the Arabic-looking couple. This time they were sitting directly behind Ken Ralsten's family.

They're here again. What is going on with them?

John was puzzled. He determined not to let them get away without speaking to them.

How long has it been since someone has attended all three morning services, listening to the same message in each one?

He smiled to himself.

This may be a first!

Soon the soloist was standing and the taped orchestration had begun. Fingering the cover of the Bible in his lap, John forced himself to focus once more on the message he was about to give.

Thirty-two minutes later, he was standing at the main door, shaking hands and greeting people as they exited.

"Good morning to you."

"Good morning." The Arabic couple smiled pleasantly as John extended his hand toward them.

"Welcome to Calvary Church. Glad you could be with us today," John said. "Your names are . . . " His voice trailed off as he waited for their response.

"I am Akmed. This is my wife, Aziza."

"I'm delighted. I couldn't help noticing you this morning. You are a very attractive couple. But what motivated you to attend all three services today? Either you really enjoyed them or there must be some other reason. People don't normally stay with us through them all."

Akmed and Aziza had been fearful that this would happen. The possibility of such a query had been discussed in the team's planning meetings, but no better alternative had been suggested. Firsthand knowledge was critical to their success. They needed to understand the Sunday morning routine of activities. What does the building layout look like? How many exits are there? How many services and which one do most people attend? Which service is televised? That was important. What sort of security is in place? Scores of tactical questions required firsthand observation before answering.

"Pastor Cain, Aziza and I have never been to a Christian service of worship before today. We are Muslims. But we are curious about the Christian religion. This is our first trip away from our families and so we took advantage to come here. I hope it was all right?"

"It's more than all right," John replied warmly. "We are happy to welcome you. Where is your home?"

"Our parents came from Lebanon to Canada when we were very small," Akmed lied. "We grew up in Toronto and met each other there. Recently, we married, and are on our honeymoon."

"Congratulations. How long will you be here?"

"We start our return journey this afternoon."

"I hope you left your address so that I can send you our thanks for your visit."

"Thank you, Pastor Cain. It would not be appropriate. Our families are very strict and for us to receive mail from a Christian church would not be looked upon with favor. I thank you just the same."

"I understand. You are welcome. We will pray that you have a safe journey and a long, happy life together. It has been a pleasure to meet you both."

Akmed extended his hand to John once again, shaking it firmly. His eyes locked onto John's.

"One day, perhaps, we will see each other again."

▼▼129▼▼

NINE

The alarm was giving off its obnoxious best. John reached over, shut it off, and turned on the bed lamp with one motion. He lay back against the pillow, rubbing the sleep from his eyes, while trying to remember why he had set the alarm for this unholy hour. Finally, his mind clicked in.

Israel. I'm leaving for Israel today.

At the same time his thoughts were falling together, John felt movement beside him.

"Hi, sweetheart. It's time to rise and shine."

A stifled groan came from underneath the neighboring pillow. Her voice was muffled. "I'll make sure Jessica is awake."

John got out of bed and shuffled toward the bathroom. Thirty minutes later, he was showered, shaved, and dressed for the day. John always traveled in casual clothes. Comfortable slacks, open shirt, definitely no tie. Today, a light jacket to ward off the early morning chill.

He could hear the sounds of Esther's and Jessica's muffled

voices coming from Jessica's room. Jeremy had decided to stay over at Geoff's house for the night. He and John had said their good-byes, rather stiffly, the evening before. As he went out the door, Jeremy shook his hand. John gave Jeremy a brief hug, but felt him quickly pull away. Things were not right, John knew, but they would just have to wait for now.

John examined the single piece of luggage he would be taking. Toiletries were stored in a fold-out, hang-up plastic case containing pockets in which to separate various items. Shaving equipment went into one. Soap, deodorant, and body lotion in another, and so forth, until everything was in its place.

Esther had selected and packed most of John's things on Saturday. She was so skilled at coordinating and packing clothing that John rarely removed anything from his suitcase until he was ready to wear it. When he did, it usually required no ironing. This made travel much easier. One case containing all he needed was prepared with such skill that it would be two weeks exactly before he reached for the final change of clothes. By that time, he would be on his way home. His only laundry would be shorts and socks he would wash by hand and dry overnight. No fuss. No need to decide what to wear. He could concentrate on the people in the group and the details of their travel. John liked the arrangement.

At ten after five, he loaded their suitcases into the trunk of the car. The girls were still wrapping things up inside when the delivery boy tossed the morning paper onto the driveway and continued peddling his bicycle along the street.

John bent down to pick it up. Sliding the rubber band from around the paper, he glanced at the front page.

....

PEACE TALKS NOW AT A STANDOFF
The United States Secretary of State prepares to return
home today after three days of negotiation efforts in the

Middle East. Both the Israeli and Palestinian delega-
tions are refusing further discussions until unrest in the
Gaza area is resolved. Five Palestinian youth and one
Israeli soldier were killed in street fighting on Sunday.
Yasser Arafat urged Hamas leaders in Gaza to join him
in an orderly resolution of differences between themselves and the PLO.

*Great. Now I suppose I'll have some reassuring to do
when we get to the airport.*

John's previous trips into the Middle East had helped
him interpret news stories of this nature. It was always this
way in Israel. However, once in the country, such unpleas-
ant activity was hardly noticed. Israeli police and the military establishment kept a tight lid on things.

His eyes scanned the rest of the page.

FIVE-VEHICLE PILEUP ON BAY BRIDGE
Upper deck closed for two hours yesterday. A truck
overturned, colliding with four automobiles . . .
WASTE-REDUCTION PACT
SHOULD RESULT IN CLEAN BAY
Palo Alto will require additional audits from some
companies.

Turning to the inside section, he skimmed through the
editorial page and the book review section. Just then, Esther
and Jessica came through the doorway. Jessica was talking
a mile a minute, bubbling with enthusiasm and the anticipation of adventure. Esther paused, checking to make certain
the door was locked behind them. Turning, she walked with
slow deliberateness to the car, as if each step were a huge

effort. John could see that her face was drawn. Though it seemed that they hardly talked anymore, he could tell that she was not looking forward to his being gone.

He laid the paper on the garage counter where she would be sure to find it later. He did not see the small article in the lower right-hand column of page three.

....

MISSING RANGER'S BODY FOUND
Glacier Park Ranger Carl Deeker's shallow grave was discovered on Sunday. Deeker had been missing for more than three days. Bloodhounds led searchers to the remote wilderness site. Apparent cause of death is believed to be a knife wound caused by unknown assailants. Authorities await the results of an autopsy. Remains of a rubber boat and outboard motor were found nearby. No known motive. Illegal entry into the country by persons unknown is a possibility. No suspects. Investigation continues. The FBI is joining in the investigation.

....

John backed the car out of the garage and turned south on Jefferson, heading for the freeway.

TEN

On the way to the airport, Jessica leaned over the seat back to talk to her mother. Esther had been quiet, smiling at her daughter, nodding her head occasionally in a kind of motherly agreement. Jessica's conversation was basically one-sided and nonstop. For once, John was grateful. At least her voice filled the otherwise empty space with sound.

He looked over at Esther now and then, at the same time keeping an eye on the lights of the cars braking in front of them. Traffic was heavy, sandwiching them on either side, as well as front and back, in the fast-slow-stop-go rhythm so familiar to California commuters. The early morning light revealed the uneven chop of the Bay's surface, stirred by stiff breezes, as they crossed the long, low San Mateo Bridge.

She did not seem sullen. Withdrawn was probably a better word. Did Jessica sense the growing rift between him and her mother? Of course they had never spoken of such a thing. But he felt the void this morning. Did Jessica feel it too? Could that be why she was chattering so?

John sighed heavily as he tightened his grip on the

wheel. Esther's eyes darted toward him. A thin smile threatened to erase the serious look on her face. Her hand started toward him. Then, as quickly as it had come, the smile faded. A familiar sadness took its place, like a dark veil covering a thousand unspoken emotions that John could only imagine were hidden inside. Her hand shook slightly, then fell back into her lap.

Jessica was suddenly quiet. John glanced in the rearview mirror in time to see her eyes move slowly from her mother's face to his own. She had noticed the movement of her mother's hand.

She's sharp, he thought guiltily. *She knows something is not right. I wonder what's going on inside her little head. Maybe the next two weeks together will give us a chance to talk. But what will I tell her? Lord, have I made another mistake? Should I have left her at home? If she starts asking questions, what answers can I give her? I don't have any that satisfy myself, much less Jessica.*

Jessica broke the silence, jump-starting her one-way conversation by rattling off trivia facts she had accumulated on her own in preparation for the journey. The rest of the way to the airport was filled with an amazingly accurate geography lesson on a land she had never seen.

John was impressed.

JESSICA SPIED EDGAR AND JILL ANDERSON talking with Shad Coleman and Mary Callahan, as her father picked up the luggage and stepped off the escalator. Shad and Mary were both in their mid-thirties and served as lay leaders in Calvary's singles ministry. Jessica knew them a little bit, but the Andersons were two of her favorite people. She was glad they were going. They were standing halfway between the ticket counter and the outer edge of the lobby, drinking coffee and laughing at something that had just been said.

Edgar looked up and waved.

"Hi, John. Hi, Esther. And good morning, Jessica! Here, let me help you with that case, young lady." Edgar reached to take Jessica's luggage from her hand.

"Thank you, anyway, Mr. Anderson," she smiled. "Daddy says I have to carry whatever I packed. So I guess I'd better get used to it."

Edgar laughed. "Oh, your daddy is one tough hombre, Jessica. But I think he wouldn't mind if I took it over there and put it with the rest of ours." He pointed to a small pile of bags near the counter.

Jessica looked at her father. He nodded.

"Okay, Mr. Anderson. Thank you."

Edgar Anderson's hair was snowy white. His face reminded Jessica of a well-worn, leather punching bag, a physiological fact of life that was not entirely without substance.

Edgar had grown up on the streets of Oakland. He fought his way up through gang-infested alleyways, at the same time avoiding the neighborhood drug pushers under the watchful eye of his mother and her sister, Aunt Ellie. Edgar never knew his father. His mother kept them in food and a place to call home by working downtown for a commercial janitorial service. She had night duty, so Ellie kept an eye on Edgar.

He began working out at a neighborhood gym when he was thirteen. It was a city-sponsored boys' program, designed to give street kids something constructive to do with their time. The rest was history. Golden gloves middleweight champion First professional fight at age nineteen. A contender for the world middleweight championship at twenty-three. Then, on the night he fought for the title in Las Vegas, he suffered a torn retina in his left eye. End of boxing career.

However, unlike many fighters, Edgar had carefully invested his career winnings. It was enough to get him, his mother, and Aunt Ellie out of their tough Oakland neighborhood and into a small but comfortable condominium in Baytown. It wasn't long after that Edgar met Jill at a Chamber of Commerce luncheon. She worked for the Chamber and was the designated luncheon hostess that day. Edgar was the guest speaker. Before lunch was over, he had asked her to join him for dinner. She agreed. That is, if he would come with her to church the following Sunday.

Though Edgar had never been a churchgoer, he was motivated. Jill was attractive, intelligent, and had a smile that lit up the world. That first Sunday, he noticed a few other African-Americans scattered through the congregation. But, hey, this was the suburbs, man. The church was mostly lily-white, sprinkled with a small percentage of upwardly mobile Mexican-Americans and Asian-Americans. At first he was uncomfortable, but he soon felt acceptance. His color didn't seem to matter much to these folk. They didn't make over his boxing background either. They just welcomed him for who he was. It felt great. Four months later, Edgar made a confession of faith in Christ. Five months after that, he and Jill were married.

Three grown children and thirty-eight years later, sixty-three-year-old Edgar had taken early retirement from his position as Pacific Telephones' public relations director. Going to Israel with Pastor Cain had been a lifelong dream for both Edgar and Jill. This morning, that dream was becoming reality.

During the next half hour, others made their way up the escalator and over to the group that was queuing up. The pile of luggage had grown to a formidable size. John asked Shad and Mary to make certain that each piece was checked and every carryon item was properly identified. They handed out rose-colored tags, watching as everyone filled them out and attached them to their bags. This up-front work would make travel easier later on. Shad counted the number of checked luggage pieces. Twenty-seven. He counted the second time, just to be sure. Still twenty-seven.

When they were finished, John had Mary collect all the passports and bring them to him. Twenty-three persons were scheduled for the tour, plus Jessica and John. Twenty-five passports altogether.

Wait. I only counted twenty-four here.

John looked around. He recounted, just to be certain. Twenty-four.

Terrific! Who's missing?

He checked his watch.

Seven-ten. We board in twenty minutes.

John ran through the names on his passenger list, checking faces in the animated group that stood nearby. Anderson, Edgar and Jill. Callahan, Mary. Cloud, Jerry and Susan. Coleman, Shad. Eiderman, Harold and Gisele. Hansen, Patricia. Micceli, Nick and Patricia.

All here so far.

Mitchel, Larry and Sandy. Smith, Adele. Sommers, Greg and Debbie. Taylor, Ruth. Thomas, Bob and Donna. Unruh, Evelyn. Watson, Dan and Phyllis. Wilson, Dan.

Wait. Unruh. I didn't see Evelyn.

John checked over the group again. People kept moving, talking to each other, as well as to family members and well-wishers who had come to see them off, making it difficult to keep track.

Still no Evelyn.

"Has anyone seen Evelyn Unruh?"

The small crowd grew silent as they looked about at one another, shaking their heads.

Everyone knew Evelyn. Small, petite, and seventy-seven. In fact, the others had been delighted when they heard that Evelyn would be traveling with them. They relished this senior citizen being part of the group. She was lively. No, feisty was a better word. A widow for nine years, Evelyn was warm and caring and amazingly aware of everything happening around her. The world had not passed her by, her friends declared, jokingly. It couldn't catch up to her!

John glanced at his watch. Seven-twenty.

A worried look crossed his face.

"Honey, there's a telephone over there. Will you try to call Evelyn? Her home number is here on the group listing. While you're doing that, I'll work the passports and tickets through the group ticket counter."

"All right. I'll be just a minute." Esther took the list and moved toward the phone.

"Good morning, sir," smiled the lady in uniform. "I'll take the tickets first. It looks as though you've got them organized alphabetically. Good. Now, may I have the passports please?"

"At the moment, we're missing one member of our group," John said, returning the attendant's smile, noting that her name was Geri, according to the name plate she wore. "It's Mrs. Unruh. Here's her ticket."

"I'll just put it to one side until she arrives. How many pieces of luggage will you be checking?"

"Twenty-seven. Plus whatever Mrs. Unruh brings. May I call you Geri?"

"Of course, Mr. Cain."

"If you don't mind, Geri, just attach all the baggage claim numbers to my ticket. It will be easier for me to keep things together that way. And I'd like them checked through to Amsterdam."

"Yes, sir. I understand. You've a nice group of people traveling with you. But I'm sure you'll be very busy trying to stay on top of it all."

She continued tearing tickets and matching them with passports. John scanned the lobby, a feeling of apprehension beginning to build.

"Is this Mrs. Cain?" the attendant asked, not looking at anyone, but seeing the name on the ticket, Cain, J. Before John could answer, she opened Jessica's passport. "No, my guess is that she's too young for Mrs. Cain. Your daughter?"

"Yes."

"How exciting for her to be on this trip with you. I hope you have a wonderful time together."

"Thank you."

"No one answers, John." Esther had come up behind him. "She must be on her way. I think her son, Donald, was planning to drive her to the airport. At least that's what Jill was told. They had offered to bring her in their car."

"Okay, hon," John responded, looking beyond her as he spoke, trying to will Evelyn Unruh into existence. "I hope nothing has happened to them."

"There you are, sir. Your tickets and passports. Baggage is checked through to Amsterdam. The claim checks are attached to your ticket as you requested. Seat assignments are in the upper right-hand corner of each ticket. Flight 311 leaves from Gate 23 at eight o'clock. In Los Angeles, you have a two-hour layover in which to transfer. You should have plenty of time for a comfortable transfer. Boarding has begun, so you had best move everyone along quickly."

"Thank you, Geri," John said. "By the way, this is my wife, Esther."

"I'm pleased to meet you, Mrs. Cain. Are you taking some time off while your husband and daughter are away?"

Esther attempted a smile, caught off guard by the introduction. "I haven't decided yet. Just getting them out the door has been the main task. Maybe some quiet time at home."

"Best wishes to all of you. I hope this will be the best of times for each of you. In fact, I'll pray that that will be the case." The attendant began clearing the pile of tickets from the countertop.

Startled, John turned back.

"Are you a Christian, Geri?" he asked.

"I am," she replied, beaming. "Two years and four months old as a matter of fact. And I'm guessing that you are a pastor and these are some of your flock?"

"Right you are," John smiled. "Thanks again, Geri, for your service . . . *and* your prayers. Maybe you can shoot one up for Mrs. Unruh."

"Already have. You run along now. When she arrives, she'll come this way, and I'll personally see to it that she gets on board. Bye."

"All right, everyone," John smiled, as the people gathered around. "Time to head 'em up and move 'em out."

"What about Evelyn?" someone called out.

"One of the airline staff has volunteered to watch for her. The rest of us have to go along. Say your good-byes now, and let's go."

Hugs and kisses were exchanged for the last time and, as well-wishers waved their farewells, the group slowly made its way toward the security check point. As carryon items moved through the X-ray machine and, one by one, the passengers proceeded down the corridor, John pulled Esther to one side. Jessica had already given her mother an excited child's hug and kiss. She was walking on ahead, hand in hand with Edgar. They were talking animatedly to each other.

"Will you be all right, hon?" John asked, gathering her in his arms.

"Do I have a choice?"

"I guess not."

"I'll be okay. Don't worry about me. Just take care of yourself and Jessica. And everybody else too," she added, returning his hug.

"Sure."

Silence.

"I wish you were going with us."

"We've been through that, John. I just don't want to go on this trip."

"I know. Still, I wish . . ."

Esther slowly pushed away from him. "John, I need to go now."

John looked into her eyes. They were dry. She looked sad, but there were no tears. The dark veil was there again. He felt pain rising in his chest. Familiar pain. It was not his heart, of that he was certain. At least not his physical heart.

This is not a good good-bye. I should not be going. I am . . . "Good-bye, John. Have a good trip. Keep safe." Esther broke away and started toward the exit. Suddenly, she stopped, turned, and stared for a long moment at John. "Remember, my darling, I love you very much."

John returned her stare, at a loss for words.

Esther hasn't said "my darling" in . . . how long? John felt warmed by this sudden expression of affection and love. Then, in a flash, the warm feeling disappeared and was replaced by a stab of anxiety and apprehension.

"I love you too," he finally replied.

She stood a moment longer, her sad eyes gazing into John's face. Then she turned and walked away. She did not look back.

John stood rooted, watching until she disappeared around the corner.

"Sir, you need to hurry. Your group is through."

With a heavy sigh, John tossed his carryon bag onto the conveyor belt and walked through the X-ray checkpoint. No buzzers. But John didn't even notice. His mind was full. Jessica was ahead of him, in the airplane. Esther was on her way to the parking lot. Jeremy was probably on his way to class by now. *And where is Evelyn?*

He slung the bag over his shoulder and ambled toward the airplane entrance.

Just then, rounding the corner and rushing toward the checkpoint, John saw the ticket attendant, Geri. On her arm was the wisp of an elderly woman, chatting and smiling as though she had all the time in the world. In her other hand was Evelyn's suitcase.

"Hi, pastor," she called out, waving with her free hand. "Isn't this just the nicest young lady? She told me she knew you and that she would take care of getting us together." Her suitcase and small carryon were moving through the X-ray machine. Geri told John to hand the suitcase to a flight attendant. It was too late to check it in here. They would need to do that in Los Angeles. A moment later, Evelyn Unruh was saying good-bye to her new young friend.

John waved to Geri, shooting her a grateful look. Then he took Evelyn by the arm. "Okay, young lady, enough chatting. We need to hurry or they'll be off to Israel without us. What happened? Nothing serious, I hope?"

"Well, it was all my fault, pastor. About halfway here, I decided to get my passport out of my purse. Well, I looked and looked, but no passport. Then, I remembered. I had laid it on the dresser so that I'd not forget to pick it up. Well, Donald just cut over that grassy sort of median in the freeway and we were headed home before I knew what was happening. We got my passport and made it back here just in time. I hope God and the State of California forgive Donald for driving like he did!"

"Good morning." The cabin hostess was smiling. "You two just made it. You are the last to board. Your seats are down this aisle."

A cheer went up from twenty-three of the passengers as Evelyn and John appeared in the cabin.

John sat down in an aisle seat next to Jessica.

The attendant helped Evelyn strap herself in as the plane began backing away from the terminal.

They were on their way!

THE DARK-HAIRED MAN folded his newspaper and laid it down on the seat next to him. He crushed the remainder of his cigarette in the armrest ashtray. As he stood, his eyes followed the attractive woman walking slowly toward the escalator. He had noticed her when she first arrived with her husband and daughter. From a distance, he watched as the group gathered together in preparation for their journey. He listened as they spoke of Tel Aviv, Bethlehem, and Jerusalem, familiar scenes crossing his mind at the mention of each name. Eventually, he had seen them disappear down the corridor toward their plane.

Now he started across the lobby, his eyes still on the attractive woman who by this time he understood to be the wife of the group leader.

Suddenly, he was being run down by a little old lady, rushing through the airport entrance. A middle-aged man, scrambling to keep up, carried a bag behind her.

"Excuse me, young man," she said excitedly, pushing by him on her way to the ticket counter.

"Mrs. Unruh?" the attendant called out behind the desk. "Is that you?"

"It's me, dear. Ready for the trip of a lifetime. Unfortunately, I'm late. You didn't let them go without me, did you?"

"No, Mrs. Unruh. We didn't. Come with me."

"Thank you, dear. By the way, what's your name?"

"It's Geri."

"Okay, Geri, let's be going. Did Pastor Cain give you my ticket? And don't you need to see my passport or something?"

"I have your ticket, Mrs. Unruh. Let me see your passport and I'll take care of everything while we're walking."

"Well, then, we don't want to keep them waiting, do we?"

"No, Mrs. Unruh," Geri laughed. "We certainly don't."

Evelyn's son handed her suitcase to Geri, kissed his mother good-bye, then dashed back through the door, smiling and shaking his head as he ran to where his car was illegally parked.

The dark-haired man turned back from this incongruous encounter and looked to where he had last seen the attractive woman walking. She was gone. He pursed his lips, paused, and took out another cigarette, reaching at the same time for a book of matches. Exhaling smoke, he blew out the match, dropping it on the marble floor. Casually, as if he had all day, the man moved across the lobby to a telephone station.

He entered ten numbers and spoke quietly into the phone.

ELEVEN

Akmed El Hussein returned the receiver to its cradle on the wall. Turning, he looked at the others around the table who were watching him.

"That was Ihab. They're on their way!"

A smile broke out on their faces. Mousa punched at Mamdouh with a clinched fist.

"How many are there?" asked Aziza.

"Twenty-five."

"The pastor? He and his wife have gone as well?"

"Not his wife. She stayed behind."

"Do we know why? She was supposed to be with him. Isn't that what they told us from Tel Aviv?"

"Yes. She must have changed her mind. She has gone on all their other trips."

"He should have known," Aziza frowned. "I don't like it when there are surprises." Her mind drifted back to Goat's Head and Ranger Deeker.

"It does not matter, Aziza," said Akmed. "Actually, this may even be better."

"What do you mean?"

"He took someone else with him."

"Someone else? Who?"

Traces of an evil smile twisted across Akmed's face. "His little girl. About twelve or thirteen."

A long silence.

Mousa chuckled. "Perhaps our people at home can find the girl a husband while she visits. Wouldn't you like to have a fresh young American girl for a bride, Mamdouh? Eh?" Mousa pushed Mamdouh's shoulder again with his hand.

Mamdouh grinned, glancing over at Aziza.

Aziza stared quietly at the center of the table. She hated it when the men began talking demeaningly about women. Even American women. It was a way of thinking common among her people, but she resented it. True, a wife had some status, but unmarried women and young girls were little more than chattel. The male/female double standard was never more evident than within the community of her own people. On that, she felt, there was no argument.

"All right, everyone," Akmed sat down in the lone, remaining chair, placing his forearms on the table edge. His hands touched in prayerlike fashion. "Let's get back to work. We were discussing the church building. Aziza, please continue with your report."

Aziza had no notes. Her memory was excellent, almost photographic. She closed her eyes, bringing back the scene, allowing its details to imprint vividly on her mental screen. Eyes open again, she glanced around the table, then began.

"As I was saying, the building has a large lobby with restrooms on either side. An information area is located inside the main entrance. There appear to be four other exits, besides the main one. The others are smaller. Inside, a hallway circles around all but the platform wall. Behind the platform is a large, stained-glass window. There are several doors leading into the auditorium, where the people gather to have their services. These doors will need to be secured with explosives immediately. Here's the way it looks."

With a felt pen and her napkin, Aziza drew a rough sketch of the church building, together with the parking lot and off-street entrances. Mousa and Mamdouh leaned forward for a closer look.

She glanced at Akmed. He nodded for her to continue.

"The auditorium is fairly large. That is where the infidels worship their God. It seats about seven hundred, but there are fewer than that at each service. There are normally three services, but we'll shorten their schedule a bit this week. They hold what is called Sunday School for the children and young people. Even adults. These are smaller classes, held in rooms off the hallway on both the first and second floors. There seem to be mostly children in attendance at the time we will arrive. Hopefully, we can let them go?"

She looked questioningly at Akmed.

He shrugged his shoulders. "Whatever is the will of Allah, Aziza. Go over the plan we discussed on our return here."

Aziza paused, reaching for a half-empty glass of orange juice. The others watched her as she finished it off. With a corner of the napkin on which she had been drawing, she daubed at her lips.

"All right. Here is the plan that Akmed proposes, now that we have been at the attack site."

0850 LOCAL TIME
BAYTOWN, CALIFORNIA

ESTHER TURNED THE KEY and opened the door. Stepping inside, she automatically reached for the alarm pad. The system light was red, emitting a piercing warning signal as she entered. Once she tapped in the four-digit code, there was silence. The red light turned green.

The color for "go." But go where?

Silence.

She moved to the center of the family room and stood still. She could feel her heart beat out its rhythm like some distant African drummer.

The quiet slammed against her with an oppressive physical force. She fell back, her knees buckling as she tried to regain her balance. She was left breathless, staring at the walls. Then at the ceiling. Was it her imagination? Or was the room really getting smaller? Esther's eyes closed tightly, then opened. Her breathing was shallow and rapid. She felt exhausted, as though she had just run a marathon race.

Shuffling toward the patio door, Esther fumbled with the latch, then threw it open and staggered outside. For a long moment, she stood still, gulping in fresh air, feeling as though her heart might take flight, at last escaping the flesh-and-blood prison that held it captive. She moved first one foot, then the other, her steps short and unsteady, until she could slump down on the nearest patio chair. Her brain was spinning. She leaned forward so that her head was between her knees, letting it remain there for a full minute, while her heartbeat returned to normal and her fear of fainting dissipated. Slowly, she raised to a sitting position and looked across the pool to the flowers in the distance.

"What on earth was that about?" Esther spoke the question out loud, needing to hear some normal human sound. The morning sun felt warm against her body, but she shook from an inner coldness.

Maybe I'm finally losing it. Maybe I'm certifiable after all. O God, John is gone. I'm here alone. What if . . .

Esther began feeling a new sensation, one that was equally frightening. A wave of intense loneliness swept in, crashing relentlessly against the shore of her already delicate nervous system. Closing her eyes, she gripped the arms of the chair, her knuckles turning white, as she forced herself to take deep breaths until the feeling passed.

At last, she opened her eyes. Her body quivered and tingled. Her hands shook so that she grasped one tightly with the other, trying to settle her nerves down. Slowly, hesitantly, Esther stood to her feet. She looked at the door. It was only a few steps away, but it seemed much farther. She was surprised when she took a step, however, to discover her limbs working quite normally. Gathering in another deep breath, she walked to the door, opened it, and went inside. She looked at the walls and ceiling again. They were still there, right where they ought to be.

It was all a figment of your imagination, she thought grimly. *You're cracking up, Esther!*

But the intense feeling of loss and sadness had become all-consuming, draining her mind of its protective capacity.

Carefully, Esther walked across the family room. Turning down the hall, she entered the master bedroom, making her way past the bed, the dresser, and through the bathroom door. Reaching up, she opened the medicine cabinet. Her hand rested on a single, white bottle on the top shelf, half hidden behind a deodorant container and some hair spray. Pulling it out, she held it up, carefully reading the instruction label. Then she twisted the safety cap off and poured the contents out on the counter. She began counting, sorting through the capsules with her finger as she counted.

0910 *LOCAL TIME*
WASHINGTON, D.C.

....

12 SEPTEMBER

The White House
Office of the National Security Director
SENSITIVE
    RE: National Park Ranger, Carl Frederick Deeker.
    AGE: 41.

FAMILY STATUS: Ummarried.

LENGTH OF SERVICE: Twelve Years.

WORK PERFORMANCE RECORD: Excellent.

REPORTED MISSING: Wednesday, 7 September.

Body found Sunday, 11 September, app. 0900 local. Approximately two miles into Glacier National Park. Autopsy shows death caused by a single stab wound. Body buried in shallow grave short way off trail. Murder weapon believed to be long, narrow knife. Not recovered. Raft and outboard motor, camouflaged with brush and tree limbs, recovered nearby. Taken to FBI office, Kalispell, MT.

Reason for murder: undetermined. Possible Deeker surprised unidentified persons entering country. FBI considers killing and equipment recovered too sophisticated for most illegal entries. *Terrorist incursion a possibility.* Number of illegals unknown. est: three to six, male.

Will advise when further details available.

....

0935 LOCAL TIME
LOS ANGELES, CALIFORNIA

"OKAY, GANG. EVERYBODY OUT." John stood in the street, near the door of the transfer bus. People made their way out into the midmorning sunshine and waited for the others.

"Are we all here now?" John asked, scanning his group with a practiced eye.

"That's debatable, pastor," quipped someone from the back. Several laughed.

"I'm glad your sense of humor is manifesting itself so soon, Dan," said John, recognizing Dan Wilson's voice. "We'll all need ample doses of it before the day is over.

"Now, we're going through that entry over there," John

pointed. "Be sure you have all your carryon items. We're not coming back for a long time."

Some cheers went up.

"Follow me. Larry, would you and Sandy mind bringing up the rear? That way we won't lose anybody."

"Sure thing, pastor." They moved to the back edge of the group.

"Okay everybody, our next stop is KLM's departure area."

John looked at the clock high on the wall to his left. It was nearly ten o'clock. Flight 2 was scheduled to leave on time, at eleven, according to the computerized display of arrivals and departures. John slowed momentarily to let an elderly Asian couple cross in front of him. The man pushed a baggage cart. She walked a step or two behind him. John smiled, nodded a greeting, then resumed his confident gait at the head of the group.

We're doing fine. No problems. Looking good. A few more minutes and we're ready to board.

TWELVE

"Good morning."

Rosa smiled, stepping to one side of the hallway so that the man could pass by. "Good morning, sir. Are you and your friends enjoying your stay?"

"Yes, very much, thank you. By the way, I want to thank you for the way you've been caring for our rooms. You do excellent work."

"Thank you, sir. I am happy that you are pleased with our service."

"We are indeed. Have a good day."

"And you as well, sir."

The man moved on, disappearing down the stairs.

Robert Jibril and his three Arab friends had turned out to be good guests. They were quiet and well-mannered, no trouble at all. Even Rosa was impressed.

Rosa had worked for the Brainards ever since Jim and Middie had moved to Booth Bay. Her parents had immigrated to New York City from Puerto Rico. She met Manuel Posadas while both of them struggled to finish high school in one of the city's toughest neighborhoods. They were kindred spirits. Both had felt the sting of ostracism because they were members of immigrant families.

While they had much in common, they were faced with an ethnic conflict, for Manuel's parents had come from Mexico City, and there was animosity between the Mexican and Puerto Rican communities. By the time Manuel reached high school, his parents were both U.S. citizens. But that accomplishment did little to stem the tide of hatred and abuse that spilled into the streets of their run-down neighborhood.

The day they graduated was a day of celebration for both families. Manuel and Rosa were both eldest children and the first in either family to graduate from high school. They lived only two blocks from each other, and Manuel's attraction to Rosa had been reason enough for the families to get to know one another quite well.

At first it had been hard. But both sets of parents were good people and they saw clearly the feelings their children had for each other. Eventually, they even came together at the Posadas' home. That night, the two fathers shook hands and glanced knowingly at Rosa and Manuel. Then over dinner, they began swapping stories about work. Manuel's father was a janitor in a nearby elementary school. Rosa's father worked with a maintenance crew in the underground maze that was New York's infamous subway system.

Rosa's three brothers and Manuel's two brothers and three sisters had so far avoided falling into the gaping manholes of failure that swallowed up so many of their peers. They were proud families, proud of each other. And, every Sunday, both families made their way to Saint Teresa's for morning Mass. Their strong Catholic faith had become a bulwark against the social and moral devastation that pummeled their grim surroundings.

On the night of their graduation, Manuel had asked Rosa

to marry him. She was quick to say yes. She knew that she loved this man more than life. The wedding took place at Saint Teresa's the following September. For six months, they lived with Manuel's family. It had been hard, but they had survived. Manuel was a good carpenter. He loved working with his hands and enjoyed the creativity and the challenge of the trade. He found that he was particularly interested in and skilled at remodeling old rooms and restoring old furniture. It was exactly the skill he needed to make a place for them in Booth Bay.

Why Booth Bay?

It was simple, really. Rosa had told the Brainards how it happened, when she first interviewed for her job at Hill House. The summer before their wedding, she and Manuel had run across a color photograph in a magazine. It was of a place that struck them as being the most beautiful they had ever seen. The companion article identified it as Booth Bay, Maine's most popular resort, with over fifty thousand visitors thronging its streets in the summertime.

They read about quaint little shops, charter boats, and offshore islands with such strange names as The Cuckolds and The Hypocrites. Visions of clambakes, flower shows, and clean schools filled Rosa's senses with the perfume of fantasy. Manuel saw something else. The article talked about auctions and antiques, weathered houses and restored sailing vessels. He pictured himself being able to make a good life for Rosa and his future family. Booth Bay would need someone with his skills as a fledgling wood craftsman.

They cut the article out of the magazine and folded it away. On early evening walks through the seamy neighborhood in which they had grown up, they would unfold the picture of this pristine bayside village. Sitting on the dirty steps of the old row house in which they lived, they held on to it together, and dreamed of living in such a beautiful place. The following March, they were on their way.

That had been seven years ago. Since then, Manuel had developed into a respected carpenter. His work was well known in Booth Bay. He had a reputation for excellent quality and unquestionable honesty. His prices were reasonable. That was important to Mainers. And his work was the best. That was important too.

Rosa came to work at eight-thirty each morning, something she had done almost every day since Hill House opened its doors. At least every day during the tourist season. She dearly loved the Brainards and enjoyed working for them. They were pleasant and kind. They had invited Rosa and Manuel to dinner soon after she began working there, an evening neither of them would ever forget. It had been the Posadas' first social occasion with people of such different background. And, of course, the Brainards were respected business people, and older, while Rosa and Manuel still felt very much like children.

Both had been nervous as they stood on the porch, ready to ring the doorbell, unsure of what to expect. Rosa walked through this door to work every day. But this was different. However, the evening was still young when they began to relax and feel at home. Later, on their way home, they decided it had been very much like being with their own families in New York City.

When their first child was born, Middie came to their small, neat clapboard house on the north side of town and took care of Rosa and the baby for three days. Each morning, she would arrive at nine and stay until Manuel returned from work.

Today, there were two children, both boys, and a third was on the way. Rosa missed Middie more than she could express to anyone. It had been like losing her own mother when Middie died. Mr. Brainard had asked Manuel to serve as a pallbearer that sad day in the little cemetery. It was an honor that he would remember always. Manuel tried to stay in touch with Mr. Brainard after that, but supporting his family kept him busy. Anyhow, the old gentleman seemed more distant of late, more withdrawn. He was different now that Middie was gone. Young Manuel was not exactly sure what to do about it, so he basically left Grandpa Brainard alone. Maybe that was best for now.

Rosa stayed in touch, however, because of her work. With the natural instinct of a woman, she occasionally brought the children over to see their "Grandpa." The children loved him and he always seemed to enjoy their visits. On cold days, they would curl up in front of the fireplace while Grandpa read stories from the books Rosa always stuffed in their packs. On warm summer days, Rosa smiled as she watched them walking across the grass in front of Hill House, each child clinging to a single finger of Grandpa's large hands.

All the rooms had been filled over the weekend. Today, however, only four were in use. One by an older man and his wife, who were leaving this morning. Another by a honeymoon couple from Boston. And the two rooms occupied by the Arab men.

Rosa knocked on the door.

"Just a minute," a male voice responded.

She heard voices speaking in low tones, footsteps, and then the door opened.

"It's your maid service, sir. But I see that you are busy. I can come back later."

The man looked over his shoulder at the others. Rosa could see two men behind him. One was seated in a chair near the window. The other stood by the bed.

"It's all right," the man said. "Come in now. We were just leaving."

The door opened wide. Two of the men reached for windbreakers hanging in the open closet, and stepped through the doorway. The third man rose slowly from the chair as he shuffled some papers into a leather case. Rosa busied herself with gathering up clean towels and bathroom supplies from her hallway cart. Out of the corner of her eye, she observed the man zip the case closed and then carefully set the built-in combination lock. He placed the case in the top drawer of the room's small writing desk, pausing for a moment, as if deciding whether or not to leave it there. Then, pushing the drawer shut, he turned and walked toward Rosa.

The man was dressed in sneakers, jeans, and a blue sweater pulled over a sport shirt with an open collar. A handsome face. Dark hair. But it was his eyes that caused Rosa to look again. They were piercing, a deep brown. She had the discomforting feeling of being looked *through*, not at. His appearance was that of a man very much in control. Still, there was about him a sense of mystery. Even danger!

Come on, Rosa. Get a grip. You've been watching too much television!

He brushed against her briefly as he moved through the doorway.

"The room is fine today," the man spoke at last. "Just make up the beds and clean the bathroom. Don't worry about anything else. Can you do that?"

"Yes, certainly. If that is all you wish."

"That will be fine," he said quietly, now standing outside in the hallway. "Nothing else is necessary."

Turning, the man walked to the stairs and soon disappeared from sight.

Rosa set the towels and washcloths down, and proceeded to open the window. A strong odor of tobacco permeated every part of the room. Rosa did not smoke and hated the way the smell worked its way into the bedding, rugs, towels, even the wallpaper. As she stood by the window, letting fresh breezes blow softly into the room, she saw the men leaving Hill House and getting into their car. The last man looked up at the window and saw her standing there. He paused for a moment with his hand on the front passenger side door, looking at her. Then he got in and closed the door. The car backed out of the parking stall and drove away.

Rosa returned to her task. As she put fresh linens on the bed, she thought about the room's inhabitants. She was used to all kinds of people. After all, she grew up in New York City where a woman needed to develop an instinct about strangers. You had to look out for yourself in the City. There were good people there, but plenty of bad ones too.

Rosa was not unattractive. Her dark, reddish brown hair had a tousled, windblown appearance that was natural. It framed dark eyes, a delicate nose, full lips, and cheeks that dimpled when she smiled. Her overall look was one of fitness and health. Two children had not diminished the appeal of her well-formed body. She hoped that the same would be true after number three.

Rosa had been propositioned by more than a few young and not so young men in the old neighborhood during her teen years. Had it not been for her strong upbringing and the powerful sense of family with which she was raised, she often wondered what might have happened to her. She was sure that her faith in God was part of what protected her. It had also been God who brought Manuel into her life. Of that she was absolutely certain. She took pride in the fact that she had been a virgin when she joined Manuel in the marriage bed on their first night together as husband and wife. In her neighborhood, that in itself was no small feat.

She had developed an acute sense for what was good and bad, safe and unsafe, while surviving those earlier years. Maybe that was what she felt this morning. Yes! That was it. The same feeling that she used to have when things became unsafe around her in the old neighborhood. It was an instinct that animals used in order to survive their predators. It had served her well on more than a few occasions in the past. But she had not felt like this for years. Not since arriving in Booth Bay. Not like this!

Rosa stopped her work. Standing in the center of the room, she stared at the drawer in the writing desk.

What is so valuable that it requires the protection of a combination lock? Why would a man bring that sort of thing with him on his vacation? It could be business, of course. That's probably all it is. Some kind of business deal that these four men are involved in together.

Having processed that thought, Rosa glanced around the room one last time before leaving. She paused at the doorway, staring at the bed. She placed the soiled linens in the laundry bag and then walked over to the bed. Kneeling, she looked underneath.

They're still there.

Yesterday, while cleaning, Rosa's vacuum sweeper had bumped something under the bed. She had bent down to look. Usually, nothing was stored under any beds. But that morning, she saw three long, waterproof bags, zipped and obviously locked, pushed against the wall. Out of curiosity, she felt one of the bags. She could not make out the contents. She pulled on the end of one of them. It was heavy.

Rosa had wondered about suitcases. The bureau drawers contained neatly folded shirts, socks, and underwear. Pants, sweaters, and jackets hung in the closet. Toiletries were carefully arranged in the bathroom.

But there were no suitcases.

And only one suitcase in Mr. Jibril's room.

One case for four men.

It seemed strange.

At first, Rosa thought the bags under the bed had contained their clothing. However, her brief investigation told her that they were full, not of clothes but of something else. But what?

Normally, Rosa was not nosy. She respected the privacy

of her guests. So what was it that was eating at her?

Rosa, you are a foolish woman. There is nothing here out of the ordinary. These are just four men on vacation. Leave them alone and hope that they give you a big tip! You can use it!

She stood, walked back to the hall, and closed the door, turning the key in the lock. Gathering her things together, she moved down the hall to the honeymooners' room. Stopping in front of their door, her mind remained on the men whose room she had just left.

One man, in particular.

He is a handsome one, I'll say that. Very strong and athletic looking. And those piercing, brown eyes!

Rosa chuckled to herself.

But no one is perfect.

She remembered the scar. His beard covered part of it, but not all. The scar ran across the cheek toward his ear.

As she knocked on the honeymooners' door, Rosa wondered how the man had gotten it.

MOHAMMED ALI ATTA eased the rented cadillac through Booth Bay's narrow streets and few signal lights until they reached Route 27. As they drove by the Booth Bay Railway Museum, Mohammed informed the others that it contained a rideable miniature railroad, a turn-of-the-century barbershop, a bank, and a country store, as well as an antique auto museum.

Their lack of response caused Mohammed to cease his attempt as tour host for the others. They drove on in silence. As they made their way through the wooded countryside, the others looked out the ample side windows at the passing farmhouses, rivers, and saltwater inlets. It was a beautiful land.

Easing onto U.S. 1, they drove through Wiscasset and on to Bath. In this city that had once served as the shipbuilding capital of Maine, they stopped for breakfast near the Bath Iron Works. From the café, they had a good view of the towering cranes and other equipment in one of the nation's busiest producers of Navy ships. The gray overcast skies turned Bath's red-brick buildings into ancient fortresses of commerce. Several looked as though they were empty, apparently conquered at last by time travelers and the death angel of economics.

After breakfast, they crossed over the Kennebec River, traveling west to I-95. The pace picked up now as they entered the multilane turnpike. According to the road signs, Brunswick was the home of Bowdoin College. Freeport's shopping outlets, off to the left, tempted tourists and locals alike. Portland, coastal Maine's largest commercial center, clung precariously to the shores of Casco Bay. They rode on in silence.

Past the Kennebunkport exit.

Yusif Shenuda sat staring out the side window.

"I wonder if George Bush is home?" he mused aloud.

"Why?" queried Safwat Najjir, Yusif's backseat companion and roommate at Hill House.

"Wouldn't he be surprised to know that we are here?"

"Would you like to drop in and say hello?" asked Marwan Dosha, looking back at them with amusement in his eyes.

"I would like to drop in, but not to say hello," said Yusif, his eyes narrowing at the thought.

"He deserves a visit from us," Safwat agreed grimly.

"Well, my friends," sighed Marwan. "Do not worry about Presidents past or present, or any of the other world leaders for that matter. In a few short days, we will bring them all to their knees. I am confident of this. Our brothers in prison will be set free. Our homeland will be ours once more. And you will be heroes of the revolution!"

Marwan appeared pleased with that idea, his face glow-ing at the thoughts of their adventure. He thrived best when living "on the edge." His daring reputation was what inspired confidence in those with whom he worked. However, Marwan Dosha was no ideological fool. Just in case his missions were not successful, he had taken the time to establish several private bank accounts in Switzerland and Brazil. These resources, secretly stored, would provide him with more than adequate income if things went badly.

It never hurts to plan ahead, he thought, smiling to himself, *just in case.*

They crossed into New Hampshire at Portsmouth. A few minutes later, they passed by a sign welcoming them to Massachusetts. The countryside was becoming more populous now as they drew closer to their destination. Quaint little villages rapidly gave way to a sprawling suburbia embracing one and a half million households.

Finally, there it was.

America's twentieth-largest city.

Six hundred thousand souls.

Fifteen thousand people per square mile.

John Winthrop's Boston.

The perfect place for a holocaust!

THIRTEEN

MONDAY, 12 SEPTEMBER, 1127 LOCAL TIME
BOSTON, MASSACHUSETTS

It was almost eleven-thirty when they entered the tunnel that took them under Boston Harbor. Traffic was heavy, but nothing compared to the morning and evening rush hours that often made two miles seem like twenty for commuters in and out of the city. Once through the tunnel, Mohammed guided the car past Faneuil Hall Marketplace; then, expertly navigating several crowded streets, he brought them to Boston Common, the city's central park.

The Frog Pond, normally filled with splashing children on a warm summer day, was peaceful and quiet. Statues, monuments, walkways, and benches were scattered throughout. Working people, taking their lunch hour, were strolling or sitting on park benches. Tourists busily snapped pictures of the State House, its gold dome shining and visible for miles. Not far away, a young couple stood on the steps of the steepled Park Street Church, absorbed in conversation.

"That's the Old Granary Burying Ground," said Marwan suddenly, pointing to a fenced-in field of weathered tombstones, adjacent to the old church. "A number of Americans who fought for their independence from Britain are buried there. Samuel Adams, John Hancock, Paul Revere. Some others too."

Yusif and Safwat leaned forward for a better view. Mohammed looked at Marwan in surprise. "You have been here before?"

"Yes."

Mohammed waited for a further word of explanation. There was none. He turned his attention back to the traffic, wondering what else he did not know about Marwan Dosha.

Having circled Boston Common, Mohammed turned onto Cambridge Street and followed it across Longfellow Bridge. The sun had finally broken through the clouds, transforming the Charles River into a watery carpet of royal blue. White sails, filled with a light breeze from the northwest, propelled sleek vessels across the river's surface. A white cabin cruiser, two men on the upper deck, disappeared from view as it passed beneath the bridge.

"That's what we want," said Marwan, straining forward to catch another glimpse as the cruiser came into view on the other side. "Where is the best place to rent something like that?"

Mohammed turned right onto Commercial Street. "The Charlesgate Yacht Club is just a short way ahead. We can look there. I dropped by a couple of weeks ago and they had three or four boats that would meet our needs. If what we want is not available, there are three other powerboat marinas on the river."

"All right," said Marwan. "Here's what you must do. Take Yusif and check out the boats. Tell them that you want to take your girlfriends out for the weekend. And you want to do some cruising and fishing. Rent it for the week, beginning Saturday afternoon. When we are ready, you will take the boat upriver aways and drop anchor. You'll wait there until I give you the signal. When it comes, you will position yourselves and be ready to do the deed. Whatever direction the wind is blowing, you will head into it. When you are finished, you will leave the boat and drive north toward Canada. We have friends in Montreal who will see that you are returned home safely."

"What about you and Safwat?" asked Mohammed.

Safwat was quiet, his eyes narrow and piercing, as he listened for the details of his assignment.

"Safwat will purchase a ticket on the MBTA Red Line. He'll begin at Alewife and work his way to Braintree. At each station, just before the door closes, he will leave a small 'gift.' From the last station, he will drive to New York City. The safe house address is back at the room in my case."

"And you, Marwan. What about you?"

"Ah, I will accept the most challenging of all roles. I will negotiate with the powers that be. But before I enter into negotiations, I intend to provide a little demonstration for our 'clients.' Hopefully, they will see their situation as intolerable and be willing to meet our terms. If not," Marwan raised his eyebrows and smiled, "then you will carry out your tasks and the infidels will die!"

No one spoke for the rest of the way until the Cadillac pulled into the yacht club marina.

1530 LOCAL TIME
BAYTOWN, CALIFORNIA

ESTHER SQUINTED as she opened her eyes. The sun was streaming through a window. Her mind was a blank slate, and for a while she could not remember where she was or why she was there. She stared at the ceiling above her. The wispy remains of a spiderweb moved back and forth, given life by a soft breeze. Esther turned her face, surprised and relieved to see the familiar outline of her very own living room. She was lying on the sofa.

Her gaze returned to the previously undiscovered spider web.

How long has it been since I've cleaned this room?

She couldn't remember.

And, if I am in my own living room, where is that breeze coming from?

After pondering that question for what seemed a more than adequate amount of time, she gave up. Then, she recognized the soft sound of the air conditioner.

It comes on automatically. That means it must be warm outside. Is it afternoon?

She moved her arm upward, until her watch came into view. *Three ten. Jeremy will be home soon. I need to get up.*

Esther rolled to one side and pushed herself into a sitting position.

That's when her head exploded!

The pain was excruciating. Both hands came up as she sank back into the sofa pillows. "Oh, my . . . " she started to exclaim. Just then, a wave of nausea swept over her. Her hand went to her mouth. She felt like she was going to throw up. Esther managed to get to her feet and stagger toward the bathroom.

I'm going to be sick. Use the kids' bathroom. It's closer.

She fell to her knees over the open toilet. At that precise moment, her stomach erupted. She continued being ill until nothing but dry heaves remained. Her body was soaked with perspiration. She was in that position, trying to let her insides settle down, when she heard a key in the front door. Then it opened.

Someone is coming in! It's got to be Jeremy!

Frantically, Esther looked for the flush handle. Disoriented and weak, she finally found it. She pulled down, but her hand slipped, banging against the bowl and falling to the floor. She reached for it again.

"Mom? Mom! What's the matter?"

The voice was close by. Esther turned her head away from the bowl and looked up.

Jeremy was standing in the bathroom doorway.

"Are you all right?"

He dropped his book pack in the hall, stepping around her and bending down. Seeing the contents in the toilet, he grimaced, reached over and pulled the flush handle down. Esther looked up, giving Jeremy a wan smile.

"I'm sick."

"I can see that. What's the matter with you? How long have you been this way?"

"That's a good question. I'm not sure I know the answer." Esther's words slurred. "Help me up, okay? Can you help me walk to the bedroom?"

"I can do better than that," Jeremy answered.

Esther felt an arm circle around her back, and a hand grasp onto her tiny waist. Another arm went under her legs as Jeremy lifted her from the floor in one smooth motion. She closed her eyes as another wave of nausea swept over her. This one wasn't as bad, though. Not like the others. She let her head sag against Jeremy's shoulder and felt her arm brush against the bedroom door. He handled her gently, firmly, as though she might break. His arms felt good.

When did you get to be so strong, Jeremy?

He placed his mother on the bed. Adjusting a pillow under her head, he stood there looking at her, wondering what to do next. Her eyes were closed, but she was breathing regularly.

"Jeremy?" Her lips formed his name slowly, as a wretched taste came churning upward into her mouth.

"I'm here, Mom. What should I do? Call a doctor or something?"

"No, no, don't. Not a doctor. I'll be fine. I just got a little upset, that's all."

"A *little* upset?" Jeremy said back to her, thinking of the way he had just found her in his bathroom.

"Would you get me a glass of water, please," Esther asked, her thick, dry lips and tongue struggling to form the words.

"Sure, Mom. Just a sec." He started toward the master bathroom.

That was when Esther remembered the pills. *Are they still there? Did I take them all? Where is the bottle?*

"Jeremy, don't use our bathroom," she said desperately, struggling to sit up. "Get it from yours."

But it was too late.

2005 LOCAL TIME
SOMEWHERE OVER THE NORTH ATLANTIC

JOHN LOOKED OVER AT HIS SEATMATE. It appeared as though she had finally decided to settle in. Earlier, she had been in the aisles, carrying on nonstop conversations with others in the tour group. Laughing, excited, happy, and twelve years old. She related easily with adults, not in the obnoxious way of a child striving for attention, but naturally, spontaneously, with bright-eyed enthusiasm that drew people into her circle. She had even made friends with one of the airline attendants, a blue-eyed, fair-skinned, blond woman from Rotterdam.

As he watched the cabin crew working the aisles after dinner, it seemed to John that all the flight attendants had blue eyes, fair skin, and blond hair.

John enjoyed the Dutch people. They were generally very pleasant and accommodating. To him, they represented that quality of confident determination that says, "No matter how hard it gets, it is never too hard. We will overcome."

Their national language was difficult. The Dutch themselves jokingly agreed that it was too hard even for them to learn. However, in the tradition of many Europeans, they then proceeded to learn three or four other languages as well. One of those was always English, the world's universal business language.

On another visit to Europe, while at a luncheon near Bern, Switzerland, John had been introduced to that country's Minister of Defense. In the course of the meal, the subject of bilingualism had become a topic of table conversation.

"Look around this room, John," the minister had said. "I know almost every person here, and I can tell you that they all speak four or five languages fluently. Of course, locally we speak mostly Dutch, as you know. What you may not know is that the Dutch we speak is not the same as that which we write. So you see, it all becomes very complicated. But one thing I can say to you with absolute certainty. When it is time to get serious about business dealings, and it becomes imperative that we are understood, we speak English."

"Lucky for us Americans," John had replied, grateful, and at the same time a bit envious of such impressive language proficiency.

He looked out the cabin window. By now, he guessed, they were somewhere over northern Canada. A heavy cloud layer enveloped the inhospitable terrain of tundra and lakes far below. Though eclipsed from view, John knew that this bleakest of all landscapes had already begun freezing over, even though winter's severest lashing was still a long way off.

The aisles were filling with passengers now, making their way to restrooms as the attendants finished their clean-up duties. The meal service had been excellent as always, in the best tradition of Holland. The movie was scheduled to begin in a few minutes. Jessica was ready, her flight earphones already in place. She was listening to the western music channel, something John didn't think she ever did at home.

"Daddy," she said, looking up at him and peeling an earphone away from her ear. "What does a cowboy get when he plays his tape deck backward?"

"I don't know. What?"

"He gets his girlfriend back, his pickup back, his dog back . . ."

John laughed. "That's a good one, sweetheart. You hear that on your down-home channel there?"

"Yup," she answered with a grin and her best cowgirl drawl. She crossed her legs and leaned back in the seat.

John reached under the seat in front of him and pulled a pocket-size New Testament out of his carryon. As he sat back, Jessica pulled the earphones down around her neck. Her finger rolled the volume control down.

"Daddy, will you read to me, please?"

"Okay, hon. What'll it be? Anything special?"

"No. I just want to hear you read," she replied, pushing her small airline pillow against him and snuggling her head on his arm. "You pick out something."

"Well, why don't we do what normally we would not do. Let's just open it up and read whatever comes. Okay?"

"Sure."

John placed the New Testament on the foldout tray. The worn binding let the pages fall open easily. He picked it up and began reading.

"That day when evening came, He said to His disciples, 'Let us go over to the other side.' Leaving the crowd behind, they took Him along, just as He was, in the boat. There were also other boats with Him. A furious squall came up, and the waves broke over the boat, so that it was nearly swamped. Jesus was in the stern, sleeping on a cushion. The disciples woke Him and said to Him, 'Teacher, don't You care if we drown?' "

John looked down at Jessica. Her eyes were closed. She was smiling.

"He got up, rebuked the wind and said to the waves, 'Quiet! Be still!' Then the wind died down and it was completely calm.

"He said to His disciples, 'Why are you so afraid? Do you still have no faith?'

"They were terrified and asked each other, 'Who is this? Even the wind and the waves obey Him!'"

He closed the New Testament, dropped it beside him in the seat, and looked again at the precious cargo leaning against him. He smiled, shaking his head.

Jesus may be awake, sweetheart. But you're not.

He adjusted her pillow slightly and with a sigh sank back into his seat, stretching his legs as far as he could, while musing over what he had just read.

He had been too busy making sure everyone was taken care of to think about other things. That, in itself, had been a welcome relief. Now, however, for the first time since leaving San Francisco, John's mind began revisiting the reality that was his life. His thoughts were disconnected, yet held together by an invisible cord. They roamed across the theater of his soul as random, unconnected scenes, broken into by some capricious hand on the viewer channel selector, before they could form any logical sequence.

The resignation letter tucked away in his office. Ken Ralsten's veiled intimidations at Saturday's board meeting. Yesterday's services. The Arab couple who attended all three services. Jeremy's anger. Esther's look of sadness at the airport. *"Remember, my darling, I love you very much."* The small cloud of apprehension appeared once more on the horizon of John's heart. She had spoken the words almost as though they were a kind of pronouncement. Had it been just the finality of the moment? Or, something else?

When the storms were the wildest, Jesus was in the boat with His disciples. Isn't He supposed to be in my boat too? That's what I tell the people at home. Well, God, if You are in my boat, it would be nice to hear from You. I've been pointing people to You for years. So where are You when I need You? Where You are concerned, I'm not sure anymore about much of anything. It feels like I've touched bottom. How much worse can things be? Are You really and truly there?

John looked down at Jessica's sleeping form.

I do know one thing, little lady. I love you!

He closed his eyes.

The familiar ache had returned.

The one that came each time he looked into a clear, sparkling pool of water.

The forboding shadow that kept haunting him.

It was there again.

His beloved ghost!

EDGAR WATCHED THE FACE of his pastor. He knew there was something important on his mind. More than responsibility for their group. There was something else. Even though John was sleeping, it was easy to make out the tenseness on his face. He looked unrested. Sad. Edgar knew that John constantly carried with him the secrets and burdens of others. That, in itself, was enough to wear a good man down.

But this was different.

Edgar wasn't sure, but he thought he might know.

And what he thought gave him concern.

He loved this man and the "Mrs." He loved their children too.

The cabin suddenly darkened as the evening movie flashed up on the screen.

He closed his eyes.

He was not watching.

He was not sleeping.

Edgar was praying.

FOURTEEN

TUESDAY, 13 SEPTEMBER, 1005 LOCAL TIME
TEL AVIV, ISRAEL

The phone rang three times before Aryeh Shamrir picked up the receiver.

"Yes?" he said, twisting the cigarette beneath his fingers in the ashtray. "How many? Yes. Twenty-five. Yes ... yes. Our man will meet them when they arrive. All right. Thank you."

Aryeh pulled open the left-hand drawer in his desk, ran his fingers quickly across the file tabs, withdrew a form with the words *Group Arrival* printed across the top in Hebrew letters, and began filling in the blank spaces. This completed David Barak's guide packet. On Wednesday afternoon, he would take it with him to meet John Cain's tour group at the airport. Aryeh knew that David had worked with Reverend Cain twice before. He liked the man and was looking forward to serving as the Cain group's professional guide during the time they were in the country. Aryeh's pen flew over the empty spaces and, when he had finished, he attached a listing of the names of Israel's latest anticipated guests from California.

Adnan Dakkad sat across the office, near the door. He had overheard every word of the telephone conversation. His understanding of Hebrew was adequate for him to know that this was the call for which he'd been waiting.

The old man turned a page in the international edition of *Time*. He had been unable to decipher the details describing the cover story. It was written in English, the language of the Great Satan. There was no escaping the power of the pictures, however, and their message served up a mystical adrenaline to his gaunt, aged body. They were done in full color. He especially liked the cover scene, captured in film only a few days earlier by a photo journalist. It was the Gaza Strip.

In the north near the security border, two young boys and a girl who could not have yet reached her teenage years, armed only with stones, were in the foreground. With fists in the air, they stood facing two well-armed Israeli soldiers. A building was burning in the background. Rocks, litter, and the bodies of three Arab comrades lay scattered like refuse across the street between them.

The peace negotiations, heralded on the White House front lawn in 1993, had done little to produce the fruit of peace in the Gaza Strip. Things quieted for a time, while Hamas leaders tried to determine the right action to take. After many extended and heated arguments, they had rejected the PLO–Israel agreement. This was followed by numerous bloody acts of terrorism as Hamas members fought to gain the upper hand. Last week, major rioting had erupted at several points along the border, seemingly signaling a further breakdown in the ability of the Palestinian residents to govern themselves peacefully.

Defiance was the unwritten motif in the picture. Anyone could see it. And as he studied the picture, his tired old eyes flickered with an ancient flame.

"Adnan."

He glanced up at Aryeh Shamrir, his occasional employer. Shamrir was used to seeing him sitting there, near the door. He had become a normal part of the room's rather sparse but functional fittings of army gray, steel-framed desks and chairs, computers, and telephones. A few travel posters were tacked to the walls and a single window let in noise, light, and automobile fumes from the outside.

Dakkad came to the office three times a week to sweep the floor, wipe off counter and desk space, and empty the garbage. When he was available, Shamrir occasionally used him as a messenger. He knew the city well and had proven his willingness and ability to follow through when given a task. He was a harmless old man who had lived out his best days. His ready smile, revealing several missing teeth, had a disarming quality about it. The few teeth that had managed to remain were stained yellow and brown from a lifetime of tobacco use. Shamrir doubted they had ever felt the hand of a dentist.

Dakkad knew that Shamrir had checked him out with local authorities. That was fairly routine, one of the indignities Arab nationals lived with in the occupied land of their birth. Adnan Dakkad was originally from Nazareth, had survived the various wars between 1948 and the present, and was now an old man, living alone in a hole-in-the-wall apartment in a poor Arab sector of Tel Aviv.

Until his failing eyesight made it impossible, he had driven a taxi, primarily in Jerusalem but also in Tel Aviv. Now he survived any way he could, mostly picking up odd jobs here and there. He had no criminal record. He always proved faithful to the task and never failed to complete an assignment, whether it was sweeping the office floor, going out for soft drinks for Shamrir's small staff, or carrying messages around the busy downtown streets of Tel Aviv.

Shamrir had been acquainted with Adnan Dakkad for the last six months. The man who formerly held this part-time job had suddenly been taken ill. A day or two later, Dakkad had shown up, indicating that he had heard there was work available. When Shamrir asked Dakkad how he knew of the opening, Dakkad simply shrugged his shoulders and smiled his toothless best. A simple soul, he was one of many poor, old castaways, living out their last years as best they could, in the land of their birth. Besides, Shamrir never gave the old man an assignment that could be security sensitive. After all, this was only a travel agency.

But there were things Shamrir did not know about Adnan Dakkad. Of that Dakkad was certain. He knew that Shamrir had no inkling of his longtime connections in the dark alleys of the Old City. He was unaware that in earlier years, Dakkad had been involved in a series of terrorist incidents in Israel, including the 1972 massacre of passengers at the Ben-Gurion Airport, where twenty-six people were murdered and seventy-six others were wounded by the Japanese Red Army, friends of the PLO. In that mission, Dakkad had served as a courier between contacts in the PLO and the Red Army. There was never any mention of his name or his connections with the groups. He had been too far down the ladder of importance to merit such visibility. Dakkar was always careful never to verbalize any political views. If he had been asked, Shamrir would have expressed serious doubts that the old man had any. That was the way Dakkad wanted it. And that's the way it was.

"Adnan, come here, please."

Adnan looked up from his magazine, his winning tooth-gap smile bringing an entirely new set of wrinkles to his wizened, bronzed face. He put the issue of *Time* down on the small wooden table in front of him and slowly stood to his feet.

"I want you to hand-deliver this to David Barak. You remember David? He was here yesterday, getting ready for a group of Americans who are arriving tomorrow."

The old man put his hands on the counter between them. Still smiling, he nodded his head.

"Yes," answered Dakkad. "I remember him well."

Shamrir wondered just how well the old man remembered anything, but gave no indication that such a thought had crossed his mind. After all, a little dignity might be one of this ancient Arab's few remaining possessions.

"I need you to take this to him. It was not ready when he came by on Sunday. He will need it in order to meet the group when they fly into Lod tomorrow. He and his wife will be having lunch at one o'clock at the Espresso Kapali on Dizengoff Square. Meet him there and see that he gets this. All right?"

Dakkad nodded and smiled. "It is not a problem. Consider it as good as in his hand." Turning, he shuffled toward the door.

Shamrir watched as he disappeared into the hallway, shook his head, lit a cigarette, and returned to his desk.

ADNAN DAKKAD WALKED up Frishman to Dizengoff. There he turned right and made his way toward the Square. Cars moved in and out, horns honked and buses belched their way through the center of town. Pedestrians strolled along the sidewalks, checking out the abundant merchandise displayed in store windows.

He saw the Espresso Kapali Cafe across the street. Dakkad stood for a moment, squinting into the bright sunlight for some sign of David Barak. Most of the customers were sitting outside, enjoying the pleasant weather. Every table was full, with a few people standing around, soft drinks in hand, waiting for others to leave.

Two young men and a woman, all in military uniforms and with automatic weapons slung casually over their shoulders. stood nearest to the door. They looked so young, like children. But the old man knew these "children" to be competent warriors. He watched them for a while. They did not appear to have any official reason for being there. Dakkar decided they probably were in line for a table and dismissed them from his mind. The Espresso Kapali was a popular place, especially with the young.

He had seen the man he was looking for only once before, but the Jewish guide should be easy enough to spot again. Sandy hair, tanned, medium build, narrow-rimmed glasses shaped in the latest modern design. Dakkad took a few steps forward, then paused again, his eyes darting back and forth from table to table.

There. Under the awning.

David Barak was leaning back in his chair, legs stretched full length under the small table. The blue sport shirt with large white fish imprinted on it was the same one Dakkad had seen him wearing on Sunday. Only today, he had on white shorts and running shoes. And his glasses were the type that darkened outdoors, shielding his eyes from the sun's glare.

Across from him sat an attractive young Jewish woman, unusually fair-skinned, with short black hair, white blouse, and khaki shorts.

Probably French. Maybe German or Russian. Who knows? These Jews come from everywhere in the world to take our land from us.

Crossing over, Dakkad approached slowly, then stopped while still a short distance separated them. He waited patiently for Barak to look his way. After a few moments, he caught the man's eye. When he was sure he had been seen, he raised his hand in greeting, at the same time revealing the paper he held. Barak nodded, saying something to the woman whom Dakkad assumed was his wife, as he rose from the table. Reaching for his glass, he downed its remaining contents in a single swallow, and began angling his way toward him, through the jumble of tables and customers.

Dakkad stayed out in the open, obviously alone. Of course, there was nothing for anyone to be afraid of. He was an old man, much too feeble and frail to be mistaken for a dangerous character. Besides, Barak had been notified that he was coming. Still, Tel Aviv was filled with nervous citizens, ever cautious when bridging the racial barriers between Jew and Arab, even on a main avenue in the middle of the day.

"You are Mr. Barak, yes?"

"Yes. And you are from the travel agency," the guide responded, making a statement instead of an inquiry.

"That is correct, Mr. Barak." Dakkad bowed his head ever so slightly. "I have the good fortune to bring you these important papers so that you may proceed with entertaining your guests from America."

Dakkad handed the forms to the handsome young man whom he guessed to be in his early thirties. Barak flipped through them quickly, then looked up.

"Thank you. These are what I need."

Dakkad stood, waiting, smiling his tooth-gap smile.

Barak reached into his pocket.

"Here, old man. Your job is finished now. Go home and take the rest of the day off." He handed him some shekels.

"Shookran," said Dakkad, nodding his head respectfully, as he took the money. "Ma-ah-salameh."

"Shalom," Barak replied, turning to go back to his companion who sat watching at their table.

ADNAN DAKKAD CONTINUED walking away from the Square down a narrow street headed west, toward the sea. When he had gone three blocks, he turned into a small Tabak store. A lone customer was waiting for the proprietor to ring up his purchases.

Dakkad smiled in silent greeting, nodding to his old friend behind the counter. They had known one another ever since the attack on the Israeli farm collective at Ma'alot in 1974. It had been a huge success. Twenty-seven dead, one hundred thirty-four wounded. For weeks, Dakkad and the store owner had remained in hiding together, while the IDS scoured the countryside, looking for two terrorists who were believed to have escaped in the confusion of the aftermath. They were never discovered.

Dakkad said nothing. He squeezed in between the crush of tables, display cases, and wall shelves filled with pipes, tobacco, and cigarettes. After fingering several different items, he paid for a pouch of tobacco and a packet of cigarette papers. Like many of his peers, he preferred rolling his own to smoking ready-made. He enjoyed the ritual of forming the cigarette in his own hands. He was also able to maintain his habit for less cost this way.

Dakkad gave the store owner a knowing glance. The man lowered his eyes and nodded imperceptibly. Dakkad moved to the rear of the little store, pushing through a curtained doorway and into the store owner's small living quarters. The single room was tiny, stuffy, and reeked a combination of lingering body odors and tobacco smells. A small, dirty sink was fastened to the wall in one corner. Pita bread, some food cans, and a bottle of water were piled together on top of a tiny cooking stove. Flies zipped through the air toward the old man, exploring his face before settling down in helicopter fashion on their pita bread landing pad.

His eye followed a cord protruding from the near wall, snaking its way along the floor until it rose to disappear under a pile of carelessly strewn newspapers. Reaching under the papers, Dakkad found a black, rotary dial telephone. Checking for the dial tone, he cranked in the numbers that had been memorized months earlier. He could hear the phone ringing.

Once, twice.

He hung up.

Waited for a moment.

Redialed.

Once, twice, three times.

"Aywah?" said a dull-sounding voice at the other end of the line.

Dakkad's heart beat rapidly with excitement. This was his great moment. A contribution, perhaps his final one, to The Cause. The culmination of months of careful placement and subtle undercover work. He wet his lips with his tongue.

"Twenty-five birds arrive at the store tomorrow. Some male. Some female. One smaller than the others, but healthy." *There are twenty-five in the group, including one small child.*

"How much will they go for?" the voice asked. *What time will they arrive?*

"Fifty-five each as late as the store stays open," Dakkad answered. *They will come at five-fifty in the afternoon.*

He heard the phone click at the other end. Then the dial tone.

Slowly, he returned the receiver to its cradle, absent-mindedly spreading the newspapers over the phone, more or less in the manner in which he had found them. Turning, he pushed back the curtain and walked into the store.

"Naharak sae'id," he said to his old friend, as he walked past the counter and out into the sultry afternoon air.

Adnan Dakkad had no idea what the result of his telephone call would be. He was only a small but important piece in a much larger puzzle. At least he *felt* important. He knew that he had done his job, and that he had done it well.

His part was over.

The Cause, however, was not.

Far from it!

It was just beginning!

"THE OLD ONE PROMISES that twenty-five birds will arrive at the store tomorrow." *Our contact confirms that the group of twenty-five persons we have been anticipating, will arrive at Lod on Wednesday.* "They are to be gathered up and prepared for resale at the first opportunity." *We will keep track of them the rest of the week. They are to be taken on Sunday.*

The voice that had spoken to Adnan Dakkad was now filling the ear of Yazib Dudori. As the words came across in low, guttural tones, Yazib felt himself growing tense with anticipation. *This is it. Everything has come down to this moment in time. Mankind is about to feel the heel print of the forces of liberation. I am a part of something that will shake the world. And it is happening now!*

"We are ready to receive delivery," Yazib reassured the voice.

The phone line went dead.

Yazib looked at the others. They had not been outside the safe house since their arrival early Sunday morning. His eyes moved across the room to Pasha and, for an instant, he relived their narrowly averted crisis . . .

. . . IT SEEMED TO THEM THAT Eilat's King Solomon Palace Hotel was grand beyond measure. They had become used to cold prison cells, spartan training camps, and traveling by camel across the hot, dry desert. This hotel rose from Israel's sands like a pyramid of Egypt. Tall and beautiful. Overwhelming. They stood silently on the steps, letting the luxury feed their starving senses.

At last, Pasha turned to speak to Yazib. Whatever she had planned to say, the words remained forever frozen in her throat. Coming toward them along the narrow street, she saw the police car! Yazib did not see it. There was no time to run and no place to hide. They had foolishly permitted themselves to be caught out in the open. In a few seconds, they would be discovered and their mission would be lost!

Suddenly, Pasha threw herself into Yazib's arms, kissing him hard and long. Surprised, Yazib caught himself, then put his arms around her, relishing the response of his own emotions to her unexpected passion.

The car had slowed. From eyes that feigned closure, Pasha saw the policeman laughing as he looked their way. He nudged his partner, pointing and saying something to him. She saw the other officer lean forward for a better look as the car rolled past.

They remained locked in each other's embrace for a long moment. Pasha felt the warmth of Yazib's responsive lips and the strength of his arms as he gathered her to himself. At last they broke free, and Pasha found herself gazing into Yazib's smiling eyes. That was when he saw the worried look on her face. She turned slightly, to look at the street behind him. It was then, in the corner of his eye, that he saw the retreating outline of the police car. Instantly, his mind raced to catch up with his emotions. The vulnerability of their situation stunned him, draining his face of its color.

"The police," Pasha whispered. "I did not know what else to do."

Her face was only inches from his. He could feel her rapid breathing.

Yazib cleared his throat as they drew back from each other. The picture of young lovers, they moved off the steps and began walking away from the hotel. He looked across the street for Imad and Fathi. They were invisible in the darkness.

"You did well, Pasha. Because of your quick thinking, we're still operational."

"I am sorry if I surprised you."

Yazib smiled. They were away from the lights now, walking along a narrow section of the street. The fear they had felt was rapidly receding. He turned to Pasha.

"It was a pleasant surprise."

Pasha pushed his arm gently.

"I knew you had not seen the police car. It was all I could think to do. It was my duty," she added demurely.

She heard Yazib's quiet laughter and felt her face grow crimson in the darkness.

"WE ARE IN BUSINESS," Yazib exclaimed as he put the telephone down. He tried to hold back the excitement that was written all over his face.

The others sat still. There was a strange silence. They stared at the phone, then, at each other.

Pasha was the first to release a sigh. "It's happening. It's really happening at last!" she said, her voice full of feeling.

Smiles broke out quickly, then laughter, as they jumped up and pounded one another with exuberant expressions of congratulations They were where they should be, doing what they had been called to do.

"Blessed be Allah!" Fathi said reverently. "Truly, he will be with us now!"

"What is our next step?" Imad asked, as he pulled back a corner of the curtain that covered the window and peered outside. They had been cooped up in this little cinder-block hovel for two days. He was ready to get on with it.

"Relax, Imad. We must wait here a while longer." Yazib saw the disappointment in Imad's eyes. He didn't blame him, really. The waiting was the hardest part. "We will move out tomorrow morning."

"Morning?" Fathi repeated in surprise. "Not at night with the cover of darkness?"

"No, Fathi," Yazib answered. "In the morning. We will not crawl like snakes to our strike point. We will cross enemy territory in style. In broad daylight!"

"Are you serious?"

"Never more so. I spoke with our host early this morning, before he went to work. It is all arranged. Early on Wednesday morning we shall be on our way."

Smiles all around again as they looked at each other. Yazib was enjoying his little secret. In the last few weeks they had become as one. Their trust in each other was rock solid. They were even beginning to think alike.

"If you are pulling our leg, Yazib, you will ride a camel all the way!" declared Fathi, pounding the table for emphasis.

"Backward!" he added, laughing as he said it.

The others agreed, offering mock threats of demeaning punishment to the man who was their leader.

"Enough, enough," Yazib said, holding up his hands in surrender. "You will see soon enough that I am a man of my word. Now, let's eat and get some rest. We have a long week ahead of us."

A stranger asked to describe this scene would have been hard-pressed not to see a group of college students, preparing to amaze their campus friends and the school administration with the ultimate prank of the year.

But these young people, made immune to the consequences of their actions by the poison of life's empty promises, were not college students. And their deadly mission was no prank!

FIFTEEN

Seasoned travelers aboard KLM Flight 2 felt the precise moment when the plane's descent began. That imperceptible movement, somewhere over the North Sea, could never be seen, only felt. In fact, it was impossible to see anything outside. This artificial recreation of earth's atmosphere, hurtling through the sky at over four hundred miles per hour, had begun working its way down through the weather that so often hides the sun from the world far below.

As the jumbo jet finally broke through the last thickness of clouds, passengers strained to catch a glimpse of God's green earth, thereby being reassured that they were not far from where all mankind belongs, namely, having both feet firmly planted on the ground.

A breathtaking patchwork of green fields rose to meet them, like some gigantic front lawn. Hours before, they had been lifted above the golden hills of San Francisco. Now, an emerald carpet awaited their descent. Exclamations were heard throughout the plane. First-timers leaned across the laps of friends to snap their memory photos. Others handed cameras to strangers sitting in the window seats, and were pleasantly obliged with their first frames of scrapbook fodder. Elsewhere, video cameras whirred in the hands of wheat farmers and professional photographers alike. Never mind that it was so overcast and damp outside that when developed, most of the pictures would miserably fail in bringing to mind the moment. Somehow, everyone would remember. Over and over again. This is Amsterdam. The Netherlands. This is Europe!

Hollanders returning home from their overseas holiday watched with jaded amusement. They had seen this before. Many times. Businessmen and women, returning home from wheeling and dealing with those acquisitive Americans, dozed in weariness from the long journey, steeling themselves for reentry into Holland's dreary weather system. They loved their land and were proud of its history and their accomplishments.

But, oh, how the sun had shone in California! They could never forget that!

Schipol Airport's expansive gray buildings flashed by the wings now. There! The sound of rubber touching runway. The long awaited, reassuring *thumpity-thump* of tires reaching out to grip cold cement. Rivets straining to help aluminum and steel come to terms with their burden. Engines screaming like mighty eagles, announcing their successful response to the pull of earth's gravity. Passengers clapping and cheering spontaneously throughout the plane. *For what?* John thought. *Don't they realize they are only part way through one of the two most dangerous moments in flying?*

Still, as the plane slowed and finally turned toward the main terminal, John had to admit that they were about to survive another flight in one piece.

Gradually, he released his death grip on the arms of the seat. Loosening the seat belt, he smiled at Jessica, then looked to see that the rest of his group was all right. Everyone seemed fine, excited, laughing. He wondered what they would say if they knew the agony he went through every time he took off or landed in an airplane. John had never even given Esther a hint of the anxiety that was a customary part of his air-travel experience. He knew his feelings were pathological. He had read numerous articles attempting to reassure air travelers in matters of safety and survival. He had prayed for relief from the abnormal fear.

All to no avail.

The jumbo airliner lumbered into the disembarking zone, finally coming to a complete stop. Outwardly, John appeared calm and pleasant. He joked a bit with Edgar and Jill, waved to the Micellis, and smiled at Shad and Mary. Inside, however, John was angry. When he suddenly realized it, he was surprised.

Why am I angry, for goodness sake?

He decided it must have something to do with his fear of flying, piled on top of all the other things that were haywire in his life.

It isn't fair, he thought. *None of it. Not Esther. Not Jeremy. Certainly not Jenny. Not the church . . . and not this stupid fear of flying! Why doesn't God ever do something?*

Mentally, he did what he had done so often of late. He shrugged the anger off, gathering up his and Jessica's things as he prepared for the familiar aisle surge as people jostled and apologized their way out. It always seemed to work itself out, although John sometimes wondered where the anger went after one of his "emotional shrugs." He had no idea. He knew it was not healthy to stuff anger like this so much of the time. He also knew that he'd been doing it quite a bit of late.

Oh, well. What's one more unanswered prayer?

ONCE PASSPORT CONTROL had been cleared and the

bus transfer had gone smoothly, John was grateful.

He remembered the time, in this same airport, that his chartered bus had failed to come at all. He had ultimately moved his group into the city by train. Even then, the closest point they had been able to reach was more than half a mile from their hotel. John found a taxi driver who spoke English, and who called for help from his friends. It probably took a taxi or two more than was really needed to haul their luggage and a few of the older travelers the rest of the way. But he had not argued. Business is business. The rest of his group had decided to walk the final lap, since it was not raining. Like most vacationing travelers, they were prepared for the unexpected and chalked it up as another "great story to tell when we get back home."

This time, checking in at the Krasnapolsky had been both pleasant and efficient. They knew how travelers wished to be handled in this, one of Amsterdam's finest hotels. Keys were handed out. Luggage immediately began disappearing from the lobby as bellmen came and went.

Following a short trip upstairs to find their rooms and freshen up, "the troops," as John often referred to them, had assembled in the dining room for dinner. Most had confessed to not being hungry until they saw the attractive table settings, smiling waitresses, and steaming food. Their enthusiasm heightened with the visible reminder that this was not airline food. Several courses and a delightful Dutch dessert later, they were all stuffed. Dinner was washed down with the guests' choice of a cup of black coffee or English tea.

Now, people moved away from the table in groups of two or three. John discouraged anyone from going out alone, especially at night. There was always the chance of being pickpocketed or mugged in the well-known tourist areas. But even greater was the chance of getting lost. Some were tired, especially those few who were up in years. Even the Eidermans had decided to call it a night.

"I think we're going to bed." Harold and Gisele came over to where John and Jessica were sitting. "It's been great so far. You've done a good job arranging all of this and keeping us together today. This place is wonderful. But I think we'll join the old folk and hit the sack."

"Thanks, Harold. I hope you have a good night's rest. Breakfast is in this room from seven to eight-thirty. Come down whenever you wish."

"What are you going to do now, pastor?" asked Gisele.

John looked over at Jessica.

"What do you think, hon? Should we go for a little walk?"

"Sure, Daddy!" Jessica's tired eyes lit up at the thought. "I'm ready if you are."

"Everyone is on their own this evening. I think some are going out. Maybe we'll see somebody we know on the street. I'm sure no one will stay out very late. They'll want to get in early tonight. We should too, so let's go. We'll take in a little of Amsterdam anyway."

John wiped his mouth with his napkin, pushed back his chair, and stood. Jessica followed suit. Only Evelyn Unruh and Dan and Phyllis Watson were still at the table, sipping tea and admiring the dining room's exquisitely blended appointments, all done in tasteful shades of green. The intricate skylight roof promised sunlight at breakfast, unless, of course, it was raining.

John took Jessica's hand as they walked up the steps and out of the dining room into the small lobby. "Wait here, hon. I'll go up and get our coats and umbrella, just in case."

In a few minutes, he was back. Jessica slipped into her coat and pushed through the lobby door. They started across the stone-paved area known as Dam Square. The shadowy outlines of ancient buildings were directly in front of them, easily seen in the semidarkness. John paused for a moment to get his bearings. Then they walked across the Square and onto the street known by most as the "walking street."

Shops lined either side of the wide pedestrian way. Anything, it seemed, was for sale: stereos, clothes, tourist trinkets, pizza, magazines, embroidery, and shoes, wooden and otherwise. Dark, narrow doorways opened off the street into mysterious, hole-in-the-wall night spots from which loud, pulsating music could be heard.

They stopped in a souvenir store where Jessica purchased several small pins shaped like wooden shoes and Dutch windmills. She'd been saving her money for this trip, part of which she had budgeted for gifts to take home to her friends and classmates. Some picture postcards, and a small, white doily for her mother. John stood by, watching with interest and a little amusement. Jessica was a very independent young lady, he thought. Busily using up the last of her preteen years.

After a while, they strolled off the "walking street" and into a residential area filled with old hotels and apartments. The row houses were narrow and tall, throwing their shadows across the sidewalk. They were headed in the general direction of the hotel, although John was not certain now as to exactly where it was located. Dark canals lined each street, crossable every so often by traversing a narrow footbridge.

"Can we take a boat ride on the canals, Daddy?"

"Tomorrow, if we have time. Otherwise, we'll be sure to do it on the way home. We'll be stopping here when we return," he promised as they turned the corner.

"There is one thing tomorrow that I definitely want to show you, Jessica. It's the house in which a young Jewish girl lived, during World War II. Her name was Anne Frank. She was about your age when she lived there."

"I've read about her, and our history teacher told us about her. She died during the War, didn't she?"

"Yes, hon, she did. It's all very sad, but I want you to see her home. She was a very brave little girl."

Jessica squeezed John's hand in what he assumed was an expression of appreciation. He looked down at his daughter. She was not looking at him. Instead, she was staring straight ahead. When he looked up, he saw what had captured her attention.

Directly ahead of them Jessica's attention had been drawn to the figure of a scantily clad woman in a store window. Only this was no mannequin. She was very real, and dressed only in brief, revealing undergarments. The young woman moved slowly and sensuously, her body swaying to the sounds of music that only she could hear. Outside the window, a young Japanese family looked on, talking and laughing among themselves before walking away. Though John had not been here before, he had often heard of Amsterdam's red-light district. Now he feared that he had stumbled into it.

As they came nearer, he could see that there were other windows with young girls similarly clad in undergarments or revealing lingerie, sitting in chairs or dancing by themselves, or simply smiling provocatively at potential customers standing along the sidewalks. A few doors down, three young men were making hand signals to the occupant in their window. Two of them jovially pushed their companion forward, pointing at him to the woman inside. She motioned to the young man who disappeared through the door, while the others strolled on, laughing and lighting cigarettes.

"What is she doing, Daddy?" whispered Jessica, staring at the young girl in the window.

John grimaced as Jessica pulled at his hand, signaling him to stop. *Wouldn't you know it. Our first night in Amsterdam and I walk my daughter straight into the heart of the red-light district! Now what shall I do?*

John could see around the corner. Ahead were still more windows with attractive young women on display. He knew there would be no getting out of this situation without an explanation.

John had never personally talked to Jessica about sex. He knew that her mother had alerted her to the changes that were on the way in her young body. Three months earlier, Esther had informed John that Jessica's menstrual cycle had begun. She assured him that Jessica knew how to take care of herself, should it be necessary while they were gone. He certainly hoped that Esther's confidence was well founded.

John remembered reading somewhere that since the turn of the century, better health and nutrition had lowered the average age of sexual maturity. He had been surprised that the onset of menstruation in girls was dropping at an average rate of three months in each passing decade. Now, the urges that once arrived at fourteen were starting to hit children at twelve. He had watched Jessica recently, noting her fresh, new interest in boys. But, he was unsure what ground the two women in his life had covered in their "little talks."

From his experience as a pastor, John also knew that young people in general these days were far more advanced in their knowledge of sexual matters than he and Esther had been at that age. It was frightening, really. Jerry Anchor, Calvary's youth pastor, recently shared with the staff that according to a recent national survey, by the time kids reached fifteen, a quarter of the girls and a third of the boys had become sexually active. John had been stunned at that figure.

Still, he knew of junior-high-age children in Baytown who were already experimenting with sex. He also knew that many young people in high school, including some in the church youth group, had been initiated into the world of sexual irresponsibility. It was like a huge tidal wave, and there seemed to be no holding it back.

Now as he looked down at Jessica, her hand still holding

tightly to his, a lump rose in his throat. He blinked back the moisture that rimmed his eyes. He looked first at Jessica, then at the young girl in the window. Then, back at Jessica again. John swallowed as he squeezed her hand.

"Jessica, honey," he began, hesitantly, not knowing whether he wanted to hear a yes or a no to his question. "Do you know what a prostitute is?"

"Sure, Daddy. Everyone knows that. It's someone who sells her body for money." Her answer was matter-of-fact and direct.

Well, so much for innocence.

She looked up into John's eyes, inquiringly. "Is that what she is doing?" she asked, turning her gaze back to the girl in the window.

"Yes, sweetheart. That's what she is doing."

They stood together, silently. The girl in the window kept her eyes on them, until finally, she stopped her slow, sensuous gyrations and sat down in a chair, still facing them. She smiled.

Jessica smiled back, her hand coming up in a timid greeting.

"But she's so beautiful," said Jessica.

"Yes, she is," John agreed. "At least for now."

"What do you mean?"

"I mean, after a few years in this business, she'll be all used up. Drugs and disease are always a danger to someone like her."

"You mean, like AIDS and stuff?"

"Yes, that's what I mean. And, how will she find a husband who will want her after a life like this? Will she have children? If she does, what will they think when they find out what their mother did? Even without marriage, unwanted pregnancy is always a possibility. For anybody really, but especially someone like her. She may go through several abortions before many years have passed. Do you understand about abortions, honey?"

"Yes," Jessica replied, a touch of sadness in her voice.
John waited.

Jessica added no further comment.

Slowly, they walked by the window. There were still
other windows to be navigated, but John could see that Jessica seemed taken by this young girl. Some kind of emotional connection had been made between them.

"Why is she doing this?" she asked, her words tinged
with a plaintive tone that caused John to look down at her
again. That was when he noticed a tear on her cheek.

He searched desperately for something wise to say.
Nothing came. "I don't know, sweetheart. Money, I guess. It
is sad, but it's the way she makes her living."

"I wish I could tell her about Jesus," Jessica said, almost
reverently, staring into the window. "She needs to know
about Him."

The girl ignored them now, polishing her nails. Slowly
they walked away, in the direction of the hotel.

John put his hand on Jessica's shoulder. "You know,
hon," he said, "you could never tell that young girl about
Jesus. You don't speak her language."

In more ways than one, he thought.

"But," he continued, "there are some Christian mission-
aries who work among the people in this area. I heard of
one missionary family who has been here for years. They live
somewhere nearby and share Christ with prostitutes and
drug addicts and others who live in this part of the city.
Perhaps they'll have a chance to speak with her."

Jessica did not respond. They walked the rest of the way
without further conversation. John was concerned. He knew
he should not have let them wander into that area. It was
safe enough—many tourists and families went through just
to see it for themselves—but this was different. This was
Jessica.

After several more blocks, they broke out onto Dam Square. Crossing over the cobblestone pavement, they entered through the hotel doors. John glanced up at the clock in the lobby. Ten-thirty.

Shad and Mary sat on a sofa on the other side of the lobby. They were drinking Cokes and chatting gaily. John nodded and smiled. They waved back.

"Time for bed, honey," he said, guiding Jessica toward the elevator.

Still Jessica said nothing.

Anxiety continued to grow in John's mind.

Once they were in their room, John encouraged Jessica to take a shower.

"You'll feel better and sleep more soundly," he promised.

A few minutes later, he heard the steady sound of running water coming from the bathroom. John sat down on the only chair in the room, leaned back, propped his feet on the end of one of the beds, and closed his eyes. They burned from lack of sleep. Tiredness gripped his back and limbs like a vise. Even his neck was stiff and tense. He thought about the shower and how glad he'd be to get in it himself.

Before long, Jessica came out of the bathroom wearing the robe her mother had packed, with her hair wrapped in a towel.

"Your eyes say, 'I'm sleepy,' " John said fondly, putting his feet down on the rug.

Jessica smiled. It was a familiar phrase from her father, one she had heard often as a small child, just before bedtime.

"Daddy?" Jessica was standing in the middle of the room. "I've been thinking."

John waited.

"You know that girl we saw?"

He nodded, waiting for her to continue.

"I'm going to pray for her every day while we're on this

trip." Jessica hesitated, then continued. "Like, what she is doing must really break her parents' hearts, don't you think?"

John felt the lump gathering. She looked so tiny and so vulnerable standing there. He fought back the wetness in his eyes.

This is my little girl. My only little girl, he thought, suddenly feeling deeply moved. *And she's growing up. There's no doubt about that.*

"Yes," he replied, his voice husky with emotion. "Yes, I am sure her parents are brokenhearted. They couldn't help but be."

Jessica came to him then, putting her arms around his waist.

"Daddy, thanks for bringing me on this trip." She suddenly changed the subject. "I'm so excited. I can't wait to get to Israel. It's so much fun being with you. Just you and me."

She thought for a moment. "And twenty-three others, of course!" she added, laughing. "But you know what I mean. Mother and Jeremy are not here. I don't mean that like it sounded. It would be great fun to have them both here, but it's the first time you and I have ever done anything like this."

She looked up at her father and hugged him as hard as she could. Then, as if she could read his thoughts, she exclaimed, "I feel so . . . so grown-up!"

"Okay, Little Miss Grown-Up, turn in and get some sleep," John replied, pushing her gently in the direction of the beds.

John went into the bathroom and turned on the shower. In the mirror, he saw Jessica reflected through the partially open door. She was kneeling beside her bed. He shook his head and reached for the toothpaste.

What did we ever do to get her? Maybe I need to let up on

God a little and give Him some credit for this one.

"Daddy?" John heard her calling, as he unbuttoned his shirt. "Daddy!"

He poked his head through the doorway.

"What's the problem?"

She was standing by the bed with an exasperated look on her face, hands on hips.

"How in the world do you get into this thing?" she asked, helplessly.

Jessica had discovered the wonderful mystery of European beds that amazes every first-time visitor to the continent!

John chuckled as he came into the room and helped her pull it all apart and then remake it. The American way! He had never learned how to do it any differently.

SIXTEEN

**WEDNESDAY, 14 SEPTEMBER, 0846 LOCAL TIME
AMSTERDAM, THE NETHERLANDS**

The next morning, most of the group arose early, ate breakfast in the sumptuous dining room, and were off to see what they could see They were not scheduled to leave the hotel for the airport until eleven, so there was time to walk, shop, take a canal-boat ride, or even a tour boat around Amsterdam's busy harbor. Most of those who had not done so the night before found their way to the canals.

John and Jessica were up early too. John knew that this would likely be the last time for the two of them to be alone together. Once they arrived in Israel, private father and daughter times would be harder to come by. The nature of this tour required that he concentrate more on the total group.

After last night's unanticipated sojourn through the red-light district, John was more determined than ever for Jessica to visit the house of Anne Frank.

"I want you to see that not all Holland is like the area we were in last night," he said. "And not all of Holland's young women work behind glass windows. There are some really wonderful people here, Jessica. They have a great history. Many of the finest artists of the world were born here. People like Rembrandt and Van Gogh. I wish the Rijks Museum was open this early. Some of the world's most valuable paintings are displayed there. But we'll just have to do that another time."

The air was brisk and they left footprints in the early morning dew. Trees showing the first signs of autumn color lined picturesque streets and canals. Fresh flowers graced window boxes and porch planters. A large green Heineken Beer sign stretched along a plain brick wall. Across the way, an even more familiar sign stood out atop an office building, announcing the presence of the Shell Oil Company.

"The Dutch are a courageous people too. That's another reason I want you to to visit Anne Frank's home."

They walked along Raadhuissstraat in the direction John had been given by the hotel concierge. He had visited the site once before and knew it was not too far. But he also remembered that it was not well marked and could easily be missed. Sure enough, they walked too far and had to double back. Finally, a short way from Kfizers Gracht, John saw the small marker identifying the Anne Frank House.

The door was closed, but a sign gave the hours during which the house was open to the public. John looked at his watch, then tried the door. It opened onto a small landing, at the bottom of a narrow, steep flight of stairs. They paused long enough to be greeted by a middle-aged lady situated behind a small ticket window.

"That will be six dollars American for each person," she replied, glancing at Jessica.

As they walked up the steps, Jessica whispered, "We didn't say anything, Daddy. How did she know we are Americans?"

John chuckled. "I don't know, hon. We must stick out. Europeans are used to identifying accents. They can tell the minute we open our mouths. Maybe this morning it was the style of our clothes. I know ... I bet she saw the American flag sticking out of your nose."

Jessica swatted his arm, grinning, obviously in a good mood after a night's rest. Her smile went away, however, as they reached the top of the stairs and she stood in the home of a little girl she had never met. Taking its place was a sober, reflective mood. John never ceased being amazed at the rapidity with which this child adapted to her surroundings. This morning was no exception.

Each room in the apartment was small. A sparsely outfitted kitchen, tiny bedrooms, a sitting area. Museum-style photographs hung on the walls, depicting vignettes of life and local events comprising the horror of World War II. Family pictures. The story of their hiding was told on placards attached to walls that were otherwise bare. Included were numerous comments from Anne's famed diaries.

They walked from room to room, John watching silently as Jessica touched a table, a lamp, a book. He sensed the totality of her absorption. She was transfixed by it all. He knew that she was there. With Anne. Imagining how it was to have been in hiding for more than two years. Never able to leave these rooms. No playmates. No running in the rain or splashing in puddles. No school plays, no recess, no sitting in the sun, no sharing lunches, or talking to friends she would get to see again tomorrow.

Only the fear.

The fear of being discovered.

Finally, that dreaded day came. Someone betrayed their hiding place. Soldiers broke in and dragged them down the narrow stairway. They disappeared from the neighborhood in the back of a military truck. Not just the neighborhood. The world. Only Mr. Frank came back, years later. He was the lone member of his family to survive the concentration camps. The others were gone. Forever.

Fortunately, Anne's diaries survived. They had been discovered and kept for her by a friend of the family in the
hope of giving them to Anne when she returned. When she
did not return, they were given to her father. Hands shaking,
and with grateful heart, he gathered in these verbal ashes
that were his little Anne. It was all that remained of his
family.

Later, the diaries were turned over to responsible people
and, at last, made public. First the nation and then the world
grieved over the senseless death of this innocent, bright,
hopeful little girl. Anne Frank was a symbol of the holocaust
that swept across a people and a continent. She became the
subject of books and stage plays as, through the pen and
pencil thoughts of a single child, humanity struggled to fathom the tragic demise of millions of its brothers and sisters.

By the time they entered the last room, others had made
their way up the stairs. They also came to see, to feel, to be
there with Anne. Two people spoke quietly, pointing to a
picture. An old woman brushed her wrinkled fingers over a
bare wall. The sounds of feet could be heard, shuffling on
wood floors. Anne's home had become a synagogue of the
soul, a kind of sacred place in which the visitors, each in
their own way, sought to recover the part of humanity that
was lost during those terrible times.

"Do you think Anne was a Christian?" Jessica asked as
their feet clicked along the cobblestone walkways on their
way back to the Krasnapolsky.

"I don't think so, hon," John answered. " She was Jewish. From her writings, though, it appears that she loved
God very much. And I'm sure He loved her back. She was a
courageous young lady, that's for sure."

They walked with hands tucked inside coat pockets for
warmth. The streets and sidewalks were noisier and busier
now. Smells of fresh bread wafted from a nearby doorway.
Lace curtains were pulled back on an upstairs window, a

woman's face appearing briefly as she checked out the day. Refuse was pushed up against the wall of a building. A beer bottle lay in the gutter, reinforcing Amsterdam's reputation as a dirty city.

"I'm glad I don't have to do that," said Jessica, after a while.

"Do what?"

"What Anne Frank had to do."

Her hand found his and sought its warmth. For a brief moment, John was moved by a sense of profound peacefulness. All seemed well with the world. Strange . . . he had not felt like this in a long time.

"I'm glad too," he said.

The sky was overcast. It was not raining, but autumn's first chill made their breath visible as they strolled together back to the hotel.

SEVENTEEN

....

14 SEPTEMBER
The White House
Office of the National Security Director
SENSITIVE
Israel Mossad reports possible terrorist activities
planned somewhere inside USA. Exact details unknown. Marwan Dosha no longer in Lebanon. Believed
headed for Europe, Canada or USA. Rumor major effort
to humiliate USA underway by Islamic Jihad organization. Goal: pressure Israel to accede to Palestinian demands. Rumor something to attract major media and
further holy war objectives. Arafat may be possible target. Nuclear possibility if connection to Iran, Iraq, or
Libya can be verified. No further details at present.
Israel concerned. Quality information source: high.

Action steps: Airports and border stations to receive copies of most recent Dosha photo. Orders to

apprehend and detain. Interpol, CIA, FBI advised. Will suggest other options and potential contingencies when available.

....

KLM FLIGHT 312 TOUCHED THE RUNWAY with such finesse that at first John didn't think they were on the ground. Then came the familiar *thumpty-thump* of tires rolling rapidly over paved surfaces, followed by engines screaming in protest as the pilot reversed power and began applying the brakes. John grimaced at the usual clapping and cheering of the relieved masses over another safe, normal landing. He did not enter into the festivities.

Fifteen minutes later, they were politely pushing their way through the crowd that milled about the Lod reception area, caught up in a kaleidoscopic sea of faces and costumes. It was a scene that never ceased to stir the soul of John Cain.

Eight or ten French-speaking Africans, resplendent in colorful national costumes, crowded around their leader, pointing at a map that obviously had them confused. Into a nearby concourse, a large jet had just disgorged a crowd of poorly dressed men, women, and children. They all converged at the same time into the passport control area. John listened until he identified their language as Russian. The men and boys all wore yarmulke skullcaps on their heads. They were well groomed, though not at all stylish, and appeared very happy to be in this humid place. He decided that they must be part of the increasing flood of Russian Jewish immigrants coming to Israel in the hope of a better life.

John waved his "troops" into this Middle East milieu and prepared to wait. Several dispassionate government workers in small booths systematically dealt with the crush of people, opening passports and examining them quickly. The agent glanced up at each carrier, back at the photo, and then handstamped the document. One by one, red, green, blue, brown passports each received the same treatment as Israel's latest pilgrims gained entrance to the Holy Land. But at this particular moment, it was hard to think of this as a "holy land."

On a scale of one to ten, the noise should rate at least a nine. John looked around at his group. They had queued in two lines, with looks ranging from serious to apprehensive to downright excited, all the while clutching their passports protectively. They were soon swallowed up in the stream of humanity moving forward an inch at a time, eyes turning first in one direction, then another, trying to gather in everything at once.

John saw David Barak standing a short distance from the passport control area. He waved to indicate that he had seen him. Tousled, sandy-colored hair, skin darkened from many hours in the hot summer sun on some of Israel's archeological digs, David was wearing sunglasses, a brown shirt, walking shorts, and well-worn tennis shoes. Looking a trifle bored, as usual, David lifted his hand in response.

While appearing to be half asleep, John knew him to be anything but. He was a brilliant young man, a skilled guide, and very patient toward those with whom he worked. In the next several days, he would draw on a lifetime in his homeland together with his formal background in Middle East history, a subject in which he had been a top student and now served as an assistant professor at Tel Aviv University. For these reasons, John had requested his services for the third time.

John felt that it was important for his group members to be exposed to the quality of knowledge and perspective that David would bring them regarding this land of Abraham,

Isaac, and Jacob. He wanted them to feel both the modern and ancient heartbeats of a people whose heritage and stories stretched for centuries across the scroll of human history. In the days ahead, he would work alongside David to bring additional insight and understanding to the group from the New Testament events that surrounded the coming of Jesus Christ to this land and to the world. Just being here once again sent a wave of excitement through John.

Greg and Debbie Sommers were the first of the group to reach a control desk. John pointed out David Barak and asked them to wait with him. Then he stood between the two lines and, as each person handed their passport to the uniformed immigration agent, he reminded them not to permit the stamp of Israel on their passport.

Israelis were used to this request; if the passport holders traveled to any predominantly Muslim country after being in Israel, they could be refused entrance if their passport revealed that they had been in Israel. In spite of recent peace accords and progress in Palestinian/Israeli dialogue, countries immediately surrounding Israel would also summarily reject the passport and the carrier, the reason being their failure to formally recognize Israel's existence as a nation. Even Muslim nations as far away as Malaysia, in southeast Asia, considered themselves "at war" with Israel.

It is a concept difficult for Westerners to grasp, but John knew from experience that it must be scrupulously adhered to. And so, instead of a stamp on their passport, the travelers received a piece of paper with a stamped entrance permit. The agent tucked it inside the blue USA passport, smiled, and welcomed them to Israel.

Bob and Donna Thomas were the last of the group to move through passport control. John then handed his passport to the agent. She looked up.

"Is that everyone, Reverend Cain?"

"That's it for this time," John responded.

"You've obviously been here before."

"This is my sixth visit."

She closed the passport over the small piece of paper containing his entry permit stamp.

"Welcome to Israel, Reverend Cain. Shalom."

"Shalom. And thanks for your courtesy to my group."

"No problem."

He took the passport and, slipping it into the travel pouch on his belt, walked to where the others stood listening as David bantered with his fresh group of American charges.

"Hello, John," greeted David. "You decided to bring some nice people with you this time."

"Hello, David," John answered. "I always bring nice people."

They hugged one another warmly. In John's previous sojourns, during which David had been his professional guide, the two men had developed a strong mutual relationship of trust and respect. After they had been together several days that first time, David had expressed to John his disappointment over the manner in which some American church groups conducted themselves. He resented the thoughtless rudeness. He was also amused and somewhat turned off by what he took to be a kind of spiritual bigotry, that considered his own Jewish heritage as something to be overwhelmed by religious tracts and jargon rather than understood and appreciated.

He had thanked John for not being that way. He acknowledged that he had led other Christian groups that were cordial and respectful, but he had not enjoyed himself quite as much as he had working with John. John thanked him for the compliment. He was proud of the way his groups conducted themselves.

Before bringing people to Israel, John always met several times with them. These meetings heightened anticipation and gave opportunity to help people realize that in Israel or elsewhere, they were the foreign guests. Their obligation to God and country was to leave genuine acceptance and respect behind with their hosts. For the most part, they had acted as savvy travelers, representing both their country and their faith in exemplary fashion.

"Your luggage is coming in right now," David pointed to a rotating carousel receiving bags and boxes from a conveyor belt. People who had not seen their luggage since it disappeared on a conveyor belt in Amsterdam eagerly helped one another identify bags. The men retrieved them, stacking and counting until all were accounted for.

"Follow me to the bus," David said, heading for the exit.

"I'm surprised there is no baggage check," Nick Micelli commented, as they hurried to catch up with David's rapid strides.

"No need," John replied. "We did all that in Amsterdam. Remember the way they examined us and our things there? They do that with all flights into Israel. Don't worry, though. You'll get a chance at a real baggage check when we leave. They'll go through your socks and shorts!"

Nick laughed as they pushed through the exit door. The afternoon's lingering heat and humidity quickly enveloped them. They saw the bus driver already placing their luggage into the underbelly of the bus. All of John's group were first-time visitors who, even though they had been promised comfortable transportation, were surprised at the sleek and modern Mercedes bus. As they stepped inside, the air conditioner's cool flow was greeted with enthusiasm.

In a few minutes, everyone was on board. As the driver guided their bus expertly away from the others parked nearby, David took the microphone in his hand.

"Shalom," he said, standing in the door well, looking into the faces of people who were now his responsibility to serve, teach, and to provide with comfort and safety.

"Shalom," the group responded in unison.

"Welcome to Israel. I hope you are all rested and ready to go to work."

He was greeted with groans from those who were beginning to feel the effects of jet lag and lack of sleep.

"No? You don't want to go out dancing tonight? Did you hear that groan, Amal? Already they complain about being tired. Wait until we are through with them," he continued jokingly, his sleepy eyes twinkling as he memorized the name tags on the shirts and blouses of those nearest him.

"By the way, this is Amal. He is an Arab and the best driver in all Israel!" The driver smiled and waved, as he maneuvered the bus out of the terminal area and onto the main road.

"My name is David Barak. You may call me David. I am Jewish," he continued, his English clear and distinct, more American in accent than British. "And, of course, I am the best guide in all of Israel!" The passengers clapped their hands as David bowed, smiling in mock humility.

"During the next few days, you will be seeing so much of the history of the Bible before your very eyes. I promise you the experience of a lifetime. You are fortunate to have a pastor who will take the time and make the effort to bring you to our land. We have worked together before. He is a fine man."

Another round of applause and a few whistles were heard as John raised both hands in the symbolic prizefighter's victory signal.

"Well, now that we have established how wonderful *we* are, you will show me during the next few days just how wonderful you are. But enough of that. Look around you." People turned their attention to the large open windows and the vistas outside. "We are leaving Ben-Gurion International, which is our international airport for the entire country of Israel. Locally, it is referred to most often simply as Lod, which is Hebrew for Lydda, where our airport is situated. I happen to know you have three such airports in the Bay Area. For us, one is enough. But anything worth doing, you Americans always do in excess."

The group laughed, feeling a rush of pride at the comparison and, at the same time, recognizing the truthful irony in David's comment.

"Have you been to California?" someone asked from the back.

"I graduated from UCLA and four years ago spent a summer in the Bay Area. My brother lives in Redwood City and teaches at Stanford."

Everyone began to relax, as John had known they would, once David joined them. The feeling of familiarity. This man knows about us, about where we live. We can relate. And in that strange way, for which American travelers are known throughout the world, they gathered him into their confidence. They had decided that he was a friend who could be trusted.

John leaned back in his seat. Jessica was next to him, her eyes fastened on this dark, handsome stranger, listening as he shared introductory facts about Israel, pointing out landmarks along the way. As they turned onto the main highway heading northwest toward the city, the sun was giving way to a magnificent orange glow that outlined the darkening, tree-covered hills.

Israel. I love this land, thought John, letting his mind wander as David talked on. He rested his eyes, smarting as they did from lack of sleep. His mind raced across ten time zones in an instant. A rush of mixed feelings suddenly made him uneasy. The pangs of guilt. *Is this real guilt or only imagined?* He did not know. Uncertainty about the future. The letter of resignation stored in his computer. *Lord, watch over Esther and Jeremy. Keep them safe in Your arms.*

Soon they were entering the outskirts of Tel Aviv. David continued answering questions as the first lights of evening began dotting the city's landscape.

AFTER DINNER, John volunteered to take everyone for a walk. All but the Mitchels and Gisele Eiderman decided to go. The Mitchels said they were too tired, and Harold indicated Gisele was feeling a bit of traveler's upset. She had been unable to eat and had remained in their room during the dinner hour. Nothing serious. She had taken something to settle her stomach and wanted to be ready for tomorrow.

David Barak had returned to his home on the north side of the city. This would be the last evening with his wife and children for a week. After tonight, he would remain with the group until they arrived in Jerusalem.

"Is it safe?"

John looked at Ruth Taylor, single, thirty-five, and about forty pounds overweight. She was already complaining about the heat. Perspiration dotted her forehead, even though the hotel's temperature was comfortably controlled by a modern air-conditioning system.

"Sure it's safe. And by now, it should be a little cooler outside too," John assured her. "Come on, Ruth, the walk will do you good. Tel Aviv awaits."

They fanned out along the wide, waterfront promenade. The white sand beach, stretching along the western edge of the city, was empty now. Before sunrise tomorrow, its daily evolution would get underway, with a group of hardy old-timers gathering to swim and exercise. As the sun came out, so would the local poseurs on parade, turning the beach into a sort of Israeli Copacabana. People would dot the afternoon sand with Israeli beach tennis, a popular game called mat-kot. Finally, as evening approached, fishing would take over, as people threw their lines at the sunset and enjoyed the glorious colors of sky and sea.

The lights from hotels, some with familiar American

names, ran together along the beach in true resortlike fashion. Several of the group exclaimed surprise at seeing a Hilton, a Sheraton, and a Ramada Continental. Surrounded by a host of other Euro-Middle East accommodations of varying quality, these vestiges of American hospitality gave a further feeling of familiarity to this strange, yet fascinating city. The Mediterranean Sea remained hidden under a blanket of darkness, speckled with pinpoints of starlight. An almost full moon was rising behind them in the east, its reflective light unseen.

Turning away from the beachfront, they strolled along a narrow connecting street, past a small Tabak shop. An old Arab was outside the door, closing for the evening. John greeted him as he walked by. The man stared for a moment, nodded, then returned to his task.

The street was not well lit, but after a few blocks it opened onto the nightlife of Dizengoff Square. A burst of neon signs. Cacophonous sounds of music. A large circular fountain, its contents spouting garishly in the glow of colored lights. John explained that the fountain had been designed by Ya'acov Agam, a leading Israeli artist, whose claim to fame prior to this was the paint job on the Dan Hotel. Most of the group agreed that he had missed his calling and should go back to painting hotels. Drink shops, ice cream stands. Even a McDavid's that a few McDonald's enthusiasts wanted to try out.

People were everywhere. Attractive young girls in short skirts and shorter shorts. Boys wearing jeans, sandals with no socks, and shirts unbuttoned halfway down the front. Young men and women in uniform, automatic weapons slung over their shoulders. Everything appeared to be so casual, so chaotic, so different from what they were used to. As they walked across the Square, John reminded them of an earlier conversation.

"You see now that what I told you back home is true. In

Haifa, they work. In Jerusalem, they pray. But here in Tel Aviv, they dance! David is a bit more blunt about it. He says that the best part of Jerusalem's nightlife is the road to Tel Aviv!"

At last, John saw the small café he had been looking for.

"Let's go over there," he said, pointing to the sidewalk tables. Several were empty. "Grab some tables before they fill up again. We'll scoot everyone together and the sodas are on me!"

The waiter and waitress helped them push tables and chairs together, then took their orders.

"Have you been here before, John?" asked one of the group as they sat, drinking sodas, eating ice cream, enjoying the convivial atmosphere of nighttime in Tel Aviv.

"Actually, no. Not to this specific café. But when I mentioned to David that we might go for a walk, he suggested this place. I guess he and his wife came here for lunch yesterday."

III

▼▼▼

As long as Islam does not take its rightful place in the world arena, everything will continue to change for the worse. The goal of the Islamic Resistance Movement therefore is to conquer evil, break its will, and annihilate it so that truth may prevail, so that the country may return to its rightful place, and so that the call may be broadcast over the Minarets proclaiming the Islamic state. And aid is sought from Allah.

— *from the* **Hamas Charter**, *Article Nine*

And did not Allah check one set of people by means of another, the earth would indeed be full of mischief. But Allah is full of bounty to all the worlds.

— The Holy Quran, *Sura 2: Baqara:251*

For God so loved the world that He gave His one and only Son, that whoever believes in Him shall not perish but have eternal life.

— The Bible, *John 3:16*

▲▲▲

EIGHTEEN

FRIDAY, 16 SEPTEMBER, 2045 LOCAL TIME
BAYTOWN, CALIFORNIA

It was warm.

Not a breath of air moved as evening shadows crept across the flower garden and onto the surface of the pool.

Esther and Jeremy sat across from each other at the patio table, the only sounds those of birds singing their September songs as instinct prepared them for their annual journey south. Between them, two partially empty iced-tea glasses formed damp rings on the table. Esther stared off toward a distant pine tree as Jeremy began twisting his glass, rolling the bottom edge back and forth along the tabletop.

Four days had come and gone since he had discovered his mother on the bathroom floor, along with the empty sleeping-pill bottle.

Over her protests, he had called 911. Within minutes, an emergency medical team was on the front steps. Esther underwent an examination and was pronounced out of immediate danger. Her vital signs were normal. On its own initiative, her stomach had already emptied itself of the majority of its contents. She could not remember how many pills she had taken, but obviously, it had not been enough. The dosage had made her ill but no longer threatened her life.

She seemed relatively calm and rational by the time they were finished, and Jeremy had volunteered to watch her during the next forty-eight hours. In addition, the medical team recommended that she see both her own physician and a psychiatrist as soon as possible. They filled out their report and left, after attending her for about an hour.

This had all happened on Monday afternoon, the day that John and Jessica had left for Europe. By about eight that evening, Jeremy had encouraged some broth and most of a cup of hot tea down his mother. She fell into a sound sleep around eight-thirty.

Jeremy went out to the garage, retrieved a sleeping bag and rolled it out on the floor between his mother's bathroom and the bed. He checked the remaining contents of the medicine cabinet. It looked harmless enough, but he didn't want to take any chances.

He lay down with one of his study books, but his mind would not focus on the subject matter. Finally, he put the book to one side, stripped down to his shorts, and stretched out on his back.

For a long time, he stared at the ceiling. His stomach churned.

He nervously ran his hand through his hair. Again. He felt unsure of himself. Of the situation. There was only one thing Jeremy was absolutely sure about.

He was scared!

What is happening to us? To our family? Mom and Dad are supposed to be the solid, spiritual leaders of the great Calvary Church. Man, that's really a joke, isn't it? The great spiritual leader, over there on the bed, just tried to kill herself!

Jeremy could hardly bring himself to think those awful words.

Dad is off with Jessica, somewhere in Europe. He'll be halfway around the world by tomorrow. Should I try to call him? I'm sure there must be an emergency number somewhere. I'll check with his secretary tomorrow. She'll know how to find him. But even if I did reach him, what could he do?

And, what about Mom? Maybe this was an accident. Well, it could be, couldn't it? Yeah, maybe that's it. Why would she want to kill herself? But, hey, I think that's just what she tried to do. O God, I can't believe this is happening! What am I supposed to do?

Jeremy kept his eyes on the ceiling. Waiting.

For what? An answer?

But, as usual, there had been none.

Now, as he turned his glass back and forth, he looked over at his mother. *What is she thinking about?*

"Mom?"

Esther sat still. It seemed to Jeremy like a long time before she slowly shifted her gaze and looked across the table.

"Yes?" she answered softly.

"Mom." Jeremy hesitated, wanting to talk, not knowing quite where to begin. Then, taking a deep breath, he plunged ahead. "It's been four days now. You've seen the doctor. You've even been to see the shrink. But I don't have a clue as to what's going on inside your head. You haven't talked to *me* yet."

He paused to catch his breath, feeling the emotion rising, working to keep his voice steady. He did not want to upset her. He was nervous about this. *Hey, this is Mom!*

The glass shook in his hand.

"What's with you?" he continued. "I need to know if you're okay. I don't know if I did the right thing by not calling Dad. I've been afraid to go to sleep at night. I get up and slip into your bedroom . . . just to be sure you're still there. I don't . . . I don't know what to think."

Her gaze was steady as she looked across the table. She spoke quietly, without any tremor, her voice matter of fact. "Son, I am truly sorry to have put you through this. I'd like to tell you that it was an accident. That somehow I blanked out and lost track of how many pills I took." She paused and looked away. Then, with a whisper she continued, "But, that wouldn't be true."

Esther twisted the end of her blouse. Her left hand clutched at the material, moving it back and forth, at first tightly, then loosening it with her fingers. With the other hand, she brushed back a loose strand of hair, as she stared down at her lap.

"These last few days, I've thought a lot about what I did, Jeremy. When I went to see Dr. Benton, he sat across from me, just like you are now, and asked me what I believed had happened. I told him that I tried to take my own life."

Jeremy could not move.

He wanted to, but he couldn't.

He sat numbly, the feeling drained from his body, staring at his hands, fingers intertwining, as he rubbed one thumb against another.

"I've no right to ask this, but I will. Can you forgive me?"

Slowly he lifted his eyes to look at his mother. The words caught in his throat.

"Mother, how . . . how could you. . . ?"

Jeremy's question died in mid-sentence.

Esther sat quietly. Her face was as calm as the evening. Her physical demeanor was perfectly composed.

That wasn't what stopped him.

It was the look in her eyes.

They were bursting with feeling. Drenched with emotion. He felt himself being drawn into her soul by the stark pain and sadness in her eyes.

She held Jeremy's gaze, then turned her eyes from his to the swimming pool. Jeremy turned to look as well. The sun's last rays danced on the surface. The water was clear. Clean. The only thing that disturbed its perfection was the dark outline of the sweep at the bottom of the pool. Even that was still. It ran only during the morning hours.

He turned back to Esther.

She continued staring silently. He could feel her drifting. She was out there, somewhere. In the water.

He followed her gaze back to the pool. And to the pool sweep!

It hit him with a force that took his breath away!

He turned again to his mother.

"It's Jenny, isn't it?" he whispered, his discovery filling him with a sudden sense of awe.

He felt the silence between them.

Esther nodded, her eyes fixed in memory on this scene of so much past family pleasure, and on the little person who haunted what had become her watery grave.

"Sometimes, when your dad didn't know I was close by and could overhear, I would find him standing here, talking to that pool sweep. He calls it his 'beloved ghost.' When I see him out here . . . like that . . . I can hardly stand it. I feel so responsible for her death. I've been so angry with God for taking her instead of me that I haven't even been able to pray for a long time. The other night, I overheard you and your father arguing. I could feel our family tearing itself apart. It just got to be too much. So when John and Jessica left . . . well, I did it."

As Jeremy listened, his feelings and thoughts spun their way into a mental metamorphosis from which, where his mother was concerned, he would never return. He was suddenly conscious of her fragility, her delicateness. Her humanity. She was a piece of rare porcelain flesh perched on the edge of a chair, in danger of falling and shattering. No

longer was Esther simply his mother. This was a woman he
had never really seen before. Not like this anyway. A stranger whom he recognized but did not really know. A prisoner
of guilt desperately wanting to be set free.

Jeremy slowly got to his feet and came to her. Gently, he
lifted her until she stood, looking up into his face.

He put his arms around her.

Silently, she responded.

Mother and son held each other for a long time.

A tear fell from her eyes.

Then another.

A crack in the dam.

The reservoir of pent-up guilt had begun its release.

Soon her shoulders heaved with sobs, and she buried her
face against his chest.

1830 LOCAL TIME
AYELET HASHAHAR, ISRAEL

JESSICA TURNED THE HAIR DRYER OFF, shaking
her long, straight hair loose with a flip of the brush. Its
chestnut color glistened in the late afternoon sun streaming
through the window. Her green eyes sparkled as she turned
to her father. "What a terrific day, Dad. And getting to be
baptized in the Jordan was a trip!"

John smiled, but said nothing. *She is beautiful. Looks
more like Esther every day.*

"What time is dinner?" she asked.

He checked his wristwatch.

"In about half an hour."

"Then let's go for a walk, Daddy. I want to see what this
place looks like in the daylight."

"I'm tired, sweetheart. Don't you ever wear down?"

John had been amazed at Jessica's twelve-year-old stamina. Ever since they left California, she had seemed ready for
anything. Some children travel poorly. Since Jessica had

never been on an extended trip like this, with only adult companionship surrounding her, John had wondered at the outset how it would work out. He had long since stopped worrying. She had always gotten along with adults. This trip was turning out to be no exception.

Within a couple of days, the group had molded into a family. Age extremes were represented by Evelyn Unruh, in her late seventies, and Jessica, who had celebrated her twelfth birthday during the past summer. Everyone was careful to watch out for them, making certain that they were included in the activities. John was continually impressed at how people who are traveling together often close ranks and differences and become friends. This group was one of the best at this that he had seen.

They had been busy since their arrival earlier in the week. Thursday had begun in the urban sprawl of Tel Aviv and Jaffa. The highlight was the time they spent in the ancient community, known in Hebrew as Yafo or Old Jaffa. The Greeks called it Joppa, David had informed them, and that's the way it is found in the Bible.

Jonah set sail from here on his great adventure. The Apostle Peter stayed in Joppa, at a tanner's house, where God spoke to him in a vision. Everyone enjoyed the restored alleyways and gardens around the port. It was delightful to wander through the artists' quarter. For hours they mingled with tourists in the little shops, and with locals who sat at tables outside tiny pubs drinking beer and wine or eating ice cream.

A few minutes north of the city, they had watched the skilled craftsmen of Netanya's diamond center cut and polish an endless supply of beautiful stones. A few miles further up the coastal highway, they tramped over the archeological site of Caesarea, Judea's Roman capital for almost six hundred years. After lunch, they drove through the seaport of Haifa, and on to Akko where cameras whirred and clicked incessantly, trying to capture the picturesque Old City with its minarets and domes and subterranean Crusader City.

By midafternoon, the group was hot and tired but still enthusiastic. They investigated Tel Megiddo, in Solomon's time a major city best known today as Armageddon, the biblical symbol for earth's last great battle. A few miles across the valley, the bus crept along Nazareth's noisy, narrow streets. The skyline of this predominantly Arab town was dominated by a large building looking a little bit like a misplaced lighthouse. It was the Basilica of the Annunciation, containing a rare collection of murals depicting Mary and the Baby Jesus, donated by Roman Catholic groups from around the world.

The sun was setting behind their bus by the time they crested the hill and first caught sight of the Sea of Galilee. Some in the group thought it breathtaking. Others were disappointed to discover that it was really only a large lake, approximately eleven miles long and five miles wide, with the Golan hills rising sharply from the eastern shore. After inching their way through the traffic in Tiberias, they drove north to their home for the next two nights, the kibbutz at Ayelet Hashahar.

Friday had also been a full day of travel by bus. A trip to the artists' colony at Safed and a visit to the community's small but quaint wooden synagogue. David Barak had grown up in this, his mother's hometown. As a child, this had been his synagogue. John could see that David felt at home here, walking through the streets, now and then greeting an acquaintance.

They traveled north to Qir yat Shemona, a short way from Metulla and the Israel/Lebanon border. Turning east, they climbed upward along the Golan Heights. David reported that some places in these hills were still unsafe, littered with undetonated Syrian landmines. It had been from this vantage point that Syrian troops had shelled the communities and farms in the valley below. They were ultimately driven back in a bloody battle by the Israeli Army and volunteers who lived in the valley. In the years that followed their occupation, some of the more desolate areas were settled by Israelis who planted numerous vineyards and orchards.

That afternoon, after a rest stop at an alligator farm not far from the Jordanian border, they drove past banana plantations and fishing villages until arriving at a point along the Jordan River, a short distance south of the lake. Here, John and the group had joined other Christian pilgrims in a baptismal service. Half an hour later, they were back in their rooms at the kibbutz changing clothes and drying hair . . .

. . . "Come on," Jessica pleaded, pulling at his hand. "The walk will do you good. You need the exercise."

"That's probably true," John acknowledged reluctantly. He rolled off the bed on which he had been resting and began lacing up his tennis shoes. "Okay, squirt, let's hit the trail."

Jessica skipped across the room, pulled the screen door open, and rushed out into the warm afternoon. The smell of freshly mown grass greeted them along the path. This was their second and final night at Ayalet Hashahar. They strolled hand in hand under the trees and alongside the various buildings of the kibbutz centrum. Farm animals, crops, exotic birds, and a major tourist trade had caused this kibbutz to grow quite large and become very lucrative. It was one of the nicest kibbutz communities for tourists.

"How do all these people manage?" asked Jessica, as they walked along the perimeter road encircling the kibbutz. Just outside the roadway, a heavy mesh and barbed-wire fence marked the border. Beyond this fence, unidentified intruders were likely to be shot. Its location was far enough north that one year, while John and Esther were visiting, they could hear artillery shells exploding a few miles north in Lebanon.

"A kibbutz is a community of people who live together on the basis of shared ownership and responsibilities. Unlike what you see back home, here there is not always a direct connection between work and wages. In other words, the type of work they do does not determine what their pay-check looks like."

"How do they live then? Don't they have to pay bills or something?"

"Sure they do. But it's like an extended family here. Suppose your grandparents and cousins all decided to come to California and live in our house."

"Wow, it would be crowded!"

"Yes, it would. So, we'd have to build on to the house, or find more property. But we could pool responsibilities. See that man over there?" John pointed to a man with streaks of gray in his hair, riding a lawn mower in front of a long two-story building. "His job is to mow all the lawns here. And someone else does the washing and ironing."

"I'll take his job," Jessica commented, watching the man turn the mower to take another swath. "I hate ironing."

"Each family has its own apartment. Sometimes all the children live together in separate quarters."

"They don't live with their parents?"

"Not always. But they visit regularly. And often they eat together or have play days with their parents. There's really no right or wrong way. That's just the way it is done here at this kibbutz. They grow up viewing all who live here as their extended 'family.' "

"How do they support themselves?"

"Almost every kibbutz has at least one factory. Some have three or four. Farming is important too. David says that by the year 2000, the kibbutzim will supply over half of all the country's agricultural produce."

They were walking past the dairy section with its barns and animals. The odor coming from the freshly churned

earth and the faded red barn caused Jessica to wrinkle up
her nose.

"Boy, that smells bad!" she exclaimed.

"You don't like the fresh country air?"

"Well, I'm a city girl and I can do without this! Yuk!"

John continued explaining the basic life of the kibbutzim.

"Places like this vary in size from one hundred people to
two thousand, and they are scattered all over Israel. They
first started here in the north, but the kibbutz movement
really began in Russia at the turn of the century. The first
one in Israel was started in 1910. Things were harsh and
very primitive back then. You can see they have come a long
way since those early days."

"Do most people in Israel live on a kibbutz?"

"No. I think it's somewhere around 3 percent. Most of
them were born in Israel, but some still come from Europe,
South Africa, or even the States. They are not just farmers
either. At least two orchestras and some internationally
known choral groups have grown out of the kibbutzim, as
well as several of the nation's leading writers, actors, and
artists."

"Where do the children go to school?"

"Right here. Normally, they are educated at the kibbutz
until it is time to go to the university."

"Are there any Christians living here?"

"Probably not, although sometimes it is permitted. Actually, most of the people living on a kibbutz are not religious.
A few groups have organized around some political ideolo-
gy. I think I read that out of over two hundred and fifty or
seventy existing kibbutzim, only seventeen are religious
groups."

"If I could live here," Jessica said, standing in front of a
huge vegetable garden, "I think I would like kibbutz life."

John smiled and took her hand again. "Let's go see if
dinner is ready. I'm hungry."

"Me too. But do we have to eat kosher food? We did that last night."

"No, we can eat from the other menu tonight. You'll like it better."

They walked up the paved street, listening to the sounds of birds in the trees. The mower could be heard in the distance. Warm, humid air tugged at their clothing and beads of perspiration trickled down John's nose. As they crossed over to the dining area, he noted that several new buses had been added to their own in the parking lot.

It would be another busy night for the kibbutz at Ayelet Hashahar.

THE SMALL, BRONZED-SKINNED MAN with a long, thin nose and a yarmulke perched precariously on top of his thinning hair finished dialing and put the receiver to his ear. Picking up the cigarette he had placed on the shelf under the pay phone, he inhaled deeply while listening to the rings.

Once, twice.

He hung up.

Wait a moment.

Redial.

Once, twice, three times.

"Aywah?" said the dull-sounding voice at the other end of the line.

The man spoke softly, his head tucked down and a hand over his mouth. If those nearby could have heard him, they would have been surprised. The man with the yarmulke did not carry on his conversation in Hebrew or English. He was speaking in Arabic.

"The shipment is on schedule." *The California pastor and his group are keeping to the schedule we were originally given.* "All the birds will be alive and well and will be delivered tomorrow as promised." *The group is still numerically the same as predicted.* "Be sure to have someone ready to receive them." *The kidnappers must be on site and ready to strike.*

"Understood," the voice responded.

The man heard a click. The line went dead.

Replacing the receiver on the wall phone, he drew deeply once more on the cigarette. Then, flicking it to the marble tile, he ground it beneath his shoe and kicked it out of sight. He walked toward the exit, stopping long enough to pick up an international issue of *Newsweek* and flip through its pages before returning it to the table. Then he casually continued toward the exit.

He reached for the door just as a young girl and a man opened it from outside. They smiled and stood back, the girl holding the door.

"Please," the man standing outside motioned to the one wearing the yarmulke.

"Todah," the man thanked the American.

"Afwan," answered the girl, with a smile.

For a brief moment, the man in the yarmulke stopped, stunned. He glared at the girl in surprise, opening his mouth to say something, not able to think of what his response should be.

"I am sorry," the American spoke up. "It is my daughter's first visit to your country. She is learning Hebrew phrases and also some Arabic words. It is hard sometimes to remember which is which."

Looking at Jessica, John chuckled. "You startled this man, Jessica, by saying, 'You are welcome,' in Arabic instead of Hebrew."

"I'm sorry," Jessica apologized, embarrassed as she saw others in the lobby begin to look their way.

The man with the yarmulke also saw people starting to stare with amusement in their direction. Without a word, he strode through the doorway and did not look back.

"O daddy, I feel terrible. I offended him."
"Don't worry, sweetheart. He'll get over it."

2000 *LOCAL TIME*
WASHINGTON, D.C.

....

16 SEPTEMBER
The White House
Office of the National Security Director
SENSITIVE
RE: Park Ranger Carl Deeker. Murder.
UPDATE: FBI and local authorities' investigation continues. Raft and motor traced to dealer in Toronto. Paid
for with cash. No physical description of customer
available. Waterton Park ranger recalls man and woman entering park evening, 6 September, with raft on van
top. Fits description. Vehicle carried province of Ontario plates. Park search has not turned up van or persons
fitting description. No one remembers seeing them at
camp sites or motels. Ranger is providing detailed description of couple. Age: twenties. Nationality could be
Arab. Artist sketch being prepared by RCMP. Will forward. Mossad and Interpol cooperating. Pictures of
known terrorists being made available to RCMP and
park ranger for possible ID. Further update ASAP.

....

NINETEEN

Rosa glanced around the room one last time. Everything was as it should be, ready for the next guests, whoever they might be. She checked her watch. Ten after one. She was running a bit late. The downstairs room that had housed the family from New Jersey had taken her longer to clean than normal. It looked as though the children had eaten chocolate ice cream in bed. Then two small hands had cleaned themselves on the wallpaper, while two others chose the carpet in the corner. Rosa wondered what the family home looked like.

She moved her cart along the hallway and knocked on the door of the room that was next to last for the day. All that remained were these two rooms occupied by the Arab men. Rosa thought they seemed a bit reclusive. Still, that was none of her business and this was to be their last night. She had actually been surprised at how each room was so neatly kept through the week of their occupancy. Her experience with male-only residents had, for the most part, been the opposite.

There was no answer.

She knocked again, this time a little louder.

Still, no answer.

They must be out again.

The men had gone out fishing on their rented boat two or three times since they first arrived.

They must not be very good at it, though, Rosa thought, inserting the key and turning it. She opened the door and entered. *They never bring anything back. At least nothing I have seen.*

"Maid service," she called out.

Nothing.

As usual, the room was in order. There was a heavy smell of stale smoke. She opened the windows. Next she emptied both ashtrays into the garbage basket. Fresh air and a thorough spraying of room freshener remained her first line of defense in any room that smokers had occupied the night before. Her sensitivity toward smells was legend at home with her men.

What is it about this room? Something keeps feeling out of place. But what?

Rosa stopped in front of the closet and looked around again.

Smells. That's it.

She went into the bathroom, picked up the used towels and washcloths, and stuffed them in the towel bag on her cart in front of the door. Gathering together the replacements, she went back to the bathroom and hung them on the wall rods. All the while, she continued thinking about smells. When she had finished wiping down the shower and damp-mopping the tile floor, her mind was made up. Rosa opened the closet door. No clothes bags. No luggage, except for the canvas bags that she thought were probably still under the bed.

No fishing poles. No tackle boxes or gear of any kind. And, no fishy smells!

Rosa had grown up with fishermen in her family. She could fly-cast as well as most men. She joined Manuel and the boys on Saturday morning fishing jaunts whenever her schedule permitted. One thing she was certain about when it came to fishing was the smell. The smell of the catch on a person's hands and clothes lingers. It isn't long before it spreads from the clothing into a room.

She never missed knowing when Manuel or the boys had been fishing, whether or not she had been told that they were going. When they returned, she knew exactly what they had been up to. Open the windows. Spray air freshener in order to eliminate the hated fishy odors.

No equipment. And no smells. That's what is missing here.

Rosa's curiosity had gotten the best of her. No clothes bags, only small shaving kits. *Now that I think of it, they are all look-alikes too, as if they were bought in the same store. But Mr. Ali said that they had not been together like this in years. In fact, he had said that they came from different cities.* Yet even the canvas bags she had once glimpsed looked alike, as nearly as she could tell.

She went to the door and checked the hallway, listening for sounds of movement on the floor below or on the stairway at the end of the hall. Nothing. Turning back into the room, she went around to the side of the bed and knelt down. Lifting the dust skirt surrounding it, she peered into the semidarkness underneath. There they were, pushed up against the wall, under the front half of the bed. Just like before.

Rosa dropped the dust skirt and sat back on her heels for a moment. Inordinate curiosity regarding other people's things did not normally trouble her. So why was this different?

Something doesn't add up. If they aren't fishing, then just what are they doing?

Suddenly, she made up her mind. Rosa trusted her intuition. It was a sixth sense that rarely led her astray. And that sixth sense was now urging her on.

Rosa leaned forward again and lifted the dust skirt, reaching underneath, stretching as far as she could. Her hand touched the nearest bag. Rosa ran her hands along its surface until she felt a handle. She grasped it and pulled. The bag was heavy, but it moved. Bracing her other hand on the bed frame, she pulled it toward her until it slid out from under the bed. Rosa stared at it, feeling guilty, her heart pounding with the knowledge that she was breaking a house rule. Never meddle with a guest's personal items.

The bag was black in color. A heavy waterproof coating made the surface feel slick. A combination padlock was in place to keep out prying hands and eyes. She tried to feel the contents that were hidden inside. With both hands, Rosa pushed and squeezed at the stiff outer shell of the bag. It felt as though there were several boxes. One appeared to be open. She pushed some more on the surface of the bag, feeling what was inside. Small, cylindrical items were attached in place in the box.

Fishing poles? No. They are too large and too heavy. Then what?

Rosa continued to feel the contents. All at once, her mouth went dry. She ran her hand along the thin, round objects, with growing apprehension.

This feels like . . .

The shape of the round objects changed as Rosa pressed her hands along the heavy yet flexible canvas cover.

This feels like . . . it is. It's a gun!

Rosa gasped, inadvertently pulling her hand away from the bag.

But these men are not hunters either. So why would they have guns?

Leaning over the bag now, she examined the lock. Realizing there was nothing she could do with it, she let it drop against the bag. Then, with both hands, she molded the shape of the bag around the contents as best she could.

Not just one. There must be four here, at least. They don't feel like ordinary guns, either. She could actually see her heart pounding now. These are different. Yes, these are automatic weapons, like in the movies!

Rosa's total concentration was on the black canvas bag. The door, left open, had been momentarily forgotten. Thick carpet muffled approaching footsteps. What happened next took place so rapidly that she had no way to recover.

The sudden awareness of someone else in the room.

The smell of stale tobacco.

A hand compressed tightly over her mouth.

Falling backward, her own hands flailing uncontrollably.

Trying to recover her balance.

Her vision locking onto the cold eyes of the man who lived in this room.

The man with the scar on his cheek.

A sudden, searing pain at the base of her neck!

Rosa fell unconscious onto the floor!

1057 LOCAL TIME
150 KM NORTH OF EILAT, ISRAEL

THE COVERED TRUCK rolled along highway 90, slowing as it neared Ketura Junction. Just before the split, the driver saw a military jeep parked at a slight angle in the northbound lane. Two soldiers stood by the vehicle, facing the oncoming truck. A third watched impassively from behind the steering wheel. One of the soldiers held up his hand and motioned the driver over, using his automatic rifle as a pointer.

Reaching back between the seats, the driver pounded three times on the wall between the cab and the cargo hold.

His forearm muscles flexed nervously as he came to a stop.

"Sabah-al-kheir," the young Israeli soldier greeted the truck driver in Arabic. In his hand was a small writing pad, together with a list of licenses that deserved 'special' attention. "What is your destination?"

"My next stop is Ein Bokek. Then on to Masada and Bethlehem."

"What are you carrying?"

"I have pottery and glassware from Eilat."

"Pull over, please, and shut off the engine."

The driver carefully maneuvered the truck onto the road's edge under the watchful eye of the soldiers. He shut off the motor.

"Get out and open the doors in the back."

Slowly, the driver climbed out of the truck's cab. There was no breeze and the heat was sweltering, though still an hour before noontime. The sun's rays baked the huge stones and rising cliffs on the left, while beating down incessantly on the salt-flat wasteland along the right side of the road. At three hundred eighty-six meters below sea level, the lowest point on earth was living up to its reputation for being uncomfortably warm. Even desert creatures were seeking refuge under rocks and in the occasional cave.

He jumped down from the cab, feigning boredom as he removed the padlock and chain and swung open the doors to the rear of the truck. The security checkpoint had been routinely set up today for all trucks moving along the Dead Sea's western shoreline. It was not done every day along this road, because truck traffic was normally light. Tomorrow, these same soldiers would be checking the flow of trucks crossing the Allenby Bridge, in and out of Jordan.

The soldier came around to the back and looked in. A handcart was strapped to wooden slats that ran the length of the inside wall. Some dirty packing blankets were piled carelessly to one side. Halfway forward, cardboard boxes and wooden crates were stacked on top of each other and tied into place.

"Pottery and glassware, you say?"

"Aywah," answered the driver. With unusual politeness, he asked, "Do you wish to look inside the boxes?"

The soldier squinted into the back of the truck, now a suffocating oven. The last thing he wanted to do was open those boxes. He hated this kind of duty, even in the Galilee region, where it was more temperate and beautiful girls were never far away. But here, at this time of the year, it was pure torture. Wanting to get this over with, he motioned to the Arab.

"Let me see this crate and that box back there."

The driver climbed up onto the truck bed and, a moment later, handed down the box that had been pointed out. The soldier pulled out his knife and attacked the box, making quick work of it. As he did, the driver wrestled the larger wooden crate over to the door's edge.

"I have nothing to open this with," he said, sweat running down on his shirt.

The soldier used his knife once more, pushing it under the lid at the corners. With a few prying motions, the cover gave way. He looked inside, ran his hand through the loose styrofoam packing, and stepped back. There was nothing unusual here. He glanced up at the driver. Nothing in his mannerisms suggested anything but the usual passive frustration of being subjected to an inspection he could do nothing about.

Now the part he really hated.

Gun in hand, he climbed up into the ovenlike interior. He randomly lifted a few of the boxes as best he could, checking the weight. They all appeared to weigh about the same as the one he had opened. Three other wooden crates were tied to one side. He thought about opening them too, then decided against it. He did not want to find anything.

Getting this inspection over with had become the goal. He peered over the tops of the boxes. They were stacked solidly, to about chin height, all the way forward.

Satisfied, he turned back to the driver who sat in the door entrance, feet dangling outside, smoking a cigarette. Sweat poured off both their faces and ran in rivulets under their shirts and trousers. The soldier motioned with his hand. Both men jumped down from the truck.

"Open the hood."

Used to this sort of request, the driver pulled the release and lifted the hood. Contraband, including both weapons and drugs, were sometimes found taped behind the engine block, in the oil pan, behind hubcaps, or inside tires. It was one of the reasons trucks often looked so stripped down. It made them easier to inspect. The soldier leaned forward for a look around the engine. Then, stepping back, he motioned for the hood to be dropped in place.

"Let me see your manifest."

The driver walked around to the cab and withdrew a clipboard containing the appropriate manifests and bills of lading indicating drops at the three locations he had mentioned earlier. The soldier flipped through the paperwork, by now disinterested in the whole task. He was already convinced that the truck carried nothing illegal. He wrote some notes down on his pad. Then, he handed the clipboard back to the driver.

"You can go."

The soldier motioned to two cars and a tour bus that had slowed their approach, stepping out of the way as they drove past.

"Shookran," the driver responded. He walked to the back of the truck and slammed the rear doors, slipped the chain through the handles and snapped the padlock into place. Smiling at the soldier, he stepped up into the truck cab. "Don't you wish you had my job now, and could get in out of this sun?"

The soldier said nothing in return. It was too hot to engage in roadside repartee. The Arab started the engine, slowly moving the truck back into the northbound lane. He smiled at the soldiers and waved. They waved back. The truck then roared its way through its respective gears.

Reaching back between the seats, he hit the wall four times.

THEY WERE GROWING ACCUSTOMED to the darkness by now. It was the heat that was rapidly becoming unbearable. The feeling of the truck rolling along the highway was their only relief. The four of them had sat motionless, cramped against the forward wall of the truck during the inspection, fearful of making any sound. Pasha's left leg was in such severe pain from cramping that she wanted to cry. As the truck bounced along, they did their best to change positions. They were soaked through their clothing, sitting in puddles of perspiration.

"Broad daylight, you said," grimaced Fathi, the darkness hiding his face.

"So what are you complaining about?" Yazib answered back, with a chuckle. "It is broad daylight. We are in Israel. Soon we will be taking a cool shower and having a nice lunch. What more could we ask for?"

"We could ask for our camels back," Fathi answered.

"No thank you, Fathi. My bottom has only recently gotten over that ride," said Pasha, rubbing her leg as best she could.

Laughter, mostly relief at not having been discovered at the checkpoint, followed her comment on their previous week's journey across the Negev.

The truck continued northward, encountering an increasing amount of traffic, mostly weekenders from Jerusalem, along with several tour buses bound for Eilat. Passing by Sodom and the Dead Sea Works, Ltd. plant, the sea itself was in clear view, with the sun casting a glaring sheen across its surface. Next came Newe Zohar's messy jumble of new and old buildings situated at the Highway 31 junction leading away from the sea into the Hatrurim Hills and on to Arad. A kilometer and a half farther, the driver reached back and pounded the wall three times. Then he turned off the highway into the parking lot of Ein Bokek's Salt Sea Hotel & Spa parking lot.

The main lot in front of the four-story hotel was about half full. In a few hours, most of the remaining available spaces would be filled. The crowd today would be typically international, with guests from as far away as Australia, Great Britain, Germany, Scandinavia, and the United States.

They came to experience the sensation of floating in the Dead Sea, sunning on its sandy beach, or taking prescribed treatments for a variety of ailments. Dead Sea water contains twenty times as much bromine as regular sea water, a component used in many nerve relaxants. In addition, its extremely high magnesium and iodine content counteracts skin allergies, clears bronchial passages, and is touted as beneficial for certain glandular functions. Rheumatism and arthritis treatments also draw the hopeful to the area.

The truck lumbered across the lot toward the back of the building. The driver looked around carefully, before stopping near the service entrance. He shut off the engine, nervously scanning the area for unusual signs of danger, then reached back and knocked on the truck wall four times. Sliding out from under the wheel, he jumped down onto the sun-cracked pavement and walked to the back of the truck, glancing about one last time before removing the padlock and chain from the doors and releasing the latch. Then he strode quickly to a hotel door marked Employees Only.

As he approached, the door was opened by a man in a

light-blue suit and wearing a sport shirt open at the collar. The driver nodded to the man holding open the door and then disappeared inside. Quickly the other man walked over to the truck. Opening the door, he saw three dripping, bedraggled men and a woman facing him.

"Which one of you is Yazib?"

Yazib raised his hand.

"Quickly," he ordered. "Through that door over there." He handed Yazib a piece of paper and a key. "Once inside, follow this map to the elevator. Your room is at the end of the hall on the fourth floor. Hurry, and try to avoid being seen!"

The shock of jumping from the truck bed down to the pavement sent stabs of pain through Yazib's feet and legs. He could see the others had experienced the same debilitation from the ride. A minute later, they were inside the hotel. Yazib held the penciled diagram up to the light, then looked around.

"This way," he said, pointing to an open door that led them into a narrow passageway. They jogged along the passage until they came to another door. It opened onto a small cement landing and a stairway. Halfway up was a landing, then more steps and another door. Cracking open the door, Yazib could see a hall leading to the main lobby area. He studied the map again. Halfway down this hall and to the left were the two elevators that serviced the upper floors. When the lobby looked like it was clear, he opened the door and they walked down the hall. At the corner, they turned toward the elevators. They could see them, a short distance from the registration desk but out of the clerk's line of vision.

Yazib pushed the button, uttering an involuntary sigh of relief as the door of one elevator opened immediately. They entered quickly and pushed the fourth-floor button. The doors started to close.

"Wait!" Startled, they stepped back as a young girl, about ten years old, slipped between the doors. Her bathing suit was dripping beneath the towel draped over her shoulders. She looked up and smiled, then punched the third-floor button.

"Hi," she said in English, with an Aussie accent. She surveyed the four of them as the elevator rose, noticing their soaked appearance. "Did you go swimming with your clothes on?"

The door opened before they could respond. The little girl stepped out, turned, and waved. "G'day!"

The door closed. The four terrorists looked at each other, then burst into laughter. On the next floor, they exited from the elevator. Yazib checked numbers on the wall signs and they hurried down the hall to the right.

Room 424.

At the door, he quickly inserted the key and turned it. They pushed their way through the opening. An instant later, the door securely shut and locked, the four dropped into chairs and onto the beds. An atmosphere of released tension filled the air. For a moment, they looked at each other, no one saying a word.

"We made it," Imad sighed, breaking the silence at last.

"Yes," agreed Yazib. "We made it. Allah be praised. We are at the Strike Point!"

Pasha stretched out on the bed, totally exhausted. Yazib noticed how her damp blouse clung to the curves of her body. Sandals kicked off to the side of the bed, her brown feet looked delicate and feminine. Yazib decided she looked good in blue denims too. Her Western-style apparel was unacceptable to their Islamic fundamentalist heritage, but necessary nonetheless. Eyes closed, her lightly bronzed face streaked with dirt and sweat was framed against dark hair and the white pillow.

No beauty in the classic Arabic style, he thought to himself, *but she is a woman created to evoke great desire in a man.*

Her eyes opened.

She saw Yazib looking at her.

Out of the corner of her eye, she saw the other two standing near the window, watching the delivery truck pull away from the service entrance and disappear around the corner of the hotel.

She turned her gaze back to Yazib.

He was watching her still.

Pasha smiled wearily.

Yazib looked away.

"Come, Pasha, get up. You are first into the shower. We want to take one too, so hurry. I am very hot and sweaty."

Yes, thought Pasha, getting up from the bed. *I am certain that you are.*

1230 LOCAL TIME
EILAT, ISRAEL

THE TWO YOUNG WINDSURFERS shot across the water on their look-alike projectiles, a stiff breeze filling their sails as they headed back to shore. Still some distance from the beach, the wind suddenly shifted. Before Dan could adjust, he was pulled off balance and headed on a collision course with Sheila. Yelling a warning, he veered past her, barely inches from a direct hit.

Avoiding injury was the uppermost thing. Flying across the surface of the gulf had become secondary. Both Dan and Sheila hit the water hard. They came up at the same time, waving the okay signal to each other.

Dan was only a few feet from his bright red sail that now floated lifelessly on the water. Sheila's board had continued on further before coming to a stop. She dove under the surface and began stroking toward it.

That's when she saw it. Something was definitely out of

place, directly beneath her. She immediately rose to the surface. "Dan! Come here."

"Are you okay?"

"I'm fine. But come over here. I want to show you something."

She treaded water, waiting as he paddled his board over to her.

"What is it?"

"There is something down there. Come with me and I'll show you."

Dan and Sheila were both expert swimmers. They dove together, slicing beneath the clear blue sea.

When they broke the surface again, they were tugging at four wet suits, two tanks and several body weights tied together and abandoned to the sea. The idea that perfectly good scuba gear would be abandoned to the sea was unusual enough. That it was discovered directly off Israel's southernmost shore was a matter of grave concern.

Twenty minutes later the equipment was on the beach, next to the rented windsurfing boards in front of the Neptune Hotel. A small crowd gathered around Sheila, curiously asking questions and staring at the equipment while Dan ran to call the police.

Ten minutes after the call, Eilat's tough, security-conscious police force had surrounded the mysterious scuba equipment that lay drying in the afternoon sun, and the two Israeli teenagers who had made the startling discovery.

TWENTY

At first, there was total disorientation.

She heard voices. They seemed close, yet far away. Was it a radio?

Where was she? Why was it dark? A moment ago, the sun had been shining through the window.

What window? At home? No. Then where?

At Hill House! It was the middle of the day. The man with the scar. The bag beneath the bed.

I have to get out of here!

Rosa tried to sit up, but for some reason she could not make herself do it.

She heard herself call for help. But no sound came out.

That was when she realized why it was dark.

ACROSS THE ROOM, the desk had been pulled away from the wall. One of the three men surrounding it glanced over at Rosa lying on the bed.

"She's awake," he said, watching her struggle and then

settle back.

"How much did you give her?"

"Not very much."

"She's been out for six hours."

"So? She had a nice nap."

The other man chuckled.

"Pay attention here, you two. We're almost finished."

On the desk lay an assortment of containers and rags. And a disassembled automatic weapon.

A cloth lay stretched over the carpet. On the cloth were three other automatic weapons, together with an assortment of ammunition, grenades, knives, and handguns. Everything was cleaned, oiled, ready for use.

The woman on the bed moved again.

"Should we take the blindfold off?"

"In a minute."

"What's her name again? Rita?"

"Rosa. She said her name was Rosa."

"There. We're done. It's ready to go. As soon as the rooms are prepared, we can leave."

"Wait."

The others looked up from their task.

"Rosa was very curious. She wanted to see what was in the bags. Take it off."

Yusif walked over to the bed. He hesitated, letting his eyes take in the attractive, helpless form in front of him. Her feet were bound at the ankles and her wrists were tied behind her back. A wide piece of adhesive tape ran from ear to ear over her mouth. Yusif pulled the blindfold over her head.

ROSA HEARD THEM TALKING, felt the presence of one of them standing over her. A stab of fear made her want to cry out as she felt the hand of a stranger touch her face. Then the blindfold was pulled over her head.

The light was blinding. She closed her eyes against its sudden brightness. As the discomfort subsided, Rosa squinted into the brightness. A stranger's face hovered over her.

One of the Arab men.

She closed her eyes again, desperately wanting the face to go away.

Slowly she opened them once more.

It was gone.

She felt like laughing from sheer relief.

It's a dream. A nightmare. Wake up, Rosa.

She turned her head.

Now there were two faces. No, three.

O God. It's not a dream. It's real!

"Good evening, Rosa." The man with the scar stepped forward. He noted the surprise in her dark eyes. "Yes, it's evening."

He glanced at his watch.

"Actually, it's ten-thirty. You've had quite a nap," the man continued softly. She watched his eyes. They were without expression, hooded, like those of a cobra. "I know you must be uncomfortable. I am sorry. You will not have to endure this much longer, I assure you."

A flicker of hope.

"I wish you had not been so curious, Rosa. You've done such a good job of caring for our rooms this week. But you are not a woman easily fooled. You knew we had not caught any fish this week, didn't you? What else did you notice, Rosa? Did it occur to you that our shaving kits were all alike? I think so. I spoke to Mohammed about that. He did not believe anyone would notice. But he was wrong, wasn't he? His mistake was in underestimating the powers of observation possessed by those who serve others."

The man moved closer, hands in his pockets.

"So you wondered just what we were doing here. And you discovered the bags beneath our bed. Rosa, Rosa. A woman of your intelligence and beauty should be doing something other than cleaning rooms, don't you think?"

He smiled.

This man. There is something about him. His smile? The scar? No. His eyes. Deep, piercing, brown eyes. He doesn't just look at me. He looks through me. These are the eyes of danger!

A chill of fear ran through Rosa's body.

"Take a look, Rosa," the man continued, motioning with his hand. "You wanted to know what was in the bags. Well, here it is."

Rosa turned her head until she could see the cloth on the carpet. Her eyes grew wide as she saw the guns and grenades. There were knives, ammunition clips, and several oddly shaped stainless steel containers. She turned back to the man with the scar. He saw the questioning look.

"Let me introduce myself. My name is Dosha. Marwan Dosha. Maybe you have heard of me, Rosa? Then again, maybe not. Perhaps you remember reading of last year's bombing in Florence, Italy? Or the attack last April on the infidel Jews in the London synagogue? Ah, yes. I see you do recall that one. May I introduce you to Yusif Shenuda and Safwat Najjir? They can describe those events to you in great detail, actually. They were the leaders of those particular strikes.

"Why are we here? I know you must be wondering. Can you understand that necessity demands it of us? Allah requires it as well. You see, Rosa, the world today is as the infidels have shaped it. They have left us with only two choices. Either we must accept this world in submission, which means Islam will die; or we can destroy it so that we can reconstruct the world as Islam requires."

Dosha leaned over Rosa, gently running his fingers across her forehead, brushing back tousled strands of her reddish-brown hair. Rosa closed her eyes at his touch.

A gentle man. Please, God, let him be a gentle man. Make

him turn me loose now. Please...

She opened her eyes.

"That's why we are here, Rosa. Allah has called us to build a new world. But first the old one must be destroyed. The East and the West are both alike. They are our enemies. Communism crumbles today because of Allah's judgment. Liberalism and socialism and democracy will surely fall as well. We do not fight within the rules of the world as it now exists. We reject all those rules. We are warriors in a Holy War that can end only when total victory has been achieved.

"Some of your people know this already and have come over to us. There are now more than two million Muslims in your country. Did you know that? What about you, Rosa? You are both beautiful and intelligent. Is it possible that you would come to our aid? Would you be willing to help us destroy the enemies of Allah?"

Rosa tensed as Dosha let his hand move past her ear and along her throat. At the collar of her blouse, his fingers touched a thin gold necklace, last year's anniversary gift from Manuel.

"What is this?" Dosha proceeded to pull it free. The last thing to come from beneath her blouse was the small gold cross attached to the necklace.

A token of my love for you and of God's love for us, Rosa.

Manuel had spoken those words the night he gave it to her. It had been the most eloquent expression that Rosa had ever known him to utter. She often remembered the tenderness with which he placed it around her neck. And how later they had made love.

Rosa never took it off after that night. Whenever she touched it, whether at home or work or at play with the children, she could feel Manuel's hands as he placed it around her neck. She could see again the look of total devotion in his eyes. *She was the luckiest woman alive. No, not lucky. Blessed. Manuel was a gift from God.*

Dosha's face hardened.

"Ah, Rosa, it is as I thought. You are one of them."

He gripped the gold cross and yanked it toward him. Rosa's neck whipped and then fell back as the necklace broke free.

"You are an infidel, Rosa! You are the enemy of Allah!"

The others watched, nostrils flaring approval of the passionate fanaticism in their leader's voice. Any doubts they may have harbored about this stranger were quickly evaporating.

Rosa turned away, her mind filled with fear and anger.

Dosha flung the necklace and cross into the far corner of the room. Reaching over, he pulled her face back toward him, fingers pressed hard against the her cheekbones. The hatred in his look burned into her soul. Rosa gave the same, both hurt and anger blazing in her eyes as she stared back.

O God, I know it's wrong. But he is going to take it all away from me. I can feel it. Lord, how can You expect me not to hate these men?

Mohammed Ali Atta had, by this time, returned to the room. He watched with interest the fiery connection between Dosha and the cleaning woman.

"How many others in the house tonight?" asked Dosha, never taking his eyes off of Rosa, who was now staring at the ceiling, listening as the men talked.

"Only two other rooms are occupied," replied Atta. "A young couple is at the other end of our hallway, in the room nearest the stairs. An older couple is staying on the second floor. And, of course, the old man is on the first floor in his room, as usual. Everyone appears to have settled in for the night. There was no one around when I came up from the reading room."

"Safwat. Put everything back in the bags," Dosha ordered. "Then take them to the car. Use the fire-exit stairs. And be quiet. Yusif, write a note to Mr. Brainard, explaining that we had to leave early in the morning rather than at the expected time. Mohammed, you will help me check both rooms. Make certain nothing is left behind. Wipe for fingerprints. We have been careful to touch only certain areas, but make sure nothing can easily be traced to us."

Rosa watched helplessly from the bed, as the men set about their tasks.

By eleven fifteen, they were finished. Just then, Yusif returned from taking the note downstairs.

"The old man is prowling around downstairs," he said, a worried look on this face.

"What's his problem?" asked Dosha.

"He says that Rosa, the cleaning woman, is missing." He glanced over at Rosa, who listened intently from her prone position on the bed. "According to the old man, she did not return home this afternoon. He asked if I had seen her. I told him, no, not since yesterday. He wanted to know if our rooms had been cleaned. I said, yes, she must have been here because the rooms had been cleaned today. I guess the woman's husband came by looking for her. They have reported to the police."

When Rosa heard that Manuel had been in the house, looking for her, a tear fell from her eye, unnoticed by the others.

So close, Manuel. We were so close and did not know it!

"It is time for us to go. This woman's curiosity may get us all in trouble," commented Dosha. "Yusif, go down and keep the old man occupied while Safwat and Mohammed take our friend here to the car. There is not room in the trunk. Put her on the floor in the backseat. And make certain there are no police lurking about.

"Give them five minutes, Yusif. Then go out the front door. Once Yusif is at the car, you two come back up the fire escape. We will all go downstairs together, say good-bye, and be on our way. If he asks, Yusif, tell the old man that some unexpected business has arisen. Tell him I have to catch an early morning plane to Chicago, and that this requires us to go into the city tonight."

Yusif nodded and left the room.

Safwat picked up Rosa and slung her over his shoulder, gripping her legs with his arms. Mohammed opened the door, looked both ways and then made for the window opening out on the fire escape at the end of the hall. Safwat passed Rosa through the open window to Mohammed and then followed after her. He was the larger of the two and so took Rosa once again, threw her over his shoulder and began the descent.

In a few minutes, Rosa was lying face down on the rear seat floor of the rented Cadillac. Yusif stayed with her. Five minutes later the others crowded into the car. Mohammed backed out of the parking stall and started down the hill on their way to Highway 27, heading north out of town. About three miles beyond the city limits, Dosha touched Mohammed's arm, motioning for him to slow down. Where the highway dipped sharply, a solitary street lamp identified a side road leading into the wooded hills. Houses were far apart in this area, with profuse expanses of trees and underbrush between.

About a half mile further, the car lights revealed a dirt road going off to the left. Mohammed turned and the car bumped along the narrow side road for about fifty yards, occasionally scraping bottom, as limbs and branches brushed against the sides of the vehicle. It appeared to be an abandoned logging road or a right-of-way used by hunters during hunting season. There were some tracks, but they did not look fresh. It was hard to tell in the uneven light as they bounced along, but Dosha doubted anyone had been through here in weeks.

"Stop here," ordered Dosha. "Shut off the motor. Lights out too."

They sat still for a moment. All that could be heard were the endless night sounds of crickets and frogs. Rosa stirred under the feet of the two men in back.

Dosha opened the door and got out. The others followed, peering at their leader in the darkness. The light of a full moon filtered through tree branches and tall undergrowth, revealing a small clearing off to their right.

"Take her over there."

Safwat grabbed at the back of her skirt, dragging her out of the car. Her face banged painfully against the doorjamb, with no way to protect herself. By now, her wrists had been tied behind her back for so long that her hands were numb and there was little feeling in her forearms. However, pain shot through her neck and shoulders with every move of her body.

Safwat carried her to the clearing, where he dumped her unceremoniously on the ground. She uttered a muffled cry as her shoulder banged hard against a rock. Safwat had torn her skirt, dragging her from the car. It fell open now, revealing a large bruise on her upper leg, apparent even in the dim moonlight.

Dosha looked across the clearing, letting his gaze run carefully through the darkened area that surrounded them. Perfect. There is no one anywhere near this remote spot. Nor will there be any time soon. He turned again, looking down at Rosa. Without warning, he reached down and ripped away the adhesive tape that had covered her mouth for nearly eleven hours. Her eyes clenched shut involuntarily and she cried out, swept away with the pain. Finally, as its intensity passed, she was able to open them again. Salty tears fell onto her checks.

The four men stood around her. Dosha placed a cigarette in his mouth and reached into his pocket for a lighter. As the flint sparked and flared, Rosa saw enough to cause her heart to sink in hopelessness. It was the eyes. Dark. Cold. Filled with hatred.

"Is there something you would like to say, Rosa?" asked Dosha. The others were smoking now as well.

She tried to moisten her lips with her tongue.

"Why . . . are you . . . doing this?" she gasped through swollen lips.

"Because, Rosa, you are in the way."

The man with the scar smiled.

"You are in the way of our most glorious achievement. Do you remember the stainless steel containers that you saw in our room? Didn't you wonder what might be in them? Even a little bit? Well, I will tell you. They hold enough anthrax to wipe out the entire city of Boston!"

Rosa's eyes grew wide in horror.

"Do you understand what that means? By this time next week, the world will have come face to face with the fearful judgment of Allah."

"But . . . why?" Rosa gasped in disbelief.

"Ours is a Holy War. It can end only when total victory has been achieved. We are not fighting so that we can be offered something. We are fighting to wipe out the enemy. In our lifetime we will see the conquest of the entire globe by the True Faith!"

"You . . . are . . . all . . . mad!" she whispered.

Dosha's gaze lingered on this defiant, helpless woman. A servant, but not servile. She knew she was beaten, but still she did not beg.

"Good-bye, Rosa."

He looked at the others and nodded.

"This infidel is my gift to you. Enjoy her. It may be a long time before you are able to have another. Take your time. I'll wait for you in the car. When you have finished with her, we will go on to complete our mission." Dosha drew deeply on his cigarette, turned and strolled away from the clearing.

Rosa returned the stares of the other three men. Fear

clawed at her throat like a wild animal. She had seen this look before. Years ago. When she was a young girl in the city.

"Please, don't do this. I've done nothing to you. I am married. I have two little boys. I am pregnant. You should not . . . please . . ."

Safwat knelt down beside her, placing his damp mouth over her lips. His breath reeked with tobacco.

Rosa bit him as hard as she could!

He fell back, cursing, while the others laughed. Rosa struggled and twisted, her whole being charged with renewed energy, fueled by fear. Desperation stoked the fires of adrenaline as she tried to get to her feet. Safwat stunned her with an openhanded hit to the side of her face, driving her back to the ground. He was on top of her. She felt him tearing at her clothes.

O God. No. How can this be happening? Mama. I'm a good girl, mama. Manuel. My darling. My babies. I love you . . . I love . . . Our Father . . . who art in heaven . . . forgive . . . as we forgive . . .

DOSHA LISTENED with a perverse satisfaction to the sounds coming from the clearing. His team would be ready after this. They would be grateful to him for the gift of the infidel woman. They would see how Dosha takes care of his own. Their trust in him would be total and complete now. They would do anything he told them to do.

Power is sometimes gained with such small price tags. He thought it amusing how little it often took to gain the allegiance he required from others. An allegiance he seldom gave back in return.

Manipulation. It was a craft he knew well.

The price tag this time was a cleaning woman that the world's number-one terrorist was sure no one would ever miss.

TWENTY-ONE

Marwan Dosha had committed his first error. He had let arrogance interfere with judgment.

This failing, so often the Achilles' heel of evil men, caused him to be mistaken about two things.

First, he was wrong about the narrow side road.

A battered once-upon-a-time-the-color-was-red pickup truck turned onto the sideroad just as the sun peeked over the forested hills. Jim Stevens and Roy Blanchard bumped along in silence. The two friends' workday had hardly begun. Jim made his living building things. He loved his craft.

Roy was a fifth grade schoolteacher who sometimes moonlighted on weekends to pick up extra cash for his young family. Normally, he enjoyed getting out with Jim and working with his hands. But it had been a long week in the fifth grade. He leaned back against the seat and closed his eyes.

"Look, Roy," Jim commented, pushing in the clutch and coasting to a halt. "Someone was in here last night. See? They turned around right here."

He slapped at the steering wheel in frustration. "I'll bet they got the stuff I left last night!"

"Doesn't that beat all?" Roy answered, yawning and rubbing his eyes. "What do they do? Just sit around somewhere, watching for you to start a new job so they can pick you clean?"

Jim put it in low and gunned the motor. They bounced along another fifty feet or so into an open clearing where he slammed on the brake, almost putting Roy's nose into the windshield.

He had spent the entire previous day hauling in lumber, bags of cement, and foundation forms in preparation for beginning a summer cottage. The Overstreets, from up in Bangor, had bought this property late last spring, and had hired Jim to build for them.

The new wing he'd been working on over at the Pates had taken Jim longer than expected, what with all the extra change orders they had requested near the end of the project, and he was three weeks behind schedule. Now, he was rushing to get the foundation in and the structure framed up for the Overstreets, before winter blew in from the north. They wanted to occupy by next June at the latest. Jim thought that with a little luck, he would still make it with time to spare.

Now the thought of pilfering made him angry. He knew that staving off young kids with nothing better to do, or dopers looking to finance their next fix, was every builder's constant problem after quitting time. Jim was partly mad at himself this morning, however. The night before, he had realized he was going to be late for dinner. He called home on the cellular that he carried on the job. That's when Sally reminded him of the conference they had scheduled with Mrs. Burdine, Jimmy's fourth grade teacher. So he left a small power generator on site, together with several cans of gasoline, thinking that no one could have figured out where he was working this early anyway. But he'd been wrong. Someone had discovered where he was on the very first day!

Jumping out of the pickup, he looked around.

There was the generator, right where he had left it.

The cans of gasoline were there too.

He shook his head.

Roy came around the front of the pickup and stood alongside Jim.

"They take anything that you can see?"

"Nope. Not a thing. Can you beat that? I wonder what they were doing in here?"

"Maybe local kids for some sex and booze."

"Well, whatever. I know someone was in here. I'm positive that there were no other tracks here but mine yesterday."

"Well, your secret lane is secret no more. We'll just have to gather everything up tonight. Let's get to work."

Roy started around the pickup to get his tools. He glanced back at Jim and stopped. Jim was staring intently off through the trees.

"You see something?" asked Roy.

There was no answer as Jim walked slowly across the building site.

"Hey, Jim. What is it?"

Roy moved toward him, at the same time turning his attention in the direction Jim was walking. He was almost up with him when he saw what had caught Jim's eye. Something white, a piece of cloth caught on a tree limb, about forty feet from where they had parked. Roy was only a few steps behind him when Jim suddenly stopped. He heard him curse under his breath as he came up alongside. That's when Roy saw what had frozen Jim in his tracks.

It was not just a piece of white cloth.

It was a woman's blouse. A badly torn blouse, looking as though it had been thrown into the air, where it remained caught on the limb of a tree.

Ahead in a small clearing, other pieces of clothing were scattered about.

"Something bad happened here, Roy. Something real bad." The grim look on Jim's face confirmed the apprehensiveness in his voice.

Roy's heart pounded out his response as they edged slowly into the clearing. Abruptly, Roy caught his breath and gripped Jim's arm, pointing over to the left.

Protruding from behind the trunk of a tree was a shock of disheveled, dark, reddish-brown hair. The face was turned down and away from where they were standing, but the long, slender arm and feminine hand stretched out on the ground bore out their worst fears.

Walking around the tree, Jim bent down to look at her face.

"Oh, no!" Jim gasped, followed by another curse. He looked up at Roy, his face an ashen gray.

"What?" asked Roy, staring at his friend.

"I know her!"

"You know her?" Roy repeated incredulously.

Jim nodded silently.

"Well?"

"It's Rosa Posadas. You know, Manuel Posadas' wife. We worked together on a job last winter." His voice choked as he added, "They've got two kids."

The two men stood silently together, looking around the clearing. Roy reached down and picked up a piece of thin cord. It had been cut. There were obvious rope burns on her outstretched wrist.

They looked at each other.

Jim's eyes filled with tears.

With an anguished cry, he smashed his fist against the only living witness to the horror that had taken place here. The tree remained unyielding and silent, its limbs extending over Rosa Posadas' battered body in regal sadness as if it too felt the unbearable pain.

Had Marwan Dosha been there, he would immediately have recognized his second mistake.

This cleaning woman had already started to be missed by the caring people who lived in Booth Bay!

0915 LOCAL TIME
BAYTOWN, CALIFORNIA

"ARE YOU READY for a waffle, son?"

As he walked into the kitchen, Jeremy was surprised to see his mother with a mixing bowl in her hand. She lifted the cover on the waffle iron and paused, waiting for his answer. It had been days since he had eaten anything but cold cereal or a piece of toast that he had prepared for himself.

She looked up and smiled.

"Well, what do you say?"

"I say yes. I'd like a waffle, Mom. Thanks."

She proceeded to spoon the batter onto the heating surface. Jeremy stood by the counter and watched.

"I know," she said apologetically. "It's been awhile."

"How are you feeling?"

"I feel . . ." she paused, placing the spoon on the tiled counter surface, "all dried up, I guess would be the best way to put it. Like I've had everything squeezed out of me. Kind of like I look, huh?"

"No, Mom," Jeremy responded too hastily, "you look great."

Esther cocked one eye knowingly.

"Well, actually," he said, with a wry smile, "maybe not 'great.' Maybe just . . ."

"Okay, okay, I get the message. And remember, Jeremy, the truth. We promised last night to tell each other the truth and nothing but, from here on out. Always. Even if it hurts."

"Yeah, we did. Well, so much for 'white lies.' The truth is, I've seen you look better. On the other hand, I've seen you look a lot worse too."

"Thank you. I think. The truth is, Jeremy, I feel pretty yucky. No energy. I'm sure it's the depression. But do you know something? There is one thing today that's different. It's a good thing too. You are the first person, outside of Dr. Benton, with whom I've been able to share my . . . the difficulty I've had accepting Jenny's death."

"What about Dad?"

Esther shook her head.

"I should have, and, at times, I've even wanted to. But I haven't been able. It's this awful, terrible guilt. I know, intellectually, that Jenny's death was an accident. I didn't cause it. God knows, enough people have reassured me of that . . . including your father." Tears began dropping onto the counter. "But it happened when I was here, Jeremy. And I just haven't been . . . able to get over that . . . at least not until now."

"Have you and Dad talked at all about this?"

"We've tried. He's told me that he knows it was not my fault. Accidents happen, and it will be all right. You know, all the encouragement stuff."

Jeremy grinned. "You mean like the pastor that he is, right? It's hard sometimes to separate whether what he's saying comes from Dad the dad, or Dad the pastor, isn't it?"

Now it was Esther's turn to smile as she brushed back the tears. "I know. And I think what he said was coming from Dad the dad. But then I would see him out by the pool . . . and I knew down inside that it wasn't ever going to be all right. I think he's tried . . . no, I know he's tried to understand where I've been with all of this, but I haven't really given him the chance. Not him or anyone really. Not until this week. There's just been too much guilt and anger. At myself mostly. But, I've been angry with God too!"

Esther opened the waffle maker and served the waffle to Jeremy. He proceeded to cover it with syrup and stuff the first bite into his mouth.

"Yeah, well, I understand that last part."

Esther wiped at her eyes with a dishcloth.

"What do you mean?"

"I mean that I've got some hangups where God is concerned too."

For the next hour Esther and Jeremy sat and talked. At one point, Esther reached over and put her hand on his, caught up, for the first time in a long time, in someone else's struggle. They looked into each other's eyes. They smiled. They even laughed.

Eventually, they became quiet.

Esther's eyes were wet again.

"Jeremy. Do you know how strange it feels for a mother to be talking to her own son like this?"

"Well, I know it's never happened to me before," he answered.

"I feel as though I've been pouring out my soul to a father-confessor. I am so sorry that I've put you through all of this. No mother wants to be remembered for her worst moments."

Jeremy covered his mother's hand with his own. "It's okay. Don't start feeling guilty again, Mom. You know what I'm going to remember most of all about this week? I'm going to remember that you trusted me enough to be a real human being with me. A person. Not just a role-player. I guess for the first time in a long time . . . I feel kind of hopeful. You know?"

Esther nodded.

Yes, son, I do know.

The house grew still around them. The events of this week had shaped a passage in life that would forever alter their relationship. Jeremy had been catapulted into an understanding of his mother that most children never know without the passing of many years. Esther was floating in a vulnerability that many mothers never permit themselves to feel with their children. Only time would reassure them as to whether or not this was good.

"Mom?"

"Yes?"

"Any chance I could have another waffle?"

With a playful slap at his hand, Esther got up.

"Some things never change, do they? Including your 'bottomless pit.' By the way, young man, what's on your agenda today?"

"Well, I'm not exactly sure . . . "

Esther felt the tentativeness in his voice.

"Look, son. I'm fine. You don't have to be worried about me. I've got a ways to go before I'm my old self, but I'm past doing something truly stupid. Actually, I'd like a little quiet time on my own without you under foot. God and I have got some things to straighten out. Okay?"

"Okay, Mom. I think I'll give Allison a call. If she's at home, I'll see if she wants to go out for a while."

"Good idea. She's a fine young woman."

"Yeah, I think so."

Jeremy picked up his dish and headed for the sink.

"Going to church tomorrow, son?"

He turned and looked at his mother.

"I'll be there. Want to go with me?"

"I'd like that. Why don't you ask Allison? Maybe she'd like to sit with us."

"Good idea."

**1400 LOCAL TIME
BOOTH BAY, MAINE**

BY TWO O'CLOCK IN THE AFTERNOON, the local police had scoured and sealed off the area. Rosa's body had been taken to the funeral home. An autopsy was scheduled.

Manuel was stunned and grief-stricken when a police officer, hat in hand, stood at his door and broke the news of their discovery. Manuel had spent the night looking for her. Now his worst fears had been realized.

Two small boys struggled to understand what it might mean to face life without their mother.

"Where is Mama? Can't she come home? Why not? How was she hurt? Is Mama in heaven with Jesus? Will we ever see her again? Why didn't she say good-bye, Daddy?"

Bad news travels fast in Booth Bay.

As word flashed through the tightly knit community, neighbors brought in food. Mrs. Cantor from next door took charge of the boys. Harriet Lawson from the church brought cookies and stayed to answer the phone calls that kept pouring in.

Father Mike, as he was known to the Posadas family, came with condolences and prayer. He promised that the congregation would offer special prayers in their behalf the next day. Manuel thanked him over and over. He and Manuel both shed tears as they hugged each other tightly.

By four o'clock, the police had arrived at Hill House to question Rosa's employer, Jim Brainard. After about fifteen minutes, Grandpa brought out the guest registration records. The two officers flipped through the most recent cards, pausing as they noted that two rooms had been vacated the night before. One officer held the card up to Grandpa.

"Robert Jibril?" Grandpa repeated. "Yes, he and these other three have been here for a week. Jibril is from Boston and, as you can see, the others are from New York City and Paterson, New Jersey."

"Have they stayed here before, Mr. Brainard?"

"No, this is the first time."

"Did they pay by credit card or check?"

"Neither. They paid in cash. Some extra even, in case

they needed something. Didn't want to take it back. I tried to reimburse them when they left."

"You saw them leave?"

"That's right. Sometime after eleven, it was. They said they had to leave early because the one fella had to catch a plane. Unexpected business."

"Did he say where he was going?"

Grandpa thought for a moment. "Chicago, I think it was. Yes, I'm sure of it. Chicago."

"Is there anything you can think of that was out of the ordinary about these men?"

"No, not so's you'd notice, at any rate. I talked with the one fella earlier, after Manuel came by looking for Rosa. Asked him if he'd seen her today. He said no. Not since the day before. Said she'd been here though. His room had been cleaned. Not that I thought for a minute that it wouldn't be. Rosa is . . . was . . . as dependable as anybody you'd ever want to know. A really good worker." Grandpa paused, then added, "And a really good mother too!"

He looked at the two policemen.

"What in the name of heaven will Manuel and those two boys do? They'll be lost without her."

The officers nodded, understandingly.

"She was pregnant, you know."

They looked at one another, then one of them pulled out a notepad. They didn't know. In his grief, Manuel had failed to mention that Rosa was going to have a baby.

"Is there anything else before we look at the rooms these men occupied, Mr. Brainard? We'd like to meet your other guests while we're at it."

Grandpa thought for a moment.

"Not unless the fact that they were Arabs is important."

"Arabs?"

"Yep."

"How many?"

"All four of 'em. Nice enough fellas, but they were Arabs all right."

"How do you know?" one of the officers asked.

"Are you serious, young man? I spent enough years in the City to know Arabs when I see 'em. They were Arabs. No doubt about it."

The policemen glanced at each other. A racial killing, perhaps? At least this was something.

"Did they arrive together?"

"No. Mr. Jibril came in alone and registered. Said he wanted two rooms for a week. Lucky for him, I had two rooms scheduled with a family from Boston, but they had to cancel at the last minute. I remember I got the cancellation the day he walked in. He rented a boat while they were here too. It's that cabin cruiser right down there," he said, pointing out the window toward the dock. "The one over by the sailboat there that's got the twin masts."

"Do you remember the name of the family from Boston? The ones who cancelled at the last minute?"

"Yep. It's all right here. He thumbed through the register. A Mr. and Mrs. Thomas Head. Two children named Amy and Sidney. The address, phone number, everything, right here."

The officers took down the information.

"Now, as I was tellin' you, this Jibril fella rented that boat down there. You asked if they arrived here together. Well, after this fella took the rooms, he told me he was goin' to pick up his friends in the boat. Said they were visiting down the the coast a bit. He went out alone. Came back with the other three. Matter of fact, I saw 'em. About two in the morning. Couldn't sleep and so I happened to be up when they pulled in. I figured he had done just what he'd said. Now, I'm beginning to wonder."

"What is it that you wonder, Mr. Brainard?"

"I'm wondering if he really did pick 'em up the way he

said. If these fellas are Rosa's killers, maybe he picked 'em up offshore somewhere. Coulda' been from a ship out at sea. There's been lots of alien folk comin' in illegally lately, according to the papers. Maybe that's how these fellas got here."

The officer continued writing. His partner sat quietly, studying Mr. Jim "Grandpa" Brainard, as the old man talked on. Finally, he interrupted.

"Mr. Brainard, we'd appreciate it if you'd show us the rooms now. We may need to see them all, but let's start with the two these four men stayed in."

Grandpa fumbled through his keys until he found the right ones.

"This way, fellas," he said, heading for the staircase.

BY SIX-THIRTY, the police had questioned the other guests, confirming Rosa's presence the day before. They had been able to determine that Rosa habitually made top-floor guests her last stop of the day, unless circumstances dictated otherwise. A thorough check of the two upstairs rooms revealed an unusual absence of fingerprints. Only a few that were too smudged to be of value. One clear thumbprint was finally picked up on the underside of a window sill.

Grandpa was standing in the doorway watching, when an officer bent down and carefully picked something up between his thumb and forefinger.

"You recognize this, Mr. Brainard?" He held it out in front of him as he walked across the room. "I found it over there in the corner. Almost missed it. It was hidden down in the carpet tufts."

He showed his find to Grandpa.

Grandpa swallowed. Tears welled up in his eyes.

"Mr. Brainard?"

"Yes. It belongs to Rosa. Manuel gave it to her on their

anniversary. She was so proud of it that it was the first thing she showed me the next day when she came to work. I asked her to sit and have a cup of tea. So she did, and we talked about Manuel and her boys and how happy she was. You could see it in her eyes. After that, I never saw her without it around her neck."

The officer wrote something down. It seemed to Grandpa that they were always writing something down.

"Mr. Brainard. Do you think you could identify these men?"

"Face to face? Absolutely."

"How about in a picture?"

"I think so, yes. Especially the one. He has this scar on his face. Right here," Grandpa said, touching his cheek.

"And you think they're on their way to Boston?"

"That's what they said."

"Good enough." He turned to one of the other men. "Joe, I think its time to call the FBI. This is a whale of a lot bigger than a local rape and murder. I'm sure of it. We have good reason to believe that these men have committed a capital crime and that they may have fled across the state line. They are suspected of kidnapping, rape, and murder. Mr. Brainard may also have given us a good idea. Perhaps these four are illegals. Make an appointment for Mr. Brainard to look at some pictures as soon as possible."

"Okay, Les. I'm on my way."

Twenty minutes later, they were all back in the Hill House reception area when Joe returned.

"The FBI is with us on this. They'll be contacting you later at the station, Les. I made an appointment for Mr. Brainard to look at pictures tonight in Portland."

"What time?"

"Eight o'clock."

"Will that work for you, sir?"

"I'll do whatever I can. I love that woman and Manuel.

They're like my own. And I'm 'Grandpa' to their boys. Now that she's gone, they'll be devastated. Believe me, I know. Will someone drive me?"

"Joe here will take you."

"Then, let me get my jacket. I need to call my Sunday helper to see if she can come in tonight. Then, I'll be ready. And can we stop for a minute at Manuel's house? I've got to see him before I leave."

**1245 LOCAL TIME
EIN BOKEK, ISRAEL**

A CLOUD OF STEAM escaped from the bathroom as Pasha emerged, wrapped in a large white towel. The others in the room were immediately reminded of her femininity as she walked over to the window and sat demurely in a chair. Crossing her long legs, she tugged at the towel, tucking its edges underneath her. Her hair was shiny black, still wet from the shower. She looked at the others and gave them an openhanded shrug.

"My clothes were soaked with grime and sweat," she said. "I washed them as best I could and now they must dry. Furthermore, I hope you will all do the same? You smell awful!"

The tension that her appearance had created broke as suddenly as it had come, laughter and agreement taking its place. Yazib nodded and headed for the bathroom.

A loud knock on the door froze everyone in place.

Yazib was closest. He peered through the security 'eye' and then reached out to open the door.

The man in the light-blue suit and sport shirt stepped inside. His eyes darted around the room, then stopped with a disapproving look directed at Pasha.

"Young woman, why are you sitting there half naked?"

"My name is Pasha and my clothes are drying. I am as modest as circumstances allow and my dress or the lack of it is none of your business!"

The man's mouth dropped open as though he could not imagine the insolence to which he had just been subjected. The others were startled by Pasha's defiant tone, and then quickly murmured their approval. She was one of them. And they did not take kindly to the critical attitude of an outsider.

Yazib stepped between them.

"You are our contact?"

The man turned his attention away from Pasha for the moment.

"Yes. My name is Amir Yassim. I am the day clerk here at the hotel. This is an envelope with your instructions. If two of you will come with me, I have the equipment you will need locked in a storage area on the first floor."

Pasha scooted forward in the chair. "I'll go," she said, adjusting her towel, obviously taunting the clerk now with her behavior.

The desk clerk's face deepened in color, from embarrassment or anger, or both. "No. It will take two *men* to carry the equipment back to this room."

"Imad, you and Fathi go with Mr. Yassim," ordered Yazib, doing his best not to smile. "Remain alert and try to be as careful as possible."

The clerk opened the door, then turned, pointing his finger at Pasha. "Young woman, I do not approve of you or your conduct. I intend to include in my report what I have found here today."

Yazib moved closer to the clerk until their faces were only inches apart. "Mr. Yassim, what you have found here are four very hot and dirty soldiers of Islam. It is not always possible for us to conform to all the rules of the faith while we are on the front lines. But I assure you that we will cooperate with you completely. And we expect your cooperation in return."

Yazib's eyes were as hard as flint.

"It would also be very unwise of you to include derogatory misstatements directed at any member of this team," he continued, his voice hard and flat. "Our lives are on the line during this mission, my friend. Yours is not. At least, not yet."

The clerk pushed backward through the door, pulling a handkerchief from his pocket and nervously wiping his mouth. Imad and Fathi went with him, one on either side. Yazib closed the door and turned toward Pasha.

"You were not very nice, Pasha," he chided. "We cannot afford to offend those who work with us."

"I know, and I am sorry," she pouted, settling back in her chair as she contemplated her toes. "But I cannot stand such pompousness. It makes me ill!"

Yazib did not respond.

She looked up. He was grinning. Pasha's face lit up with relief.

"I will take my shower and wash my clothes as directed earlier," Yazib mocked her.

"Good," she retorted. "You stink."

He went in the bathroom and started to close the door.

"Yazib."

He poked his head back into the room.

"Thank you."

His eyes locked with hers for a moment, and he thought about how lovely she looked sitting there, and how he wished they could have met in a different life than the one they were in.

He nodded and closed the door.

A moment later, Pasha heard the shower running.

WELL INTO THE NIGHT, the four of them worked quietly over each weapon, grenade, and explosive device that Imad and Fathi had retrieved from the clerk's hiding place.

Everything would need to be ready for instant use and then repacked carefully. There would be no further time to prepare, once the Strike was under way.

2048 LOCAL TIME
PORTLAND, MAINE

GRANDPA HAD BEGUN FEELING the emotional drain of this day. Rosa's death was starting to sink in. Spending those few short minutes with Manuel had been poignant and stressful, to say the very least. During the ride to Portland, there had been little conversation. The grimness of their mission precluded much in the way of small talk. Finally, at eight-fifteen, they pulled into a parking space in front of an obscure, gray building in downtown Portland. On the second floor, they were greeted and ushered into the brightly lit offices of the FBI.

They were ready for him and, once he was settled in, it didn't take Grandpa long before he looked up and motioned one of the agents over.

"This is Robert Jibril," Grandpa said, pointing at the face of Mohammed Ali Atta. "At least that's the name I knew him by."

"This is the man who rented two rooms from you a week ago?"

"One and the same."

"Are you sure?"

A worried look came over his countenance.

"Absolutely."

"All right. Thank you, Mr. Brainard. Will you continue looking through these photos. Perhaps you will find the others as well."

Thirty minutes later, Grandpa looked up again and motioned excitedly to the agents.

"I've got another identification," he said.

The men all crowded around to see.

"This one."

A sudden stillness enveloped the room.

Grandpa looked up, quizzically.

"Are you sure, Mr. Brainard?"

"I've never been more positive in my life," Grandpa assured the agent. "See the scar? It runs along his cheek and into the beard right here. Just like in the picture. That's the man. Why? Who is he?"

He saw the men throwing glances of genuine concern at each other. Finally, the Special Agent in Charge spoke.

"His name is Marwan Dosha, Mr. Brainard. You have just identified the world's most wanted terrorist! This picture was taken when he was in prison. You're absolutely certain?"

Grandpa nodded emphatically.

"And your 'Mr. Jibril' has been under suspicion as a terrorist link ever since the Trade Center bombing in New York. We've been watching him, but no one has been able to connect him. Then a week ago he dropped out of sight. We lost him. Until now, that is."

Grandpa tried to absorb what he was hearing.

Terrorists? At Hill House? Unbelievable!

"Steve, get the word off to Washington. And contact Ellis in Boston. Have them cover Logan and every bus and train station and car rental in the area with these pictures. Hurry. Mr. Brainard, keep looking. See if you can spot the other two."

Grandpa spent the next forty-five minutes sorting through the remaining pictures of known Arab terrorists from around the world, but with no luck.

TWENTY-TWO

The Israel Tours bus drove under the entry canopy of the Salt Sea Hotel & Spa at about six-thirty. The sun was low in the west, but as the passengers stepped down from the bus, they felt the blast of hot, desert air hit them. It didn't take them long to push through the front door and crowd into the lobby area. A young employee in a white jacket moved among the weary travelers with a tray containing small glasses of fresh orange juice. There was no lack of takers.

David Barak went to the registration desk where he spoke to the man in charge. After a brief exchange, the desk clerk stepped around the end of the counter and walked over to the group.

John thought him to be a bit overly effusive.

"Good evening, reverend," the man gushed, as, with a half bow, he held out his hand in greeting. John briefly grasped it with his own, silently reaffirming his displeasure of limp handshakes.

"I am so glad to welcome you to our hotel. We have been looking forward to your arrival. As you see by my badge, my name is Amir Yassim. You may call me Amir. Whatever you need, we will do our best to provide. I am at your service!"

John smiled and thanked him politely.

"And this little girl is your daughter?"

"Yes. Jessica, meet Mr. Yassim."

"Masa'al-kheir," said Jessica, with a smile.

"Ah, Jessica. How wonderful. You honor us. You have been in our land for only a few days and already you are speaking our language! It is a distinct pleasure to greet you."

Amir began checking David's passenger list against his own. The others lounged about, watching the driver unloading their bags. Still twenty-seven. None lost. Most were heavier than when they started, because of souvenirs purchased along the way.

"You can go swimming tonight, if you wish," Pastor Cain told the group. "And tomorrow is a 'rest and recreation' day. We'll not be leaving until late afternoon. This gives everyone an opportunity to sleep in, wash clothes, relax in the sun, or whatever. The idea is for us to arrive in Jerusalem at sunset tomorrow. It should be spectacular.

"Breakfast will be served from seven until nine-thirty, at your leisure. Lunchtime is twelve noon and we eat together. The bus will leave at four-thirty. Your room is available to you only until three, however. Then you have to be out. I would suggest a walk or a quiet time of reading between checkout and four-thirty. Also, don't forget that tomorrow is Sunday. We'll have a worship service by the seashore at nine-thirty. Any questions? Okay, you're on your own. See you at dinner. We'll be eating in the dining room. It's across the lobby and through that far door."

Names were called, keys handed out, and roommates disappeared into the elevators. Most were pleased to see that they would be staying on the fourth floor. The fourth was also the top floor and held the promise of less noise and possibly even a good night's rest.

ESTHER SAT NEAR THE WINDOW at which she had spent so many hours since Jenny's death. Outside, a hummingbird darted around the red hibiscus, striking a series of graceful poses in its never-ending quest for nourishment. Esther loved hummingbirds. As she watched, she thought of Jessica and John and the others.

I wonder how they are doing?

Absentmindedly, she picked up the Bible lying nearby. It automatically opened to Job.

How many times have I read your words, Job? I used to hate what you had to say. You were too depressing. But now I understand you so much more than I ever did before. I used to read your thoughts from an intellectual point of view. Now I know that your writings must be read with one's feelings, not simply one's intellect. Thanks, Job. Sorry I gave you such a bad rap for so long.

Esther thumbed through the dog-eared pages, stopping to read aloud some of the underlined verses.

"For hardship does not spring from the soil, nor does trouble sprout from the ground.

"Yet man is born to trouble as surely as sparks fly upward.

"But if it were I, I would appeal to God; I would lay my cause before Him.

"Blessed is the man whom God corrects; so do not despise the discipline of the Almighty.

"His wisdom is profound, His power is vast. Who has resisted Him and come out unscathed?

"Though He slay me, yet will I hope in Him."

She stared out the window. The hummingbird was gone.

Like my Jenny!

But, there is nothing I can do about it. No one else to turn to. Lord, help me, please. I know that she is gone and I don't understand why. Were You angry with me? I've surely been angry with You.

Esther felt ashamed as she prayed.

Lord, I'm so sorry for my anger. I've blamed You for not being here when I needed You. Still, I know Your wisdom to be so much more profound than mine. I've "resisted" and I've not come out "unscathed." Lord, forgive me. I hurt so much. I need You to cleanse my mind and heart of this incredible, debilitating guilt. I've got to break out of this depression. Please help me to live again, Jesus. I mean really live!

She continued her page-turning journey through Job. Several chapters were without underlined verses. Then she came to one she could not remember underlining. But there it was, and done with a different colored marker than she remembered using.

"But He knows the way that I take; when He has tested me, I will come forth as gold."

Lord, I don't remember this verse being here. Did I mark it? Or was it John? Maybe You marked it for me. In any event, thank You for the reminder. I am so grateful that You know the way I take. By faith, I am holding on to this as Your promise to me. Lord, let the tests You take me through cause me to "come forth as gold!"

She wept as she knelt in front of her window. Tears flowed freely as Esther felt the power of divine reconciliation released within her heart. It was not something of her own making. No. She felt certain that at this very moment the Greater was taking the initiative with the lesser. He tenderly touched her weakened spirit. A tremendous wave of emotional release rushed through her. Faith soared upward. Lightness replaced heaviness in her heart. God was reconciling her to Himself, as He had Job centuries earlier!

Then, Esther's window unexpectedly opened onto a mysterious, sacred altar.

She saw herself kneeling before the altar, cradling a child in her arms. She could feel the elfin heart beat as she hugged this little body to her own with a mother's recognition. She basked in the child's winsome smile and sparkling eyes. Then the little one wiggled free and, on tiny feet, ambled innocently toward the altar. It was much taller than the child, so she stood beside it for a moment, running her hands over the rough stones from which the altar was built.

Then, turning, she smiled and waved.

Esther started to get up to reach for her, but she could not. She could only watch as the child climbed up the side of the altar. There were no handholds visible, and Esther watched in amazement as she made her way easily to the flat surface at the top.

She caught her breath as a man appeared on the side of the altar opposite to her. He was dark-skinned. No. Wait. Was he light? It was hard to tell. There was such a "presence" about him! He wore a white suit. And his face was kind . . . loving. Esther had never seen such a face before. She was drawn further into the scene by the man's eyes. There was no doubt as to who he was.

He looked directly at her and an indescribable compassion transferred between them. Its diffusion was so real that she actually experienced what seemed like a physical touch. She could not speak. She could not move. There was nothing she could do.

Nothing but watch.

The child was standing on the altar now, in front of the man, her back to Esther. They appeared to be talking to each other. Esther strained to listen, but couldn't hear what was being said. Slowly the child turned. Her eyes were dancing with delight. She lifted her hand and waved. Then she turned to the man who stood beside the altar and lifted both her hands high above her head. Those little hands, stretched high above her head, were such a familiar sight. Both she and the man in white were laughing, as he reached out to her. She ran to him and he lifted her, ever so gently, from the altar's surface.

And then they were gone!

Esther blinked.

Outside, the hummingbird danced a ballet in flight over the red hibiscus. It pirouetted to the window where for one brief moment it posed, holding Esther's gaze.

And then, it too was gone.

Nature's *Amen* to eternity's drama.

A holy moment.

One she would never forget.

She dabbed at her tears and looked up, smiling.

You were there with her all the time, weren't You? I should have known!

2130 LOCAL TIME
NAPA, CALIFORNIA

IN SIMILAR FASHION to the others embarked on this mission of terrorism, Akmed and his group worked into the night, cleaning, oiling, checking, and double-checking. Strewn about the living room in semiorganized chaos were automatic weapons, hand grenades, plastics, detonating devices, knives, pliers, wire cutters, a small hammer, screwdrivers, a miniature set of wrenches, and as many rounds of ammunition as they could carry.

There was little banter. The business of the next few hours was serious.

In the corner, a television had been turned on earlier in order to watch the news. Its volume was barely audible now and almost forgotten by those present in the room. It was the faint sound of a crowd cheering that caused Akmed to glance up. A rerun of the day's football contest between the

University of California and the University of Oregon was playing itself out on the screen. Halftime had just been reached and the teams were running off the field. Moments later, Akmed watched as a camera caught the players heading into the locker room. The door shut behind the last blue California jersey, and the station cut away for a commercial break.

Filled with these fresh images, Akmed turned his thoughts to the realization of what was ahead. Like any team sequestered in the locker room at halftime, the young men and the woman in this room were ready. They were poised, trained, well equipped, and primed. They were as seasoned as they could be. All that remained was for them to play out their part of the final half.

Looking around at the others, busily checking and rechecking the tools of their trade, Akmed determined that there was one big difference.

Win or lose, it was unlikely that his team would be going home.

2210 LOCAL TIME
BOSTON, MASSACHUSETTS

THE BOAT that Mohammed and Yusif had chartered earlier in the week was an eight-year-old, thirty-four-foot trawler. Mohammed had taken it out for a run, during which he'd been asked to show routine docking and navigational skills. He had checked out on all the boat's systems and electronics at the same time. Papers were signed under the name of Robert Jibril, and the $1,200 charter fee for the week was paid in cash.

Darkness set in as the four men came on board, carrying their gear. The anthrax cannisters and weapons were quickly stored below in the stateroom. Safwat had shopped for provisions at a nearby supermarket. Now he stowed the perishables in the galley's refrigerator.

At nine-thirty, Mohammed returned the rental car to the agency at Logan Airport. He left the agency in their shuttle bus, as though he was headed for the terminal to catch a flight. At the terminal, he went in and waited until the bus moved on. Then he walked outside and hailed a cab. By ten-fifteen, he was back at the boat slip. Lights were out and everyone was settled in by eleven.

The last few hours had been busy. Preparations were complete.

The cleaning woman named Rosa was a fading memory. They needed a good night's rest.

Tomorrow, the Strike would commence!

2215 LOCAL TIME
WASHINGTON, D.C.

TO: Secretary of State
FROM: NSC New East/Asia Bureau
RE: Intelligence Update Israel
DATE: 17 September 2215 EDT

Intelligence Alert
Recent intelligence indicators point to some disquiet-
ing undercurrents which, to date, have not been pieced
together. German sources have passed rumors that at
least six canisters of anthrax spores — labeled as industrial chemicals — were passed through a Munich export-
ing house for reshipment to an unknown destination.
Possibly Athens. Sources in Lebanon report Islamic Jihad organization planning for a new attack — possibly
in Europe or Israel — or in America. Word has it that this
operation may already be underway. Also, Marwan
Dosha's present whereabouts still unknown. View here
is that he may be connected.
    Source quality: Very reliable.

Action Steps

This situation continues to be monitored. Intelligence data has been passed to our counterparts in the Middle East and Europe. Interpol and CIA have been advised. Recommend that you keep the President apprised of a potential "situation" on American soil.

....

....

TO: Secretary of State
FROM: FBI, Office of the Director
RE: Illegal Entry by Known Terrorists into USA
DATE: 17 September 2230 EDT

Incident Report

FBI, Portland, ME reports positive civilian identification of 1. Marwan Dosha, and 2. Mohammed Ali Atta. Both men wanted for questioning regarding the murder of one Rosa Posadas near Booth Bay, ME. Both men linked with terrorist organizations in Middle East. Two unknown others reported to be with them. All believed to be Arab extremists. Very dangerous. Possible location: Boston, Chicago, or New York City. Have been living in Booth Bay, ME, at a guest house for approximately one week.

Action Steps

Continuing investigation. Notifying our offices and local authorities in Boston, New York City, and Chicago. Descriptions and/or pictures of suspects are being provided. Airports, train and bus stations, and car rental agencies are being checked.

Will keep you advised.

....

SUNDAY, 18 SEPTEMBER 0930 LOCAL TIME
WASHINGTON, D.C.

....

TO: Office of the Director, FBI
FROM: Agent S. Keeler, Kalispell, MT
RE: Illegal Entry by Terrorists into USA
DATE: 18 September 0930 MDT

Incident Report

Acknowledge notification re M. Dosha and other potential Arab terrorists in Eastern USA. Have been in touch with Portland office concerning possible link between their case and the murder of Glacier Park Ranger Deeker on 6 September. Body found two days later. Death by single stab wound. Also recovered raft and outboard motor. Traced to Toronto dealer. Purchased cash by customer believed to be Arab nationality. Waterton Park ranger has described Arab man and woman entering Waterton Park with the raft on blue minivan. Ontario plates. Van and occupants have not been located. Theory: Van removed from scene and raft carried at least four or more persons to the USA side of Lake Waterton. Deeker surprised them and was murdered. Descriptions, sophistication of equipment, and efforts to conceal same lead us to believe likelihood that extremist Arab terrorists may be responsible.

Hypothesis: We should consider the possibility that our situation may be linked to Booth Bay terrorists. They may represent a coordinated terrorist offensive within USA, as per earlier CIA and Mossad alerts.

Action Steps

RCMP continues effort to locate mini-van believed to be somewhere in Canada. Artist descriptions of the man and woman have been created and distributed to our of-

fices in all Western states and Canadian provinces.
Advise re hypothesis.

··

The message from Kalispell's FBI office was received midmorning on Sunday. Helen Cartier put down her lukewarm cup of coffee and pulled the message, glancing at its contents. She knew that the Director had returned to Washington only hours earlier, after speaking at a law enforcement convention in Atlanta on Saturday night. Sunday mornings usually found him and his family attending services at Messiah Lutheran Church, near their suburban home.

She looked at her watch.

Helen was not sure whether the Director would be sleeping or attending church.

She smiled. Maybe he was doing both.

In any event, this could wait. At least for a few hours.

She dropped the message in his folder and returned to the paperwork scattered across her desk.

IV

▼▼▼

Allah is its Goal.
The Messenger is its Leader.
The Quran is its Constitution.
Jihad is its methodology, and
Death for the sake of Allah is
its most coveted desire.

— *Motto of the Islamic Resistance Movement, Hamas*

Of a truth ye are stronger [than they] because of the terror in
their hearts, [sent] by Allah. This is because they are people
devoid of understanding.

— The Holy Quran, *Sura 59: Hashr:13*

You will hear wars and rumors of wars . . . nation will rise
against nation. . . . Then you will be handed over to be per-
secuted and put to death, and you will be hated by all nations
because of Me.

— The Bible, *Matthew 24:6-9*

▲▲▲

TWENTY-THREE

SUNDAY, 18 SEPTEMBER, 1000 LOCAL TIME
BOSTON, MASSACHUSETTS

Certain Defense Department officials had called anthrax their choice for the ideal biological weapon. It enjoys the dubious distinction of being the granddaddy of biological weapons. Winston Churchill recognized its military possibilities as early as 1925.

In 1942, British researchers actually turned fiction into fact at the Porton Down Micro-Biological Research Establishment, when they exploded the first anthrax bombs on a rocky outcrop of an island known as Gruinard, off the northwest coast of Scotland. When sheep tethered in concentric circles died within days, it was hailed as a great success. The following summer, a bomber dropped another anthrax bomb on the island. Since then, it has been determined that anthrax spores can survive for well over fifty years. To this day, Gruinard remains contaminated and off limits to all human life forms.

By 1944, American researchers at Camp Detrick, the U.S. center for biological warfare research, had produced five thousand anthrax bombs, and military strategists conceived a plan for their use designed to wipe out six German cities. This saturation bombing with anthrax never took place because the war ended. If the plan would have been consummated, however, the cities of Berlin, Hamburg, Frankfurt, Stuttgart, Aachen, and Wilhelmshaven would still be contaminated cemeteries today.

In the early 1960s, the U.S. phased anthrax out of its arsenal of biological weapons because it was discovered to lurk in the soil indefinitely, denying the target area to friend and foe alike. However, in June 1979, stories were told of a terrible accident at a secret biological weapons research facility in Sverdlovsk, an industrial city of about one and a half million people, in the gently rolling hills of the Ural Valley, eight hundred fifty miles east of Moscow.

Reports posted the death toll at a thousand, with additional thousands injured by the dreaded disease of anthrax. Later reports from Russia insisted that the anthrax outbreak was due to natural causes, the result of eating contaminated meat. Experts, however, believed the reports of swift death had to mean inhalation anthrax, which kills within a matter of hours to two or three days. Inhalation anthrax occurs only when some force propels it into the air, thus giving further credence to the story of a biological accident resulting from an explosion.

Following the breakup of the U.S.S.R., economics dictated the closure of the research and development center in Sverdlovsk and other similar institutions throughout the countryside of the former Soviet republics. Numerous scientists, skilled in biochemical warfare techniques, were displaced and forced to stand in bread lines. When it became obvious that their future was nonexistent in the Soviet Union, large numbers left for other countries, where their services were well reimbursed. Syria, Iran, Iraq, Egypt, Lebanon, and Libya were all bidders in the mad dash to acquire mass destruction weapons, capable of annihilating hundreds of thousands of people at a time.

It was in a secret terrorist training camp in Lebanon's sunbaked Baaka Valley that Dosha, together with Yusif and Sufwat, had been schooled in the use of the deadly anthrax spores. Mohammed had no training in biological warfare, other than what he had gathered the last few days, listening and observing as the others rehearsed the steps they would be taking. He was an excellent boatsman, however, and also knew Greater Boston better than the others. He was not expected to have to work with the special weapons, except as a last resort.

While everything hinged on whether or not world leaders acted on their demands with all due seriousness, there was little doubt that their demands would be rejected and that they would use their biological weapons in order to bring the world to its knees. Well, they were ready. In fact, they would be disappointed if they didn't get the chance to display the power they possessed.

At ten o'clock Sunday morning, they split up. Yusif cast off the lines and hopped on board the chartered trawler. Mohammed expertly backed the boat away from its slip and into deeper water. Then he brought her about and headed slowly out into the Charles River.

Dosha and Sufwat, each carrying a backpack, walked away from the slip until they reached Commercial Avenue. There they parted, Sufwat checking into a nearby hotel, while Dosha ordered a cab to take him into Boston. At the corner of Charles and Beacon Streets, Dosha paid the driver and watched as he drove off. He looked at his watch. Nearly eleven o'clock. Eight o'clock on the West Coast, where he knew that their team was ready to attack the unsuspecting congregation in Baytown. He also knew that the team in occupied Palestine was poised to strike as well.

He smiled. The climax was near. He was beginning to taste the excitement that always came to him just before turning an unsuspecting public into victims of the Holy War.

Dosha walked over to a park bench and sat down. He pushed the straps away from his shoulders and placed the pack in his lap. Thirty or forty people, probably half of them children, lounged, read, or played in nearby Frog Pond.

Not so many, but enough for the "demonstration," he thought.

He reached into the backpack and pulled out a radio transmitter. It had been preset the night before on the boat. First, he held it up to his ear and listened to the sound of static. Then he pushed a button on the side four times. Holding it to his ear once more, he waited.

One click.

About five seconds passed.

Two more clicks.

Dosha smiled. One click came from Sufwat in his hotel room. The other two were from Mohammed and Yusif.

Everyone is ready to begin.

Dosha leaned back, closing his eyes at the sudden rush of pleasure that filled his body. He locked his hands behind his head as soft September breezes played around his face.

Sounds of laughter filled the air as little children splashed their way in and out of Frog Pond. They did not want this glorious day to end.

But in a few short hours it would.

1000 *LOCAL TIME*
BAYTOWN, CALIFORNIA

OVER FIVE HUNDRED PEOPLE were singing the opening hymn in Calvary Church's second service when a 1991 Chevy van with California license plates turned into the main parking lot. This Sunday's three volunteer parking attendants had just finished their assignment and were walking up the steps to the church's main entrance when the van came to a stop in one of two remaining handicap spaces next to the north entrance.

One of the men stopped to look.

"Someone is late," he observed. "Think we should go help them?"

The others turned to check out the van.

"Naw, let's go in. Looks like there's a young person driving. They'll be okay. I want to find the wife before the singing is over."

They needed no further encouragement. Serving as parking attendants was a ministry that the three of them enjoyed. Smiling. Helping people. Welcoming and giving directions to newcomers. But when it was their week to be on duty, it always meant getting into the service after it started. So they hurried through the door.

Songs of praise could be heard coming from the sanctuary as three men and a woman jumped out of the van. Akmed, Ihab, Mousa, and Aziza scooped up bags and boxes and ran for the entrance. Mamdouh waited anxiously, hunched over the rest of the supplies. Mousa and Ihab rushed back to the van and quickly gathered all but two of the remaining boxes in their arms. Mamdouh picked those up and followed after them in the direction of the door.

They stacked their "tools" along the inside wall of the empty hallway that circled the sanctuary. Akmed and Aziza had earlier determined that there were four public entrances leading into the worship area, plus one on either side of the platform. Six altogether. Since there were only five of them and it would be impossible to begin the Strike by physically covering all doors, they had decided on a bold plan, full of surprise, deception, and bluff. No one had ever done what they were about to do, so they felt confident that shock and surprise would work to their advantage.

As the congregation stood en masse for the pastoral prayer, to be led today by Terri White, the sounds of collective movement just beyond the door startled Calvary

Church's five visitors. For an instant, they remained frozen. Then a woman's voice could be heard guiding the congregation in prayer.

Beads of perspiration formed on their faces as they tore into one of the bags and drew out the freshly serviced and already loaded automatic weapons. Akmed's mind was racing. He remembered that during the services he and Aziza had attended, people had sometimes moved toward the exits immediately following prayer. They needed to be in position before then.

"They are praying," he hissed to the others. "They stand and close their eyes for prayer while someone leads them. Get inside before they finish!"

Aziza peeked around the corner into the main lobby. It was completely deserted. The information desk was unmanned, and the ushers had gone inside to prepare to receive the offering. "Now!" she ordered, leading the dash across the large, empty space. Their feet were silent on the thick carpeted floor, but she was feeling more vulnerable than she had ever felt in her life.

In seconds, Aziza was at the far door. Akmed took up his position at the central entrance. Mousa was at the door nearest the cache. Ihab and Mamdouh remained in their kneeling positions, busily arming the detonators and preparing plastic explosives. Neither man looked up.

Akmed threw a glance at Mousa, then at Aziza. Through small viewing windows in the doors, they could see the congregation, still focused in prayer.

"And Lord," Terri was nearing her conclusion, "we especially pray for Pastor Cain and Jessica and all those who are with them in Israel this morning. Watch over them. Keep them safe and free from danger . . . "

Without warning, a young boy, about six, came out of the restroom and walked straight up to Aziza. His big, brown eyes took her in from head to toe, and then fastened themselves on the gun in her hand.

"Watcha doing, lady?"

Aziza stared at the lad, speechless. Desperately, she looked up at Akmed, whose attention had been diverted in her direction by the sound of the boy's voice.

The lad continued to look up at Aziza.

"Are you a Sunday School teacher?" he asked, finally.

"Yes," Aziza whispered. "Now, go over there and sit down." She pointed to a folding chair against the wall.

"No. I have to go back to my mom and dad." Before she could react, the little boy pulled open the door and slipped inside.

" . . . and lead us not into temptation . . . " The congregation recited the Lord's Prayer together.

Akmed nodded, reaching for the door. A split second later, the three of them were inside.

" . . . and deliver us from evil. For Thine is the kingdom, and the power . . . "

They hid their weapons behind them, hugging the back wall as tightly as they could.

" . . . and the glory forever. Amen."

The congregation sat down.

The little boy tugged on his father's jacket. "Daddy, look. That nice woman over there? She's a Sunday School teacher."

The boy's father glanced in Aziza's direction, wondering who his son might be referring to. He saw a beautiful woman standing near the door, her back against the wall.

All at once, a sudden burst of gunfire directly behind him wrenched at his gut!

**1545 LOCAL TIME
THE DEAD SEA, ISRAEL**

IT SEEMED AS THOUGH they had been over their plans at least fifty times, though twenty might have been more accurate. Their weapons had been checked and checked again. Tension filled the room as Yazib looked at his watch. Five minutes had passed since he had looked at it the last time. The only sound was that of the room's air conditioner, providing them with one of the last vestiges of comfort they would enjoy for some time. Maybe forever.

Pasha was nearest the door when the knock came.

She opened it.

Amir Yassim, the desk clerk, stepped inside. He greeted Pasha with a hard look of animosity, running his dark eyes up and down the white jacket, blouse and light-blue skirt that was the Salt Sea Hotel & Spa registration desk uniform, but said nothing. Instead, he pushed past her and stood before Yazib.

"It is time."

Yazib held the desk clerk's gaze for a long moment. Then he turned away to the others.

"This is it, then. We are ready." He spoke to Yassim. "Where is the driver?"

"He has gone to start up their bus. It takes a little while for the air conditioner to bring down the temperature inside."

Brilliant. How many more inanities does this fool carry about in his feeble brain? thought Yazib.

"Their bags have been placed in the bus. The group is gathering in the lobby area. They plan to leave on time," he continued.

"You have been a great help, Mr. Yassim," Yazib said, as he guided the man to the door. "You had best return to your duties now. Thank you for your hospitality."

The desk clerk nodded. He stood still a moment longer, as though waiting for a tip. Seeing that none was offered, he licked his lips nervously and glanced over at Pasha one last time. Then he closed the door behind him.

The four stood in a circle, silently holding out their hands until each was touching the other, almost as though they were an American basketball team, ready to go out and do damage to their rival. Slowly, they removed their hands and stepped back. Yazib smiled.

"Allah u akbar! Go, Pasha. And hurry. We will soon follow."

TWENTY-FOUR

For one unbelievably long moment, there was stunned stillness.

People twisted around in the pews in an attempt to comprehend the reality of what they had just heard. Terri White, halfway from the pulpit to her chair, turned and gaped at the scene before her.

All eyes immediately fell on the young dark-skinned man, dressed in a peach-colored sport shirt, denims, and tennis shoes. He held an automatic weapon in his hands.

Then pandemonium broke out!

Frightened screams. Cries for "Mama." Shouts of "What's going on?" and "What is this?" could be heard throughout the sanctuary. Some people jumped to their feet and started rushing toward the aisles.

Another burst of gunfire, this time to the left of the sanctuary, froze everyone in their tracks. Faces swiveled in the direction of the new sounds. A beautiful, dark-haired woman stood in front of the exit door, feet spread apart, holding a gun in front of her, looking very professional and very serious.

"Sit down, please," Akmed ordered. "If you remain in your seats, you will not be hurt. Do not worry. Eventually, you will all be released."

A man on the front row, dressed in an usher's jacket, suddenly leaped to his feet and ran for the door located to the left of the platform. He bounded up the three platform steps and covered the remaining distance in three steps. When he was almost at the door, Yazib leveled his gun and fired. Bullets thudded into the wall to his left. Then, a string of bullets cut through the back of the man's jacket as he fell across the platform.

Screams of horror erupted. An elderly woman sank between the pews in a faint.

"Silence!" roared Akmed.

Once again, it became still as the inside of a tomb.

Every eye was riveted on the handsome man in the center aisle. The man who had just shot Jake Lunder, the head usher.

"Understand this," Akmed spoke loudly, pausing as he stared hard at the people in the pews. "You will not be hurt, unless you do something foolish. If you try to run, you will be shot. Even as I speak, the doors are being sealed with explosives. If you try to come in or go out, it will mean your death, and the death of others. Nothing is to be gained by foolhardy actions. Remain calm, do what you are told, and you will not be harmed."

Lowering his voice, he nodded at Crystal Abrams. "Now, if you please, may we enjoy some organ music?"

Crystal did not move, paralyzed by the fearful events happening in front of her.

"Play," Akmed motioned at her with his gun. "We enjoy the organ music. It will help calm us all."

Slowly, Crystal moved her hands to the organ keys and placed her feet on the pedals. Soft music began to flow from the large speakers overhead. Though the song was not familiar to the three unwelcome visitors, its meaning was not lost on the people of Calvary Church, who recognized the soothing strains of "It Is Well with My Soul."

On the far right near the back, a well-dressed man stood to his feet.

"Sit down," Mousa commanded sharply. Akmed looked over in that direction.

The man remained on his feet, careful to make no sudden move that could be wrongly interpreted by these strangers. His voice shook at first, becoming stronger with each word directed at the man standing in the center aisle.

"I do not know who you people are or what you want. But I am a doctor. The man you just shot is our friend, Jake Lunder. We know him. We know his family. He needs medical attention. You must let me go to him."

The congregation was still, their attention fixed on this new element of drama.

"Please," Dr. Orwell pleaded, hands extended outward, palms up.

Akmed directed his gaze at the man who had spoken out.

"What is your name?"

"Sidney Orwell."

"All right, Dr. Sidney Orwell, you may examine him. However, I can assure you that it is not necessary."

Sidney Orwell touched his wife's shoulder reassuringly as he moved past her into the aisle. Three center aisles converged on the platform, in addition to the aisles at the far left and right of the room. Pews were arranged in the shape of a gentle crescent. The floor sloped gradually toward the pulpit and platform. This design permitted everyone to participate with the awareness of others being present, while at the same time never losing sight of the pulpit, Communion table, and choir.

Dr. Orwell hurried down the right center aisle and crossed over the open area between the front pews and the platform. He went up the steps and onto the platform. Every eye strained to see as he knelt beside Jake Lunder, feeling for a pulse. Carefully, he turned Jake over, and bent down, laying his ear against Jake's chest. He could not hear a heartbeat. Sadly, he ran his fingers over Jake's eyes, closing them for the last time. Standing up, he turned toward the others who waited for an official pronouncement of what they already knew in their hearts.

Dr. Orwell glared angrily at the young man with the gun. "You were right. The man you shot ... *in the back* ... is dead!"

The crowd's exhalation of breath was followed by soft sobs. Whispers of, "Oh, no," could be heard through the sanctuary. Somewhere in the back, a child began crying. Dr. Orwell scanned the crowd, looking for Thelma and Lucy, Jake's wife and daughter. He felt relief that he did not see them there. It was strange, though. The Lunders were so faithful. They never missed church.

Unless one of them is sick!

Dr. Orwell's mind raced as he looked into the lenses of Calvary's three television cameras. When he saw the red light on Camera Three, he suddenly remembered that the nine-thirty worship service, televised live each Sunday and fed by cable to a local Baytown station for immediate airing, was going out right now. Those cameras were windows through which the viewing audience had to be seeing the crisis developing inside Calvary Church. A wave of relief swept over him. Help will surely be on the way. Then his stomach churned.

If Thelma and Lucy are at home, sick ... they may have watched this whole tragic affair! What must they be going through right now? Take care of them, Lord. And us too.

JEREMY WAS COILED LIKE A SPRING, sitting on the

edge of the pew in third row center, watching the astonishing events taking place around him. As Dr. Orwell started to leave the platform, Jeremy felt a sudden movement to his left. He glanced over at Allison, instantly registering the concerned horror on her face. Jeremy was sitting between Allison and his mother.

Allison's attention was fixed on her father. As he walked back across the front, she leaned forward to call out. Jeremy, seeing what she intended to do, clutched at her arm and pulled her back.

Startled, Allison turned toward Jeremy. With a slight head motion, he signaled her to be quiet. Her body was tense against his arm, but she did not move, her eyes following her father to his seat. She saw her mother's worried look and tried to catch her eye. But she was watching her husband as he came up the aisle.

Jeremy glanced at Esther. Her face was pale, her eyes closed.

How will Mom handle this? Will it push her over the edge?

He started to reach for her, then stopped. With relief, he saw her lips moving silently. His mother was praying.

HELEN GARVEZ TOOK THE CALL at exactly ten-fourteen.

"Hello, you've reached 911."

"Hello. I've been watching the telecast of Calvary Church's worship service. I think something is wrong. There are people with guns and somebody was just shot! They need help."

"Your name, please?"

"Sylvia Wall."

"You say you're watching television?"

"Yes. I can't get out to church anymore, so I watch Calvary Church of Baytown. Their service comes on at nine-thirty every Sunday. But I just saw people with guns there. And they shot somebody!"

"Are you sure this is not a television movie you're watching?"

"No. It is a church service. I see it every Sunday. You've got to do something!" The caller's voice was becoming agitated.

"All right, Sylvia. Calm down. Do you know the church address?"

"I can't remember it exactly. They show it at the end of the program, though."

"We'll find it, Sylvia. The police will check it out immediately. You did say that someone has a gun?"

"Not just someone. I'm watching right now and it looks like two or three people with guns."

"Thank you, Sylvia. We'll check it out."

The operator turned to her coworker. "I've heard some strange ones, but this is right up there. I've got to send a policeman to a church because a woman thinks she sees somebody there with a gun. She's getting all this from her television set!"

"God works in mysterious ways," the other operator chuckled, leaning forward in her chair to answer another call.

"Hello, you've reached 911."

"Yes. I know this will sound a bit strange, but I've been watching Calvary Church's worship service on television. And I think something is wrong. It looks like there are people with guns in the auditorium. I think somebody was just shot!"

The operator glanced over at her coworker. "Helen, I've got another one about the church!"

But Helen didn't respond. She was busy with another incoming call.

"HEY, FRANK, turn the tube on, will you? 911 is getting calls about some people with guns over at Calvary Church. They say they're watching it on television."

"What channel, Joe?"

"How should I know? They have a service on TV every Sunday, but I've never watched it. My kid goes to their school, though. He's in the fourth grade. Doing great too. It's that big church over on Twenty-First Street."

Frank Castor waited momentarily for a picture to appear on the screen. Then, starting at channel 4, he began flipping through the channels. Cartoons. News interviews. A rerun of yesterday's UC-Oregon game. MTV. More cartoons. He paused at Channel 17, KMAN, an independent, originating in Baytown. Their studios were only a few blocks away, on the top floor of the Burton Building.

"Here it is," he said, stepping back from the set.

Joe got up from his desk and came around to stand beside Frank. Their mouths dropped open as they stared at the picture on the screen. It was Calvary Church all right. Joe remembered being there for a meeting that included all the school parents. There were so many that the sanctuary had to be used. He and Emily had sat over there, on the right-hand side. He noted the location mentally, while trying to discern what was going on.

The organ was playing.

A man was kneeling over someone on the platform.

Joe leaned forward.

It looked like a man was stretched out on the floor. The other man stood and turned to the audience. The camera moved in on his face. It was flushed. He was obviously fighting to keep from exploding in anger. They heard him speaking to someone off camera.

"You were right. The man you shot . . . *in the back* . . . is dead!"

The man's face faded from view and was replaced by

that of another man. Young. Good looking. Fade. A full room scene came up on the screen.

"Joe, look. That guy has got a gun!"

Lt. Joe Randle whirled around and poked his head through the door. "Cindy. There's a guy over at Calvary Church with a gun. Looks as though he's shot somebody already. APB our guys on patrol. For starters, I want every street closed off around that church!"

"Yessir, got it." The dispatcher began relaying Joe Randle's orders over the police radio channel.

"Frank, see if you can get hold of that guy with the Oakland PD. You know, the one who talked that woman with the baby off the Bay Bridge last week. Was his name Cole? Something like that."

"You want a negotiator?"

Joe Randle did not answer. He was staring at the television, motioning with his hand for Frank to be quiet.

The camera shot revealed most of the sanctuary now. Joe could see at least three people holding automatic weapons. A fourth person was kneeling at one of the sanctuary doors, working with something.

Joe swore.

"See that guy? Over at the door? He's got to be sealing it off with explosives! Isn't that what it looks like to you?"

As Frank watched, he shook his head.

"I wouldn't believe this if I wasn't standing right here watching."

"Do you see what I see, Frank?"

"What?"

"Look."

Frank scanned the picture on the screen.

"There! See? At least three men and a woman are in there with weapons. They're sealing the doors with explosives. Now. Keep looking. Notice anything?"

The screen began picking up the faces of the four persons with guns.

"I don't know who the operators are, but they've got guts. I wonder if those hoods know they're on *Candid Camera*?"

Suddenly Frank saw what Joe had seen.

"They all look like . . . "

"Arabs!" Joe confirmed. "Come on."

They rushed for the door. "Cindy, you'd better contact the Chief. I'm not sure, but, I think we may have a group of terrorists holding a church full of people hostage, so stay alert."

The dispatcher looked up in astonishment.

"Terrorists?" she repeated. "In Baytown? Are you serious?"

But the two men were already out the door.

Cindy quickly looked for the number on her display and made the call.

TWENTY-FIVE

Four adults. Five small children.

They will do fine, he thought.

Like rats in a laboratory.

Confirming messengers of death!

Two were men, sharing a blanket and a Sunday morning edition of the *Boston Globe.* One offered up a disgruntled groan while reading yesterday's score of the Red Sox game.

Every April, Bostonians touch their beer steins together and declare this to be the year of the Red Sox. Come September, true Sox fans sink into an undeniable "Fenway funk" in the realization that their team will not make the playoffs again this year. These indefatigable sports fans, refusing to weary of the hunt, then turn their attention to football. In the spirit of the season, Mr. Sports Pages rolled over onto his elbows, spreading the newspaper out flat on the blanket, engrossed in an editorial declaring that, despite the New England Patriots' 0–3 preseason record, their opener today at Sullivan Stadium promised potential victory. Heavy on *potential!*

The other man skimmed the front section, including a page three article about yesterday's rape-murder of a married woman in Booth Bay, Maine. She had two sons and a third child on the way. No motive was cited and no suspects had been identified. He glanced up at his own two children, bending over the edge of the pond, splashing in the water. His wife was engrossed in conversation with her best friend. They were together. Safe. That's all that mattered. He turned the page.

The two young mothers were facing each other, yoga style, tracing imaginary lines through the grass with their fingers, engrossed in a discussion of what they were going to do this fall, now that their youngest had joined the rest of their children in school. The man sitting on the bench couldn't hear their conversation, but the one with long, blond hair threw back her head in laughter, while her dark-haired friend reached out a hand in mock protest over whatever had been shared, resting it on the other woman's knee.

He got up and strolled toward this tiny, tranquil gathering. As he drew near, the blond squinted at him, the sun directly in her eyes. He smiled politely and she looked back at her friend who was saying something else. Three or four steps past, the man appeared to fumble something, dropping it in the grass. He bent over to pick it up and walked on.

More sounds of laughter.

Life is good, isn't it?

If someone had looked in the grass where the dark-skinned man had stopped to pick up what he had "dropped," they would have realized that just the opposite had happened. He had not picked anything up. He had left something there.

A tiny three-inch stainless-steel canister.

He was counting on the fact that no one would notice.

No one did.

No one, that is, until five minutes later when it exploded

with a muted pop.

A small cloud of spray was momentarily visible, engulfing the four adults. They looked up, startled.

"What was that?" the dark-haired woman asked.

"Got me," the other replied.

They brushed at their clothing and looked in the direction from which the sound had come.

Meanwhile, pushed by a soft September breeze, the tiny cloud dispersed and floated toward the children.

**1300 LOCAL TIME
BOSTON**

"YOU'VE REACHED WBZ, channel 4. How may I direct your call?"

"I'd like the newsroom, please," the slightly accented male voice answered politely.

"Hello, newsroom."

"Listen very carefully," the voice instructed. "The people of Boston are in grave danger. If the reasonable demands of the Islamic Jihad are not met, we will loose an epidemic of death in this city on a scale never before experienced in the world. I will present you with our demands in one hour. Be ready, and understand that this is not a hoax."

"What are you trying to pull, whoever you are? You can't expect me to believe you are serious!"

"To illustrate to you just how serious we are," the voice continued, "less than one hour ago, at the Boston Common, nine people were exposed to a lethal dose of inhalation anthrax. There may be others. We are prepared to kill hundreds of thousands of Bostonians the same as was done to these two families. The city itself will be left in irreparable desolation for decades. You will be contacted again in exactly one hour."

The line went dead.

1330 LOCAL TIME
Boston

THE POLICE CAR pulled to a stop near the Joy Street steps. Both officers exited from the car and paused, looking around.

"Lots of people out today, Jim."

"Yeah. Where is this thing supposed to have happened?"

"Somewhere in the Common. That's what dispatch said. A creep called a local TV station and claimed nine people had been exposed to inhalation anthrax."

"What in the world is inhalation anthrax?"

"Who knows? I think anthrax is something you get from eating bad meat. Can it be released so that you breathe it?"

"I don't know. This has got to be somebody's joke."

"Yeah, you're probably right. We live in a crazy world, don't we? Well, as long as we're here, let's go see if we can find anybody who might know something."

They walked across Beacon Street and into the fifty-acre park located in the heart of downtown Boston, known simply as the Common. Making their way toward the east end of the Frog Pond, they stopped a family that looked like tourists.

"See anything unusual in the Common?"

"No, we haven't."

"Got a report that there might be a sick person here."

"Haven't seen anybody."

They moved on, circling the southern side of the concrete depression that is used as a children's wading pool in the summer and as a skating rink in winter.

"Seen anyone who looked sick?" the officer asked a group of teenagers cutting across the park toward the Esplanade.

"No," they answered, giggling as they pushed and shoved one another playfully.

"Let's angle over to Charles Street and then back around."

"Okay. Hey, wait. Over there. Didn't dispatch say nine people?"

He pointed to four adults standing near the west end of the pond. Just beyond were five small children, rolling in the grass and kicking a beach ball between them.

The policemen waved and called out, "Hello."

"Hello, officers."

"You folk seen anything strange around here? Anybody who looked like they might be sick?"

The woman with long, blond hair looked curiously at the officers.

"As a matter of fact, about an hour ago, there was a sort of 'pop' and a kind of puffy cloud of something or other. Came from over there." The woman pointed to her right. "Some of it got on our clothes. Why? Is there anything wrong?"

"Do you feel okay, ma'am?"

"Well, actually, no. I'm having a bit of difficulty breathing. It's probably my allergies. That's why we've decided to cut the afternoon short and go home. Why do you ask?"

"We had a report that we think is a crank, but we're just making sure. Someone claims to have exposed nine people to something called inhalation anthrax. We saw nine of you here and so we came over to check you out."

"Inhalation anthrax?" the youngest looking man repeated. "Never heard of it."

"Me neither," replied the officer. "Oh, well, sorry to have bothered you. Have a nice afternoon."

The two policemen walked away.

The adults finished putting their picnic stuff together.

About halfway between Frog Pond and Charles Street, the officers heard a loud commotion!

Turning, they saw the youngest of the children thrashing about on the path. The officers ran back. The child, gasping for breath, was clawing desperately at his shirt.

One policeman knelt beside him and took the boy's hands. The other whipped out his radio transmitter.

"Get a medical team to the Common. On the double. We're near the west end of Frog Pond. Child down. Breathing is labored. We're here responding to a call concerning possible exposure of civilians to some sort of anthrax."

Radio static.

Followed by a woman's voice.

"Emergency medical team is on the way. ETA, five minutes."

MOHAMMED ALI ATTA and Yusif Shenuda smoked and drank mineral water, watching the shoreline as they slowly drifted under the Harvard Bridge connecting Cambridge with Boston along Massachusetts Avenue. A small radio receiver/transmitter lay between them on a box. The constant, irritating static was suddenly broken by one click. Silence. Two clicks. Silence. Then three clicks.

A few seconds passed.

One click. Then three clicks. Sufwat's response from his hotel room.

Yusif picked up the transmitter and pushed the button twice.

Wait.

Then three times.

They looked at each other and smiled.

The Strike had been launched!

TWENTY-SIX

Amal sat in the driver's seat of the orange and blue Israel Tours bus, while the engine idled and the air conditioner cooled the interior. It was "September hot" at the rim of the Dead Sea—over one hundred degrees. He relaxed in the familiar manner of a veteran driver, used to waiting for the passengers who provided him, and his family of five in Bethlehem, a decent living.

He glanced down at the instrument panel, making certain that the motor did not overheat. Amal hoped that David and his group would not be too much longer. He had been reminded earlier that they wanted to arrive at Jerusalem at sunset. He looked forward to it. Leaving the heat here at thirteen hundred feet below sea level, and climbing up to Jerusalem's hills, some twenty-five hundred feet above sea level, would be a cool and welcome relief. Sunset was also one of this city's most beautiful moments, a spectacle in which even the natives took delight.

Looking up again, he noticed a woman coming out from the shadows under the entry canopy and heading in his direction. She was dressed in a white jacket and light-blue skirt, the uniform of a hotel employee. Three other stragglers who were also out, apparently forced by necessity to shuffle through the sweltering heat, did so slowly and with lethargic pace. This woman, however, seemed oblivious to the heat as she walked swiftly across the lot toward the area where four tour buses were parked.

Since he was the only driver preparing to leave, he decided that she must want to speak with him. As she came near, Amal bent forward, pretending to be busy with something beneath the instrument panel. He acted as though he had not seen her, and he did not look up until she knocked.

Amal opened the door, looking inquisitively at the woman. *Very nice. I have not seen her before.*

"You are the driver for the Reverend Cain's tour group. Yes?" the woman queried in flawless Arabic.

"Yes, I am Amal, and this is his bus."

"Please, come with me. Your guide, Mr. Barak, wishes to speak with you."

Amal hesitated for a split second, then slid out from under the steering wheel. Stepping down and out of the bus, he turned to lock the door.

"Is there a problem?" he asked the woman, while he made sure the bus was secure.

"He did not say. Follow me."

The driver smiled as he happily obeyed the woman's instruction. He kept his eyes on the light-blue skirt that came to the knee, in Western style, and flowed smoothly with each graceful movement of her body. On her feet, she did not wear the sandal, so customary in the Middle East. Instead, she had on low-heeled dress shoes that accented her very attractive ankles.

"I have not seen you here before," Amal said as he tried to keep up with her.

"I am on duty at the desk this evening," she replied over

her shoulder. "I have been sick for two days."

Friendly too, the driver thought. *Some of the women who work behind hotel desks will not speak to mere bus drivers. They get too much freedom and authority and begin thinking they are really somebody.*

He continued to admire the view that she provided as they drew near the hotel building.

"Mr. Barak is waiting inside. We will go in here."

The woman walked up three cement steps and inserted a key in a door marked Exit Only/Use Front Entrance. Opening the door, she hesitated long enough for Amal to put a hand on it, before stepping through in front of him.

Inside, the light seemed dim in comparison to the brightness of the late afternoon sun. About halfway down the hall, a man could be seen standing in front of an open door. Noting the presence of others in the hall, the man disappeared through the doorway. As he drew near, Amal recognized that it was a maid's room stacked with towels and linens.

The man inside had his back turned, hands on hips, apparently checking over the inventory, or perhaps the condition in which the maids had left the room at the end of their shift. Anyway, it did not matter to Amal. His attention had quickly returned to the woman in front of him.

PASHA FELT THE HEAT from the moment she stepped through the service door and made her way around to the front, careful to stay out of view of the bus parking area. It was the first time she had been outside Room 424 since their arrival on Friday. Her borrowed costume fit fairly well, but the shoes she wore were too tight. They hurt her swollen feet, but they would have to do for the moment. Her legs were bare, a grateful concession to the temperature.

As she walked up to the bus, she could see the driver

inside, bent down, apparently working on something. The motor was running. Pasha knocked on the door. When it opened, she delivered her message to the driver and requested that he follow her. She made a mental note about which pocket he placed the key in after locking the bus. And she was conscious of the level of his gaze while she walked ahead of him, purposely moving with just enough sensuality to guarantee his attention.

Pasha climbed the steps leading to the south side entrance, withdrawing from her pocket the key that Yassim had left in their room. With it she unlocked the door, waited for the driver, then continued along the hall ahead of him.

She saw Imad waiting at the entrance to the maid's room. He stepped inside as Pasha and the driver walked by. As soon as they had passed, he came back through the doorway, taking three quick steps that positioned him directly behind the driver.

Amal heard something.

He started to glance over his shoulder.

It was too late!

He fell quickly and silently to the floor.

They hurriedly dragged his inert body into the maid's room. Pasha shut the door and locked it from the inside. Then she removed the bus key from the driver's pocket and handed it to Imad.

"Will he live?" asked Pasha.

"I hit him with a simple spinal chop to the neck. He'll be out for a couple of hours. I did not kill him."

"He has seen my face."

"It does not matter."

"But he can identify me."

"It makes no difference. In a few hours, all our faces will most likely be on the front page of the *Jerusalem Post* anyway," Imad grinned.

Pasha didn't like the sound of it, but said nothing. Imad

took a roll of tape from his pocket and secured Amal's hands and feet. Several strips of tape were wrapped around his head, covering his mouth but leaving room to breathe through his nose. A large stack of dirty towels and sheets lay piled in the far corner, awaiting the washing machine. Imad and Pasha scooped them back, dragged Amal over against the wall, and covered him with the linens.

"It will be awhile before he is found," said Imad, reassuringly.

"I think we should kill him," Pasha declared emphatically.

"He's an Arab," Imad protested.

"He has sold his soul to the Jews," Pasha responded passionately, her eyes blazing. "He works for *them*. He takes their money. He kisses the hand of our enemy!"

"Come on, Pasha. Enough. He is unimportant. Let's get out of here."

Reluctantly, Pasha backed away.

"We have bigger fish to catch," Imad reminded her. "We must focus our attention on them. The driver is only a pawn. He is of no consequence. We are after the king."

Pasha looked at Imad and, with mock reprimand in her voice, she asked, "And what do you know about the game of chess? Was it not forbidden in your house?"

Imad looked a bit sheepish. "I have watched a game or two in my youth. But how did you know I was describing the players on a chessboard?"

Now it was Pasha's turn to look away.

"My brothers," she said, simply.

"JUST A MINUTE."

David Barak was rinsing his mouth when he heard the knock on the door. He pushed his toothbrush into the travel kit and tossed it on the bed, alongside his small travel bag.

He would take care of it after answering the door.

"Who is it?" he called, squeezing through the narrow space between the bed and a small writing desk.

"A message from Reverend Cain," the muffled voice responded from outside the door.

David felt in his pocket for some tipping money. Then he opened the door and reached for the note. For a brief moment his eyes widened in disbelief. The man standing in front of him held a handgun with a silencer attached.

Two muffled pops!

David felt himself driven backward into the room by the force of the two lead projectiles slamming into his body. He staggered, clutching at his bleeding chest, as he fell against the bed.

The hallway figure stepped inside the room.

In an instant, David knew.

He was helpless to defend himself.

The eyes that stared over the gun were cold, unmerciful.

David felt a sudden sadness.

Life should not be over so unexpectedly. Not like this!

The man elevated his gun slightly, until David could see directly into the barrel opening.

A third pop!

AT TEN AFTER FOUR, John and Jessica walked into the Salt Sea Hotel & Spa lobby, glad to escape the shimmering heat.

An hour earlier, they had placed their luggage outside the door of their room. Hotel staff would gather all the group's luggage within the hour and, under Amal's supervision, place each piece in the bus baggage hold.

With nothing left to do, they had walked out to the pool. John dropped the appropriate change into a Coke machine and handed one of the cans to Jessica, keeping the other for himself. They sat beside the pool, removed their shoes, and dangled bare feet and legs in the water. For the next hour, they remained there, the afternoon shade from the hotel structure making the sweltering heat bearable. It was the first time in several days that they had had any time alone, other than late at night in their room.

Jessica let her feet stay in the water as she lay back on the warm cement. John knew that she did not feel well. She had complained of an upset stomach which, he assumed, was probably from something she had eaten the night before. It was hard to say. She had taken several antacid tablets and spent more than the usual amount of time in the restroom. He sat quietly, watching as she appeared to doze off. Her color looked better than it had earlier.

What a sweetheart! I'm so glad you came with me on this trip. We've gotten closer. I can feel it. You are truly God's gift.

John checked his watch. He hated to rouse her, but it was time.

"Wake up, Jessica. It's time to go."

Her eyes opened and looked into his. She smiled wanly, as she sat up and pulled her feet from the water.

"Are you feeling any better?"

"A little."

"Think you can stand the bus ride?"

"I hope so."

"Okay. Let's go gather up our crew. You can get a good night's rest in Jerusalem. Then you'll be ready to go tomorrow."

Everyone was in the lobby prepared to leave when John and Jessica entered.

"Time to hit the trail, pastor." Edgar slapped him on the shoulder as he walked by. "And I am ready! This place feels like it is too close to you know where." Choruses of "Yes," "Me too," and "Amen to that," were heard around the room.

"Daddy, I'm going to the restroom," Jessica whispered

in his ear. "I'll be right back."

John nodded and then smiled, turning to the group as he wiped beads of perspiration from his face with a tissue.

"It is a little warm today, isn't it?"

Groans filled the lobby.

"Well, we'll fix that. An air-conditioned bus ride will be just the ticket. By the time we arrive in Jerusalem, you will have forgotten all about Masada and Jericho and the Dead Sea. We'll be basking in the fresh, cool air of the Judean hills."

"Can't be too soon for me," complained Ruth Taylor, sprawled in a large chair that suited her ample frame.

"Reverend Cain?"

Mr. Yassim was walking toward him, a message memo in his hand.

"Yes?"

"Mr. Barak was looking for you about thirty minutes ago. He received an emergency call from his wife in Tel Aviv. Their son was hit by a car while riding his bicycle home from school. He was injured severely. The hotel loaned Mr. Barak a car and he has gone to be with his family."

Concern etched John's brow.

"Oh, no. We were out by the pool. Was the injury critical?"

"I am sorry. It sounded serious. But we have no further information."

"Perhaps I should call their home."

"Later, after you are in Jerusalem, Reverend Cain. Mr. Barak will not yet be in Tel Aviv, and Mrs. Barak is at the hospital with her son," the clerk lied nervously. "He asked me to arrange for someone to take his place on your journey to Jerusalem."

"That will not be necessary. We can do quite nicely with our driver, Amal. I can serve as guide for this short period."

"Oh, no, Reverend Cain. The tour company would be upset if we sent you on without a proper guide. I have asked one of our employees to go with you. She is extremely competent. It will not inconvenience her, as she lives in Bethlehem."

"Amal is from there."

"Oh, really?" Yassim feigned surprise.

"Perhaps they will know each other."

"Yes, it is possible." The clerk wiped perspiration from his face with a white handkerchief. "Ah, here she comes now."

An attractive woman in the uniform of a hotel desk clerk walked up and bowed her head in greeting. Yassim moved away as she introduced herself.

"How do you do, Reverend Cain. I am Pasha. I am sorry to learn of Mr. Barak's family difficulty. I trust that his son will recover very soon. In the meantime, it will be my honor to attend to your needs on your journey to Jerusalem. I understand you wish to be there by sunset. Is that true?"

John nodded affirmatively, his mind still on David's need to be at his family's side. His sudden departure was disconcerting.

"Then we must hurry. Please tell your people to board immediately. Your driver has already stored your luggage and is waiting. The bus is cool inside and comfortable. We can explain Mr. Barak's situation as we travel. He has assured us that he will meet you tomorrow at your hotel. If that is not possible, the agency will send another guide to serve you. Shall we go?"

John pondered his circumstances for a moment. It was not like David to disappear without a word. But he probably was so distraught that he didn't take the time to check the pool area.

"All right, everybody," John said in a loud voice. "Head 'em up and move 'em out. We're on our way."

People shuffled and struggled to their feet, gathering up cameras, carryon bags, and miscellaneous possessions. They started for the exit, continuing a collage of conversations as they moved through the doorway.

"You will wait for me, please, Reverend Cain?" the attractive hotel employee said to John. "I must get my handbag."

She disappeared around the corner. John walked over to the window, watching as the bus door opened and people crowded around it, anxious to get in out of the heat.

A moment later, the hotel employee reappeared.

"I'm sorry. What was your name?" John asked.

"It is all right. You are upset because of Mr. Barak's misfortune. My name is Pasha. You are ready?"

"I believe so."

"Then we shall go. Yes?" The woman opened the door.

"Yes," he said, his thoughts jumping from the group and their upcoming bus ride, to David and his son in the hospital.

They started across the parking lot together. Suddenly, John stopped. "Oh, I almost forgot . . . " He felt a sharp jab in his side.

"Keep walking, Reverend Cain!" It was the voice of the woman, no longer warm and friendly, but harsh and cold.

"But . . . "

"Walk!"

He looked at the woman the hotel had sent as an interim guide. Her eyes were hard as she pushed him forward. His mouth dropped open as he saw the gun in her hand.

"What is this?"

"Keep walking. Get into the bus. Quickly!"

John stepped up into the bus and knew at once that everything was wrong. A stranger sat behind the wheel.

"Where is Amal?"

Pasha pushed John forward and stepped in behind him.

The door closed and the bus began to roll.

John looked across the group. They were stone silent, faces pale, terror etched into every pair of eyes. The front rows of seats, normally the first to be filled, were empty, except for two large canvas bags and two evil-looking young men, both armed with automatic weapons.

"What is the meaning of this? What are you doing?" Even as John's questions spilled out, he sensed that he already knew the dreaded answer. "What have you done with David and Amal?"

The bus pulled onto Highway 90 and headed north. Salt crystals jutted upward from the sea on the right like monstrous snowflakes. Just ahead on the right were the man-made canals dug into the Lashon Peninsula, jutting out from the Jordanian eastern shore. These canals, filled by pumping stations located at Israel's Dead Sea Works Ltd. and Jordan's Arabic Potash Corporation, are the waterways that keep the southern portion of the Dead Sea from drying up altogether.

John remained standing in a hunched position near the front seat while such scenes as these, normally pointed out by David, passed by unheralded.

"I asked what you have done with David and Amal." John's voice was tinged with indignation and anger.

The young man in the seat across the aisle leaned forward and gave John a vicious shove. He fell sideways across the front seat, his shoulder slamming painfully into the bottom of the window frame. The man was on him like a hawk, talons poised, ready for the kill.

"You will stop asking questions," he snarled, his face inches from John's.

John opened his mouth, starting to respond.

The man hit him with a stinging blow that jarred John's teeth, causing him to bite his tongue. Blood trickled from the left side of his mouth.

"Reverend Cain, it is important that you understand this. You are no longer in charge! You and your friends from America are now our prisoners. Allah u akbar! You are honored by Allah to be an important part of what he is doing in our world. You are now a vital element in an international battle that will ultimately bring the world to its knees in praise to Allah."

The other man was intently watching the people huddled in the back two-thirds of the bus. He turned and whispered something to the first man who, in turn, gave his attention to John.

"I am informed that there are only twenty-four people on board. Yet there were to be twenty-five. Who is missing?" asked the first man.

John remained silent, looking steadily at the man.

The man's hand suddenly shot forward. In it was a handgun with a silencer attached. Pressing it up under John's jaw, the man's voice shook with anger. "Now you tell me who is missing!"

"My ... my daughter," John replied hesitantly.

"Where is she? Why is she not here?"

"She ... was in the restroom. Not ... feeling well."

The man cursed and then hit John across the side of the head with the handgun. He fell unconscious against the seat. Frightened screams escaped the lips of the horrified onlookers.

"Shut up!" the other man roared, waving his weapon wildly. "Another outburst and you will regret it! Just sit back and keep your mouths shut. We have a long ride ahead. Do not talk at any time. Not even to the person beside you. And do not try any heroics. It will only end in getting people killed."

THE BUS ROLLED PAST Metzada Junction. Masada's

cableway could be seen on the left, carrying tourists to and from the imposing mountaintop fortress. Evelyn Unruh stared out the side window at the site they had visited only two days earlier. A subconscious need to touch the familiar tore at her mind. Masada's story was as familiar as anything could be for now. She forced herself to think about it, to run as many details of it as she could through her mind, in an effort to escape the frightfulness of their present moment.

She and the others had enjoyed their visit to the top of Masada, in spite of the heat. They had sipped bottled water almost constantly to avoid dehydration. As they walked through the ancient ruins, David had given them a lesson in history. He explained that the wilderness summit had first been fortified by Alexander Jannaeus. Later, around 43 B.C., Herod the Great turned it into a formidable and luxurious palace refuge, completing the work about 35 B.C. Or was it 38? No, David had said 35 B.C.

Jewish zealots then captured it, turning it into a refuge for themselves and their families in A.D. 70, at the same time the Romans were putting down a Jewish insurrection and recapturing Jerusalem. The zealots remained in control of Masada for three more years. Ultimately, eight camps of Roman soldiers, totaling about fifteen thousand men under the command of Flavius Silva, laid siege against nine hundred sixty-seven men, women, and children atop Masada. Evelyn remembered the rock-outlined border of the camps far below that she had viewed from the top.

The Romans ultimately used Jewish slave labor to build a ramp of stone on the western side, managing to reach the defenders who, in response, committed suicide rather than surrender. Choosing lots, ten were chosen to kill all the others, then nine of the ten killed themselves, leaving the lone survivor to set fire to the palace before killing himself. When the Romans finally stormed the complex, two women and five children who had survived by hiding were able to tell what had happened.

Looking up, Evelyn remembered David Barak standing with them at the Tanner's Tower next to Masada's Western Gate, reciting the ancient story. He told them that Masada has become a symbol for the modern state of Israel. " 'Masada shall not fall again,' is the clarion call to the hearts of modern Israelis," he had said.

She recalled seeing a group of schoolchildren visiting the site as a part of their curriculum and watching a unit of the IDF hold their swearing-in ceremonies atop the mountain fortress. Two Israeli jet fighters screamed low over the site, waving their wings in a grand salute to the men below. It had been an awesome experience, a dazzling composite of ancient and modern, burned indelibly in the minds of all who had witnessed it.

Slowly, Evelyn permitted her mind to reenter the present.

Is this real after all? Or is it only a bad dream?

Jerry Cloud and Shad Coleman were nearest to the gunmen. They gave each other knowing looks as they silently measured the distance and the odds between them. Gradually, each saw the other ease back in their seats. It was no use.

JOHN CAIN BEGAN TO STIR. With a groan, as pain shot through his head, he pulled himself to an upright position. There was blood on his shirt. His own, he presumed.

"Ah, Reverend Cain. I am pleased that you are once more with us."

The young man sat across the aisle, straddling both seats with his legs, as he spoke.

"I was about to tell your friends here what is happening. Now you are available to listen as well. My name is Yazib Dudori. This lovely woman is my partner, Pasha Bashera. Over there is Fathi Adahlah, and at the wheel our expert driver, Imad Safti. We are a key factor in the greatest offensive battle ever mounted by a small group of oppressed people in modern times."

"You cannot possibly get away with this," John said forcefully.

"You are wrong, Reverend Cain. We can and we will," said Yazib. "You see, we not only possess you who ride with us in this bus. Others, with whom we work in this coordinated offensive, are right now preparing to turn your city of Boston into a field of the dead."

John felt his stomach churn. *They must have a nuclear bomb.*

Yazib moved closer, leaning over the seat as he spoke directly to John.

"We also have your wife and the congregation you left back home!"

John's mouth dropped open. He stared at Yazib in shocked surprise!

JESSICA CAME OUT OF THE RESTROOM and walked into the center of the lobby. It was empty, except for two people working at the hotel desk.
Where is everybody?
She went out the front door.
The bus is gone!
Incredible! Had they had gone off without her?
This can't be. They wouldn't leave me behind.
Jessica walked the length of the building. From the corner, she could view the rest of the parking area. But the familiar orange and blue bus was nowhere to be seen.

A stab of panic caused additional upset to her already delicate insides.
What should I do now?
She ran back through the entrance doors and crossed

the lobby to the desk. Both clerks were working quietly, busy with reservation forms for the final tour group of the day, expected to arrive at any moment.

Jessica hesitated, her anxiety continuing to mount.

"Excuse me."

"May I help you?" the man asked, looking up.

"Yes, I am Jessica Cain. My father is the leader of a tour group that has been staying here. I think they just left without me."

"Your group left without you?" the man repeated, coming around the side of the desk to stand in front of her. "How could such a thing happen?"

"I don't know. I was not feeling well, so I went to the restroom. When I came out, they were gone. But, surely Daddy would have missed me. I sit in the seat next to his when we are on the bus. What should I do?"

Jessica fought back the tears that kept threatening to spill over onto her cheeks. She waited for something to happen. Anything. She tried to act as grown-up as she could, but she felt helpless, like some forlorn little waif. The desk clerk was staring at her. She assumed that he was trying to decide how best to handle her situation.

After a long moment, Jessica felt the man's reassuring hand on her shoulder. She looked up into his toothy smile.

"Don't worry, my little friend. We live in a small country. They probably have missed you already and are turning back. In any event, it is no problem at all. I'm sure we have your father's itinerary here somewhere. I will personally call ahead and let them know you are safe and well, in case they go all the way without you. Meanwhile, there is an extra room available. I will get the key and show you where you can wait. Don't worry. They will contact us before long, one way or another. Come with me."

"Maybe I could just wait out here in the lobby." Jessica did not like this man. There was no particular reason, really

She just remembered that her father had not appeared to like him either.

The clerk smiled and took her hand.

"It is no trouble at all, Miss Cain. This unfortunate event should never have happened. But since it has, I will show you to a room and bring you something to drink. How would that be? Would you like a Coke? Or juice, perhaps? If you are not feeling well, you should have somewhere to lie down. When your father returns, you'll be feeling much better."

Reluctantly, but not knowing what else to do, Jessica followed the clerk to the corner of the desk and waited while he checked through the registration listings for a vacancy. She watched as he reached under the counter and pulled out a key.

Motioning for her to follow, he walked to the elevators.

Jessica was nervous, but tried not to show it. She walked behind him.

The elevator door opened and an elderly couple, dressed in swimsuits and conversing in Danish, stepped out.

She followed the clerk into the elevator and watched as he pushed the fourth-floor button.

"Thank you for your help, Mr. . . . I've forgotten . . . what is your name?"

"Yassim. My name is Yassim."

The elevator door closed.

"Terrorists? Get out of here! At a church? You're pulling my leg, right?"

Police Chief Jim White was the first African-American to be named chief of police in Baytown. Lieutenant Joe Randle was, by now, used to the chief's slow, deep voice. At the time of White's elevation to police chief, Joe had hoped to be his successor in the narcotics division. Instead, another minority officer, Peter Sanchez, had gotten the promotion.

Initially, the whole process had rankled him. He hated the idea of positions being filled because racial quotas required it. Eventually, he came to terms with his lack of promotion by admitting to himself that both of the other men were good officers and probably deserved what they got, regardless of ethnicity.

"Rejoice with those who rejoice," his mother always used to tell him. Of course, his mother, a very religious woman, used to tell him a lot of things, most of which he'd just as soon forget, not being very religious himself. Well, he might not be able to rejoice at being passed over, but he was determined to live with it. All he ever wanted was to be a good cop. He knew that sounded like a Clint Eastwood movie cliché, but it was true of Lieutenant Joe Randle.

Randle also knew when he was in over his head. He felt as though this was rapidly turning into one of those days.

"Turn on the tube, chief," Joe responded, as Frank turned onto Second Avenue and headed across town. "You can see for yourself. At least we could five minutes ago at the station."

"Okay. Listen, I'll meet you there," Chief White said. "Should be with you in ten minutes. And don't turn on any sirens!"

ON THIS SUNDAY MORNING, so far as the San Francisco regional office was concerned, the entire FBI world was in the hands of two people. Doris Lander was the clerk on duty and Steve Jackson was carrying out one of his least favorite tasks, that of Agent on Complaint Duty.

"Hello, FBI."

"Yes, my name is Holanda Seers, and I want to talk to somebody about my civil rights bein' violated!"

"Ms. Seers, I'm the only agent on duty today. Would it be possible for you to call back tomorrow morning?"

"Hey. Who do you think you are, Mr. FBI? I ain't got no time to call you tomorrow. I got to work tomorrow. Ain't got no cushy job with a big pension, all for sittin' behind some FBI desk and answerin' the stupid phone when it rings! Are you tryin' to violate my civil rights too?"

"No, Ms. Seers. I'm here to help if I can. But you'll have to wait one moment. I've got another call coming in. I'm putting you on hold and I'll be back as quickly as I can."

Steve punched the hold button. Then, line two.

"Hello, FBI."

"Yes, my name is Dr. James Novell. I am prepared to

present you with undeniable data regarding an unauthorized landing of Martians near the university campus in Berkeley. It happened again last night."

"One moment, Dr. Novell." Steve put the second caller on hold and reached for the "nut box." Under "N," he found an index card. In the upper left-hand corner was the name, *NOVELL, Dr. James.* Underneath the name was a San Francisco address and phone number. Handwritten times and dates indicated previous calls taken by other complaint duty agents. *This guy's a nut case,* was the card's summation comment. *To deal with him . . .*

Steve read the instruction, smiled, put the card down and punched the caller up again.

"Dr. Novell, are you ready with your information?"

"Yes, thank you, I am," was the polite reply.

"I need to record your statement, Dr. Novell."

"I understand. I've done this before many times."

"All right, sir. When you hear the click, go ahead and begin."

Steve pushed the hold button again. He chuckled as he thought about "Dr." Novell reading his statement. He'd check back in ten minutes. If he was still reading, he'd put him on hold for another ten. If there was a dial tone, he would know the treatise had been delivered. At least for today.

"Now," Steve said under his breath, "what shall I do with Ms. Holanda Seers' civil rights?"

He was thinking of several options, none of which would be palatable to Ms. Seers or the FBI, when the phone rang again.

"Hello, FBI."

"Hi, Steve. It's Jim Cantor. How's complaint duty going?"

"Like a root canal, Jimbo. What's up?"

"You watching TV?"

"No, should I be?"

"Tune up Channel 4. They're running a news bulletin. Unconfirmed. Says a hostage situation is developing in a church in Baytown. Big time. Any word?"

"You're the first."

"Wait a minute, Steve. Bernstein's their anchor and he's just come on. Just a sec ... okay, he's confirmed it. Better make some calls."

"Thanks, Jim."

Steve hung up the phone. He thought about the people on hold. "Dr." Novell would eventually run out of space aliens and hang up. Ms. Seers' civil rights would have to wait. Steve dialed Frank Lyons' beeper.

SOME PEOPLE COMPLAIN about having to wear one beeper. Frank was a round-the-clock, two-beeper man. One was for general calls from the office. But when the other one went off, Frank knew it meant trouble. It was his SWAT team emergency number. The moment it beeped, he put down the paper, leaped from his chair in front of the television, and reached for the phone.

"Get your boys to the garage, Frank."

"What's up?"

"It's the world's 'biggest something'!" Steve answered with a phrase often used by agents, when there was no time for explanations or not enough information to give.

Frank hung up, took a deep breath, and began calling his team leaders.

PAUL DANVERSEN, Assistant Special Agent in Charge of the San Francisco office, returned Steve's call from Carmel, where he and his family were spending the weekend. While they conversed, he calculated the time it would take for someone to fly to nearby Monterey Airport, pick him up, and then fly back to San Francisco. Two hours, minimum. Probably longer. Paul would drive instead. Code 3. He could do it in an hour and forty and he was on his way. Steve got the number of the hotel where they were staying and assured him that the department would send a car down later in the afternoon for his family.

Next, Steve dialed the beeper number of Special Agent in Charge, Duane Webber.

"THIS IS WEBBER."

So much of FBI work, like all police work, is dull and routine. Big time cases, the ones that pump adrenaline into a law enforcement officer's body, are few and far between. But when they come, they generate excitement and draw cops to danger like moths to the flame. This morning, Duane Webber listened as Steve filled him in, sensing that just such a case was coming his way.

He stood alongside his neighbor's backyard pool, drying off with a towel as he cradled the cellular phone to his ear. The beeper on the table by the lawn chair had gone off moments earlier, while he was still doing laps.

Duane loved feeling the tensions fall away as he plowed back and forth through the water. A stylish swimmer he was not, but he knew he wouldn't drown either.

Their neighbors, the Carringtons, were in Hawaii for a month and had invited Duane and Janice to use the pool in their absence.

His voice sounded even more raspy than usual when he got excited. And he was excited.

He glanced up and waved as Janice came through the side gate and walked over to him. He continued his phone conversation.

"Get whoever is available out to Baytown ASAP. Code 2.

Fly them, if necessary. I want a team assembled on site in one hour. Be sure you reach Don Raley. It wouldn't do for us to go without the field director getting a wake-up call, now would it?"

Janice stood next to him, watching and listening to the one-sided conversation, as her husband plied his stock and trade. Duane looked up again at the statuesque features of the woman who was his one and only true love. Her olive-colored skin required absolutely no sun for her to look stunning in whatever she wore. At least that's the way Duane felt about it. And the white, one-piece swimsuit she had on this morning was no exception to the rule.

He winked, but his face looked serious.

She smiled back, the knowing smile of a wife used to being stood up by a husband whose life was regulated, twenty-four hours a day, by a beeper.

Webber listened as Steve informed him of some extraordinary luck. FBI agent-pilot, Sam Seitzman, had "the bird" in the air right now. He was alone this weekend. His wife was visiting her family in Fresno. With nothing else to do, he had decided to check the helicopter out following yesterday's replacement of a broken rotor blade.

"Get him over here. I'll be at Webster High School in twelve minutes. Have him pick me up on the football field. And tell him I don't want to be kept waiting, okay? Thanks, Steve."

He pressed the off button and, receiver still in hand, he looked solemnly at his beloved and beautiful forty-seven-year-old wife. How he loved this woman, his only regret the fact that they had not been able to produce any children.

"What is it, Duane?"

"Terrorists in a church in Baytown. Can you believe it? In a church! They think they might be Arabs. Come on. Drive me over to Webster High. I'll change in the car while we're driving."

FRANK AND JOE DROVE as rapidly as possible, but without siren. The streets were nearly empty, the only real activity centering around Baytown Mall. It looked as though there was probably a pretty big sale going on today. More cars than usual in the parking lot. Women were hurrying toward the shopping mall's main entrances, the doors having opened at ten.

Radio static and conversations between patrol units being called into the Calvary Church area filled the airways.

"Car eleven."

"Eleven here, Cindy."

Her voice carried with it an edge of excitement.

"Someone's on the phone from the FBI. He asked for the officer in charge. I told him 'Lieutenant Randle.' He said, 'Great, let me talk to Joe.' "

"Okay, Cindy. Patch him through."

Joe looked at Frank and smiled.

"Just between you and me, it's better than okay. We're going to need this guy."

They were turning into the church parking lot when Webber's raspy voice came through the car radio receiver.

"Hey, Joe, good to hear your voice. How ya doin'?"

"Not so good this morning, Duane. A little while ago I thought about taking some vacation time and getting out of town, but I guess it's too late for that. It looks as though we've got major trouble here. A hostage situation. A church full of people being held by at least four heavily armed persons. So far, we've seen three men and a woman."

"Seen them?" asked Webber. "How?"

"On television."

"Are you serious?"

"Calvary Church televises one of its Sunday services live each week over Channel 17. We started getting calls from viewers and then turned it on ourselves. Looks like the real thing. May already be one victim. Not sure about that."

"Sounds like we might be interested."

Joe paused. What would Chief White say if he accepted the not-so-subtle invitation being offered? He was all too aware of the intense rivalry between law enforcement agencies. Politics. Joe hated the politics. Each department wants in and hopes to gobble up the glory. Jurisdiction is a line over which careers are sometimes won and lost.

Then he thought about the people in the church.

"Get in here as quickly as you can. I think we can use the help."

"Find your local judge and get a warrant issued, Joe. We've got to have that before we can move a muscle. How long will it take?"

"I'll get it going right away. If we're lucky and the judge is home, inside of an hour."

"Okay, Joe. I'll get things moving over here. You sure about this?"

Joe wasn't certain whether or not Webber was asking about the situation or the invitation.

"I wish I wasn't, but yeah, I'm sure. We're pulling up to the church's front entrance right now. We're the first to get here. Nobody outside. Looks quiet. Got a blue van parked near a side entrance in a handicap zone."

"So?"

"So the side door is wide open and nobody's around it."

"All right, I'm on my way. Be careful, Joe."

"Count on it."

"Sounds like you know each other," Frank commented as he stopped the car directly in front of the main entrance to the church.

"Remember when White was named chief? About a month later he asked if I'd like to go to the FBI National Academy. He had an invitation and couldn't make it. The Department sent me to FBINA instead."

"Lucky, man. You've got to be pretty special to get to

take that in. How long were you there?"

"Four weeks. That's where I met Duane."

They sat talking, looking for some sign of movement in the building. There was none.

"Cindy, we're in front of the church. Nothing going. What do you see? Are the cameras still on?"

"Yes. It looks like they're just standing around. The people who have guns, that is. The rest are still sitting down."

Two black-and-whites turned into the parking lot and sped toward Joe and Frank.

A uniformed officer jumped out of the first car and jogged around to where Frank and Joe sat as they sized up the situation.

"All the streets leading in or out are shut down, lieutenant. We've got the place locked up. Starting to divert the traffic coming in for the eleven o'clock service."

"Thanks."

"What do we do now, sir?"

"Good question. For now, we sit here and wait."

ELEVEN MINUTES AND THIRTY SECONDS later, Duane stepped out of the car and scanned the sky. Janice came around to where he stood, still in her swimsuit but with a royal-blue blouse covering her shoulders and tied loosely at the waist.

"There he is. Over there. See it? He'll be here in a couple of minutes." Duane glanced at his watch. "Not bad. Not twelve minutes, but not bad."

"You're the bad one," Janice chided him playfully, moving her arm around his waist. "How you can go from a wet swimsuit to a business suit, replete with tie, socks, and shoes, while driving down the road, I'll never know."

"I wasn't driving. You were," he responded with a chuckle.

"What do you suppose some of those people we passed thought you were doing?"

"It'll give them something to talk about."

Duane strapped the black fanny pack around his waist. It was standard for an agent, looking very much like the money pouch worn by many tourists. In this pack, however, was a lightweight but very deadly SIG-Sauer P22K handgun, together with extra 15-round ammunition clips. Standard equipment for all agents. He pulled on his jacket as the helicopter settled down in front of them.

Duane gave Janice a quick kiss.

As he started to go, she wrapped both arms around his neck and kissed him hard on the lips.

"You be careful, Duane Webber."

He saw the serious, worried look that had become a familiar trademark in moments like these. He guessed that it was a little different for her to send her husband off to work than for some women.

He nodded.

"Not to worry. I'll be home as soon as we're finished."

Janice stood by the car as he ran under the helicopter's rotating blades and climbed inside. A moment later, he was off the ground and on his way. Looking down, he saw her still standing by the car as they swept across the field and out over the Bay.

While flying northeast, the San Mateo Bridge could be seen on the right. Oakland's International Airport was straight ahead. Duane donned the extra helmet and began talking to ASAC Danversen on Danversen's cellular phone. He was now en route.

"Paul, I'm closer than you, so I'm on my way to the site. Head into the office and take charge there. I want a local command post established at the church, first thing. Get on the horn and arrange to have the Winnebago brought over from the city. We'll put it as near to the church as we can safely get."

The Winnebago was a twenty-four-foot recreational vehicle that had become government property thanks to one of the largest drug raids ever on the West Coast. It had been retrofitted with television monitors, communication links to every city, county and state police agency, and the latest in cellular gadgetry, tracing and recording equipment. It would serve as the on-site command center.

"Steve has called up the SWAT team. They may get there before I do. This could be a bad one, Paul. I talked with Joe Randle, the local PD guy on the scene. He sounded worried. If they really intend to hold an entire crowd hostage, we've got major problems.

"Gene's our best negotiator, but he's on vacation. Where did he go? Back east? He's out then. Let me check when we get there. Maybe there's somebody available from Oakland or San Francisco PD. I doubt that Baytown has any. Listen. Patch me through to Washington. I need to let the Boss know what's coming down."

Duane looked over at the pilot. "How much longer?"

"Five minutes."

"Sir, Washington's on the line."

"Hello, this is Duane Webber, SAC in San Francisco. Who am I talking to?"

"This is Special Agent Lawford. What can I do for you today?"

"I'm en route to Baytown by chopper. Local PD is on location. They think they've got a hostage situation in a church."

"A church? How many involved?"

"Don't know for sure. Report is at least four people, well armed. Word has it that the gunmen may be Arabs. They are holding an entire crowd at bay. Exact number of hostages is not yet known. Maybe several hundred."

"When do you arrive?"

Webber glanced over at the pilot, who held up three fingers.

"ETA is three minutes."

"I'll notify SAC Johnston. He's heading up the international terrorist desk these days. When can you verify that these are Arabs?"

"Soon. We'll establish a command post on site, first thing. Let the Boss know, okay?"

"Yessir. And call as soon as you can verify what's happening."

"You've got it."

They skimmed the top of the last hill that loomed between them and the campus of Baytown's Calvary Church. Duane had been in Baytown several times. It was the first time he had flown in, however. Houses neatly laid out in suburban tract fashion. A downtown area in which the highest building was only five stories. Schools, playgrounds, city parks. It was a fine, new, upscale community, the sort of place people moved to in order to get away from crime and violence. Twenty-six thousand people within the city limits. Several other larger, contiguous communities surrounded it on three sides. The fourth side backed into the golden hills for which the Bay Area is so famous. In a few months, with any decent amount of rainfall, they would turn into a rolling carpet of verdant green.

The pilot pointed. Just ahead, several police cars could be seen near the front of a large structure, the highest point of which was a cross mounted on a steeple.

Calvary Church.

"Set us down in the parking lot. Over there." Duane pointed to the north side of the large lot filled with cars that had brought this morning's worshipers to church. Duane was not much of a churchgoer himself and so was quite impressed with the number of cars he saw as they drew near. The helicopter settled down as Duane unbuckled his safety harness, opened the door, and jumped to the pavement. He walked briskly in the direction of three police cars. Several uniformed patrolmen were standing around the cars, looking in his direction.

"Hi, Joe," Duane greeted one of the men, extending his hand.

"Hello yourself, Duane. You're looking fit. Sorry to have to call you out, but this one looks like we could use a little help."

"Glad to oblige," Duane answered, his eyes on the main entrance, as he wondered what might be happening just beyond those closed doors. "What do you know for sure?"

"We know that there are at least four people inside armed with automatic weapons. Maybe others, we don't know. Looks like they have plenty of firepower and are ready to stay. We saw one of them working on a door. My guess is that the doors are loaded with explosives by now. It looks like they've killed one man. Can't say about the others."

"You say you've seen all this on TV?"

"Yep. The church televises its morning service every Sunday. They're on the air right now."

"Do you think these guys are aware that they're on the tube?"

"At first I didn't, but I don't see how they can help but be by now. They've made no effort to shut it down. Maybe that's part of the deal."

"Could be," Duane mused, staring at the building. "Our boys will be here within the hour. We'll set up a command post in the Winnie. Then we can watch them ourselves. Who's your main man going to be?"

Joe glanced up at the car turning into the entrance to the parking lot. "Chief White's coming in right now. He's the boss."

"Okay, let's get to work. Have your men spread out and

circle the building. Doesn't look like they plan to come out any time soon, but let's not take the chance. All roads closed down?"

"Tight," was Joe's terse response. He wished that he could be the main man in this operation. But he would take a backseat when Chief White arrived.

"Good. You've done everything possible and you've done it well," said Duane, sensing the frustration in his voice. His hand rested on Joe Randle's shoulder. "Now, introduce me to your boss."

TWENTY-EIGHT

The twenty-four-foot Winnebago RV was rapidly being turned into the Central Command unit. It was parked about a hundred feet away from the church's main entrance. The whirring of a power generator could be heard each time the door opened. Inside, several agents squeezed back and forth past one another in the narrow walking space. The air-conditioned interior of the vehicle was crammed with electronic gear, telephones, radio sending and receiving equipment, and several television screens.

At the moment, three of those screens all revealed the same picture. The scene being transmitted by Baytown's Channel 17 looked grim to Webber as he watched the images over a technician's shoulder.

"Are we ready to talk to Washington yet?"

"Yessir."

"Okay. Tell 'em I'll talk in a few minutes. Just as soon as we can figure out for sure what's going down. Tell 'em what you see on the screen. I'll be right back."

Webber stepped out of the trailer and started around the

side, just as one of the agents inside stuck his head out of the door.

"Sir. Come here quick. One of the bad guys is wanting to talk."

Webber whirled, ran back up the steps into the trailer and stood in front of the screens. He saw the face of a handsome young Arab.

Can't be very old. Twenty-five? Twenty-six, maybe.

He was speaking into the camera.

" . . . so, I assume by now that the law enforcement agencies of the Great Satan are at the door. May I warn you against doing anything rash. All of the entrances to this place of worship have been seeded with enough explosives to take out anybody trying to enter. The explosion will also kill these people."

The figure on the screen paused as his image dissolved and another took its place. On the screen was a group of at least ten men and women. One had a baby in her arms. They were huddled together on the floor in front of a door.

Webber swore beneath his breath.

The speaker's face reappeared on the screen.

"If any of these people do not cooperate with us, they will be shot," he continued, matter-of-factly. "If you try to overpower us, you will force us to kill them. I hold the detonator in my hand, as you can see," he continued, holding up a small black object with several red buttons.

Webber swore softly.

"If these people or anyone else tries to overwhelm us, we will shoot them. But first, I will push this. The result will not be a pretty sight." Webber's face tightened as he watched the man's finger brush over the buttons.

"I have one small request to begin with. I would prefer to talk with you over a telephone. However, there is none available. If you would be so kind as to place one inside the lobby area near the door closest to the main entrance, I would be grateful. I would also appreciate the provision of a television set. I'm told there is such a set and an extension phone in the church nursery. Bring them." The man smiled at his own politeness. "Knock when these things are available. We will disarm the door and retrieve the items. There is an extension outlet here on the platform. We will plug the telephone in and speak further at that time.

"Please do not do anything more or less than what I have requested. All the other doors will remain armed and ready to detonate. Anyone trying to force entry will be summarily shot. If both items are not at the door when it is opened, someone with us will die. Do not tamper with the items before bringing them to us. I have an electronics and explosives expert with me. If there is evidence of tampering, I assure you others will die." The man smiled into the camera once more. "In fact, the possible loss of life in here is tremendous, so, please, act with the greatest of care. You have fifteen minutes. Do not disappoint us."

Chief White watched along with Agent Webber and the others. "The phone will be an advantage. But why does he want a television set? You think he just wants to see himself on the screen?"

"No," Webber answered. "He's got other plans. And he's got the upper hand. I think we have to give this character what he wants this time around. Is there any other choice? Did you see that guy on the platform? He was alive when he went to church this morning. Now, he's deader than a doornail. We've got to establish communications with these people."

Webber looked at Joe standing beside his boss, then back to White. "How about it, chief?"

Chief White frowned as he watched the images on the screen. Then he grunted affirmatively. "Joe, take Steve with you, get that stuff out of the nursery, and pound on the door. But be careful!"

Joe wheeled about and disappeared through the RV door.

THEIR HEARTS WERE BEATING doubletime as they walked up the steps and onto the large, Spanish-style patio. The midday sun was warm, but it was the secondary cause for beads of perspiration needing to be wiped with uniform shirt sleeves. They crossed to the entrance and paused, examining each of the four double doors as best they could from the outside. There did not appear to be anything unusual.

Joe looked at Steve and nodded. He reached for the door handle and opened it. Stepping inside, they stared at the sanctuary doors. They walked across the lobby, eyes darting back and forth in both directions. Joe motioned to Steve. There was a sign to the left identifying the nursery.

Opening the door, Joe's heart suddenly skipped a beat. Two startled and very frightened women stood in the middle of the room, a baby in each arm! A wall-mounted television was flashing the telltale scenes from inside the sanctuary.

"Oh, thank God! We thought . . ."

"I'm Joe Randle. This is Steve Smith. Baytown Police. How many children are in here?"

"Six. All babies," said the one woman, tears of relief spilling from her eyes.

Joe glanced at his watch. Seven minutes left.

"Steve, get the telephone and the television. I'll get the children and these women out of here."

Joe carefully scooped up the other two sleeping infants. He smiled at the women. "You've done great so far. These are the quietest six kids I've ever seen. Now, follow me and let's see if we can keep on being quiet."

The two women followed Joe down the hall and across the lobby to the entrance. He pushed the crash bar and opened the door with his hip, both arms full of babies. The women followed him outside and started running across the patio.

"Careful," Joe called after them.

Several policemen came forward to meet them and they disappeared behind the trailer. Joe handed the two babies he carried to another policeman and turned to go back into the church.

"Officer," a female voice called.

Steve stopped and looked back. One of the two women ran toward him, followed by a policeman.

"What is it?"

"I am sure that there are more inside."

"We know. We have seen them in the auditorium."

"No. I mean in the classrooms upstairs."

"Upstairs?"

"Yes. We have a children's Sunday School during this hour, in conjunction with the worship service. They must still be up there!"

Joe looked at the other officer.

"Get some men together, quickly. Let's get in there and check it out. Thanks, lady. You've been very brave. Now, go on back with this man."

Eight uniformed patrolmen trotted up the outdoor steps and through the main entrance. Four started up the stairwell on the right. The other four followed Joe across the lobby and up the steps to the left.

The stairs opened onto a landing and a hallway with doors on both sides. The hall was silent and empty, except for the images and voices that came from a ceiling-mounted TV monitor near the landing. Slowly, Joe opened the first door Inside, a group of small children sat, in a circle, heads bowed, holding hands. The man and woman sitting cross-legged with them looked up and smiled with relief at the sight of the policemen.

"See, children? We asked Jesus to send help and these

nice men have come."

Joe stood in the doorway.

"I want you to follow us down the stairs and outside. Okay? Here, young fellow. You take this policeman's hand. Form a line and stay together. Walk very quietly. Understand?"

Twelve heads nodded gravely, eyes big. They looked frightened, but did exactly as told. One little girl looked at Joe.

"Are my mommy and daddy all right?"

"They are fine. Everything will be okay. Now, you do exactly what I asked you to do."

The little girl's eyes remained on Joe, as though trying to discern whether or not he was telling the truth. Then she disappeared with the others down the hall.

Door after door repeated the same scene. Some children were crying, but there was no panic. After the initial warning from the hall monitor, the adults who worked with them had kept them together and comforted, while waiting for help to come.

Joe was amazed at how well this was going. Not a sound was heard as they passed in orderly lines through the hall and down the steps. He jogged down the stairs as children and their adult workers streamed out of the building and ran toward the big, black trailer.

Steve had finished placing the television and extension phone near the sanctuary doors. Joe looked at his watch. Less than a minute left. Children were still coming down the stairs. Joe motioned for them to hurry.

Fifteen minutes gone. Exactly.

Patrolmen appeared on both landings at almost the same time, waving. Everyone was on their way out.

Joe hesitated, his heart pounding as he watched the last of the human stream rushing out of the door.

As the last child's foot touched the lobby floor, Joe

checked his watch. Thirty seconds beyond the deadline! He pounded sharply on the door. Then he and Steve followed the others outside. Standing on the patio, he watched as at least two hundred children, and the workers who had remained with them, scattered quickly across the parking lot, directed by the officers outside. Cries could be heard now, together with excited voices and sounds of frightened relief.

Joe looked back at the lobby. Through the glass doors, he could see the telephone and television set, still on the floor in front of the sanctuary auditorium. He noticed another sign he had not seen before. It was an attractive, free-standing wooden sign, just to one side of the sanctuary doors.

> Thank you for being quiet.
> Service is in session.

Joe turned and headed for the trailer.
You're welcome, he thought to himself.

AKMED CHECKED HIS WATCH. Eighteen minutes since he had spoken into the cameras. It was unnerving not to be able to see outside. He said nothing to the others, but his stomach was churning. He was bothered. What was going on out there? Was he talking to the wind? Was anyone there?

He motioned to Mamdouh, who was leaning against the back of the last row of pews, gun in hand, watching the small group of people huddled near his assigned door.

Mamdouh walked up to the group and poked one man with the barrel of his gun. "Move away from the door."

The man started to get up.

"No. Do not get up. Move!"

They stared at each other for a moment, silently measuring, as antagonists often do. Slowly, the man scooted forward, the others following his example, clearing a space in front of the doors. He looked to see that Akmed had disarmed the explosive charge. Then he pushed the crash bar down and slowly opened it, peering outside as best he could, wary of some sort of trap. The lobby was empty.

He pushed the door open all the way. There they were, as ordered. A telephone and a television set. Reaching out, he dragged the television inside the door. Then the telephone. Just before he closed the door, he looked out across the lobby and through the glass on the far side. What he saw took his breath away.

A recreational vehicle was parked straight out from the main entrance, about a hundred feet away. It was surrounded by police cars. Men in blue and brown uniforms could be seen everywhere.

He closed the door.

We've done it, he thought. *We've awakened a sleeping nation. Allah u akbar!*

JOE WATCHED FROM THE CORNER of the RV. He saw the door open and a man reach down and drag the television inside. He then reappeared and picked up the telephone. He stood up momentarily, and looked out at the scene in the parking lot. Quickly he backed in and shut the door.

Joe cursed and walked around to the RV door.

TWENTY-NINE

Barely two and a half hours after the first shots were fired, the local command post was well on its way to being established. Baytown Police Chief Jim White, and the FBI's SAC, Duane Webber, were acting as top commanders, representing both local and federal law enforcement. Paul Danversen, Assistant SAC, had arrived at the San Francisco office. Lieutenant Randle had been cast into the unofficial role of advisor to the commanders. Baytown's mayor was also on the way to the scene and would, undoubtedly, demand to participate in the process as the community's elected leader.

The pieces were beginning to fall in place.

Two behavioral specialists were being called in from Oakland. They had been part of a recent negotiating training seminar for law enforcement personnel that Joe Randle had attended. Dr. Dale Hummel served as an on-call consultant for the Oakland PD. Dr. Sandra Hinkle worked with the Alameda County District Attorney's Office, as an expert in the field of hostage negotiation. She was also a professor in the Criminology Studies Department at the University of California in Berkeley.

Police calls were routinely monitored by the offices of the *San Jose Mercury-News* and the *San Francisco Chronicle.* The media was beginning to arrive on the scene at a Communications Center, temporarily set up near the entrance to the church parking lot. Sgt. Frank Castor was assigned duty as press officer.

Public utilities personnel arrived with blueprints outlining the various gas, water, and electric underground routes leading into the facility. The location of cutoff valves was being determined. The mayor ordered City Planning Department personnel to find and deliver blueprints of the church facility to the Command Center. Emergency medical teams and equipment were arriving. Hospitals in the area were being alerted as to possible massive emergency and trauma center needs. Weapons and tactics specialists from Baytown PD and the FBI were arriving in a steady stream. Personnel were marshaling in an area about a block away, out of sight of the hostage-takers.

Inside the Command Center, Webber, White, and Randle, together with the technicians, continued to watch the television screens. They observed someone carrying the television to the platform where it was plugged into an electric socket. Now, one of the congregation's members could be seen stringing a long cable down the aisle, apparently from some TV cable source, off camera. He attached the cable to the set. He also plugged the telephone into an extension outlet on the platform. The terrorist, who seemed to be the one in charge, turned on the set and watched for a picture.

"What channel are we on?" he asked.

"Seventeen," responded the man who had laid out the cable.

The man in charge flipped the dial until he reached Channel 17. He stopped, looked up, and smiled. He had just seen his own picture.

He picked up the telephone. As he turned it over, he seemed to be looking for something.

Chief White swore and hit the work bench with his fist. "We didn't give him a number to call! That's what he's looking for."

They watched as the man slowly put the telephone down in a chair beside the one in which he sat.

"Dial 911," a young man sitting near the front suggested. "Then ask to be connected with the police."

The man on the platform eyed the younger man for a moment, as though he were evaluating what he had just said. Then he picked up the phone and dialed. In a few moments he was on the line.

"Good morning ... or, I should say, good afternoon?" the man said with a cheerful tone. "Time flies, doesn't it."

Joe wondered how fast time was "flying" for the people who had been sitting in the pews now for almost three hours.

Probably not very. And by now, the need to relieve themselves must be reaching a critical point for many. How's he going to handle that?

"To whom am I speaking?" the man asked, leaning back in the chair.

"My name is Webber. Duane Webber."

"Well, Mr. Webber, who are you? What qualifies you to be talking with me just now?"

"I am with the FBI."

"Ah, the FBI. Good. And what is your position there? Are you one of those trained negotiators we hear so much about? If you are, forget it. I do not wish to speak with a negotiator. *I* am the negotiator! I am also the leader of this commando unit and I wish to speak only with the leader of the FBI. Are you the top man?"

"I am Special Agent in Charge of the San Francisco

office. I am in charge of this region. Now that I've introduced myself, perhaps you would be kind enough to do the same."

"Yes, you'd like to know who we are. I will tell you in a moment. But first of all, we have some personal needs to attend to. You will find it of interest to note that we have counted four hundred eighty-seven people who remain here as our guests. We are very much like a jumbo jet filled with passengers. Only we are not flying anywhere."

The man paused, then continued.

"That is not exactly true." He motioned toward the body lying on the platform. "You can see that one individual has already been judged by Allah. He is in hell with the rest of the world's infidels who refuse to acknowledge Allah as the one true God. There will surely be others, if you decide not to assist us in meeting our demands. But for now, the comfort of our guests is important to us."

"Look at him sitting there with a dead body, talking about the 'comfort of his guests,'" snorted Chief White.

"Shhh. Listen." motioned Webber.

"We have been here together for about three hours. There is a need to use the restrooms. Here is what we will do. One of my associates will be in the lobby for purposes of security. Our guests will be numbered off, in groups of twenty, and permitted to use the restrooms. Once they have returned, the next group will be permitted to go, until everyone has completed the task. Should anyone fail to return..." he paused, looking around, his eyes growing dark and hard. "Two of those remaining inside will be killed for every individual trying to escape! An eye for an eye!

"This is the plan. The doors are charged with explosives. We are deactivating one of them. Twenty people are ready to leave. Please let them do so without endangering those who remain. Oh, there is one other very important request. While we are caring for these mundane personal needs, I want you to see to it that we are linked up to NBC, ABC, CBS, and CNN. This must be accomplished within the hour. If it is not done, five people will die. For every hour of delay thereafter, five additional souls will be deposited in hell until you comply. This is not a threat. It is a promise. This is a non-negotiable request, so do not waste precious time talking. Just do it."

Webber and Randle looked at one another.

White swore again, a look that almost bordered on admiration in his eyes.

"They've got us," he said. "And they know it."

They watched as a group of people shuffled out of the door to the far left of the main entrance. Webber knew that this was going to take some time.

"I still don't know your name," he said into the telephone.

"Ah, yes. How impolite of me. But first, we must attend to the further needs of our guests."

"He's taunting us!" growled White.

"We will need diapers and some baby food. There are three infants with us here."

"Why don't you just let them come out with their mothers?" asked Webber.

"Perhaps later. Not just yet. It is also past the noon hour. We are all getting very hungry."

"What would you like to eat?" asked Webber.

"Something quick. How about McDonalds? Tell them to bring us enough for five hundred people. Oh, I almost forgot. You will want to add to that number your own people outside. How many extra will we need?"

"Don't worry about us, but thanks for your concern."

"It is my pleasure," the man inside responded with a smile. "Don't forget. You have fifty-five minutes for a national news hookup."

Webber and the others could see people returning now

from the restrooms. Others were forming a line pointing toward the exit.

"Can you believe this?" Joe asked, as he watched the screen. "There's a side exit about twenty or thirty feet from that door. If someone went for it, they could probably get away. But there they are, going back inside."

"It's a plot hatched in hell!" White said savagely. "What are we going to do?"

Webber sat silently, staring straight ahead. *I don't know,* he thought.

For the first time since arriving on the scene, Webber's mind drifted back to Janice. He saw her standing by the car, her lithe form growing smaller as the helicopter lifted off the ground and flew away.

I love you, Janice Webber.

Webber mouthed the words silently as he watched other people's husbands and wives and children filing in and out of that auditorium.

"Food and drinks will be delivered within the hour," Webber was back on the telephone. "We're working on the network links. Now, I will not continue our conversation until you have identified yourself. In our culture, we do not carry on discussions with people we do not know by name."

"Ah, you are very perceptive, Mr. Agent Webber of the FBI. You see that we are not from your own people. Is it our skin color? No, there are many in your country with our skin color. What causes you to know we are from a different culture?"

"I repeat, I will not continue our conversation until you tell us who you are."

"Yes, of course. Please. My name is Akmed el Hussein. My friends and I are a part of the Palestinian Islamic Jihad. We represent the poorest and most oppressed people on earth. You may have heard of us?"

White looked at Webber and shrugged. Webber said

nothing. He knew that this group was on the FBI security threat list and that they were an extremely radical and dangerous organization.

"Of course I have heard of the great Palestinian people." said Webber. "Perhaps I have heard of the organization you claim to represent, but I'm not sure. Can you enlighten me?"

"Yes, of course. The PIJ has been in existence for several years. We are committed to the creation of an Islamic Palestinian state. The Jews have shown themselves to be our enemies by usurping our land and suppressing our people. In spite of the PLO's efforts to the contrary, there can be no meaningful negotiation with the Jews. It has always come to naught. This is in large part due to the strong support they continue to receive from America. So we come to you because we have no other choice. And make no mistake about it, we are ready to die, if necessary.

"The Jihad used to be a condition of faith among early Muslims. It was their sacred duty to engage in Holy War, to kill anyone who did not embrace the one true faith. Today many of our Muslim brothers have left the path of our ancient forefathers. It is for this reason that Allah has called a new generation of the faithful to give themselves to restoring the faith in our day."

"So just what is it that you want from us? May I call you Akmed?"

"If you wish."

"Why are you holding these people?"

"Because you ignore the plight of our people. It is the only way we can gain your attention and that of the world. For this reason we are here. But we are not alone, Mr. Agent Webber. Today, 18 September, will be a day to remember in history.

"We demand that America require Israel to release all Arab political prisoners. It must be done immediately. Within twenty-four hours.

"We demand that the United Nations Council force Israel to retreat from the Gaza Strip and the West Bank and restore it to its rightful people, the Palestinians.

"We demand further that the UN Council establish a Committee of the People, together with a strict time limit for the restoration of all lands that were wrongfully usurped from the Palestinian peoples in 1948.

"We demand that Palestine be accorded full statehood by the nations of the world.

"We demand the immediate removal of all Israeli Armed Forces and police from these territories.

"And, we demand that the United States cease its interference with these goals through its financial and military aid to our enemy, the illegitimate nation of Israel!"

"They don't want much, do they?" whispered Joe.

"You have exactly twenty-four hours to accomplish these tasks. After twenty-four hours, if all has not been completed, or at least adequately undertaken with agreed-upon limits insuring their timely completion, two persons will die every hour, until all of them or all of us are dead! Am I being clear enough, Mr. Agent Webber?"

"You are being quite clear, Akmed, though I cannot imagine that one human being would do such a heinous thing to another."

"Imagine, Mr. Agent Webber. You will do well to imagine, for it will happen if we do not achieve our worthy goals. And not only two each hour, but thousands elsewhere."

" 'Thousands elsewhere'? What do you mean?" asked Webber.

"Exactly what I said," Akmed replied. "Listen to your newscasts and you will see."

ELIZABETH AND GEOFF RALSTEN stood directly in front of Ken. Ken's mind was racing. He was angry. And he had never been more frightened in his life. These fools were crazy enough to kill them all. He was sure of it.

Wouldn't you know something like this would happen while Cain was off cavorting about in Israel with his little fan club? When I told him in the board meeting that he shouldn't be going on this trip, I had no idea . . . We've got to get away from here!

As they shuffled nearer the door, he whispered into Geoff's ear, "Get ready. As soon as we get through the door, run for the side exit!"

Geoff looked startled.

"But, Dad, what about . . ."

His father squeezed his arm until it hurt.

"Tell your mother. Be ready and don't let anybody stop you!"

"But . . ."

"Be ready!"

Geoff moved closer to his mother and whispered in her ear. Her face blanched, but she said nothing.

They were almost through the door.

MAMDOUH WAS TIRED of standing in the hallway, watching people move back and forth between the restrooms and the sanctuary of the infidels. He reached into his shirt pocket and found the pack of cigarettes. It had been a long time. He tapped one out and fumbled for a match. Striking it on the matchbook cover, he leaned forward to touch the flame to the cigarette.

Suddenly, there was pandemonium!

Amid shouts and screams, two figures darted for the side exit. A third was half-dragged before falling to the floor. The doors flew open and the two were gone before Mamdouh could react.

Mamdouh fired his gun into the ceiling. Some people

dropped to the floor. Others pushed their way back inside. Mamdouh's brother, Mousa, ran out into the lobby, stumbling over people who had fallen on top of one another in their fright and panic.

"Back inside. Everyone, get back!"

People scrambled to their feet and hurried back into the sanctuary.

Elizabeth Ralsten was the last one in before the door closed.

"WHAT'S HAPPENING, AKMED? We heard shots being fired." Webber leaned forward, trying to ferret out the corners of the television screen that were off camera and left to his imagination.

Akmed was watching the commotion. Then Webber saw one of the other terrorists run down the aisle and say something to him.

"A small problem. It seems two of our guests chose to leave us without requesting permission." He added grimly, "You know what that means."

ASSISTANT NEWS DIRECTOR Jody Ansel hurried through KFOR's main entrance on San Francisco's Stockton Avenue. Paulo, the friendly Hispanic security guard, looked up from behind the reception counter. Three security monitors displayed their pictures in front of him.

"Hi, Paulo," Jody waved as she walked by the modernistic and decidedly ugly statuary in the center of the lobby. She glanced up at four Sony overhead monitors, all tuned to Channel 4. Today, the Eastern Division NFL Game was just getting under way. Jody thought that whoever had the clever idea of placing four monitors in the lobby entrance, all tuned to Channel 4, deserved an award. Just what kind of award she had not as yet determined. She hated it. But it was a fact that television stations have monitors in every hallway and on every desk. Anything worth doing is worth overdoing.

She pushed the elevator button at the same time that her eye caught the familiar worn sofa, chair, and end table on which lay a scattered jumble of the *San Francisco Bay Guardian* weekly and a pile of brochures with the message, "Sponsor a Rubber Duck!" While she frowned at the disarray, the "Rubber Duck" flyer did promote something that she believed in strongly—support for Oakland's Children's Hospital. Her own daughter had spent six weeks at Children's right after she was born for a heart disorder that doctors corrected with surgery. Amy was four now and perfectly healthy. That was the good news. The bad news was that the promotional event had taken place two weeks ago. Jody reached for the out-of-date brochures.

On the second floor, she stopped by her desk, depositing her purse into one of the drawers and dumping the "Rubber Duck" brochures in the wastebasket. Without sitting down, she proceeded to The Desk and began sorting through the latest newspapers as well as wire bulletins from Reuters and the Associated Press. Her watch said ten-twenty-five. The same as the clock on the wall. She was late, but it was Sunday.

Things were quiet in the newsroom jungle. She could see Sally across the room, trying to coax the coffee maker into doing its thing. It had gotten especially stubborn of late. Jerry Leighton, copywriter, was busy at his desk. She knew that Vern McNair was overseeing the control room on the third floor. Sunday morning's skeleton crew. And only an hour and a half until the Channel 4 Noon Update.

Get with it, Jody.

Her phone rang. Once. Twice.

"Jody Ansel."

"Jody!" The voice on the other end sounded excited.

"This is Jim Wilson at Daystar. Check out Channel 17. We're feeding live from Calvary Church in Baytown. They've got a hostage situation under way!"

"A what?" Jody lowered the phone and waved to get someone's attention. Sally looked up. "Sally, bring up Channel 17."

"What do you know about it, Jim?" Jody knew Jim Wilson on a casual basis. Daystar Cable Corporation had a contract for daily televised news updates by KFOR anchors. These news briefs were used on various cable channels that were a part of the Daystar system.

"Just what you see."

"Thanks, Jim. I've got to run."

Sally was staring at the images coming over the monitor into the news center. She turned to look at Jody.

"Check the police calls. I'm going to run a crawl line." Jody dialed the control room intercom.

"I'm sending you a crawl line, Vern. It's hot. Get ready for a busy morning!"

Jody fed the notice into the computer and sent it to the control room on the third floor. A few seconds later, the black crawl line made its way across the newsroom monitors, just below the green and red jerseys that were slugging it out back in Philadelphia.

....

This is a special Channel 4 news bulletin: unconfirmed reports indicate a hostage situation may be developing at the Calvary Church in suburban Baytown. Sources report unidentified persons, armed with automatic weapons, are holding church attendees hostage. Stay tuned.

....

The crawl line was repeated three times.

Jody pulled her list of emergency home numbers out of the side drawer. She began punching numbers as fast as her fingers could move.

But it *was* Sunday morning.

"You've reached the residence of A. Foster. We can't come to the phone right now. At the beep, leave a message and we'll get back to you as soon as possible."

"Alice. This is Jody. We've got a hot one. A hostage situation at a church in Baytown. I need you in here." Alice Foster was the KFOR News Director, Jody's immediate superior.

"Hello." The familiar television voice of Thomas Bernstein sounded hoarse and groggy.

"Tom, this is Jody. Sorry. I know you were out late last night hosting the benefit at the St. Francis, but you've got to get in here now!"

"What's up?"

"A hostage situation. Some crazies have an entire congregation hostage out in Baytown."

"Confirmed?"

"I'm watching it happen in front of me. Daystar is showing a live feed from inside the church."

"I'll be there in fifteen." The phone clicked. Jody checked the time again. She knew that Tom lived in Marin County. His commute across the Golden Gate Bridge should take twenty-five minutes on a good day.

"Sally, help me make some calls. We've got to get a crew going."

Jody called the home of George Mason, KFOR's corporate president. She knew that he and his family were vacationing in Hawaii, but she wanted her message to be on his voice mail. That way, at least, Mason would know she had thought of him. Betty was next.

"Hello?"

"Hi, Betty. I'm glad I caught you." *Lie.* "We've got a

story coming over Daystar. People being held hostage in a Baytown church. I thought you'd want to know." *Of course she'll want to know. This could be "big time." She'll want to have both sets of claws in the middle of it!* "The Masons are in Hawaii." *I can see drool dripping at the reminder.* "You're the senior person, Betty." *Yes. That's what she wants to hear!*

"I'm coming down as soon as I get dressed. Do you have confirmation?"

"I'm watching a direct feed from the church right now."

"What have you done so far?"

"I've called Alice. Left a message. Tom is on his way. We're putting a crew together. As soon as we have one, I'll send them down the road. We should be on site in forty-five. Maybe sooner."

"Alice is spending the weekend with her kids in Mendicino. I don't know how to reach her. Push for sooner, Jody. I want us to be the first on site!"

Why am I not surprised?

"You've got it."

Jody put the phone down. If there was one person she disliked intensely, it was Betty Filtcher, the station's senior vice-president. Conniving. Conceited. Controlling. Ambition personified in a tight-lipped, feminist package of dyed hair and plastic surgery. She had had a face-lift during her last vacation. Only God knew what else she had lifted in the last few years. She was bossy and inclined to bad decision-making, and Jody dreaded her interference if this story really took off. But there was nothing she could do about it.

"So goes life in Medialand!" she murmured to herself.

SCANNING POLICE CALLS brought further confirmation that a big story was breaking.

Exactly twenty minutes from the time he had hung up the phone, Tom Bernstein burst into the newsroom.

"Sally. Find somebody to park my car when you get a break, will you? Here's the keys. It's out front. Thanks. What's happening, Jody?"

"Channels 2, 5, 7, and 20 are all at crawl-line status. Nothing else. We were first up," she added smugly.

"Get me on the air. Maybe being first up to bat on this thing will help our ratings. God knows they need some help!"

Tom's shirt was open. He had not taken the time to put on a tie. He threw his jacket on the back of his desk chair and walked over to the Update Desk, a small cubicle located at the far end of the newsroom and designed for special bulletins and update reporting. He was unshaven and did not take time to put on makeup. Part of the station's economic crunch had forced the news personalities to take care of their own television makeup. He would do that later.

He glanced at a script outlining details known at the moment. Jody had typed it herself. Spelling and punctuation were unimportant.

"Fifteen seconds."

Tom looked up and grinned.

Jody had put on a headset and was acting as the floor director, taking her cues from Vern upstairs. She stood by the camera, her hand signals counting down. Five, four, three, two, one . . .

"Good morning. This is a special news bulletin from Channel 4's Twenty-four-hour News Desk. I'm Tom Bernstein. It has been confirmed that at approximately ten o'clock this morning, the worshipers gathered at Baytown's Calvary Church had the quiet peacefulness of their church service shattered by gunfire. Just who the gunmen are and what they want is not known. Unconfirmed reports indicate that it is a group of Arab terrorists and that they are currently holding hostage the entire congregation, estimated to be several hundred in number.

"The pictures you are now seeing were part of an earlier, live telecast of the church's weekly service, as seen on Channel 17. Authorities have surrounded the church. All streets leading into the area have been blocked off. If you have family or friends who may be in attendance at Calvary Church, please stand by. Law enforcement officials are requesting that you do not call the church or local police at this time. All lines must be kept open. Continue to watch this station for further information."

Yes!

Jody smiled at Tom.

For once, KFOR is first with the news. All right!

THE DOOR TO THE RV opened and a policeman stuck his head inside. "Two of the hostages managed to escape, sir."

Webber stepped to the door and looked down. The teenager was weeping uncontrollably, oblivious to the strangers around him. "But, Dad," he cried, shaking the shoulder of the man standing at his side. "You said we had to get away. I did what you said to do."

The man's face was pale. He appeared to be in shock.

"What's your name, sir?" Webber asked.

The man looked blank, staring straight ahead.

"Sir?"

"Ralsten. Ken Ralsten. This is my son, Geoff. My wife didn't make it," he added dully. "Elizabeth didn't make it."

He looked at the boy.

"She should have gotten out." His voice was getting shrill. "You let go of her!"

"I tried, Dad. I pulled her with me. She wouldn't come. Let's go back. Something terrible is going to happen to her. You heard what that man said about people trying to escape. Let's go back, please."

"I'm sorry, son," Webber injected. "I can't permit that."

"But . . ."

"Officer, take these two over to the medical unit."

Webber turned and ducked back into the RV. He was chilled by what he heard the man saying to the boy. "It was our only chance, Geoff. You should have had a better hold on your mother!"

Webber closed the door and looked at the others. They shook their heads.

"The shrinks are going to have their work cut out with that kid," Joe said. "His old man has already dumped a truckload of guilt on him."

"I can't blame them for wanting out," White mused. "But what a price to pay!"

Webber said nothing. He returned to his seat and stared at the picture on the screens.

"SWEETHEART, THAT'S THE CHURCH we visited last Sunday. The one we liked so much. If Terry wasn't sick this morning, we'd be there right now. Can you believe that? They think that it's Arab terrorists. Say, do you remember that couple who sat right in front of us? Next to the pregnant lady? We decided they were probably Arabic. Remember? You don't suppose . . ."

"WOUDJA GET A LOAD OF THIS, Marge? Hey, this is why I don' go to church. You can get yourself kilt goin' to church! Looks like some poor meathead already did. Who's doin' it? I don' know. Some crazy Middle-East fanatics. Prob'ly didn' get enuff in the offrin'. Now we got this stupid show on instead of the Eagles. Ain' nobody got any priorities any more? Hey, babe, I know it's early, but bring me 'nother beer, okay?"

THIRTY

"You know our policy is not to negotiate with hostage-takers, Duane." The FBI Director's voice sounded adamant over the direct line hookup between the Command Center and Washington.

"Yessir. I am well aware of our policy. But I'm here in the middle of something, with nearly five hundred lives in my hands, and I believe we need to give them some quarter in order to buy time. If we don't, this has the makings of a disaster that will make the Branch Davidian compound in Waco look like a walk in the park! They've killed one man and are threatening more. If we don't give them network television access in one hour, they say they will kill five hostages. I believe them. They're going to do it."

"And if we give it to them, they may do it anyway. Hold on just a minute, Duane." The line went dead.

Webber looked at the others. Their unanimous recommendation a few minutes earlier had been to permit a network linkup. Was there any way to make them think they were on network television without actually doing it? None of those present knew. They had sent a runner to the media corp at the Communication Center to ask about the possibility. The runner had not yet returned.

Webber took a long sip of Cola, sat back in the chair, and stretched. With every passing hour, tension was increasing inside the black trailer. He could feel it all around him.

The young man who spun dials, listened with earphones, and operated most of the equipment surrounding them, turned to Webber.

"It's for you sir. Washington."

"Hello. Webber here."

"Okay, Duane. Sorry to break away like that. It looks as though we're in even deeper than we thought. We just got a call from Boston. Some guy called WBZ, the NBC affiliate there, and told them Boston should 'prepare to die.' He declares the city is going to be the victim of a biological holocaust unless their demands are met within twenty-four hours. Said there were some people already exposed, as a kind of 'living illustration,' at Boston Common near Frog Pond. You ever been there?"

"Sure. A couple of times."

"Well, they thought it was a hoax. Sent a couple of uniforms down to check it out. When they got there, they found two families getting sicker by the minute. They are all in the hospital now. The littlest one is already dead. Apparently this guy used some kind of inhalation anthrax. A fellow from up in Maine was able to I.D. two potential suspects. They stayed for several days in his guest house. Get this. He put the finger on Marwan Dosha!"

"Dosha. Are you certain, sir?"

"Ninety-nine percent."

"You think there's a connection with what's happening here?"

"Possibly. Ask your friend there."

"Dosha," he repeated, half to himself. "That will certainly be a 'magic name.' Shall I use it when I talk to the leader here?"

A pause.

"Yes. Go ahead. Test the waters."

"We'll keep this line open, sir. Can you give us a permanent tenant there on your end of things?"

"Will do."

Webber turned to the screen. Akmed was sitting in a chair on the platform, smoking a cigarette. There were no ashtrays, so he flicked the ashes onto the carpet. The irreverence seemed so out of context. Webber dialed. He heard the phone ring over the television set at the same time that it was heard in the room. He watched as Yazib picked up the receiver.

"We're working on the network hookups, Akmed. I'm doing the very best that I can. I'm not sure I've got the clout to force such a decision."

Akmed made a point of looking at his watch. "There is not a great deal of time remaining. Rest assured that if you fail, five people will die. That is not a threat, Mr. Agent Webber. It is a promise!"

Just then the runner stuck his head inside the trailer. He moved it from side to side and motioned 'thumbs down.' They could not pull it off.

"The networks are ready, but it's too 'iffy' to try to fake it," he whispered to Randle. "They may have someone else outside who will let them know whether or not they're really on."

Randle nodded. "Thanks. Stand by, in case we need you again."

"OUR RECOMMENDATION at this end still stands, sir. We're unanimous, and we're running out of time." Webber could hear the murmur of voices on the other end of the line. Then it was silent.

"Okay," the Director's voice came through, wrung out with resignation. "This is a mess, Duane. We may be dodging debris just so we can hit an iceberg, but get busy anyway and set it up. Try for something big in return. Like a few hundred hostages. I've got to talk to Ellis up in Boston. Hang in there."

"Yessir. Good luck."

"Joe, take charge of getting the media hooked in. Make certain they don't go off half cocked. Remember Harry's Bar."

Joe did remember Harry's Bar. How many years ago had it been? In Berkeley, a nut with a gun had taken over a local bar and was holding the patrons hostage. When television crews arrived to provide live, on-the-spot coverage, the 'basketcase' saw what was happening outside the building by watching the television in the bar.

As news reporters described police activity, complete with pictures that documented their commentary and revealed members of a SWAT team positioning themselves for an assault, the nut began killing everyone inside.

Eventually, he too was killed, but the fat had already been dipped into the fire. Lives had been lost unnecessarily, and fingers of guilt were pointing in all directions. Coverage of the tragedy came under major scrutiny, resulting in more stringent and strategic guidelines for cooperation between law enforcement agencies and the media.

As he headed for the communications center, Joe tried to mentally prepare himself for what was ahead.

"LOOK, AKMED. I'm doing everything I can," Webber's voice revealed an edge of frustration as he spoke. It was the exact mood that he wanted to convey. "I'm pulling all the strings I've got. Give me something to negotiate with. Give me the hostages. Let me come in and take their place."

"Are you serious?" responded Akmed. "These people are our ticket. If we gave them up, you wouldn't begin to meet the needs of our people."

"If you won't give them all up, then give some of them as an act of good faith. Without that, I'll not be able to pull together enough support for hooking you up to national television."

Akmed let his eyes wander across the crowd seated before him.

The other two operations should be well on the way by now. It's time to play the next card.

"Mr. Agent Webber, this is the deal. When I see proof that we are linked into the major networks, guests will be released."

"How many hostages can I say will be coming out?"

Akmed placed his hand under his chin, pausing long enough to feign the appearance of giving the question thoughtful consideration. In actuality, he had already made up his next move days ago.

"NBC, CBS, and ABC are each worth fifty. CNN will be worth a hundred. That is my best and final offer. Not one more or less. Do not attempt to stall."

"Look, Akmed, this is very difficult. How about giving us an extra hour to work out the details?"

"No."

"Thirty minutes. Surely you can give us thirty minutes?"

"Mr. Agent Webber, you are beginning to get on my nerves. The answer is, and will continue to be, *no*. Not an extra hour. Not an extra half hour. Not an extra minute. And please do not try to fool us with treachery or dishonesty. By now you must be aware that ours is not the only matter before you."

Webber knitted his brow and licked his lips.

"What do you mean?"

"Come, now, Mr. Agent Webber. Have you been in contact with your headquarters in Washington?"

Webber hesitated, wondering where this conversation was going.

"Yes," he answered, finally.

"And have your people there expressed concern over the welfare of the city of Boston?"

Webber looked up at White and the mayor.

"Well?"

"Yes, an unverified threat has been received. What do you know about it?"

"I know that you would do well to consider it seriously. If the United States requires Israel's acquiescence to the righteous demands of the Palestinian Islamic Jihad, there need be no further bloodshed. If she does not, then your troubles have only begun.

"If our demands are not acceded to, we will be forced to release a weapon of incredible death and devastation on the people there. You may also be interested to know that we also have in our possession the pastor of this church and twenty-four of the church's members, who have been sightseeing in Palestine."

Akmed allowed a dramatic pause while this unexpected bit of news was absorbed. Then he continued.

"So, if this offer is not accepted, we will begin by executing five persons here immediately. We will continue to do the same every hour after that until you accept our demands. One way or another, you will have your wish regarding the release of our guests. You get to decide if you prefer them to come out dead or alive. You don't have much time left before the hour is up."

"HE KNOWS ABOUT BOSTON. Says they've got some 'incredible weapon' and that they're ready to release it. He also claims that they've got this church's pastor and twenty-four church members hostage in Israel."

"I'll have it checked out," the Director answered.

"I decided not to mention Dosha at this stage, though I'm not exactly sure why," Webber added, wiping sweat off his forehead. Even though the trailer was air-conditioned, perspiration continued to pop out on his body, an indication of the stress he was feeling.

"It's just as well. If no point is served, there is no purpose in divulging things we know," the Director responded. "We've verified anthrax as the weapon of choice on the little boy at Frog Pond. An inhalation variety. He had skinned his elbow earlier in the day. The doctors say that and his asthma are the reasons he went so soon. The others are goners too, according to the medical reports. It's only a matter of hours. Doesn't seem to be much the doctors can do, once the spores are ingested."

"This is much more sophisticated than a run-of-the-mill terrorist operation, sir," said Webber. "It also looks to be more deadly. I don't know about the Boston situation, but these people here appear to be ready to die for the cause."

"What's your overall status, Duane?"

"Our Command Center is one hundred percent. We've set up a Communications Center a couple of hundred yards away and out of sight. I've not been down there, but I'm told it's already loaded with media peeps. We just delivered hamburgers, fries, and Cokes enough for five hundred inside the church. We've gotten everyone out of the peripheral rooms; you know, all the Sunday School kids and the adult workers who were with them. I guess it pays to volunteer for Sunday School work. At least it did today. Two other people escaped about a half hour ago—a man and his teenage son. His wife is still in there. And in five minutes, we go on live network TV."

"You got a SWAT team there?"

"Came in about twenty minutes ago. They've taken up positions near the building."

"What about the building layout?"

"Got the blueprint copies from the Planning Department about a half hour ago. The SWAT team leader is checking them out now."

"Who is he?"

"Hendrickson."

"Don't know him. Is he good?"

"The best."

"Great. Stay in touch."

ESTHER HAD REMAINED quietly in her pew from the beginning of this whole bizarre event. The only time she had moved was to use the restroom with the others. Then back to her seat again.

At first, she had prayed. Since no one was permitted to talk to their neighbors, a good number of those being held spent the time in conversation with God. She glanced out of the corner of her eye in both directions, something inside her needing the reassurance from others.

No, it was more than that.

She was possessed by an inner longing that she recognized, one with which she had never fully come to terms—the need to be reassured that somehow, everyone was all right. It was a feeling she and her pastor wives' friends had occasionally talked about over a cup of afternoon coffee; how that, even after being ground into powder by congregational criticism and thankless behind-the-scenes tasks that nobody else would do, they had this need to know that everybody in the church family was okay. Even if they themselves were not.

Now Esther Cain was experiencing that same mysterious concern. It drove her, once again, to her silent vigil of prayer. Surrounded by frightened souls, rendered helpless by armed and dangerous beings whose cause she did not understand, she sought and found her refuge in communion with the God whom she was rediscovering to be the *God who is there.*

At first she glanced at Jeremy, sitting next to her. She caught his eye and then looked away, not wanting to draw attention to their relationship. Next to him was Allison. Beautiful Allison. She seemed so strong in her faith. A stand-out in terms of physical attractiveness, she carried within her a spirit that was equally beautiful. Esther tried to think of a time that she could remember seeing her in church without her Bible. In fact, there it was in her lap. A young girl undergoing the transforming metamorphosis from adolescence to womanhood. She possessed what Esther liked to call a "fair" beauty, one that spoke of purity, flawlessness, and freshness.

Why am I thinking like this? Why is my mind wandering so? Come on, Esther. Pull it together. You've got to stay calm and alert.

As she let her gaze move beyond those next to her, she saw some with heads bowed, obviously praying. Others were comforting family members and keeping an eye on the intruders. She was surprised to discover that more than a few pairs of eyes were on her. Watching. Perhaps they were wondering what she was thinking, what she would do.

Esther tried to read the lips of the man on the platform, sitting there in her husband's chair. He was talking with someone; she did not know who. She hoped it was a negotiator. She had read about such people in the newspapers. Their verbal heroics had seemed so otherworldly, however, that it had never been more than a passing curiosity. Now she found herself straining to interpret any discernable lip movement, and praying that the world's best negotiator was on the other end of the line!

What's going to happen now that Ken and Geoff have escaped? The man threatened to ...

Esther could not bring herself to even think those fearful words.

If only John were here.

THIRTY-ONE

SUNDAY, 18 SEPTEMBER, 1830 LOCAL TIME
SOMEWHERE IN ISRAEL

The sun was low over the Judean hills, as the orange and blue Israel Tours bus made its way along Highway 90 to the main road between Jericho and Jerusalem. Turning left, the long, winding ascent from two hundred fifty meters below sea level to eight hundred twenty meters above was slow going, and the passengers were silent.

John's last question, directed at Yazib, remained unanswered.

"What do you mean you have my wife and our congregation? You expect us to believe you have taken them hostage too? That is impossible."

"Be quiet. I have told you what you need to know for now," was his only answer.

Talking among themselves had been forbidden by the terrorists. No one was to speak unless first spoken to.

The sun readied itself for the day's final encore by turning clouds into fiery curtains and throwing giant shadows across the audience of the ancient hills. Under normal circumstances, it would have been a grand finish to another glorious day of adventure. But today the actors were unappreciative, as their commandeered bus turned off the main highway and bounced over potholes onto a side road leading past a marker that declared Nebi Musa to be just ahead. Shortly thereafter, they pulled into a deserted parking lot in front of an ancient mosque.

"Enjoy a brief rest while we wait for darkness to come. This is a good place, no?" asked Yazib, looking at John Cain. "Do you know where you are?"

John stared at Yazib, resentment choking his throat with anger at their predicament. He nodded once.

"You may speak to your people now, Reverend Cain. Tell them where we are. I'm sure they would like to know."

John turned his gaze slowly, pain shooting through his head as he shifted his body in the seat. His eye and cheek were swollen, as well as part of his lower lip. It was hard to speak clearly. He wanted to bring words of comfort to these frightened disciples who had followed him halfway around the world.

They had often stood together on the threshold of eternity back home. There, as the funeral dirge echoed in their ears, they had waited for their pastor to make some sense out of death's senselessness. And somehow, by digging deeply into his soul and into the Scriptures, he had come up with a word time and again. But today no words came that could erase the collective fear he saw staring back at him.

"Tell them!" Yazib spoke sharply. "That is, if you even know where we are," he added with a smirk.

"We are at Nebi Musa," John began, flinching at a sudden stab of pain under his eye. "Muslims believe that this is the site where Moses is buried. From here you can see Mount Nebo across the Jordan Valley. According to Deuteronomy 34, that is where Moses was shown the Promised Land by God. It is where he died. Because Muslim tradition holds this to be Moses' final burial place, there is a large cemetery here in which many of their people have chosen to be buried. If I remember correctly, Mohammed's favorite wife, Aisha, is also buried here."

Yazib and the other team members had all turned their attention to John, as he spoke.

"Very impressive, Reverend Cain," said Yazib. The others passed raised-eyebrow looks and Imad nodded his head appreciatively. "I am surprised that you are so aware of our Muslim beliefs."

"Your beliefs and traditions are a very important part of the history of this land," John responded, grimacing at the pain, and wondering if his cheekbone had been broken by Yazib's blow.

"Where are you taking us?" Evelyn Unruh suddenly demanded, in a loud, clear voice, from two rows behind John.

"Shut up, old woman," Yazib answered curtly.

"I will not 'shut up,' young man," Evelyn retorted, her eyes flashing defiance. "I have lived too long to be treated this way. Furthermore, I am an American citizen, as we all are. You may think you are making some kind of political statement by taking us hostage, but the way you are acting is most certainly not in keeping with your own Muslim traditions."

"I said to be quiet," repeated Yazib.

But Evelyn was on a roll as she leaned forward in her seat, her finger pointing and slicing through the tension in the bus to emphasize her words.

"I don't know a great deal about your beliefs, but I do know about mine," she said hotly, "and I am not afraid of you. I also want you to know that I deeply resent the way you have treated Pastor Cain. He is our spiritual leader. *We* would never hit *your* spiritual leader. I cannot imagine Mohammed respecting what you are doing to us. He would certainly show an old woman some respect!"

Yazib seemed at a loss for words, put off guard by this

elderly woman's challenge.

It was Pasha who finally stood and approached Evelyn slowly.

"What is your name?"

"My name is Evelyn Unruh."

"Where are you from, Evelyn Unruh?"

"I was born in Omaha, Nebraska. My family moved to California when I was six years old. I've lived there ever since. I have a son and three grandchildren."

"I see. Do you have some pictures of them?"

"Yes, as a matter of fact, I do. May I show them to you?"

"Of course."

John watched in amazement as Evelyn worked her grandmotherly charm on the gun-wielding terrorist. She reached into her purse and withdrew a well-worn picture laminated in plastic, and handed it to the woman.

"They are very beautiful," she said quietly, handing the photo back to Evelyn.

"How old are you now, Evelyn Unruh?"

"I am seventy-seven years old," she answered emphatically.

"Come with me. Some fresh air will be good for one as old as you."

"I am fine just where I am, thank you," Evelyn answered emphatically.

Pasha suddenly grabbed Evelyn by the hair and yanked her from the aisle seat. Screams of surprise and protest erupted from the other group members. Three of the men nearby rose to try to stop her.

"Sit down!" ordered Yazib, pointing his gun at them. "You must sit down. Now!"

Meanwhile, Pasha dragged Evelyn down the aisle by her hair. John, aghast with horror, reached out to stop her, only to be brutally hammered back into his seat by Fathi Adahlah's pistol chop to the back of his neck. A split second later, Pasha hurled Evelyn out of the open door!

Pain from the blow paralyzed John's brain, making any further movement momentarily impossible. He felt himself slam against the window and he heard a pop. Then another. Was it a bone? Had he broken something? He was too stunned and in too much pain to tell.

"O God, please, no!" John heard Patricia Hansen's voice. He could make out others sobbing uncontrollably. John wanted to tell them that he was all right, they didn't need to worry. But he could not move. A hot, electric current of pain was streaking through his body.

Then, out of the corner of his eye, he saw the woman they called Pasha. As she withdrew from the door, John saw the weapon in her hands. Her face was expressionless, her eyes dark and cold. Slowly he forced his brain to concentrate as a stab of apprehension forced its way through him. He pushed himself up from where he had fallen, until he could peer out the side window.

There in the dirt by the side of the bus Evelyn lay motionless, staring up at the darkening sky, the pictures of her grandchildren clutched in her hand.

Evelyn Unruh.

Born in Omaha, Nebraska.

Moved to California at age six.

Died in Israel at age seventy-seven.

Cause of death: two shots fired at close range, after being thrown to the ground from a bus by a young woman not even a third of her age.

Another victim of Pasha Bashera, terrorist!

John stared at her lifeless form. He lifted his hand to brush at the tears in his eyes, and was surprised to discover there were none. That's when he realized that the tears he felt spilling over were on the inside of his soul, dropping onto the floor of his heart.

My God, what have I done? We should not be here. We

should be home, with our children, in America. What is happening to us?

He heard weeping behind him. Regret came crashing in on him like falling rocks. He wanted to tell everyone just how sorry he was. He wanted to hold Esther and Jeremy. And especially Jessica.

But it was no use.

It was too late.

THE SUN HAD DISAPPEARED behind the hills when Imad started the motor, ground the gears into place, and turned the bus in a tight circle around the parking lot, heading back in the direction from which they had come.

Almost every eye strained to catch one final glimpse of Evelyn.

A moment later, she was out of sight.

John looked at her empty seat. Inches away sat Mary Callahan, her seat partner and roommate. Mary's face was chalky white as she continued wiping tears away with nervous hands.

Their kidnappers said nothing as the bus turned left and continued westward up the Jericho–Jerusalem Highway.

They had gone only a few kilometers when Yazib turned to face the group, the guide's microphone in his hand. His look was grim. "You see what happens when you show disrespect. Such tragedies are unavoidable in war. And you must understand, we are at war. What part do you play? You are nothing more to us than pawns in a game of chess. You are property. Chattel for purposes of negotiation. Your lives mean nothing to us, unless your country understands that the only way to get you back is to meet the demands of our people."

He paused, but no one moved or spoke up.

"Fathi is coming among you now. He will bind your

arms and tape your mouths. I warn you not to panic. Do not attempt any heroics. If anyone does anything out of the ordinary, that person will be shot. If some of you die, it does not concern us. Enough of you will remain alive for our purposes. And if you cooperate, you will all live. It is as simple as that."

Fathi moved silently among the hostages, beginning with those seated in the back of the bus. Pasha's eyes never left them for an instant, her weapon held in firing position.

Their mouths were taped over with a wide brown adhesive. They were then made to stand while the same tape was wrapped around them, binding their arms to their upper body, from shoulder to wrist. Returning to a sitting position was difficult, forcing them to sit up straight or lean forward, with hands tucked behind their hips.

John was the last to be bound.

"Do his arms, but leave his mouth free for now," Yazib ordered.

Fathi made no effort to answer, but quickly drew the tape around and around John's torso. His shirt was short-sleeved, and the tape clung tightly to his bare arms. John remembered that most of the group were dressed similarly, all in short sleeves, several in walking shorts. When the tape was removed, it would be painful. *If* it was removed...

John looked into the eyes of the man who was wrapping the tape. He was cold, matter-of-fact. A man seemingly void of any of the feelings that John felt slamming around inside his head. A skilled employee, well trained and dedicated, busy with the day's work!

A stab of remorse!

What if it is true? What if they do have Esther and the Calvary Church family held hostage? How could they possibly have done it? It's probably just a bluff to make us more uneasy, more willing to cooperate. Still, how did they know about the church? Poor Evelyn. She will never see it again.

Will any of us ever see it again? And what of Boston's inhabitants? Could it be possible? Could they really have a bomb?

The more he thought, the more concerned he became. Finally, his mind returned to the hotel by the sea, where the nightmare had begun. To Jessica. Both relief and concern filled his mind as he thought about his sweet, lovely Jessica.

What has happened to her? She's a very resourceful twelve-year-old. Obviously they expected her to be on the bus. And I almost drew attention to her at the last moment. She is probably safe, but will she know what to do?

He prayed silently.

Thank You, Lord, for allowing her to not feel good today. Thank You for keeping her safe in the restroom during all of this. Once again, You've taken something bad and turned it into good. Help her find someone at the hotel who will take care of her and keep her safe. And, Lord, please watch over Esther and Jeremy back home. I don't know what is happening there, but You do. Keep Your protecting hand on them. Enable Jessica to reach them by phone soon, so that they can arrange to get her home.

The burning inner concern and a feeling of real physical pain swept through John once again.

If what these people say is true, please, Lord, I beg of You, keep my family and the church family safe. Remove them from danger and watch over them until we are all together again.

Even as he silently prayed, Evelyn Unruh's dead body, lying there on the parking lot pavement, haunted his thoughts.

The bus abruptly veered to the right, onto a road identified by a sign as Highway 437. John peered out into the darkness, then back at the road again, now dimly lit by the bus headlamps.

Where are they taking us? We must be fairly close to Jerusalem, but I don't remember ever having been on this road.

After what seemed to be about eight or ten kilometers, the driver, the one they called Imad, made a sudden sharp left turn and then pushed the accelerator to the floor once again. Along the edge of the road, another sign caught John's eye.

Ramallah. We must be circling Jerusalem, coming around to the north.

"Do you know where we are now?" Yazib asked. He sat across from John, leaning back against a large canvas bag that John assumed must be filled with ammunition and other weapons.

John shook his head. He was not going to reveal that he had any idea of direction or location. Even at best, his sense of where they were was sketchy.

"We are coming soon to a small village. We will be met by other soldiers of the revolution. Ten of your group will be taken into their custody. The rest of us will continue on."

"Why are you separating us?" asked John.

"We are, as you say in America, 'hedging our bets' when it comes to dealing with our enemy. If you are all in one place, and that place is discovered, we are much weaker than if you are scattered. Our power to negotiate is heightened by keeping some of you on the black squares and others on the white." Yazib paused, then asked, "Do you like chess, Reverend Cain?"

John said nothing.

"It is a game forbidden by some of the very strict in our Islamic community. However, I have found it to be great mental exercise. Perhaps we can play together one day, when this is all over and done with."

John continued looking straight ahead, watching for other road signs that might reveal a familiar name. Before long, another flashed by indicating an interchange on Highway 60: Ramallah to the north, Jerusalem to the south. Highway 60. John knew where he was now. It was only a short distance to the city. Ramallah and Shechum/Nablus lay along the highway to the north. They did not turn toward the north or south, however, but continued along in a westerly direction another four or five kilometers before the bus slowed and eventually rolled to a stop, halfway off the road.

From out of the darkness several shadowy figures emerged, gathering at the side of the bus. Imad opened the door and one of the men stepped up into the entry well.

Yazib strode down the aisle, tapping first one passenger, then another on the shoulder.

"Move. Hurry." Yazib spoke roughly to the first few until everyone got the idea of what they were supposed to do. Patricia Hansen, Mary Callahan, Shad Coleman, and Debbie Sommers stood to their feet and shuffled toward the exit.

Nick Micceli stood, expecting to see Yazib tap Patricia's shoulder as well. It did not happen. John watched as concern etched its way into the lines in Nick's face, visible above the tape that circled his head and covered his mouth.

"Move!" shouted Yazib, giving Nick a shove. There was no opportunity for pleading to be removed from the bus together; no time for good-byes. Nick staggered under the force of the blow, then made his way along the aisle.

Adele Smith, Dan Wilson, Jill Anderson, Dan Watson, and Sandy Wilson.

John watched as each one quietly moved past the man standing in the door and disappeared into the night. Finally, with a broad smile and a wave of his hand, the man followed Sandy out the door.

The door closed and the bus roared to life, lurching back onto the roadway. Amidst the grinding of gears, it headed west, but only for a kilometer or two. Then Imad made a sharp left, and John was certain they were headed south toward Jerusalem. He closed his eyes as a flush of emotion coursed through his body. Every bone seemed to ache. He was suddenly consumed with weariness.

Lord, I implore You. Keep each of those people safe! I am responsible for their being here, but there's nothing I can do to protect them. I don't know where they are being taken. But You do. Keep Your arm of protection around them, and around the rest of us too.

The deployment of the ten hostages had taken probably no more than a minute, maybe two. It had been only a few hours since leaving their hotel on the Dead Sea.

But it seemed like an eternity.

THIRTY-TWO

Two more stops were made, but John was not sure where. At each stop, figures came out from dark, shadowy buildings to meet them, and more of his flock were swept into the tenebrous depths of the city.

Ruth Taylor, Larry Mitchel, Susan Cloud, Harold Eiderman, and Donna Thomas.

John was heartsick as he saw how carefully Yazib selected and separated husbands from their wives.

What is his purpose? Will we be easier to control this way? Do the terrorists anticipate greater cooperation from us?

John wished he had taken more time to read regarding the psychology of hostage-taking. Over time, he had scanned articles on the Stockholm Syndrome, Pan Am 103, the New York Trade Center bombing, and other articles on terrorism presented in popular news journals back home. He had even watched a film about Terry Anderson's seven-year saga as a hostage in Lebanon. But these had evoked only a passing interest, in that the prospect of any real involvement with terrorists seemed no less incredulous than playing the starring role in Tom Clancy's *Patriot Games.*

Who could ever imagine a pastor and the people in his church taken hostage, to serve as pawns in a diabolic scheme of international political blackmail? Now, however, John was discovering what had escaped him before, when reading about acts of fundamentalist Muslim terrorism around the world.

The *intifada* was not simply a racial-political issue, spawned by mutual hatred and distrust between Arabs and Jews. Listening as these Arab youths spoke quietly among themselves, mostly in Arabic but occasionally in English, John was becoming increasingly aware of one thing. This was not about a piece of dirt. This was a religious battle. A Holy War! At its core was a commitment to spiritual re-awakening and moral purification, a return to the soulish roots of the Muslim faith.

Apparently John, his family, and church had been chosen as human vouchers, flesh-and-blood currency with which a people hoped to barter their way out of the rock-strewn streets of the Gaza and the refugee communities of Israel's West Bank, that for generations had kept them under the boot of poverty and the domination of their hated enemy.

The felt need was for a platform, a nation that would serve as the springboard from which to launch a Muslim renaissance throughout the world. Since Islam is not known for its tolerance of religious pluralism, it offers little room for persons of other faiths to coexist in mutual harmony. The most radical of religious Muslims hold that all outsiders are infidels who must either be converted or destroyed.

We are even more than currency to these people, John thought, as the bus started to move once again. *We are symbols. Symbols of a false religious group that has befriended the Jew and blocked the Middle Eastern Muslim from having his day.*

It was not a thought to nurture hope.

The second stop was on one of Jerusalem's narrow, dark side streets. Through the window, John could make out the familiar, well-lit, ancient walls of the Old City, with the Jaffa Gate and David's Tower in the distance. Phyllis Watson, Greg Sommers, Sandy Mitchel, Jerry Cloud, and Patricia Micceli disembarked and were quickly loaded into two vehicles. One appeared to be a taxi. Both drove away from the scene, but in opposite directions.

John looked around. The only persons remaining in the bus now were Edgar Anderson, Bob Thomas, Gisele Eiderman, the four terrorists, and himself. They were rolling again, moving out along Karen ha Yessod, past the YMCA and the King David Hotel. Eventually, they turned onto Hativat Yerushalayim, took a right down the hill and then a left along Silwan Road. Eventually, they came to a stop at a place that was familiar to John, even in the darkness. They were in the parking lot in front of the Gihon Spring, at one time the sole water supply for ancient Jerusalem.

Around 1,000 B.C., King David had captured the city and made it his capital. Although his son Solomon eventually built the Temple above it on higher ground, the main residential portion of the ancient city remained clinging to the hill called the Ophel, located just above the Kidron Valley. The site had been chosen because the Gihon is at the foot of the slope.

This was a favorite place of John's, one to which he had hoped to bring the group during their visit. But definitely under different circumstances.

The spring was located in a cave on the floor of the Kidron Valley. This meant that Jerusalemites of old were in constant danger of being cut off from their water source when the city was under siege. About three hundred years after David, King Hezekiah carried out a stunning engineering project. He connected the spring to the Siloam Pool, more than a quarter of a mile *inside* the city.

On several occasions, John had tramped through the dark, connecting tunnel, candle in hand and knee-deep in water. Now he wondered if this was to be their final destination. And if so, why? What was the purpose in all this?

Pasha, still dressed in her hotel clerk's costume, came up to John, pulling on the roll of adhesive tape in her hand. Without a word, she wrapped it several times around his head, covering his mouth. Then she drew a knife from the bag she had carried when leaving the hotel. The knife startled him, especially in the hands of one as calloused to killing as this woman appeared to be. She reached around him and cut through the tape that bound his arms to his torso. "Do not attempt to remove the tape over your mouth. Just tear the tape off your arms."

She repeated the task with the others, giving them the same instruction. John removed the tape as cleanly as he could, tiny hairs pulling away as he yanked it from his arms. He could hear the same process being repeated behind him. He rubbed his arms. It felt good to be able to move them again.

The terrorists gathered up their gear in preparation for leaving.

"Everybody out," Yazib ordered, looking at John.

John went first, followed by Gisele, Bob, and Edgar. It wasn't until everyone was out of the bus that John noticed the old car parked near the entrance to the tunnel. It was an ancient Mercedes taxi cab, filthy dirty, and with license plate numbers beginning 666. He could not make out the rest in the darkness.

"Over there." Yazib pointed toward the car, his voice gruff, signs of tension filtering through.

They walked rapidly toward the parked car. John assumed they were about to leave the area in it.

"You men, inside quickly. In the back." He signaled to Gisele. "You, stand here. Fathi, keep your knife near the woman's heart. Anyone attempts to escape and the woman will be killed first." Yazib looked at John. "Do you understand?"

John nodded.

"All right," he looked at the others. "Let's get busy. You know what to do."

Imad and Pasha opened the canvas bags, removing automatic weapons, grenades, ammunition clips, a large amount of explosives, two radio-controlled detonators, and a few other nondescript items. John was surprised to see a coil of rope with a grappling hook, each prong covered with what looked like a rubber substance.

What are these people up to?

Pasha withdrew some clothing from the bag, tossing pieces to Yazib, Imad, and Fathi. Then she moved behind the car and began undressing. With what appeared to John as an unusual amount of feminine immodesty for an Arab woman, she removed the hotel clerk's uniform and dropped it to the ground, kicking it under the car, together with her shoes. A moment later, she had donned the uniform of an Israeli officer, her feet ensconced in combat boots. She shrugged her way into a backpack the color of her military blouse. Yazib smiled at her and patted her shoulder in approval.

By the time she had finished, the others had also changed. Only they were in the uniforms of Arab policemen. The contents of the larger bag were being transferred into packs and strapped on each of their backs. At last, they were ready.

"Come," Yazib motioned to them. "We are going."

John and the others, their mouths still taped, got out of the car.

"Follow me. We will walk single file. Watch your step. The stairs are uneven. You could easily injure yourself in the darkness. If you fall and hurt yourself, so that you cannot continue to keep up, we will have to go on without you," Yazib said very matter-of-factly. The sinister implication of his warning, however, was not missed by anyone.

They moved out from the vehicle and started up a series of irregular steps, carved out of earth and stone. John remembered having walked down these steps from the upper part of the Ophel, some years before. It was much more difficult in the dark, however, with no illumination other than moonlight. The temperature was definitely cooler here in the Judean hills, but the night air was still warm. There was no need for a jacket.

Yazib led the way, moving swiftly, steadily up the side of the hill. After a few minutes on the steep incline, the hostages were breathing heavily. John wiped perspiration away from his eyes. There was a sharp ache spreading throughout his chest as his lungs struggled to cope with this sudden burst of exercise. Though he and the others were in better than average physical condition, the strain of the last few hours and the physical exertion generated by this climb were maxing out his strength. He wondered about Gisele and the others. Surely they were at the end of themselves as well. Would life ever return to normal? John was suddenly overwhelmed by a wave of emotion. His family was so far away. It was another life altogether than the one they were living now.

Will I ever see Esther and Jeremy and Jessica again? Where are you, Jessica? Are you all right?

A feeling of hopelessness added its weight to John's shoulders as he climbed. He forced himself to turn his attention back to what was at hand, not to what might never be again.

Focus. Pay attention to the present. Let the future take care of itself.

At the apex of the climb, they stopped to catch their breath and to view the City of David excavations. Evidence of the archaeological dig that had been going on for some time was everywhere. John knew this to be a scene of great controversy and violent protests staged by religious zealots who claimed that ancient Jewish graves were being violated. Diggers refuted the accusations, declaring that the site was too important to leave buried.

As a result, ever so carefully, the earliest incarnation of Jerusalem, some three thousand years ago, was being unwrapped by the tools of the experts.

Its ragged stone steps and high walls were bathed in the glow of bright lights. A broken pillar could be seen still standing upright on its base. Several others were horizontal to the ground where they had fallen centuries before. Even in this danger-filled night, John could feel himself giving way to the glories of the past that reached out to him from these ruins.

As he surveyed the scene, John also believed he was starting to see what the terrorists intended to do. But their ultimate goal still eluded him.

"We are going over there," Yazib pointed across the road to a part of the wall that formed a forty-five-degree corner and, unlike the rest of the area, remained in dark shadows. John wondered about the darkness, then noticed that two of the lamps pointing toward that area had been broken. This really was beginning to feel like a well-organized, sophisticated operation. The mix of daring and detail was impressive.

These people must have major backing from someone. This is not a few hotheads running a slam-bang program of indiscriminate terrorism. If what he says is true about other teams in America, this is shaping up to be a major international event. And I'm so close to the middle of it that I can't gain perspective.

They waited for a couple of minutes. There was very little traffic on the road at this hour.

"Now!" hissed Yazib.

As the last vehicle passed by, they dashed across the road. For about a minute they were out in the open, Yazib leading the way, then the hostages, followed by the others. It was an opportunity for someone to see them, to question their presence, and to stop them from going further.

Sixty whole seconds!

They reached the shadows of the wall that stretched above them into the inky blackness of the night. They leaned against the stones to catch their breath and to determine if they had been seen. Nothing happened to indicate that they had been discovered. No shouts. No sirens. Nothing unusual.

John was consumed once again with disappointment.

Where are You, God, when we need You? Here we are, in the very place that You Yourself walked. Have You forgotten us?

OFF TO THE LEFT and around the corner from where these unwelcome visitors huddled was the Dung Gate, so called because in ancient times the area around the gate was the local rubbish dump. It provided the nearest access into the Old City. Paul Levi leaned against the corner of the wall, designing figure eights in the dust with the toe of his boot. Asher Ras was looking into the Old City toward a deserted street. Their weapons hung loosely at their shoulders. The two young IDF soldiers were bored with another tour of uneventful guard duty.

"Yesh mashehoo?" asked Paul. *Do you have something to eat?*

"Khafisat shokolad," Asher answered, reaching into his pocket for the candy bar. He broke it in half and handed one of the pieces to Paul.

"Ani rotseh bakbook birah," Paul mumbled as he bit

down on the candy. *I'd like to have a can of beer.*

"Ken," agreed Asher, licking his lips. *Yes.*

"Remember those two American girls who came through here a couple of hours ago?"

"The blond? And the one with the tan?"

"Yes."

"How could I forget?"

"Nice looking, huh?"

"The best today. I wonder what they're doing now?"

"I know what they're not doing."

"What's that?"

"They're not having as much fun as they could be if we were off duty!"

Both guards laughed and strolled into the center of the gateway. The Bab el-Magharbeh, its official name, meaning "Gate of the Moors," was typically quiet at this time of the night. The only extraordinary sights they had observed through the evening were a few tourists moving in and out of the Old City through the gate. Mostly Japanese and American. Occasionally a young woman worthy of a second look. Other than that, nothing.

A short distance away, the visitors who might well have earned these two soldiers medals and accolades from their superiors went unnoticed.

FATHI HAD PRACTICED for this throw. He had hurled stones and chunks of driftwood high and far, letting them fall into the sea off the Gaza coastline. He had also coiled and thrown this very rope and grappling hook a hundred times under a desert sky.

He was ready.

With one expert fling, Fathi saw the hook disappear and soundlessly hit the rampart floor. He pulled back on the rope until it was firmly anchored against the upper wall.

Then they waited, straining to hear whether or not a guard above them might have noticed, looking to see if any accusing face stared down at them. There was none. John felt the tension that gripped the shadowy figures huddled at the base of Suleiman the Magnificent's sixteenth-century legacy to the City of Gold.

A legacy that John now understood they were about to climb!

John guessed that the thick Ottoman walls must rise thirty or forty meters straight up into the dark shroud of night. Scrub bush, broken pillars, and fallen stones lay scattered along the base. One false move and it was all over. *This is not the way to enter the Old City!*

"I will go first," Yazib said, looking up to the point where the rope disappeared. "Pasha, you are next. Then you, Reverend Cain, followed by the other men. The woman comes last. If you try to do anything but cooperate, you will be killed and her throat will be cut. Understood?"

The men nodded.

Gisele's eyes were wide with fear. Unintelligible sounds were coming from behind the tape across her mouth. She made desperate motions with her hands as she shook her head.

Yazib stepped up to Gisele. "Be quiet. You *must* do it!"

Gisele was shaking now. Tears rolled down her cheeks.

"There is only one other choice," said Yazib, his hand on the gun that rested in its holster. He paused.

"What will it be?"

John moved over to where Gisele could see him. He put his hands together in prayerlike fashion, fingertips pointing heavenward. He nodded as if to say, *You can make it.* Then he put his arms around her and held her until he felt her stop shaking. He stepped back and nodded affirmatively again.

Gisele swallowed the bile that retched upward from her

stomach. She brushed back her tears and nodded. *I'll try.*

John watched as Yazib grasped hold of the rope and put his weight on it. It held. He climbed slowly but steadily, always careful to remain in the shadows. A short distance away, the climber would be invisible to all but the most discerning onlooker. Here at the base of the wall, however, one could see with clarity. The wall was high enough that those standing below were offered the illusion of Yazib's body growing smaller as he climbed. A careful hesitation at the top as he peered over the edge. Then he was out of sight. A moment later they saw him motioning for them to come.

Pasha took hold of the rope and began climbing. All too quickly, John thought, she was at the top. Now it was his turn. He took the rope in his hands and placed both feet against the base of the wall, as the others had done.

One hand over another. *Don't look down, John.* The pain from blows received earlier in the evening was accentuated now as he tried to fight off the pounding in his head. Then his foot slipped, throwing him off balance. The rope started sliding through his hands. Desperately, he held on, his elbow scraping raw against the stones. The thought of free-falling onto the stones below pumped fresh adrenaline into his body. Struggling to regain upward momentum, John felt his foot brush a large crack between the stones and he jammed his toes into it. His heart was hammering. *Keep going up!* John felt the rope tearing into the flesh of his hands. *Don't look down!*

The rope was tighter against the wall now. *I must be nearing the top.* The thought of airplanes flashed randomly through his brain. *Flying should be a piece of cake after this, if I make it.* Sweat ran in rivulets down the inside of his shirt. He forced himself not to panic at the thought of how high he was from the ground. Then there were hands under his armpits, another on his wrist. They dragged him over the side where he fell, exhausted, on the rooftop of the El Aksa

Mosque, at the place where it served as part of the fortress wall.

John rolled over and sat up, leaning against the wall as he sucked air into his exhausted body. *One more thing they didn't teach me in seminary*, he thought, as he braced his hands and knees and prepared to get up.

The others were looking over the side, their guns propped up against the wall. John began a stealthy crawl toward the nearest one. A voice inside him shouted, *It's your chance. Do it!* Just then, Edgar's black hand reached over the wall's top edge. Then he was pulled over the top. John stood up, his legs still shaky from climbing. He glanced again at the gun. It was not to be. Even if he saved himself, the others would never make it. And that, John knew, he could never live with.

Bob Thomas was over the top now. That left Gisele. The three men looked at each other. The same thought seemed etched in all of their faces. *Can she do it?*

John closed his eyes and silently prayed for Gisele.

When he opened them, he saw that Edgar and Bob had followed suit. They were sitting with their backs against the wall. Pasha had retrieved her weapon and stood a few paces away, facing her hostages. Yazib was leaning over the side.

John started toward the wall's edge.

"Stop!" Pasha, her voice low and threatening, lifted the gun and pointed it toward him.

John hesitated, then two more quick steps placed him next to Yazib. Yazib glanced over at him but said nothing, his attention on the woman clinging to the rope.

Gisele was struggling. Halfway up, she seemed to be running out of energy. They could see her waiting longer between letting go with one hand and crossing over the other. With about ten meters to go, she attempted to place her foot in a crack between two stones.

That morning, Gisele had decided against pants or

shorts. They were going to Jerusalem. She would wear a skirt. The multicolored, cotton skirt was lightweight and came to mid-calf. It would meet the day's requirements very nicely. She had chosen a short-sleeved cotton blouse and canvas walking shoes to complete her outfit.

Now, as she placed her foot in the crack, the toe of her shoe became entangled in the folds of her skirt. She looked down, and attempted to pull loose. That's when she saw just how far up the wall she had come.

And with that, Gisele froze!

John looked in horror at her awkward struggles. With each passing second, it became apparent that she was not going to make it. Without thinking, he reached for the tape around his head. He tore it away, pulling hair and skin at the same time. Yazib heard the sounds, but by the time he turned to John, the gag was hanging limply around his neck.

"Gisele!" he called, in a low voice. "Hang on. I'm coming to help!"

Yazib grabbed at John's shoulder to stop him, but John shrugged him off.

"You are not going anywhere!" Pasha hissed, swiftly moving forward, until the black barrel of her rifle was only inches from John's face.

"Shoot me, if you wish. You'll wake up Jerusalem if you do. That woman is my friend and I intend to go after her!" John turned to Yazib. "Is there another rope?"

Yazib shook his head. His surprised gaze never left John's face.

John let out a long, anxious breath. "Then I'll just have to do it the hard way," he said, as he threw his leg over the side.

Edgar and Bob scrambled to their feet, unable to speak, but concern filling their eyes. John gave them a smile and said, "Pray, fellas. I'll be right back."

He let himself drop over the edge into the dark shadows.

Hand over hand, he made his way down to where Gisele hung helplessly. By the time he reached her, both hands were raw and bleeding. *Don't go too fast. You'll knock her off the rope.*

Holding onto the rope as tightly as he could, he came to a stop when he gauged that he was close to her. He shoved his toes into some cracks in the wall and then looked down.

The world turned!

Dear Lord, what am I doing up here?

The height was dizzying to John. Going up, he had purposefully not looked down. Now he *had* to look down, in order to see what he was doing. What he saw made his stomach churn. His arms ached as he adjusted his grip, but the foothold gave him a brief respite, enabling the release of some tension while he got a better hold on the rope with his bloody hands. Then he looked down again.

"Gisele. Nod your head if you can hear me."

John was surprised by the sound of his own voice. It was calm, quiet, confident, the same voice he might have used in a counseling session in his office. It did not betray the fear and anxiety that flowed like molten lava into every part of his body.

Her face was against the wall, her eyes closed.

"Gisele?"

Her head moved. She nodded, but did not look up.

"I'm about four or five feet above you. I'm coming down now and when I'm right over you, I'll swing out and drop in beside you. Did you hear me?"

Her head moved again.

"Hang on tight. I may bump you, so whatever else you do, don't turn loose! Okay?"

She did not move.

John put his face against the wall and took a deep breath.

"Jesus," he whispered, "I'm all Yours now. It's just You

and me."

He moved his toes out of the cracks and slowly descended. When his feet were only inches above her head, he lowered his left hand on the rope as far as he could reach. Then he took a deep breath. Twisting away, he dropped down and in against her. He came into her harder than he had hoped. Gisele groaned with a muffled release of air on impact. In the same movement, he drove his left foot into the narrow crevice beside hers. A stab of pain shot up his leg. He threw his arm around Gisele, desperately feeling for the rope.

They hung precariously, their bodies swaying with the impact of John's movements.

Where is the rope?

His left arm ached and he felt his hand starting to slip. At last, his right hand touched the rope underneath Gisele's body. He grabbed it and hung on with every ounce of energy until they stopped swaying.

"Gisele," John whispered through gritted teeth, "we're going to make it, so hold that thought. The fellas are on top praying. Listen carefully to what I want you to do. Keep your feet where they are for now. Face me and put your arms around my neck."

She turned her face toward him.

"That's right, Gisele. Turn loose from the rope and put your arms around my neck. Hurry. Do it now. We'll apologize to Harold later for this."

John felt her body balance against his as she released one hand, then the other from the rope. Clinging to his neck, he felt her head cradle into his shoulder, her hair brush the side of his face.

"Keep planting your feet in the cracks as we move, Gisele. That will help. Don't look down, because we're going up. Push upward with your feet when you can, but mostly just don't turn loose. You're a lightweight, so I'll pull us both up really easy. Not to worry!"

Liar. You're a dead man. Your hands are torn up and your energy is used up. How do you think you are ever going to make it back to the top?

John leaned his head against the wall. Then he looked at Gisele.

"What did you say?"

She returned his look, inquisitively.

Even as he asked, he remembered the tape wrapped around her head, covering her mouth. *She didn't say anything. But I could have sworn she said, "We'll do it together."*

"Okay, Gisele. Here we go."

Okay, Lord. Come on. I need Your help.

John pulled as hard as he could. He heard himself grunting as he strained to move upward. Every ounce of energy was focused. Hand over hand. The world had become a tiny place in which only the two of them existed. It was a simple world, consisting of a few rough-hewn, centuries-old stones piled on top of each other. The stones were fighting back, resisting his efforts at overcoming them, scraping knuckles with every move. Darkness. All feeling gone. *Maybe this is it. I tried ...*

The weight. It's gone. Gisele. She must have turned loose. O God, no. I've lost her!

Strong hands were reaching under his arms ... dragging him up and over the rampart's edge for the second time ...

Almost ... almost, Gisele ... I'm ... so ... sorry ...

Then darkness fell in upon darkness!

THE RIGHT SIDE OF HIS FACE felt the blow ... No, it was the left side.

What's happening ...

John opened his eyes and saw Edgar hovering over him. His big hands were slapping first one side of John's face, then the other. A look of relief flooded his face as he saw

John coming around.

"Edgar . . ." John tried to sit up, only to slump back on the rooftop. He waited until he could gather his strength; then he rolled over and pushed himself into a kneeling position. With Edgar's help, he stood up.

Imad and Fathi were on top with the others by now. In Arabic, and with low voices, they were talking among themselves, with an occasional glance in their direction. Bob was sitting nearby, Pasha's gun pointed at him in a threatening manner. All at once, John remembered. Tears filled his eyes.

"Gisele . . ." he choked out her name. It was all he could say, remorse at his failure to rescue her flooding his emotions.

Edgar gave him a puzzled look. Suddenly he understood. He put his hand on John's shoulder and turned him around.

Gisele was sitting by herself, knees drawn up, her face buried in the folds of her skirt. She lifted her head and saw John standing there. Slowly, she rose to her feet and came toward him. Her mouth was still covered with tape. There could be no words, but her eyes, brimming with tears, said everything. She placed her head against his chest.

"I'm so glad to see you, Gisele," John whispered hoarsely. "I thought . . . I thought that I'd lost you at the very last. Thank God you are safe!"

Her arms went around him, holding onto him tightly. Then, reaching up, she touched his face with her hands. Standing on tiptoes, she drew him toward her until her adhesive-taped cheek touched his. First one side, then the other. He started to put his hands on her arms, but stopped when he saw how dirty and bloody they were. She noticed them too, as she stepped back. Staring at his hands, more tears began spilling down her cheeks.

"Don't worry, Gisele," John said. "These hands will heal fast. If there are some scars, they'll just remind me that you are alive."

"WHAT DO YOU MEAN, 'An empty bus'?" Elijah Pazer leaned forward in his chair, gripping the edge of his desk so hard that the knuckles of both hands turned white.

"Just what I said, Eli. It's confirmed. An Israel Tours bus was reported missing this evening at 2145. The group was more than two hours overdue for dinner at their hotel. The manager finally contacted the tour company. They had no word of any problem, so they called the Salt Sea Hotel & Spa in Ein Bokek. The group stayed there last night. The hotel manager told the agency that the bus left around 1630. No one noticed anything out of the ordinary. That was the last anyone saw of them, until about twenty minutes ago."

"So what happened twenty minutes ago?" Elijah Pazer inquired of his young associate.

"IDF reported the sighting of an empty bus parked along Silwan Road near the Gihon Spring."

"Any signs of life?"

"None."

"No explosives involved?"

"They weren't sure at first, so they brought in the bomb squad. As it turns out, there was nothing."

"Well, an entire busload of tourists just can't have disappeared!" Eli exclaimed. "How many people are supposed to be in the group?"

"Twenty-five, plus the guide and driver."

Just then the phone rang. Eli picked up the receiver. "Halo!"

The young man watched nervously as Eli's face grew somber. "Todah, le-hitra'ot." he said at last, putting the receiver down slowly, while staring at the desk.

"Eli?" Even though Benjamin Hertzel was a generation younger than his commanding officer, he felt free to call him by his first name. It was often this way in Israel, where there were more open collars than ties, and informality was a way of life. In this unique land, respect was earned, not simply accorded to someone because of age or position.

"They found the driver of your bus, Ben. Tied, taped, and stuffed unconscious under a pile of laundry in a maid's room at the Salt Sea Hotel." Eli rose from his chair and walked around the desk. "So they sent someone up to check each of the rooms that the group members had used. They were all empty . . . except for the guide's room. It was David Barak. I know him . . . *knew* him. My wife and I had dinner with his family two weeks ago."

Eli's young associate was silent, shocked by what he knew was coming, waiting as Eli struggled to continue.

"He's dead. They found his body with three bullet holes."

The young man swore softly.

"That means . . . "

"That means," Eli interrupted, "twenty-five American tourists are somewhere in this city, held captive, or maybe they're even dead by now, 'offed' by some hotshot Arab terrorist. Only God knows. This looks like an unholy mess!"

"So what shall we do?"

"Put out the word. Close the city down. Tight! Shut down all routes in or out. Lock up the borders in the morning. Call in all off-duty personnel. Oh . . . and impound that bus!"

"The bus is already secure," Ben replied, writing the instructions on a notepad, using the same ancient Hebrew script as had been used centuries earlier by lawkeepers in King David's day.

"Good. Have it dusted. We probably won't get anything worthwhile, but do it anyway."

"Done. Anything else?"

"Yeah. See if the travel company has any pictures. I'll pass the word along to the chief. He'll probably want to contact the Man."

"The Minister? This early in the process?"

"Yeah." Eli walked over to take his jacket from off the wall hook. "There's more to this than you know, Ben. I took a call around eight o'clock from Mossad HQ. They had just been contacted by the NSC in Washington about a hostage situation out in California. Some terrorist nuts who claim to be members of the PIJ have got five hundred people rounded up in a church in the Bay Area."

Following his superior to the door, the younger man suddenly stopped.

"Did you say the Bay Area? In California?"

"Yeah," Eli turned and looked at his assistant. "What?"

"That's where the group in the bus is from."

"Say what?"

"Baytown. They're from a place called Baytown, somewhere near San Francisco."

Eli paused, then began walking slowly down the hallway, toward the situation room. His mind was racing.

"Eli," a female voice called out from behind them. "Another message from Mossad HQ."

The uniformed woman's heels clicked on the marble floor as she walked across the hall and handed a piece of paper to Eli. He scanned it swiftly, then looked up at Ben.

"Now the word from Washington is that Boston has received a threat from terrorists. They claim that they're going to cover the city with anthrax spores if the USA doesn't put the screws on Israel to meet their demands."

"Are they taking it seriously?"

"One person is already dead; others are in the hospital. Anthrax was confirmed to be the killing agent. Apparently some people were chosen at random, nearly as the police can tell, to provide a little demonstration proving these killers have the power and intend to use it. Anthrax! Good grief, man. That stuff's lethal enough to kill everyone for miles around and for years to come, if they actually release it."

"Do you think this is tied together?"

"Is our Father's name Abraham? Let's go. We've got work to do!"

THIRTY-THREE

Light and shadows.

No guards appeared to be on the rooftop tonight. John was not sure whether to be disappointed or relieved. He knew their lives were inconsequential to their captors. What he did not know was why such a great effort had been made, with extra chances being taken, to get them into the Old City. He couldn't figure what they wanted. It would have been much easier for them to climb the wall without these inexperienced Americans.

Imad, Fathi, and Pasha were crouched together, engaged in animated discussion with Yazib, under cover of the darkest shadows of Al Aqsa's circular, silver-capped dome. The tone of their voices was subdued but intense, and the language of the moment was Arabic. John could not understand what they were saying.

Yazib shook his head vehemently. Then he turned and spoke to John in English.

"You must continue to do exactly as you are told. Do you understand?"

"I want my friends to have their gags removed," John countered.

"Impossible."

"No. It's not impossible. We refuse to move further until you take the tape from their mouths!"

Yazib stared through the dark shadows at John.

"You are an interesting man, Reverend Cain. And a brave one too. Is this woman your . . . " he nodded toward Gisele, grinning " . . . special friend?"

"I understand what you are implying and the answer is no. She is not my special friend."

"Why else would you risk your life for her?"

"She is a member of my church. She and I have two things in common. We are human beings and we are Christian friends. That is our relationship."

Yazib continued looking at him, his eyes gleaming in the starlight.

"They might call out."

"I assure you, upon my word, we will not call out."

"Your word," sneered Yazib. "The word of an American infidel pastor to a soldier of the Holy War? It is not much."

"It is all we have remaining."

"This is true." Yazib pulled the revolver from his belt and touched the barrel against John's lips. "You make a single sound and you're a dead man. Furthermore, I assure you, the woman will die more slowly than you *and* more painfully!"

John nodded, feeling both apprehension and triumph.

"Cut off the gags," Yazib motioned to Fathi.

Fathi shifted about so that he could follow orders, though a look of concern crossed his face. He slipped a wicked-looking combat knife from its sheath. Gisele shuddered when the cold steel touched her neck. A moment later, the tape was cut. She began pulling it away from her face and hair, grimacing as it came loose. The others followed suit.

When Fathi finally stood in front of John, knife in hand, their eyes locked. Then he cut the tape that hung loosely around John's neck.

"Put the tape in here," ordered Fathi. He held out his open backpack. "We do not want to leave anything lying around, do we?"

John dropped the gag material into the bag.

"Come. Follow me and do exactly what I do. Our guns will be trained on you and ready to use if you do anything out of the ordinary."

"You've made your point," John retorted.

Yazib moved out of the shadows of the dome. Bending low, he strode swiftly over the rooftop, careful not to get close to the wall's edge where they could more easily be seen from below. The others followed after him in single file.

John felt a strange sensation of deja vu as they walked across Al Aqsa's rooftop. The familiarity of these surroundings was uncanny. He had been inside this large, rather plain mosque on several occasions. Plain, that is, in comparison to the eye-catching Dome of the Rock situated just off to their right, with its gold-leaf aluminium dome rising majestically over the Kubbet es-Sakhra, the sacred rock on which Abraham prepared the sacrifice of his son, Isaac. This same rock is the place from which, during his mystical journey to Jerusalem, Mohammed is said to have mounted his steed and ascended into heaven. The great Dome was magnificent tonight, silent, with not a soul in sight.

Directly underneath them, Al Aqsa was a vast complex, accommodating up to five thousand worshipers at one time and serving essentially as a prayer hall. Many believe that it was built on the remains of an ancient Byzantine basilica. Below this are the huge underground chambers of Solomon's Stables. John remembered some Jewish friends calling it Midrash Shlomo, the School of King Solomon.

John looked across to where, in a few hours, hundreds of

Muslim worshipers would stop at the fountain in front of the mosque. There the people would ready themselves for prayer by ceremonially washing head, hands, and feet. Once inside, they would prostrate themselves until their foreheads touched the carpeted floor, in acknowledgment of the majesty of Allah. Tonight, however, it was quiet, a cavernous chamber listening to the sounds of the intruders' footfalls on its strictly off-limits roof as they made their way to the edge.

Without hesitating, as though he had done this many times before, Yazib slipped over the wall and dropped to the roof of the Islamic Museum, a long, rectangular structure attached to the west side of the mosque and holding exhibits depicting the many centuries of Muslim life in Jerusalem.

About three-quarters of the way along the roof, facing into the vast esplanade known as Haram esh Sharif, the Venerable Sanctuary, the slender, lofty tower of a minaret pointed the way to a Muslim heaven. Near the top was a square balcony covered by a miniature dome, marking the place where the muezzin stood and called the people to prayer each day at sunrise, midday, afternoon, sunset, and evening, reciting the Adhan.

Allah u Akbar.
God is greater.
God is greater.
I witness that there is no god but God.
I witness that Mohammad is the prophet of God.
Rise to prayer.
Rise to felicity.
God is greater.
God is greater.
There is no god but God.

As a Westerner, John had felt the mystery of the call of the minaret the first time he had come to Israel. His soul-

expanding emotions were tempered somewhat by the discovery that the ancient "mystery" had succumbed to modern technology. In most minarets, an electronic recording
has long since taken the place of the muezzin.

John followed Yazib, dropping down onto the museum
rooftop and waiting while the others followed. The strain of
the past few hours was starting to take its toll. John was
exhausted. Still, adrenaline flowed from some unknown reservoir as he watched Yazib motioning to the others. He signaled for quiet as they walked to the edge of the roof and
looked out upon the esplanade. Responding to another hand
motion, they dropped onto their stomachs and peered over
the edge into the area below.

Haram esh-Sharif, known to Jews and Christians as
Mount Moriah or the Temple Mount, stretched out before
them, a fantasy of long shadows and moonlit plazas. John
understood that they were looking down at a locale with the
potential of igniting the religious and political passions of a
billion people around the world. Tonight, however, it was a
place of quiet gardens, where a gentle breeze sighed its way
through tall trees.

The narrow Morrolo Gate, one of two gates through
which tourists could enter the Haram during the day, was
closed and under guard. Patrols of plainclothes Muslim
guards, uniformed Arab police, and IDF soldiers maintained
security. Tonight, as on other nights, they watched. But no
one could be seen moving about.

Yazib attached the grappling hook to a lip that protruded
from the roof. Next he threw the line over the side and
quickly rappeled to the ground. John went next. One by one
the others followed. Then, with a flip of the wrist that would
have made Clint Eastwood proud, Fathi snapped the rope in
a manner that caused the hook to release and fall to the
ground.

"Come, quickly," whispered Yazib, sounds of danger and

excitement cracking his voice. He ran to the southeast corner of Al Aqsa mosque. John recognized this to be the area
identified by tradition as the site of the ancient Temple's
pinnacle. Here, tradition said, Jesus was tempted by the devil. John had not been here before, because it was off limits to
the general public.

They hurried down a stairway leading to a solid, wooden
door, one that was always locked and could be opened only
by an official of the Supreme Muslim Council. Well, almost
always. Yazib pushed on the door. Whoever had turned the
key earlier had done well. It opened immediately and the
small group of captors and captives crowded inside.

They were in a large underground room. Damp, musty
odors greeted them in the darkness. Yazib produced a flashlight that revealed a few of the dozen pillars supporting the
esplanade above. They walked across the room to the far
side. At first, John did not see it. Not until they drew close
did he become aware of a door tucked in behind one of the
pillars. Yazib pulled it open far enough for everyone to
squeeze through, closing it after the last person was inside.

He ran his flashlight back and forth until it revealed a
single, bare bulb and a pull-chain. Reaching up, he pulled it
and dim light filled the room. John guessed the room to be
about twelve by fifteen feet in size. Two of the walls were
cement. The other two had been roughed in by carpenters
more intent on finishing in a hurry than they were on quality
of craftsmanship. Bare boards, no insulation, and no windows. It gave the appearance of having been thrown
together, probably quite recently. A makeshift room built for
one purpose alone. And they were it.

There was a table, four chairs, and three beds. The beds
were outfitted with blankets and mattresses. A stack of
bread, cheese, and several bottles of mineral water heaped
in a pile on the table by an unknown benefactor reminded
John of the fact that it had been many hours since any of

them had eaten. Chains that looked to be six or eight feet in length were attached to one of the walls. Each was fitted with a steel ankle bracelet. A crude bucket at the far side of the room was also filled with water. John recognized its purpose, though the other Americans did not.

"Sit down," Yazib commanded, motioning toward the chairs. "This is where we will remain for the next few hours."

"Why did you bring us with you?" John asked, standing near Yazib.

"Patience, Reverend Cain. You will be made aware of everything in due time." In spite of the coolness of the room, Yazib wiped perspiration from his brow as he turned his attention back to his team of kidnappers and killers. He spoke to them in Arabic.

"Congratulations. We have done well, my friends. We have crossed the desert and the sea. We have entered, undetected, into the heart of the land that belongs to our people. Praise belongs to Allah."

His teammates nodded.

"He has enabled us to do what others thought impossible," Yazib continued, "by bringing us safely into the Sacred Zone. Now we wait. Our brothers are at work, tightening the noose around America's neck. By this time, the world has awakened to its danger and its responsibility. We can no longer be ignored. They will be forced to meet our demands or mortgage their own future!"

Imad and Fathi smiled as they took in the words of their leader. Pasha's eyes were on Yazib, but her face was a mask. John could not tell what emotions were gathering there. He wished he could understand what they were saying.

In English Yazib said, "These two beds are for use by the Americans. Imad. Fathi. Move the one on the right away from the others. We will use it. We will do guard shifts of four-hour duration. You two will be first. Pasha and I will remain here with the Americans. I want one of you just outside this door. The other will stay nearer the outside entrance. Hide behind a pillar. If someone should come, do nothing unless absolutely necessary. We must keep our presence unknown as long as possible. Understand?"

Heads nodded.

"In four hours, come and wake us. We will spell each other this way."

"Some of us need to relieve ourselves," John mentioned, as the others prepared to leave.

"I regret the absence of the privacy to which you are accustomed, Reverend Cain. You may go outside, in the large room, one at a time. These two will be with you," he said, glancing over at Imad and Fathi. "Take the bucket."

Gisele looked at John, puzzled.

"There is no toilet paper," said John. "This doesn't appear to be a five-star facility."

The puzzled look faded into a stare of incredulity, followed by a shrug of resignation and a tight smile. It was a moment for earthy humor. Unfortunately, the seriousness of their plight did not permit its full exercise. Gisele picked up the bucket and gamely followed the two guards out the door.

Yazib looked at John.

"You and the others may take turns when she returns. You see the chains attached to the wall? As you return, you will be fettered with those. Pasha will personally see that they are securely locked around your ankles. Then I believe we should all try to get some sleep. Do you agree?"

John said nothing.

"All right. Pasha, break open some food and water while I move these packs nearer to the table. And please, gentlemen, relax and rest." He looked at the three of them, his countenance suddenly hard and unyielding. "Do not even think about escaping. I am sorry. For you there can be no escape."

His words struck John with forboding finality. He looked over at the others. Their faces mirrored his own fears. John knew that Yazib's threat, veiled in polite conversation, had not escaped their attention.

Just then, Gisele stepped through the door opening. "Next?" she said, offering a weak smile to the men.

"Shortly after ten o'clock this morning, gunmen invaded the worship service at Calvary Church in Baytown, California. Authorities have moved rapidly to close off the area surrounding the church. Both local police and the FBI are working toward the resolution of what is being viewed as an extremely dangerous situation.

"As you can see, a large crowd has gathered near the Communications Center at the far side of this parking lot. We are told that many are church members who were on their way to the eleven o'clock service. Some are friends and relatives of those inside the building. Many appear to have come from the surrounding area, drawn to this macabre scene by the extraordinary media coverage, of which we are a part. CNN has a long-standing news arrangement with San Francisco's KFOR . . ."

"Honey, come here. You're not going to believe what is happening!" CNN's *Travel to Europe* had been interrupted moments earlier with the special news bulletin.

" . . . as a part of the negotiation process, network coverage around the world has been agreed upon by officials at the Command Center, located in that recreational vehicle you see on the right-hand side of your screen, and by a consortium of network news bureaus. Our news staff is at the church right now to bring us the latest developments. Off-duty fire department emergency crews and law enforcement personnel in Baytown have been requested to report immediately to their duty stations. This is Ann Stewart at CNN. We'll be going live to the scene just moments from now."

"ABC NEWS IS TAKING YOU live to Baytown, California, an East Bay suburban community, where gunmen have taken hostage an entire congregation of several hundred people . . . "

"THIS IS A SPECIAL CBS news bulletin. I'm David Shaw. We are going direct at this hour to Baytown, California, where earlier today an undetermined number of gunmen took an entire church congregation hostage during one of their worship services. Little is known at this moment but Sherry Ellison of station KGNA is at the site. Sherry, what can you tell us about this situation?"

"Well, David, at approximately ten o'clock this morning . . . "

"OUR NBC affiliate KFOR in San Francisco is joining us in a national hookup, as we abandon our regularly scheduled programs and focus coverage on one of the most bizarre acts of terrorism ever perpetrated on our shores. Several gunmen, believed to be of Arab nationality, are currently holding hundreds hostage in a church in Baytown,

California. We are going live now to KFOR news anchor, Tom Bernstein."

"Hello, everyone. A quiet Sunday morning in the East Bay suburb of Baytown has been shattered by the staccato of gunfire. At least one parishioner is dead. Calvary Church is an interdenominational church that has served its community and the surrounding area for more than thirty years. This is what we know at present. At about ten o'clock this morning . . . "

AGENT WEBBER shook his head as he watched the additional monitors disgorging details of the crisis he faced as the FBI's Special-Agent-in-Charge. It had to be done. But he didn't like it. Score one for the bad guys. This eruption of coverage across the globe was not going to make his task easier. It was, however, the currency needed to buy more time. And time was what he desperately needed.

The RV door opened and Special Agent Hendrickson poked his head inside.

"We've got a couple of ideas, boss. Take your pick." Hendrickson was holding a partially folded blueprint of the church building in his hand.

"Let's take a look," Webber said, motioning the SWAT commander inside.

AKMED WAS NEARING THE END of his rambling oratory that included a list of demands directed at the United States, the UN, and Israel. He had been standing in front of the cameras for forty minutes. His gun was leaning against the platform chair, next to the one he'd been sitting in before he began his "Conversation with the World," as he so modestly put it.

At each door, small groups of ten to fifteen people sat

huddled on the carpeted floor. A few, weary of the strain and discomfort, leaned against the ends of pews or fell back onto the floor itself. Directly in front of the central entrance, thirteen people had been herded into position as human fodder in case of a surprise attack.

Earlier, everyone had been required to pass purses, wallets, keys, and any other personal belongings to the aisle. These were gathered up under the supervision of the woman they called Aziza. The considerable volume of items was piled indiscriminately in the altar area between the platform and the first pews.

As people divested themselves of their possessions, all men wearing suit jackets had been made to stand and open them, confirming to their captors that no dangerous weapons remained hidden. None had been confiscated, but none had been anticipated. Still, through this systematic and thorough process, the entire congregation had been relieved of credit cards, car keys, make-up, checkbooks . . . everything that would normally be carried to church by normal parishioners.

Everything, that is, except for one item held by one person.

That person reclined on the carpet, propped up on an elbow, in the center of the group. She had kept her secret to herself. And, now, she had made up her mind that it was time to put it to use.

While observing the confiscation procedure, Connie Farrer had slipped a weapon of sorts from her purse and pushed it under the folds of her full skirt. She had been carrying it for the past five weeks, ever since landing her new job. Before she was made to go to the back of the sanctuary and take up a position at the door, she had secured it under the belted portion of her skirt, making it possible to carry unobtrusively.

She looked around and took stock of her situation.

The strikingly beautiful, female terrorist stood barely a half-dozen paces away. In addition, there were two young children, five men and six women surrounding her in the group. The children concerned her the most. If they saw what she was about to do . . . *can't think about that. Just do it!*

Connie sucked in her waist and tugged on the hidden item. A quick glance around, just to be sure. She slipped it out and pushed it under the arch of her arm and shoulder. She could feel her heart beating against *her weapon of choice!* Nervously, she ran her fingers over the buttons until she was sure of their position. Then she began punching in the numbers she had only recently committed to memory.

Pause.

The muffled sound of the cellular phone startled the person next to her. He jumped, then slowly turned his head until he could see her out of the corner of his eye. Connie's heart skipped a beat as she glanced up at the woman with the gun. She evidently had heard nothing. In fact, she seemed totally absorbed in the speech that her leader was giving, momentarily allowing her attention to be distracted from the group huddled on her left.

Perfect, thought Connie, as the phone rang the third time.

"Hello. Jody Ansel here."

Connie froze, then quickly punched down the volume. She looked over at the Arab woman. She was still watching the man next to her.

"Hello. Can I help you?"

"Jody, it's Connie," she whispered.

"Hello. This is Jody Ansel. I can hardly hear you. Can you speak up?"

"Jody. It's Connie Farrer."

"I'm sorry. We're very busy now and I can't hear what you are saying. Can you call back later?"

A stab of fear sliced through Connie's stomach.

She's going to hang up. No! Don't! Please!

Connie leaned forward until her mouth was almost touching the instrument cradled on the floor, beneath her arm.

"This is Connie Farrer."

"Connie. Where are you?"

Thank God, she's recognized me!

Hers was the name and voice of the newest kid on the block. Connie had been afraid that Jody Ansel might not even remember her. They had talked briefly only a few times since Connie had gone to work for the station. Her feeling of relief was overwhelming.

Get control of yourself, Connie.

"I'm in church."

"In church?" she heard Jody repeat . . . then followed a long pause. Her voice took on a new, quieter tone, when she spoke again. "You mean *the* church? You're at Calvary in Baytown?"

"Yes," Connie whispered.

"Oh, my . . . ," she heard Jody swear softly. "Just a minute, Connie."

Connie could hear muffled sounds of conversation. Then a male voice.

"Connie, this is Tom. Are you okay?"

She looked about her. Others in the group had become aware of her whispers into her armpit. There were looks of concern and fear on their faces.

"In a manner of speaking," she whispered.

"What can you tell me?"

"Not much. Talking is dangerous. I'm only a few feet from one of the terrorists. There are five altogether. Four men. One woman. We are stacked in front of the doors to discourage rescue attempts. They aren't fooling. The doors are set to blow. One guy is already dead."

"We're getting pictures from inside the auditorium,

Connie. We're on NBC now. Plus CNN. I still can't believe we've got a reporter *inside* the church!"

"Believe. And answer the phone next time on the first ring. Got to go." Connie flipped off the cellular phone and returned it to its private hiding place in the folds of her skirt. As she did, a drop of perspiration surprised her as it fell into the crease of her eye.

She wiped it away.

"BUT, YOU'VE GOT TO GO WITH IT, Tom. So far the word has been that *four* terrorists are holed up in that church. Now, we know there are not just four. *There are five!* This is incredible! We have someone inside. With a phone, no less! We'll absolutely scoop everyone else!"

Betty Filtcher, the station's senior vice-president, was standing in front of Tom Bernstein, her back to the eyes of the three large robo-cams that stared vacantly at the newsdesk. No matter. At the moment, KFOR was showing the live feed coming from inside the church, with a voice-over interview between Tom Brokaw and Dr. Al Zenbari, a UC professor at Berkeley with expertise in Middle-East history and culture.

"What we should do is let the FBI know what we know." Tom was looking not at Betty but at Jody. Jody nodded in agreement.

"No!" Betty's voice rose slightly, fists clinched at her side.

Every hair remained in place. Her makeup was classically faultless. The royal-blue suit and burgundy blouse didn't have so much as a wrinkle that showed. Only her fists revealed anything other than perfect control.

And her eyes.

Her eyes were a shade too close together and when she became angry, they narrowed, giving her face a squinty, hard sort of look. It was the only uncontrolled reflex Jody had ever noticed her making, and then, only on those rarest of occasions. Like right now. Jody couldn't help but wonder how Betty could put herself together like this on such short notice, and whether or not the woman ever perspired.

Tom Bernstein, on the other hand, didn't look a bit better than when he had jogged in a few hours ago. His shirt was still open and his five-o'clock shadow looked more like seven or eight. His sandy hair was tousled and appeared as though he had jumped out of bed and never put a comb through it. Which, of course, was exactly what had happened.

It was another reason that Jody liked Tom. His was an honest face for the moment at hand. His unkempt look sent a message of urgency and sincerity to the viewing audience. He reminded her of Dan Rather during the days of Desert Storm. Tom made the audience come together around their television sets. He connected with them. They identified with him. This man could be their husband, brother, or father. Right now, he was all of these and more. He was their link to a world that was both familiar and strange. Most of them had been to church before. But no one had been to church with terrorists!

"No," Betty said again, quickly regaining her composure, fists unclenched. "Not yet. Not until you've done your job, Tom. And your job is the news! We've got her number. Call her back. Find out what's really happening inside that place. Then report it. Don't you understand what's happening here, Tom? We've been scraping the bottom of the ratings barrel for a solid year. Finally, it's our turn! "

Jody saw their eyes lock in battle. It was going to be very interesting to see who would win this war of power and restraint.

"Betty, if we go on the air with this now and the terrorists see it, we will put that girl's life in danger. To say nothing of the others. This is a delicate situation, not just a news piece. She risked a lot just to get in touch with us." Tom glanced up at the monitor. "Look at the pile of stuff they've lifted from the rest of those poor souls. Somehow, she kept her cellular hidden. If they find out who she is and that she's been in contact with us, who knows what they'll do to her?"

Jody could feel Tom's identification with the pictures on the monitor; his mental absorption with the circumstance and the people. She knew that this uncanny ability of his to "feel a story" was what set him apart from so many other newspeople.

"Then, what good is she to us, if we don't use the stuff she gives us?" KFOR's senior vice-president spat back at her chief anchor.

"We're on again in ten," floor director Matt Hershey's big voice came booming through the tenseness surrounding the studio desk.

"Just do it!" ordered Betty, staring down at Bernstein's lined face. She opened her immaculately manicured hands in a gesture of disgust. "And for goodness sake, get some makeup on. They can't see your eyebrows, Tom!"

"Five, four, three ... "

Matt's fingers kept falling with the count.

His eyebrows? Jody wanted to laugh and hit her at the same time. *All of this and you're concerned about the man's eyebrows?*

"Two, one!"

"We're back in San Francisco again." Tom Bernstein's unshaven face filled the screen.

Betty's right about one thing, mused Jody, her eyes on the monitor. *It is hard to see his eyebrows.*

"You've been listening to a discussion between Tom Brokaw and Dr. Al Zenbari, Middle Eastern expert and professor at the University of California in nearby Berkeley. We continue to bring you live coverage of this morning's unprecedented takeover of a church's worship service by Arab terrorists.

"The number of hostages, claimed by a terrorist spokesman inside the building, has been set at four hundred eighty-seven. One is known dead. There is no word as to that person's identity, although the victim appears to be male. There is word that two persons have escaped from the church sanctuary and an unknown number of children, together with their adult teaching staff, have been rescued from Sunday School classrooms located in the building.

" 'Sanctuary' is a word that usually describes a protected place of refuge. A house of worship. Today, however, the sanctuary at Calvary Church in Baytown, California has been turned from a haven of tranquility into a house of terror.

"At the scene now, the church parking lot, is Sandra Marshall. What's the latest from your vantage point, Sandra?"

"Tom, the only word that can adequately describe this situation is ... "

Betty Filtcher, senior vice-president, stomped away, furious.

Tom Bernstein, KFOR's chief anchor, remained in a quandary.

Jody Ansel, assistant news director, felt guilty.

She was glad to see someone stand up to Betty Filtcher. God knows she'd wanted to do it herself many times. She felt a growing concern over Connie Farrer's life-and-death situation. Connie was young and new in the business, and could easily make a tragic mistake. But these were not the reasons Jody was feeling guilty.

The real reason was that this had turned into the most exciting day of Jody Ansel's entire career. And she loved it!

JIM "GRANDPA" BRAINARD stared at the television.

The night before, an FBI agent had deposited him at the Sonesta Hotel, along the banks of the Charles River. Get some sleep, he'd been told. He was tired all right. And despondent. When he let his thoughts return to Booth Bay, it was not his beautiful Hill House that filled his mind. First, it was Rosa. Then came the faces of the murderers of this beautiful child who had been the daughter he'd never had.

Now as he watched the news from California, he became angry. *How dare these people disrupt society as we know it? Why don't they just leave us alone? What ever did we do to them? What will they attempt to do next?* He wanted to turn off the television. Go to bed. Get some sleep. But he couldn't.

By Sunday evening, the networks were all giving round-the-clock coverage. CNN and NBC were coordinating efforts somehow. It was beyond Grandpa's understanding; he recognized that television news was a medium of tremendous power. No wonder the Arab in that church was determined to get air time. This kind of coverage was unprecedented. There had been nothing to equal it since Desert Storm.

He was watching NBC. Tom Brokaw had just finished interviewing some professor of Middle Eastern affairs from Berkeley. Now the San Francisco anchor, Tom Bernstein, was back. Grandpa liked this young man. He guessed him to be in his late thirties.

Pretty sensitive when it comes to reporting. Doesn't pander to the sensational. Maybe his station manager has put the screws on him. Who knows? I like the guy, though. Doesn't look like he's taken the time to shave all day. Wonder how long he can stay with this without being spelled off? Looks tired. There is something disconcerting about the man too. What is it?

He watched the newscaster closely.

Maybe it's his eyebrows. You can hardly make them out.

THIRTY-FIVE

John leaned his head back against the makeshift wall and looked up at the light bulb. It couldn't be more than forty watts, he decided. The low wattage and the dust that clung to the bulb resulted in a room that was, at best, dimly lit.

Yazib and Pasha lay close together on the bed farthest away, her back turned toward him, his arm thrown across her waist. Yazib's heavy breathing confirmed that he was sleeping soundly.

John sat on the floor, knees pulled up as a headrest. He was between the two beds designated for the prisoners. His body ached. His face was bruised and cut from the beatings on the bus. He was sure that a cheekbone was broken. His hands were raw from the wall climb. Every muscle in his body cried out in frustration over the way they had been treated during the last many hours.

Gisele Eiderman occupied one of the beds. Edgar and Bob had argued with John over who would use the other. John insisted that he was fine and that if he wanted to sleep, he would do so on the bed Gisele was using.

In actuality, however, he had no intention of doing so. The beds were not large and two people would inevitably touch in their sleep. John felt such contact would be embarrassing to them both. Holding on to each other while climbing the wall of the Old City was one thing. That had been a matter of necessity, of life and death. Sleeping on the same bed was something else. He could not bring himself to do it.

Besides, he had discovered something. Where his chain was attached to the wall there was a small crack in the cement. John decided that the cement work was probably recent. After the others had fallen asleep, he tried to wiggle the fixture. At first, there was nothing. Then, just as he was about to give up, a small piece of sand and cement broke loose and fell to the floor. Heartened, he continued his efforts with renewed energy, checking every so often to be sure his captors were still sleeping.

Both Edgar and Bob were stretched out in the deep sleep of exhaustion. They each had an eight foot chain securely fastened to one leg.

John looked over at Gisele, huddled in fetal form near the far edge of the bed. She too wore the ankle chain. As he watched, she shivered, whether from the cold or from the stress of the day's events, he could not tell. John scooted along the floor until he reached one of the blankets at the foot of the bed. Unfolding it, he carefully laid it over her shoulders. She stirred, but did not awaken.

"Pastor John?"

John looked over.

"Pastor John, either you get up on that bed or I'll do it myself."

John shook his head and smiled briefly. "Keep talking, Edgar. Your words are long, but your chain is too short. You couldn't, even if you wanted to."

"John, there's nothin' immoral or immodest about you

gettin' up on that bed and gettin' some sleep. The rest of us need you to be at your best and you ain't goin' to be if you keep sittin' down there. Now, what's it goin' to be? Either you get up there or I'm movin' over."

John grinned sheepishly.

"You know me like a book, don't you?"

"It ain't hard to read a book with large print, Pastor John."

"Or blank pages," John added ruefully.

He looked up from where he was sitting, sighed, and then pulled himself up until he was sitting on the edge of the mattress. Carefully, so as not to awaken Gisele, he lay down. Slowly, he stretched out and let himself relax. Every bone in his body affirmed that this was a decision well made.

"Good night, Pastor John."

"Good night, Edgar."

ALL FOUR PRISONERS were sound asleep when the changing of the guard took place. Had they been awake, they would have seen Yazib and Pasha check the contents of the backpack on the table to make certain everything they needed was there. Had they been awake, they would have been impressed, even awed, with what they saw.

Several compact packages containing powerful explosives; a detonator; and a collapsible, telescopic device with a magnet on one end and a release button on the other.

Yazib replaced the items in the bag and threw it over his shoulder. With one arm, he gave Pasha an affectionate hug. Their heads touched briefly. Then they went out together.

SUNDAY, 1635 LOCAL TIME
BAYTOWN, CALIFORNIA

"I'VE JUST BEEN HANDED this special news bulletin." Tom Bernstein paused, then looked off camera. "Are we certain of this?"

The voice of a woman could be heard in the background. "The White House confirmed it five minutes ago."

Bernstein turned back to the camera.

"Earlier today, terrorist spokesman Akmed el Hussein indicated that in addition to the hostages being held in Baytown, California's Calvary Church since approximately ten o'clock this morning, other terrorist activities are underway elsewhere. He specifically mentioned Israel as a target.

"It has now been confirmed by the Israeli government that an American tour group visiting in that country for the past seven days is missing. An Israel Tours bus was found abandoned near the entrance to the Gihon Springs, just outside the Old City in Jerusalem. Further investigation has determined that this same bus left a hotel near the Dead Sea at about four-thirty this afternoon. That would have been eight-thirty this morning, here on the West Coast. Lending a further bizarre twist to this day's incredible events, authorities in Israel have confirmed that the missing group is being led by Dr. John Cain, the senior minister of Calvary Church!"

Bernstein paused, rubbing at the side of his cheekbone.

"This is unbelievable. Authorities in Jerusalem have heard nothing from any member of the group, nor from any would-be kidnappers. However, Israel Tours in Tel Aviv has verified that there are twenty-five persons in the group, including Dr. Cain. All of them are missing. It seems they have simply disappeared. Vanished!"

He sagged back into his chair, sighed, then looked straight into the camera.

"It doesn't take a genealogical researcher to determine that with a name like Bernstein, my roots and heritage are Jewish. Both my wife, Ruth, and I are proud to be American-born Jews. A little over a year ago, we visited Israel for the first time. When we arrived there, we witnessed a small group of Yemenite Jews at the airport, in the process of entering their new homeland. Yemenites. Russian Jews. Jews from Poland and Hungary. Even Jews from the United States. All coming to Israel because it is their homeland.

"I remember that moment as if it were yesterday. As a Jew, I tell you it was a strange, discomforting feeling. Ruth and I are Americans. We've always been and always will be. I served for six years in the Marine Corps. We pay our taxes and complain about it, like everyone else. We're proud to be Americans.

"But my heart went out to these people, many of them with nothing more than what they had on their backs. Happy to be in a place they could call their own. A little piece of the world's dirt, not much larger than the Greater San Francisco Bay Area. I can tell you, it was hard for these two Americans to fully comprehend.

"Later, we followed these people to the Western Wall, the most sacred spot on earth for Jewish people. Ruth and I watched as they stood for a long time with their eyes closed and faces within inches of the Wall, bodies swaying back and forth, prayers being offered to God. Then I went to the Wall. I wrote out my little prayer on a piece of paper and stuck it in a crevice between two stones. It was an indescribable feeling for me to stand there, where thousands of other Jews have stood throughout the years. To know that I belonged.

"I walked back to where Ruth was waiting and we held hands together for a long time. We offered up prayers for the peace of Jerusalem. Tonight..." his voice faltered. He rubbed his eyes with the back of his hand.

"Tonight..." he repeated, clearing his throat, "it all seems so long ago and far away. What we have seen today is not an answer to our prayer. It is instead the prelude to our worst nightmare."

Bernstein opened his mouth to continue. Then, as if he

suddenly remembered where he was, he leaned forward, eyes filled with a sadness that fully transferred into the minds of millions of viewers.

"This is Tom Bernstein reporting from San Francisco. I'll be back in a moment."

It was quiet on the set.

Off camera, Jody wiped at her eyes.

Sally choked back a sob and ran toward the restroom.

Betty sat on the edge of a nearby desk, watching, unaware that she was chewing her carefully manicured nails.

Upstairs in the control room, the director had been momentarily caught off guard. He was absorbed by Bernstein's sudden, heartfelt expression of personal feelings. Now he moved quickly to fade the newsroom from the screen. He punched up KFOR's signature and viewers heard a voice-over say, "You've been watching KFOR's twenty-four-hour news coverage of today's hostage crisis in Baytown, California. In a moment, we'll continue. Stay tuned."

It was an unnecessary command.

Tom Bernstein's emotion-packed comments had riveted NBC and CNN viewers to their television screens across America and around the world.

"TOM, YOU DESERVE A BREAK in the action." The floor director was leaning over the desk, looking sympathetically at his favorite anchor. "Go lie down for a while."

"I'm tired, but I'm okay. Let's keep going."

"You're starting to crack, Tom," Betty Filtcher chimed in. "That last bit was too personal. Not objective enough. You probably just ran off all of KFOR's Arab audience with your remarks."

Tom looked at KFOR's senior vice-president in charge. His eyes shot sparks of anger.

"Get off my back, Betty. I'm fine. I expressed some personal feelings, that's all. It doesn't hurt our viewing audience to know that their news team has feelings. Once in a great while, it's okay not to come off like some wooden Indian! And I suppose you'll say *that's* a racist comment, guaranteed to wipe out our native American viewing audience. Get a life, Betty!"

Tension crackled like electricity between the two super egos of KFOR.

At that very moment, a small man in work clothes came around the desk and walked up to Tom. Hesitantly, he reached out a bronzed hand, his dark eyes brimming with emotion.

"Mr. Bernstein, my name is Beni Hamill. I am called in today, especially for purposes of security. They say for me to lock the doors downstairs and double-check everybody coming in. Paulo and I have been doing this all day. We watch you just now on monitors downstairs. I asked Paulo could I come up to tell you that I am also sad today? He say yes.

"I am from an Arab family, Mr. Bernstein. My people are Palestinians. They are living in terrible circumstances. It is not right what they have to suffer. But it is not right what is happening today either. It brings us all more pain and suffering. I pray for peace in the world, as well as you. I am sorry that Allah has not chosen to answer our prayers."

Tom stared at the man for a long moment. Then he came around the corner of the desk and gathered him into his arms.

For a small moment of time, in a place normally filled with cynicism, confusion, and chaos, there was peace on earth.

....

VOICE OF PALESTINE, ALGIERS
Today, in the Gaza Strip, the IDF shot four Palestinians dead, among them a twelve-year-old retarded boy. A Palestinian youth stabbed five students and a princi-

pal in a Jerusalem high school. The IDF has sealed the
assailant's home. Students and other Israelis rioted,
damaging West Bank automobiles and wounding two
innocent bystanders.

ISRAEL TELEVISION NETWORK, JERUSALEM
The IDF in the Gaza Strip today quelled an unprovoked
attack, initiated by as many as a dozen Palestinians.
Rocks were thrown, and at least one assailant fired a
handgun at Israeli police as he ran down Gaza's main
street. Two Palestinians were confirmed dead and two
more wounded during the clash.

A Palestinian youth stabbed five students and critically wounded the principal in a Jerusalem high school.
The IDF has sealed the assailant's home. Protesters of
the incident rioted in a West Bank suburb for about an
hour this afternoon. The IDF reported that two persons
sustained minor rock injuries. No other substantive
damage was experienced.

Authorities have also reported the recovery of an Israel Tours bus, missing for several hours. It was discovered near the entrance to the Gihon Springs. The driver
of the bus was found bound and gagged at the Salt Sea
Hotel & Spa in Ein Bokek. The tour guide has been confirmed as a victim in what appears to be a hostage-taking incident. He had been shot to death. His name is being withheld until relatives can be notified. Hotel
management has verified that the group of twenty-five
are United States citizens, here on a religious pilgrimage. They were last seen boarding the bus at about
four-thirty in the afternoon. If anyone has information
regarding this bus, or its occupants, please
contact . . . "

SUNDAY, 1730 LOCAL TIME
BOSTON, MASSACHUSETTS

"THIS IS NOT A TEST. Please check immediately with the local radio or television station designated to provide Boston's citizens with emergency information. Those stations are . . .

"Police have confirmed one death and several critically ill, resulting from the ingestion of a deadly anthrax spore, apparently released near Frog Pond in Boston Common . . . there is no reason to panic . . . police and the FBI have determined that an orderly evacuation of the city should begin. In this unprecedented move to insure the safety of Boston's citizens, all major automobile thoroughfares, turnpikes, and expressways have been closed to incoming traffic. All lanes are reserved for outbound traffic only . . .

"Logan International Airport is diverting all incoming flights to Newark and New York City's LaGuardia and JFK Airports. Commercial and privately owned aircraft will be permitted outgoing flight status only, until advised otherwise. Fares are being suspended.

"All MBTA Orange, Blue, Green, and Red Lines will continue outbound operation for the time being, moving passengers away from downtown. You may board at any station. All of MBTA's one hundred sixty-two bus routes will provide outbound service until further notice. Fares are suspended. Amtrak trains will be operating outbound service every two hours from South Station and Back Bay Station, beginning at ten P.M.

"The following is a further list of public transportation being made available in your area. Greyhound Lines . . .

" . . . lock your doors and windows. Turn your car radio to

the emergency band for traffic updates and other information . . .

" . . . and so the decision to evacuate was issued following a closed emergency session in the mayor's office, after receiving a terrorist threat concerning the use of a biological weapon with deadly anthrax spores as its base. At least one death and several others in critical condition are known to have resulted from inhaling anthrax spores at Boston Common earlier today . . .

" . . . here are the pictures of two individuals wanted for questioning regarding the alleged terrorist threat to the citizens of Boston. Mohammed Ali Atta, also known as Robert Jibril, is believed to be living and working in the Boston area.

This second picture is the most recent likeness available of one Marwan Dosha, the man with the dubious distinction of being the world's most wanted terrorist. It is now believed that at least four men of Arab descent are working together here in Boston in an effort to carry out their threat . . .

" . . . medical authorities confirm that small amounts of anthrax spores can create a catastrophic situation here in the city . . .

" . . . a small island off the coast of Scotland was the location of a secret study regarding the use of anthrax as a potential offensive weapon during World War II. Every living animal was killed. Still today, more than fifty years later, this island is off limits to all visitors as a result of the lingering effects of contamination . . .

"Please, do not panic . . . "

GRANDPA BRAINARD LOOKED at Agent Morse. "Now there's the media understatement of the year. 'Please, do not panic!' "

They sat still, staring at the pictures on the screen, listening to the commentary. Suddenly, Grandpa sat up on the edge of the couch.

"I've got an idea," he exclaimed.

The younger man smiled.

"I know. I think getting you out of town is a good idea too. I'm going to check with my boss and see if we can get you out of here."

Grandpa shook his head emphatically.

"No. That's not what I mean. I know where they are," Grandpa said, pounding his fist into an open hand. "Why didn't I think of it earlier?"

The young agent watched him carefully.

"Are you serious? *You* know where they are?"

"Come on," Grandpa shouted, jumping to his feet. "Get your boss on the phone. I've got to talk to him!"

Morse hesitated, sizing up this exuberant senior citizen who was fairly bouncing in front of him. It was difficult to know how seriously he should take the man. Grandpa suddenly stood still, his eyes boring into those of the young agent. His look had become determined, his countenance rock hard.

"Hurry!"

Morse hurried.

TWENTY-SEVEN MINUTES LATER, Special Agent in Charge Ellis was wrapping up a five-minute, emotion-charged conversation with the Director.

"It makes sense," the Director said, his voice sounding detached now, as though evaluating the recommendation of an out-of-town business associate regarding the latest pending company deal. The lower his voice became, the more the charismatic energy that had helped bring about his rise to the top FBI post seemed to flow. Ask any SAC. That's what they would tell you about dealing with the Director.

"I've shared your idea with the Attorney General," he continued. "She's at the White House with the President and the boys at NSC. It's a go. I'm sending you every agent within three hours of Boston. Anybody we can drive in or fly in. Logan has been notified that we're coming. I'll have an HRT underwater unit on its way within the hour.

"Meanwhile, take the old guy with you. What's his name? Brainard? He sounds pretty sharp and he's the last person to have seen these vermin. Concentrate on this Ali Atta character. I'd like to be wrong, but I'll put money on Dosha already being long gone. He's not going to stick around for the party.

"That's why he's got these other three nuts. He's on his way somewhere to watch it all happen on television! We'll cover all the airports, train stations, and rental car agencies. We've alerted U.S., Canadian, and Mexican border agents. Maybe we'll get lucky.

"I've got an HRT unit on its way to California too. It may be too late to do any good, but we're leaving nothing to chance. This is war. Nothing less. They've been telling us this for years. Maybe this time, we'll believe it.

"And, listen. Do your best to keep your troops on point. That's all I ask. We don't need another Waco up there. What we need is a win. I'll guarantee you, if we don't, the world won't be the same ever again!"

**2047 LOCAL TIME
WASHINGTON, D.C.**

AT EXACTLY 2047, A C-130 Hercules lifted off the same runway from which its identical look-alike had departed three hours before. It climbed rapidly into the dark skies, the lights of the nation's capital flickering in the distance.

Inside, a full array of the latest equipment, including a jet-black Messerschmitt twin-engine helicopter and a high-speed power boat, both equipped for night surveillance, was dispatched along with a small core of the nation's most uniquely trained federal officers. They were members of the FBI's Hostage Rescue Team, a cadre of persons trained in the necessary skills needed to accomplish exactly what their name implied, anywhere they were needed in America.

They sat quietly, listening with rapt attention, as their leader laid out the possible options for their team as soon as they landed at Logan.

THIRTY-SIX

From the islands of Hawaii to the down-east villages of Maine, unusual, spontaneous gatherings were beginning to take place. In churches where Sunday night services were still a regular part of the religious menu, pews long sparsely populated were filled with seriously troubled souls.

They did not dress up for the occasion, but came in the casual afternoon attire of sport shirts, jeans, and even shorts. They obviously were not concerned about the lack of childcare. Their children were with them, sitting quietly in pews next to their parents, or standing along the walls and in the aisles, if seating was not available. Even the little ones seemed to sense the gravity surrounding this weekend.

Pastors and priests who served churches normally locked and dark on Sunday nights were filled with amazement as they drove into the parking lots and stepped out of their cars. Parking spaces generally empty at this hour were filled with automobiles. Inside, most often there was no music, no liturgy, no formal leader in charge.

In a small Congregational church in Manchester, Vermont, an elderly couple stood in front of the lectern, guiding the people in an informal time of corporate prayer.

A tiny Roman Catholic church in the old section of St. Augustine, Florida overflowed with tourists and locals, their heads bowed as a young priest led them in the reading of Scripture and in prayers.

In the shadows of tall grain elevators, an Assembly of God church in an eastern Washington farming community was filled with young and old alike. They wore simple work clothes, and lifted their hands and hearts in a time of united intercession for a part of their world that most had not experienced and did not understand.

The pastor of a Baptist church in urban East St. Louis, Illinois sat in the back row of the old, red brick building in which he had faithfully preached for twenty-seven years, weeping silently, listening while deacons took charge of the unscheduled prayer meeting. The occasion that brought them together that evening filled the white-haired preacher with grief. The event that he saw taking place in the church, however, was a dream come true!

A synagogue in a well-to-do New York suburb opened its doors to the concerned members of its congregation. The rabbi led in a discussion of the events and in a time of prayer.

The San Jose Mercury-News sent a photographer and reporter to a mosque in Fremont, California where Muslims gathered, some to pray and others simply out of fear of retribution from neighbors angry over the day's events.

In thousands of homes and churches across the land, believers paused to pray for their brothers and sisters held helplessly in a church that most of them had not known about before today. They prayed for the missing pastor and church group in Israel. And they wept for a city and its people who at this very moment were desperately trying to escape from their own unbelievable holocaust.

THE CHURCHES IN BOSTON and its contiguous towns and villages were empty. So were the synagogues and the mosques.

Downtown was a virtual ghost town. Only the most rumor-hardened citizens remained. They were the Harry Trumans of Boston. Nothing was going to dislodge them. Not even impending death.

From Faneuil Hall Marketplace to the Prudential Center, and from Old North Church to the Bull & Finch Tavern, only an occasional shadowy figure could be seen running toward a subway station.

Boston Common was empty.

Traffic was creeping along in every outward direction on the inner city streets and avenues.

Even the Combat Zone along Washington Street between Avery and Stuart, normally buzzing with its strip shows, porno films, and generally sleazy diversions, was devoid of patrons.

Fenway Park and Schaefer Stadium, thirty miles away in Foxboro, were empty.

Across the river, Harvard and M.I.T. campuses were deserted.

Inexpensive studio apartments and finely appointed row houses were vacant.

Theatres were dark.

Restaurants were closed.

Hotels were locked.

Massachusetts General Hospital was almost entirely evacuated.

Buses were full.

Trains were full.

MTBA Lines were full.

The Massachusetts Turnpike was full.

Fitzgerald Expressway was full.

Gridlock was reigning.

Tempers were flaring.

An occasional fight was breaking out.

Even random gunshots could be heard.

IN MONTREAL'S downtown Sheraton Hotel, a man sat by himself in his room. He sipped from a bottle of mineral water and toyed with the Caesar salad he had ordered from room service. The television blared out the latest on Boston's evacuation crisis.

He watched thoughtfully, his finger lightly touching the scar on his cheek.

2105 LOCAL TIME
BOSTON, MASSACHUSETTS

AT LOGAN INTERNATIONAL AIRPORT, THE C-130 rolled to a stop. The giant cargo door in its belly dropped open.

The jeep came out first. Without stopping, its occupants raced out onto the runway and through a nearby open gate. A boat and trailer were next, followed by the helicopter. Men readied the machine for flight, while others attached lines to the boat. Within a few minutes, the helicopter's engines sputtered to life and lifted into the air, hovering noisily over the boat. The lines were linked to a cable lowered from the helicopter. A moment later, the boat rose from its trailer bed and disappeared into the darkness.

A television traffic helicopter appeared suddenly over the terminal building and touched down near the C-130. Four men dressed in scuba gear trotted down the ramp and climbed on board. The red and white machine lifted from the runway, and moments later it too was gone.

"WE'VE LOCATED THEM, sir. They rented a powerboat at one of the marinas along the Charles. We found the fellow who rented it to them, just before he split. He recognized the one guy. It's Ali Atta. He's been trying to reach the boats he has out. Says that he called these two and alerted them to the danger. Ordered them to hightail it in. They told him they might try to land at a dock closer to where they're located."

"How far away are you?"

"I'm not sure exactly. Couple of miles, maybe. They have been sighted by our agents in a television station chopper. You got a Boston map there?"

"In front of me."

"Right now they're about a quarter of a mile beyond the Harvard Bridge. Do you see it?"

"Yep."

"They're not moving. I don't know what they may have going, but we've dropped our boat in further upriver, about a mile beyond them. We'll approach them SEALS style, put our men in the water as we go by. They'll hear us, maybe even see us. But they should think we're just pleasure boaters, anxious to get back to a landing and out of the area."

"You say there are only two on board?"

"That's the word."

"Be careful."

"Thank you, sir. We'll do our best."

THE ENGINE ROARED TO LIFE AT THE FIRST touch of the ignition. The pilot looked back at the men in black. All four gave the OK sign. He put it in gear and headed downriver. Cambridge on the left and Boston to the right. Solid ribbons of light on the main traffic arteries stood out against the unusual darkness of the cities on either side. The pilot turned his attention back to the river and to the task of finding the craft that had been spotted a short while earlier by an agent with night-vision field glasses.

There!

The pilot lifted a hand and pointed in the direction of the target, floating silently well ahead and to the left. He stayed on course now, keeping his boat at the same speed and to the right side of the target. There could be no slowing down, nothing that would cause suspicion that he was anything other than just another poor victim trying to escape with his life before it was too late.

One!

Two!

Three!

Four!

They were gone.

Swallowed up by the river like stones from a child's hand!

The powerboat roared on into the night.

MOHAMMED ALI ATTA and Yusif Shenuda extinguished their cigarettes. The sleeves of their sweaters not only provided warmth against the chilly night air. They offered protection. And protection was what they were interested in. Surgical masks and gloves covered their faces and hands. They understood the gravity of what was about to take place, at least as much as any human being could. And in spite of special rewards promised to those whose death occurs while waging Islam's battles, both men had secretly decided that they wanted to live.

Their day had been spent reassembling two model airplanes. The same two they had assembled and flown before, while rehearsing for this great moment.

At eight-thirty, Mohammed had looked across the balsa wood wingspan at Yusif and nodded.

"We go forward with our plan. There can be no turning back now. The infidels think we are fooling. They do not believe we will destroy their empire. But Allah is greater!"

Yusif grunted.

They continued working on the airplanes.

Three hours later, working with a small light attached to the cabin door, they were ready.

It's time.

From a cloth-covered, plastic container, Yusif slowly withdrew one of two square objects located inside. Each was exactly four inches in diameter. Carefully he attached it to the specially designed aluminum mounts awaiting on the top side of the model, just behind the single propellor.

Then he paused.

In the distance they heard it. A motorboat coming at high speed in their direction.

Both men stared out into the darkness until they saw it, looks of concern forming above their surgical masks. Mohammed checked the seat beside him. The fully loaded and deadly, silencer-equipped Cobray M-11/9 remained inches away from his hand.

This inexpensive but reliable submachine gun had been created specifically for close military combat. Mohammed liked it because it did not need to be aimed, only fired. He had obtained it easily, another reason he was partial to this particular gun. It had been purchased from a suburban high school student who had acquired it from an unlicensed dealer.

Anyone in its path of fire would be snuffed in an instant. Like the two young Israeli soldiers he had murdered with a similar weapon three years ago, as they strolled along a sidewalk in Jaffa.

The boat roared past them now, without letup, continuing off into the darkness. There appeared to be only one person on board. Mohammed smiled, his gloved hand caressing the model plane as he would a fine woman. He turned his attention back to the task at hand.

His watch read eleven fifty-seven.
Three minutes to the appointed hour!

THE FOUR HRT frogmen swam swiftly, silently under the surface of the river. The lead agent checked his watch. Eleven fifty-eight exactly. He continued stroking toward the target.

YUSIF STOOD UP, grasping the model airplane by its underbelly. He primed the motor and sent the signal to the starter. In a moment, it would rise into the darkness, headed toward Boston. Mohammed sat, eyes glistening with excitement, holding the second model, destined for Cambridge. Yusif lifted the airplane high, grasping the controls in his left hand. He looked at Mohammed and nodded.

THE FOUR AGENTS broke the surface of the water without making a sound, two on either side of the boat, just as one of the Arabs stood, holding up a model airplane. The two on board were oblivious to the men in the water. The cabin light outlined the scene, defining in an instant the method of delivery planned for Boston's demise. With one hand, Tom Riley ripped off his scuba mask and with the other reached desperately for his knife.

"ALLAH U AKBAR!" shouted Yusif, as he released the model airplane, with its deadly cargo! A second later, grunting with surprise, he turned toward his companion. Mohammed stared in disbelief at the handle of a knife, protruding from Yusif's chest!
Desperately, Mohammed twisted away from the side of

the boat, fumbling for the weapon lying on the deck chair. It was all a blur of motion. A dark face behind where he had been sitting! He pulled the trigger, releasing a hail of bullets!

The face disappeared.

Yusif fell forward against Mohammed.

Another dark form.

Then another!

They were on top of him, a fist crushing into his mouth.

A chop to the neck.

Darkness!

Yusif's left hand went out to break the continuation of his fall. In the motion, the radio control unit broke free.

It flew past Tom Riley's outstretched hand. Frantically, he scrambled in a desperate effort to catch it. Too late! He watched as it disappeared into the dark waters of the Charles River.

"IT'S WHAT?" shouted the director. "The stuff is on a model airplane headed for Boston? Are you serious? A model airplane?"

"I'm sorry, sir. We were a split second too late." SAC Ellis sounded like a condemned man. "One of the terrorists is dead. The other is in custody. We lost Abramson. He took a direct hit from a submachine gun. And the airplane's radio control unit was lost during the attack."

There was a long silence. When the Director responded, his voice sounded distant and hollow. "I'm sorry too. Dear God in heaven, I'm sorry too!"

TOM RILEY PUT DOWN his radio pack. He watched as the others took Abramson below and laid him gently on the bed. He had died instantly, with three bullet wounds visible in his face. The Cobray had sprayed its pellets of death in a matter of seconds. Tom looked away into the night sky.

Somewhere ... out there ... still more death was on the wing.

The tail section on the second model plane had been broken by Yusif's fall. Tom bent down and picked up a cloth covered plastic container. He pulled back the cover.

"Hey. Check this out."

The others moved in to take a look. They spied the second square container, instinctively understanding what it was. A spray valve protruded from the top. But, there was something else as well. Tom lifted it out.

A model airplane radio transmitter!

"For the second plane," he said, turning it over in his hand. "Do you suppose it will work the first one?"

"If they haven't already altered the radio frequencies. My kid's got one almost exactly like this at home," Larry Becker said. "I've run it a few times. Want me to give it a go?"

Tom handed the unit to him.

"Be careful. Even if it works, can you bring it back?"

"I don't think we want it back," Larry responded dryly. "We just need to find it. Then ... maybe ... "

"Maybe what?" Tom's hand was on Larry's arm.

"Maybe, if we can find it, we can land it somewhere in one piece. It's a long shot."

"Let's try. Gene, get this tub going and head for shore."

"Wait a minute. Be quiet and listen," said Larry, staring up into the dark night.

The others were quiet. There was only the lap of the water against the boat together with night sounds from the city and the constant flow of traffic in the distance.

Then they heard it.

"Look for lights! Look for lights!" Larry exclaimed excitedly.

"Lights?"

"Yeah, this model has wing lights. The one out there

probably does too. Do you hear it?"

"Yes. Yes, I do."

"I think it's circling. It's ... there, see? At about ten o'clock. See the lights? Going away, the red one is on the right; green on the left. Coming toward us, vice versa. Got it?"

"Got it, Larry. Looks like red is left now. Must be coming our way."

"It is. And look. I've got control!" He wiggled the wings a bit and the lights bobbed up and down.

"All right! Then let's head for shore. Okay?"

"Okay. I'll work the plane and keep it up until we get to the riverside. Then, we'll try to land her." said Larry, as he concentrated on the device in his hands. "There is one more problem, though."

"Another problem?" *What else could there be?* This was the worst night in Tom Riley's twenty-eight years.

"I'm not sure what triggers this baby off. I've got a feeling it's this button here. But there's no way of knowing for sure. And we don't know when or how it's set to disperse. We may get there just in time to see it go off."

"That's a happy thought, old buddy," Tom answered. "I tell you what. Just be very careful!"

THIRTY-SEVEN

"I believe we should go with the SWAT leader's recommendation. It's our best chance. But I have to be honest, the definitive word here is 'chance.'"

Webber stared at the television monitor, as he talked to the U.S. Attorney General, who at this moment was standing in the FBI Crisis Management Center at Tenth and Pennsylvania, in Washington, D.C. alongside several high ranking AG personnel and the Director of the FBI.

"Duane, I know time is critical there, but do you think we've done all we can do in negotiation? What if someone higher up could talk with them? How about a local Muslim leader there in the Bay Area? Have we exhausted all our good ideas?" Her voice was quiet, but firm and thoughtful.

"We'll do what you decide, of course. But I think I hear you asking for my opinion. I don't believe any further 'wait and talk' tactic is going to get us anywhere. We've bit into the apple already. The longer we wait, the less apple we have left. We need to get in there now."

"I know you do, Duane. But, after all this time, we're still living in the shadow of the Waco decision. And that hit we took last month in Chicago is looming over us like . . . hang on a second. I'll be right back."

Webber sat still, watching a scene of relative inactivity being projected from inside the church. Akmed was pacing back and forth in front of the first row of pews. He stopped to whisper something to one of the other male terrorists. The man smiled and nodded, then backed away. Now it looked like he was speaking to someone seated in the congregation. He was not near a microphone and so it was difficult to figure what he was up to. *I wish I could hear what he is . . .*

"Yes, I'm still here." Webber shifted his feet as the Attorney General came back on the line.

His face tightened as he listened.

" . . . it looks grim, Duane. We were so close! Anyhow, there's still two of them on the loose up there; we've got a model airplane in the air ready to drop a cargo of anthrax on the city; there's a bus load of Americans missing in Israel; and your church full of people are living on borrowed time out there in California. Other than that, it's business as usual here in D.C."

"I hear you, and I don't envy you one bit." Webber paused as silence fell between them. "So what will it be?" he asked softly.

He waited.

"Duane, I'm ordering you to get in there and get those people out. Do it as quickly as you can. Put your SWAT team to work!"

"Okay. Right now we're still waiting for the release of all the hostages that were promised when we got the networks involved. A couple of hours ago, our friend indicated they would be coming out soon. If and when that happens, we'll execute your order immediately," he responded, leaning forward in his chair. "I will stay in touch as things unfold here . . . oh, and by the way . . . "

"Yes?"

"Good luck!"

"Thanks, Duane. Good-bye."

Webber heard a soft, feminine sigh on the other end of the line.

Why did I think of it being "feminine"? Maybe because I'm still not used to a woman having to make some of the toughest, grittiest decisions any person ever has to deal with. Including the President. Well, get used to it, Webber. It's a new day!

Webber looked over at the others. "It's a go."

He got up from his chair and stretched. "Let's find Hendrickson and make sure we're ready to take these characters out when the time comes. I could also use something to eat."

Turning his back to the monitors, he headed out the door with Chief White following close behind.

MONDAY, 19 SEPTEMBER, 0025 LOCAL TIME
BOSTON, MASSACHUSETTS

AGENT GENE JONES guided the boat slowly, steadily, all the while keeping an eye on Larry Becker. Agent Becker peered up into the night, watching the red and green wing lights blink out their presence above them. Sweat beaded on his face, even though the night was cool.

Handcuffed and with feet bound together, Mohammed Ali Atta observed the unfolding drama with a sense of resignation from the bottom of the boat. He was going to die. He knew it. There was no way these fools would ever be able to bring that model plane down. The dreaded spores were sure to get them all.

Tom Riley kept an eye on both men and on the shore as they drew closer. Jones maneuvered the boat alongside a small floating dock. The moment they bumped the dock, Riley leaped out and secured the boat.

Larry never let his concentration waver. Jones and Riley carefully helped him out of the boat, Jones keeping a hand on his waist as they walked barefoot toward the edge of the river.

The floating dock moved unsteadily under their feet as they neared the shore, causing Larry to lose his balance. Jones tightened his grip, at the same time staying low and away from the transmitter controls hanging by a strap from Larry's neck.

"You're doing great," Riley said, encouragingly, as they stepped on shore. "This way."

The red and green lights on the plane continued to circle the men who desperately endeavored to control it from below. Walking at a rapid pace, they came to the edge of the street paralleling the river.

"Okay, Larry, take your pick," Riley said. "We've got a paved street, a cement sidewalk, and some grass here between the walk and the river."

Larry glanced around quickly, then back at the red and green lights. His fingers were not as nimble as he wished. They had not had a chance to warm up from being in the Charles, and now they felt swollen and cold. The level meter looked okay and he had managed not to bump the power switch so far. The only button he did not recognize from his son's model airplane he assumed was the trigger device that released the spores.

"Grass. Let's do grass. It's softer. I'm going to try to bring it in tail down, nose up. If you guys would like to leave, now's your chance."

"Hey, Larry. You do this right and we'll all go home together. Mess it up and it won't make much difference where any of us are standing when you bring it down." Riley gave Larry a pat on his bottom. "No pressure though, buddy. For an old model airplane man like you, this is a piece of cake."

Larry smiled at Riley's effort to ease the tension.

"Okay, frog people, here we go."

The zippy sound of the tiny motor inside the plane could be heard clearly now as Larry adjusted the throttle trim lever. Their eyes were riveted on the running lights as he moved the rudder lever and began the final delicate adjustments on the aileron and elevator trimmers. Even Mohammed Ali Atta strained to see what was happening, but he was too far away.

"There," Riley exclaimed. The plane was dropping into the light projected by the street lamps and the buildings across the way.

Larry carefully maneuvered the plane toward the strip of grass along the shore. At the last second, it veered toward the sidewalk. No! He pulled it back. *Tail down. Nose up. It's coming in too fast. Too fast! Stall. Stall! Power off! Drop!*

The other two later said they'd never seen anything like it. The plane looked to them as though it was coming in too fast. But at the last possible moment, the nose lifted and the tail dipped down. Larry cut the engine and the plane dropped onto the grass. It bounced once, twice, and then nosed into the turf, before it fell to one side and twisted around on the tip of one wing.

No one moved at first. They simply stared at the child's toy that had been turned into a lethal bomb. Larry lifted the strap from around his neck and placed the control box on the grass. Then he sat down beside it. His hands began shaking uncontrollably.

Riley and Jones walked over to the plane. There, attached to the upper part of the model, was the lethal cargo, still intact.

The two of them looked at each other and grinned.

"Yes!" they exclaimed, high-fiving and pounding each other and running back to where Larry sat on the grass. Both men stopped as Riley picked up the box and laid it carefully on the sidewalk. Then the two of them pounced on Larry, rolling in the grass like boys playing in the park.

"You did it!" Riley panted, finally, amid their laughter and release of tension. "Becker? How does it feel to have saved the world?"

They broke into howls of laughter again.

"Stupid Americans," Ali Atta muttered to himself, as he listened from the bottom of the boat.

GRANDPA BRAINARD and Agent Morse ran to catch the MBTA Commuter Rail Green Line at Science Park. Morse had just spoken with the Assistant Agent in Charge by phone. He had been told to get Brainard out of the area as fast as possible. A model airplane carrying the deadly anthrax bomb was on its way toward the city.

"Get out of there now!"

Morse was surprised at just how agile the older man was. He thought of being sixty-something as old. His father had died at age sixty-two of a heart attack. Of course, he had been a lifetime smoker, but still, Morse had never seen a man who seemed more fit for his age than Jim Brainard.

Both men, of course, were highly motivated. The fear of the unknown that surrounded this invisible, deadly disease, that could fall like rain in the night and kill an entire city, was indescribable. There was no time to notify any persons still trapped in Boston's city limits. The worst case scenario had just been confirmed. They both knew they were probably dead men. But they ran anyway.

The Green Line was the only train carrying passengers toward the downtown area. The other lines were running empty into downtown, then racing back along their respective lines, gathering up evacuees at each outbound station. The need to move people out of the area between the Charles and downtown had caused MBTA officials to schedule the

Green Line to run empty to Lechmere Station, reversing back through downtown and on to Boston College or Cleveland Circle Stations.

Science Park Station was the second stop.

Grandpa Brainard and Agent Morse scrambled on board just as the departure signal sounded and the doors closed. They had expected the train to be packed. Surprisingly, there were still a few seats available. Grandpa surmised it was because the majority of people had already been evacuated. No one really had known, before this crisis, just how rapidly a large population might be removed from the center point of danger.

He looked around. Few people were talking. Most sat huddled in their seats, looking out into the night or staring across the aisle at their neighbors. Grandpa saw two vacant seats across from a mother and her young son. The boy was eleven or twelve, Grandpa guessed, and was wearing a baseball uniform and a cap with the Red Sox emblem on the front. Morse was behind him as they reached the seats. He smiled at the mother and patted the lad on the shoulder. Then he started to slide in so that Morse could have the aisle seat.

That's when he saw him!

SAFWAT NAJJIR sat hunched down in a side seat from which he could see everyone coming on board. He had boarded at Science Park Station also, just moments before Grandpa Brainard and Agent Morse. In a small case clutched in his lap, he carried enough death to turn Boston into a mass graveyard!

Beginning at North Station, the very next stop, he intended to take up a position near the doorway. At the moment the signal indicated the doors were closing, he would toss out a small egg-shaped object, barely two inches in circumference.

The object looked very much like a small light bulb and was just as fragile. It was an ingenious, innocent-looking device that would break on impact against a rail or a cement wall, delivering anthrax spores into the city's underground where huge air-conditioning units would eagerly pump the virus into the streets and buildings above them. Above ground, stations would receive the same gift of terror and death, with nature's wind currents doing the rest.

When Safwat saw Grandpa Brainard stepping onto the very car in which he was sitting, he could not believe his eyes!

How can this be? It's the old man from the fishing village. He's the one person who might recognize me. But will he have sense enough to connect me with tonight's events?

The train was moving. He opened the case and withdrew his first "egg." He held the device delicately, fearful of breaking it as he covered it with his other hand. He would be ready for the toss. It was for a moment such as this that Allah had called him. He would not fail.

He glanced over again at the innkeeper. The man was walking toward him! It looked as though the young man behind him was a companion too. Involuntarily, he tightened his grip on the death device. He watched as the innkeeper stopped and prepared to sit down. The old man smiled at the little boy across the aisle, patted his shoulder, and then looked up.

That's when their eyes met!

Safwat saw the old man turn and whisper to his companion. Now he was staring at him too. A rush of anxiety streaked through Safwat's body. He felt the danger. Slowly he stood, clutching the case in his left hand. In his right hand he held onto the "egg." He knew that *they* knew. He was no longer a secret. And suddenly the terrorist was terrified!

THEY WERE SLOWING FOR North Station. In a few seconds, the train would stop and the doors automatically open. People would be crowding onto the car. It would be impossible to fire a weapon.

Agent Morse had never been in a situation like this before. If Jim Brainard was right and this was the man, he had to take him now. His mouth felt like cotton as perspiration broke out underneath his shirt. He never took his eyes off the Arab.

He was standing now, holding onto a small case. Morse thought he had something in his right hand too; but if he did, it was not a gun.

Morse reached across, and with two deft moves, unzipped his fanny pack and withdrew his handgun. Even before he said a word, passengers nearby caught sight of the weapon. One young woman screamed.

"Don't move, fella," Morse called out. "FBI."

The train rocked slightly as it continued to slow down.

What happened next was destined to become a legend along Boston's Green Line!

GRANDPA BRAINARD stood in the aisle, only a few feet behind Agent Morse. Emotions ran unchecked as he glared at Safwat Najjir. He remembered the first day he had opened his doors to the man at Hill House.

Anger welled up as he thought of what had been done to his "adopted daughter," Rosa. Fear gathered like bile in his stomach when he caught sight of a small object in the man's right hand.

"Stay back," Safwat cried out, sliding out of the seat and moving nearer to the door.

"FBI," repeated Morse. "Give it up!"

He steadied his gun with both hands and pointed it at the Arab's heart.

The train was barely moving now, as it rolled into North Station.

"Don't come any nearer," Safwat shouted back. "This is anthrax. If I drop it, we all die!"

The train jolted to a stop.

Safwat glanced around quickly.

None of the passengers moved.

Then with an underhand motion, he tossed the egg well back into the car!

The door opened.

The Arab turned to run. But there was no place to run. People on the platform jammed the doorway, fighting to get inside.

Agent Morse fired his weapon.

Passengers screamed.

Safwat Najjir crumpled to the floor. The Holy War checked off its latest martyr!

Grandpa watched the flight of the egg. The instrument of death slowly made its journey toward him, and it seemed to take forever. It arched over Agent Morse's head and flew straight toward Grandpa Brainard.

A miniature missile filled with bitterness and hatred and jealousy and cruelty.

A biological bomb destined to end forever Grandpa Brainard's life and the lives of all those around him.

A tiny egg on a slow-motion, airborne journey of death and destruction.

At the last moment, there was a flash of brown in front of his face. Grandpa blinked and steeled himself for the inevitable.

But there was nothing!

He looked to his right and there, standing on the seat in his Michael Jordan specials, was the young lad in the baseball uniform. The one whom he had seen when he got on board. On his hand he wore a first baseman's mitt.

Carefully, the boy opened it. He glanced down at his mother who sat horror-stricken, unable to move. Then he looked over at Grandpa Brainard and grinned.

Timothy O'Neil had just made the catch that would be talked about for years to come, from Boston's Back Bay to Fenway Park.

In his glove lay the unbroken egg!

**MONDAY, 19 SEPTEMBER, 0147 LOCAL TIME
WASHINGTON, D.C.**

"ARE YOU SURE? You're one hundred percent certain? That's wonderful!" The Director leaned back in his chair. "Thanks. Yes, I'll pass the word."

He put down the phone, folded his hands across his chest and looked around the room. It was filled with high-level people laying various contingency plans for sealing off the doomed city of Boston.

"Let's wrap up Boston and give it back to the people, folks!"

All activity stopped as the men and women turned to hear the Director.

"Ellis has confirmed that the model airplane has been recovered and its cargo contained."

A cheer broke out as people clapped and hugged with a spontaneity seldom seen before in that room. Next came the questions.

"How did they do it?" "Have the people been told?" "When will they be allowed to return?"

"What about the other two terrorists?" asked the Attorney General. "Any word?"

"They think Dosha is long gone. He's not the sort to stick around for the dirty work. His pattern in the past has been to put things into motion and then skip. The educated guess is that he's three states away by now. Maybe even in Canada. We'll concentrate every effort toward finding him. But he's a cool one. The remaining terrorist was recognized and apprehended on a subway by one of our agents and the gentleman from Booth Bay. You remember him? The fellow who owns the bed and breakfast place where these lunatics stayed for a week?"

She nodded.

"Wait until you hear this though. Talk about your miracles."

The Attorney General and the others listened as the Director recounted the capture of Safwat Najjir and the heroics of a young lad named Timothy, who possessed the meanest first baseman's mitt in Boston.

The room was buzzing as people gathered in groups, drinking Cokes and coffee, the feeling of relief washing over them like the first cool rains of autumn. Along with the relief came the added affirmation that somehow they had made a contribution toward resolving the crisis.

Occasionally, they glanced over at their boss.

She was busy on the phone, talking to Duane Webber in California.

THE MAYOR OF BOSTON went on radio and television at five-fifteen in the morning. The tone in his voice and his personal demeanor confirmed the message that he presented.

"The evacuation is over. It is safe to come home!"

Along auto-clogged expressways and turnpikes, horns began honking. In homes crowded with friends, relatives, even strangers who had been taken in, cheers went up. There was lots of hand-clapping, hugging, and dancing going on among what was perhaps the largest late-night viewing and listening audience in regional radio and television history. Old-timers reminisced that they had not seen the likes of it since the end of World War II.

GRANDPA BRAINARD was being congratulated by the Mayor and Special Agent in Charge Ellis. Television lights warmed the cool of the early morning at Logan Airport. Newspeople and cameramen were stretching both cables and tempers back and forth across the runway pavement. In the background, the FBI's HRT personnel were already reloading their equipment on board the plane in which they had arrived a few hours earlier. Its huge motors were just starting to turn over.

A stretcher shrouded in black was lifted from a police van and solemnly taken up the ramp, disappearing into the plane's belly. Television cameras captured images of the tired faces of the three remaining agents who had overcome impossible odds and saved the city. They were unavailable for comment.

Following his interview, Grandpa took SAC Ellis' arm and pulled him to one side.

"Do you have any idea how long it will be before Logan opens up to commercial flights?"

"No, but I can find out. What do you have in mind?"

Grandpa hesitated. Then he looked up at Ellis.

"I want to go to California."

Ellis looked at him quizzically.

"It's hard to explain, but a couple of hours ago, I started to feel as though I need to go to California. It has something to do with that pastor's family and the church situation out there."

"Do you know those people, Mr. Brainard?"

"Nope. Haven't even been to California. Besides, I'm a Catholic. Never met a Protestant preacher in my whole life. But before my wife died, God love her, she would get like this once in a while. She used to call it 'a leading of the Lord.' More often than not, she was right.

"Well, I have to be honest, I don't actually know much about 'the leadings of the Lord.' Now that I think of it, that's kind of sad for a man in his sixties to have to say, isn't it? She'd get determined though, and follow through on whatever it was that she believed God might be telling her to do. I know it sounds kind of corny and all, but it's almost like she's here again, only I know she isn't. This time," he lifted his eyes to the stars, "I guess the good Lord's talkin' directly, tellin' me to go to California and be with that family. It doesn't make much sense, but . . . well, I've really got to do this."

Special Agent in Charge Ellis studied the man's face. An honest face, clear-eyed and earnest. Then he made a decision.

"Mr. Brainard, if it weren't for you, this city would be a graveyard. The entire country would be devastated. The more I begin to think about the last couple of days, the more awesome it all becomes. I go to church regularly. I've always believed in God and I pray every day. But this experience has me thinking that there's something about my faith that I've never tapped into before. I'm a Lutheran, by the way; one of those 'bad kids' who left the Catholic Church."

"You may be one of God's 'bad kids,' " Grandpa chuckled, "but tonight you've done okay by my standards. And I think you've met *His* standards pretty well too."

"The same goes for you," responded Ellis warmly. "I'll tell you what, Mr. Brainard. It could be hours before commercial flights resume at Logan and, then, who knows how long before you can book a flight out. But, we've got a C-130 here that's just about ready to leave. If you'd like, I'll get you on board. You can fly to Washington and, by the time you arrive there, we'll have a seat for you on the next flight out to San Francisco. How does that sound?"

"I like the way you work, Ellis," Grandpa chuckled, as they shook hands. "Come and walk me up that ramp so that your boys don't decide to toss this old geezer out on his ear."

THIRTY-EIGHT

Word of the events in Boston reached Webber and his team early in the morning hours. What had appeared to be headed toward a monstrous tragedy was now an incredible victory. The news lifted the spirits of the tired men inside the Winnebago command center.

However, in Baytown, there was no change. Nearly twenty-four hours had passed since shots first rang out in Calvary Church's sanctuary. In spite of every effort to the contrary, no hostages had been released. Webber had kept the SWAT team back while he urged Akmed to release those that had been promised freedom earlier. But, it was to no avail.

Finally, at 0845, Webber left the RV to stretch his legs and get some fresh air.

AKMED PACED BACK AND FORTH at the front of the sanctuary. He laid his weapon on the Communion table and motioned for Ihab Akazzam.

Ihab listened as Akmed whispered instructions in his ear. He nodded, smiling as he stepped back.

Akmed then turned and looked at the weary crowd sitting before him.

"Mrs. Cain!"

Esther jumped involuntarily at the sound of her name.

"Ah, Mrs. Cain. There you are. Come here, please."

"What . . . " her voice cracked. Esther swallowed and cleared her throat. "What is it that you want?"

"Please do not ask questions, Mrs. Cain. What I want is for you to come here. Now come!"

"Let her alone. She's not been well."

Jeremy was on his feet, even as Esther tugged at him.

"Jeremy, sit down. Please!" Esther drew him down into the pew. Then she stood and began moving sideways past the others toward the aisle.

"Wait!"

Esther froze.

"And who might Jeremy be?" asked Akmed, his eyes having never left the young man who had just spoken out. He recognized him as the same person who had directed him earlier to dial 911.

Esther cast a desperate look at Jeremy and then back to Akmed.

"Who is he? What is he to you, Mrs. Cain?"

"My son," she whispered, her head down, hating herself for divulging the information, not knowing what else she could do.

"What? Speak up so that I can hear you clearly, Mrs. Cain."

"He is my son," she said again, this time clearly and distinctly.

"Ah, Jeremy. Jeremy Cain. And Jeremy Cain, who is this young lady sitting next to you? Your sister, perhaps?"

Jeremy stared back, not moving, saying nothing.

"You will answer me, Jeremy Cain, if you know what's good for you. Is this your sister?"

"No."

"Then, who?"

Jeremy remained silent. Esther saw Akmed reach for the weapon lying on the Communion table. Her eyes filled with horror, and in desperation she started to speak. But she was interrupted by another clear, steady voice.

"My name is Allison. Allison Orwell."

Startled, fear squeezing the breath out of her, Esther looked over and saw Allison and Jeremy standing together.

"Orwell, Orwell." Akmed rolled the name over, his hand releasing the weapon to the table. Then his face lit up with recognition. "Your father is the good doctor, sitting back there. Is that correct?"

Allison looked back at her parents.

"Yes. My father is the *good* doctor. He spends every day *saving* lives, not taking them," she answered firmly and with a touch of defiant pride.

"Very good," Akmed said, admiringly. "A very fine answer indeed and your point is well taken. Am I to assume that you and young Mr. Jeremy are good friends? Perhaps even best friends?"

There was no response.

He waited for a moment, his eyes flitting across the crowd that was now at attention, weariness forgotten as this new scene unfolded before them.

"Mrs. Cain. Please, come and sit here in the front pew." He looked around again. "Mrs. Ralsten!"

Elizabeth Ralsten stood to her feet.

"Thank you, Mrs. Ralsten. Please join Mrs. Cain here in front. No, don't sit down," he motioned as Jeremy and Allison made a move to do so. "I want you to come here also."

Jeremy and Allison looked at each other, concern clearly etched on their faces.

"YOU'D BETTER GET THE BOSS. Something's going down in there!" The technician turned away from the monitors and looked toward Randle as he spoke.

But Randle was already scrambling out the door.

"THERE IS ANOTHER COUPLE that my associate and I met while visiting with you last week." Akmed's excellent English and polite mannerisms were an enigma to all who watched and listened to him. The man who had been sitting next to Esther had whispered that Akmed should be in graduate school somewhere, preparing to make a contribution to society and to himself. Esther had nodded her agreement.

"I do not recall their names, but I recognize them both sitting over there." Akmed pointed in the direction of the Heidens. "Aziza, would you be so kind as to escort them to the front, please?"

Esther turned to watch as a young couple stood and started down the aisle, Aziza following, her weapon held ready. She did not know them, but she recognized their faces. John had mentioned that they were from the Seattle area. They had not been at Calvary Church for long. And the young woman was obviously very pregnant. Esther wondered what effect this tension might have on her and her baby.

"Please. Come with me." Akmed turned and mounted the three steps onto the platform. "You too, Jeremy and Allison."

The four followed him up the steps.

"Turn around, please, and face the people." Akmed took the microphone in his hand. To the Heidens, he said, "I apologize for not remembering your names."

"Heiden," Phil responded nervously. "I'm Phil. This is my wife, Sherri."

"I am pleased to meet you again," Akmed responded warmly. "It is regretful that it must be under such circumstances."

Esther tensed. Though his mannerism was warm and cordial, there was a steely look in his eyes. *This man is evil,* she thought. *He's capable of doing anything.*

"WHAT IS GOING ON?" Webber demanded, as he burst into the command center vehicle, his eyes riveting immediately on the monitors. White and Randle were close behind.

"I'm not sure. We couldn't hear at first. He just now picked up the microphone. He's got a young couple that he and the woman apparently met last week at church. Our friend Akmed and the woman he calls Aziza must have been here checking the place out. That's them, standing right there. She's the pregnant one. The young fellow over here is Cain's son. His name is Jeremy. That's his girlfriend, Allison Orwell. Her father is the doctor who checked out the dead guy earlier on."

"Any idea what he's up to?"

"I'm not sure, sir. But a moment ago, he ordered those two women down to stand near the front pew." He pointed them out on the screen. "One is Mrs. Cain, the pastor's wife. The other is Mrs. Ralsten."

"Oh, oh."

"Is the SWAT team going in, sir?"

"Yes. I just hope and pray we're not too late!"

"WE HAVE TRIED to make you comfortable during this stressful experience. We have even permitted all of you to go to the restrooms to relieve yourselves. It was extremely disappointing to note that our generosity and consideration was earlier taken advantage of by . . . I believe it was your husband and son, Mrs. Ralsten. Am I correct?"

Elizabeth Ralsten's eyes were downcast. Her lip trembled.

"Mrs. Ralsten?"

Elizabeth felt a hand slip into in hers. She glanced over as Esther squeezed and then released it. It wasn't much, but it was the courage that she needed.

Elizabeth stood up straight and looked Akmed in the eye. "Yes," she replied. "It was my husband and my son."

"Mrs. Ralsten. Do you not recall my saying that anyone who escaped would result in the death of two others?"

Elizabeth stared at him.

"Do you?"

Numbly, she nodded.

"Your husband and your son escaped. I am told they tried to take you with them. Is that true?"

Again she nodded.

"Why did you not go with them?" asked Akmed, curiously. "You would be safe now."

"I could not," she replied evenly, her eyes now focused onto Akmed.

"Why?"

"Because I believed you. I could never live with myself knowing that, as a result of saving my life, others had died."

Akmed studied her face. At last, he nodded, as if he clearly understood her motive. "You are a brave woman, Mrs. Ralsten. You have the spirit of a Muslim warrior! Sit down."

Elizabeth Ralsten sat down. She was visibly shaking and near to tears.

"Mrs. Cain."

While Esther remained standing only a short distance from Akmed, she quietly prayed, *O Lord Jesus, let me be strong for You just now. Help me honor You through Your strength and not disappoint You with my weakness.*

"Mrs. Cain, it is important that you and all these people, as well as those making decisions outside these walls, know that Akmed el Hussein is a man of his word."

Akmed paused. Esther said nothing.

"Our people have nowhere else to turn. We are ignored, killed, deprived of our possessions and our land. We are desperately seeking an end to all this pain and suffering. Your people have contributed to our tribulation. We come seeking relief in the only way left open to us. 'An eye for an eye, a tooth for a tooth.'

"It is your political and religious leaders who are at fault. They have caused this disaster because of their refusal to heed our repeated warnings. Politicians like your President. Religious leaders like your husband, Mrs. Cain. All are guilty. All must repent or be severely punished by the fires of hell.

"Just look at what has happened here. Even in such a simple thing as an order given to enable the use of the restrooms, you are guilty of disobedience. Now punishment is at hand. I said earlier that two people would die for every one who tried to escape." Akmed paused and smiled beneficently. "Two plus two equals four, does it not?"

Esther's knees buckled, then she caught herself. She suddenly realized what he intended to do. It hit her with hammerlike force. Jeremy and the others were going to be sacrificed!

"However," Akmed went on, "to show you just how generous I can be, even though four deserve to die, I am presenting you with a gift. A gift of the undeserved mercy of Allah."

He smiled, looking at the four young people before him.

Esther stopped breathing.

"Two may live, according to the mercy of Allah," he declared, looking down at Esther. "It is only necessary for two to die."

Fear pierced through Esther's body.

"And you, Mrs. Cain, must now decide which two will live and which two will die!"

DUANE WEBBER SWORE, pounding an open hand with his fist. "He's an animal. A diabolical madman!"

"Here, sir. This headset. Put it on. Hendrickson wants to talk."

Webber grabbed the headset and put it on. "What is it?" he growled angrily.

"AH . . ." Hendrickson's voice hesitated. He sensed something was wrong. "Our man has been in the air-conditioning duct for ten minutes. The rest of us are in place and ready."

"How much longer?"

"I can't be sure, sir. He's got to move carefully in order to avoid making noise."

"What's he using?"

"A .308."

"Is this guy the best you've got?"

"Absolutely. He's the best sniper, period. He can shoot the eyes out of a snake at a hundred yards."

"Good. He's about to run up against the biggest snake he's ever taken out."

"Yes, sir."

"By the way. What's his name?"

Hendrickson groaned. He had hoped that Webber would not ask that question.

"It's Hamdi, sir."

"Okay, then, let's . . . say again?"

"Hamdi."

"But that's an . . ."

"I know, sir. Hamdi is an American-born Arab. He's also proven himself in five years of excellent service. And he's the best there is."

"But do you think it's wise to put him in this situation? For his sake, if nothing else?"

"He's the best I've got, sir. This is not an issue of race. It's a matter of duty and honor. If he makes it all the way in, he will do the job."

"But..."

"Sir, remember what happened in WW II?" Hendrickson plunged ahead. "We told a lot of American Japanese that they couldn't fight and that we didn't trust them to even walk on our streets. But after all was said and done, they turned out to be some of the best soldiers on the battlefield."

There was silence at Webber's end.

"Sir?"

"You did the right thing, Hendrickson. We're staying with you from here on until you're inside." Webber kept his eye on the scene unfolding in front of him in living color. "We'll let you know where the bad guys are when you're ready to move. Looks as though something may be happening right now. He's pulled a few people out of the crowd. Says he intends to kill two of them as retribution for those two who escaped. Move as fast as you can."

"Yes, sir."

Hendrickson breathed a sigh of relief. Quietly gathering the team together in the church lobby, he got to work.

It was almost over.

IN THE WINNEBAGO, Webber stood and stretched his tired body. Every muscle felt fried. He listened to the radio receiver as Hendrickson deployed his team across the church lobby. He watched the people on the screen, weary of this drama that provided him no commercial breaks with which to relieve the tension. Soon every citizen in America would begin exercising their constitutional right to second-guess the results of their action.

He heaved a long sigh and wondered what Janice was doing.

THIRTY-NINE

MONDAY, 19 SEPTEMBER, 0932 LOCAL TIME
BAYTOWN, CALIFORNIA

Esther was stunned.

He's serious. They intend to kill Jeremy. And the others too. O God, how could You let this happen? You've already taken Jenny. I don't know where Jessica and John are, or even if they are alive!

Just then, she heard a voice beside her.

Quiet, firm, composed.

It was Elizabeth Ralsten.

"Sir, it is not right that these people should die for something done by my husband and son." She paused, while taking a deep breath, and then continued. "Let me take their place. It's not right that anyone should have to die here today; but if you feel you must kill someone, then kill me."

A look of amusement came over Akmed's face.

"I will say it again, I am impressed with your bravery, Mrs. Ralsten. Even if it is utterly foolish. Your husband and son would do well to examine themselves in the light of your courage. It is more than I would expect from the likes of all of you. But I'm afraid I must decline your most generous offer."

▼▼477▼▼

"It is not just a 'generous offer.' It is what Jesus did for us," Elizabeth continued, remaining on her feet. "He died for our sins. He took our place, though He did not deserve to die. The only 'sin' that my husband and son have committed is wanting to escape from this terror you have heaped upon us. If that is a 'sin,' it is one of which all of us in this room are guilty in our hearts. Perhaps they were unwise to act as they did. Perhaps they lacked courage in that particular moment. But I am certain that they would not wish for anyone in this room to die needlessly and without just cause for something that they did."

Akmed's gaze never left Elizabeth.

"And so I ask you again," she said softly but with definiteness, enunciating each word. "If someone must die to appease your 'word of honor,' then let it be me. Let these young people go!"

The room was still.

Not even the sound of a foot shuffling.

Esther felt a flood of pride as she watched Elizabeth.

"Sit down, Mrs. Ralsten."

Elizabeth did not move.

Akmed took a step toward her. "If you do not sit down, Mrs. Ralsten, I will make you sit down. And I assure you, it will be painful. Learn from your husband's and your son's errors. Obedience is best."

Elizabeth sat down.

Akmed smiled. Then he turned to Mamdouh Ekrori.

"Make certain that the cameras are facing the wall until I say otherwise. We will use them again later." He put the microphone down on the floor and moved away. "What we must do now will best be done without the world looking on. Aziza, Mousa, Ihab. Come."

"HE'S GETTING READY to kill some people. How

much longer before you're ready?"

Webber paused, listening for a response from inside the church building.

"We have the lobby doors and windows blacked out. Our entry teams are ready. Hamdi thinks he's about two-thirds of the way. Maybe ten more minutes. He can hear voices. But the turns are tight to get through. He's got to go slow. If they hear him, it's history. And so is he!"

"I know, I know," Webber's voice was filled with resignation. "Look, we've got more trouble here. Our friend Akmed has just turned all the cameras toward the wall. The only thing we can make out are the bumps in the wallboard. He's away from the microphone too. Whatever he intends to do, he's not about to show and tell. At least not until he's finished. I think he's moving his troops though, and we're not going to be able to tell you where they're at."

Hendrickson swore and bit his lip, hard enough to draw blood. Everything was timing. Timing down to the second. If they did not know where the bad guys were, the rescue plan was never going to fly!

Webber's voice crackled over the radio. "Any bright ideas?"

"Yeah. Pray for a miracle!"

CONNIE FARRER had been doing just that. She desperately wanted to call the station back again, but Aziza was too close. She hadn't dared to risk exposing the fact that she had a cellular phone in her possession. But the miracle she'd been praying for had just happened.

Akmed was calling the others forward. Each of the groups remained huddled in front of the doors, but the terrorists were well removed from where they were sitting. Connie tucked in her stomach and once again pulled the instrument from its hiding place. She punched in the numbers to Jody's desk.

"Hello," the voice answered before the first ring had finished.

"Jody?" Connie whispered, conscious of the anxious looks being given her by others in her group.

"Yes! Oh, thank God you're okay and you've still got the phone."

Yes, thought Connie. *Thank God.*

"Connie, what's happening? They've turned the cameras and shut down the microphones. We're not getting anything from inside."

"I know. Listen carefully. They're getting ready to kill some people! I think it's going to happen at any moment. Is anybody out there going to help us?" Her voice filled with desperation.

"The police and the FBI are all outside, Connie. I'm sure they're doing everything they can. But now they can't see inside, so . . ."

"They can if I can talk to them."

"What?"

"Patch me through to whoever is running the show, Jody. I can tell them what they need to know. I can see everything from here. But hurry. I really think they're getting ready to kill somebody!"

"I'm putting you on hold, Connie. I'll be right back."

Connie looked toward the front of the church. They were all still standing there, talking together in Arabic.

JODY ANSEL LOOKED AT THE CIRCLE of anxious faces around her desk.

"Well?" demanded Betty.

"They've shut the world out because they are going to kill some people. Connie's watching it all and hoping somebody comes quickly."

Betty swore softly, her face alight with excitement, her

hands clenching and unclenching over slightly damaged nails. "It's what we've been waiting for."

"What do you mean?" asked Jody.

"Get her back on the line. We can give a blow by blow report of the situation. We'll scoop every network with the biggest story we've touched in years. This is it, Jody! It's our big break." Betty threw her hands in the air. "The ratings game is about to be won by KFOR!"

"Betty, you're crazy!"

Everyone turned toward Tom Bernstein. "You're talking ratings and people inside that church are about to die. Good grief, woman, have you no soul?"

Betty stared at Tom, hatred boiling in her eyes.

"Tom Bernstein, I want . . ."

"He's right, Betty."

Jody could hardly believe whose voice she heard speak up. It was her own.

Betty's jaw dropped open as she looked at Jody. Then it clamped shut. Tight!

"You're fired, Jody. And so is the Great Tom Bernstein! Both of you get out of my studio!"

"I'll be happy to leave," Jody heard herself saying, gathering courage with each word. "But only after this is over. Right now I'm calling the FBI, so get out of my way and stay off my back!"

Betty started to say something, stopped, then looked again at KFOR's lead anchor. Everyone else stood frozen in place, watching their off-camera minidrama work through to its climax.

Tom Bernstein smiled. "I'm with her, Betty," he said, with mock innocence, nodding toward Jody.

Betty's face turned crimson. Her hands went to her hips. Her eyes darted back and forth between these two mutineers. Then without a word, she turned and flounced out of the studio.

IN LESS THAN FIVE MINUTES, Jody Ansel was talking with SAC Duane Webber of the FBI, explaining the situation to him.

"You have a what?" was his incredulous response.

"A reporter from KFOR went to church there yesterday, before coming in to work. She's still in there and I've got her on a cellular phone."

"Hold on . . . what's your name again?"

"Jody Ansel."

"Hold on, Jody. I'll be right back."

Webber flipped on his radio phone.

"Hendrickson!"

"Yes, sir."

"I think we just got our miracle!"

"Sir?"

"Channel 4 has a reporter inside the church. She's been there all along. And she's got a cellular phone. I'm going to speak with her right now. Hang in there a bit longer. By the way, where's Hamdi?"

"He needs another five, sir."

"I'll be right back."

He switched off the radio and picked up the cellular phone.

"Hello. Who am I talking to?"

"My name is Connie Farrer," whispered a female voice.

"This is Duane Webber, FBI. Connie, Jody Ansel vouches for you that you're the real thing, and not a plant, so here's the deal. We're about ready to send in a SWAT team, but I need your help. I need you to be a part of the entry team. Okay?"

"Yes."

"We need your eyes. We can't see anything in there right now. I've got a sniper moving into position. Maybe five more minutes. I've got SWAT teams at each door. We have to take out the leader so that he doesn't have a chance to blow the doors. Do you understand?"

"Yes," the voice whispered.

"Connie, when we come through the doors, we have to know where the bad guys are. By the way, we count five of them. Do you agree with that?"

"Yes."

"All right. Tell me exactly where those five people are located and give me an idea of what's happening in there. Why did they turn the cameras away?"

Connie Farrer whispered her story into Duane Webber's ear.

"MRS. CAIN? Do not delay any longer. What is your decision?"

Esther stared at the four people standing on the platform. The attention of every person in the room was riveted on the wife of Calvary Church's senior pastor, the mother of one of Akmed's chosen victims.

"Please," she said, her voice low and strained. "I cannot do this. I cannot make such a decision. What you are asking is impossible."

"Then all four will die," Akmed said abruptly, motioning toward one of the terrorists who stood near by.

"Wait!" Esther cried out.

Akmed stopped, then turned back to Esther.

"Oh, please. Don't do this terrible thing."

"Then decide, Mrs. Cain! Who should live? Who will die?"

Akmed waited.

Tears fell down Esther's cheeks as she looked at the chosen four.

"Mrs. Cain, you are wasting our time. Let's not protract the inevitable any longer. It is within your power to save two lives. Isn't that what you and your Christian husband do?

Save lives?" The smile that crept across his face was countered by the hard glint in his eyes. "That is what you claim to do, is it not? So I am giving you an opportunity to fulfill your vocation. If you refuse, all four will die. Two unnecessarily, and all because of you. That will remain on your Christian conscience for a long time, will it not?"

"But this is my son. My own flesh and blood. And Allison has done nothing to deserve this. And the Heidens. What have they done to you? You can see that this woman is with child. Take her life and you take the life of her unborn baby. These are innocents. What purpose will be served? In the name of God, what can you people possibly hope to achieve with such calloused madness?"

Esther's voice was strong. Her tears fell to the floor.

Akmed's eyes were darker now, forboding, like some terrible thundercloud. His voice stirred with sudden passion, his hand twitching involuntarily as he spoke.

"What purpose will be served, you ask? I will tell you what purpose. We will show the world that it has no alternative. Palestine must be granted the right to live again or every one of her enemies will remain under the sentence of death. Not just two or four," his hand swept dramatically across the congregation, "but four hundred or four hundred thousand! The enemies of the people of Palestine are the enemies of Allah. We will strike you again and again, until justice prevails at last!"

"But we are not your enemies," Esther cried. "We don't even know you!"

"Ah, yes," Akmed smiled grimly. "Perhaps that is the problem. You do not know us. But you will. That I can guarantee you. And you will give us what we want. Sooner or later. No, Mrs. Cain, you must choose. And you must do it *now!*"

Esther slowly moved toward Akmed. She felt weak. Numb. Desolate. Defeated.

"Akmed," she spoke his name softly.

She had heard the others call him by name. But she had never let it cross her own lips. To do so, she felt, would make this evil intruder a person. It would give him a mother. A father. Perhaps brothers and sisters. It would permit the inhuman to become human. Esther had not allowed herself to think in those terms at any time.

Until now.

Now she knew she must. She did not understand what drove these persons to such desperate deeds. But they were people. They were not things. They were not animals without souls. They were flesh and blood people.

And they had names.

"Akmed," she said again, her eyes shining. "If you must kill someone, kill me."

"No!"

"Please, Akmed. Hear me out. Let these children live. Let them live to understand the plight of your people. Think about it. My death will serve your purpose in a far greater way than theirs could ever do. You'll be killing the leader's wife. You claim that my husband is in your hands in Israel. Perhaps he is dead already. Don't you see, Akmed? You will serve your purpose far better by taking my life than by killing them. Let the children live!"

Akmed hesitated, folding his arms. He held the detonator in his left hand, running a thumb across the switch as he considered what Esther said.

Suddenly, without warning, he fell backward, clutching his throat.

The detonator dropped from his hand to the floor.

He looked at Esther in disbelief.

Then, the entire room was swept into darkness!

"I HAVE HIM, SIR."

Hendrickson heard Hamdi's voice crackle into his earphone. It was a high voice and always reminded him of a young boy, not yet past the age of puberty. *A boy's voice for a man's job.*

"Hold it."

Hendrickson took a last look around at his men. At each of the three doors he could see, five-member teams were standing ready. He knew the scene was identical at the two doors beyond the periphery of his vision.

Each man wore Kevlar headgear, a solid piece looking a little like a biker's helmet fitted with goggles. Fatigues worn in a pants-in-boots style. Combat boots. A flack jacket. And a radio pack on the back with a receiver attached firmly in the ear. From head to toe, they were dressed in black.

Each team was now positioned less than three feet from their respective door entry. Like dominoes, they were stacked together, every man pressed against the one in front. Attached to the hip, each one wore a SIG-Sauer P226 handgun loaded with a twenty-round clip. Team leaders carried sawed-off shotguns with Heckler and Koch MP-5 submachine guns strapped on their shoulders. The others held submachine guns in their right hands. Attached to each weapon was a slender laser light to enable them to find targets in total darkness. In their left hands, the men held onto battering rams.

Jim Corry was the lone agent assigned to the entry plan who was not a regular member of the SWAT team. He had been relegated to the electrical control panel located in the basement. His hand was on the master switch that provided power to the sanctuary. It tightened as he listened over the receiver in his ear.

Hendrickson grinned.

"Everyone is in position," he spoke into his radiophone.

"Go when ready," Webber responded from the command center.

"Team One?"

"Ready."

"Team Two?"

"Ready, sir."

"Team Three is ready," Hendrickson said for the benefit of the others. He would be leading Team Three through the center doors himself.

"Team Four?"

"Ready."

"Team Five?"

"Ready."

"Corry."

"Ready."

"Hamdi?"

"Ready, sir."

"All right. We'll do it just like we've rehearsed. Tell me when he's down, Hamdi."

The following four seconds seemed like minutes.

"He's down!"

"All teams," Hendrickson spoke firmly into the radio phone. "Execute! Execute! Execute!"

FORTY

Esther saw Akmed stagger back and reach for his throat.
That was all.

Then a curtain of darkness descended and pandemonium broke loose!

Pitch black erupted with the sounds of splintering wood.

Two flash-bangs exploded near the center of the sanctuary. Their sudden brightness blinded Esther. The noise was so painfully loud that she thought her eardrums were bursting. Narrow swords of light sliced through the darkness from every direction.

"Down! Down! Down!"

Strange voices shouting.

The rush of many footsteps.

People throwing themselves onto the floor.

People scrambling for cover under the pews.

People sprawling flat in the doorways and aisles where earlier they had been ordered to sit.

People desperately trying to survive!

Connie Farrer lunged forward, banging her head against

the side of a pew as she fell. She cried out as shadowy figures kicked and crushed her back and legs while charging through the darkness. Something long and heavy dropped on top of her exposed legs, pinning them in an awkward position.

On the platform, Esther defied the order to get down, throwing herself instead in the direction in which she had last seen Jeremy, Allison, and the Heidens. She stumbled over the kneeling forms of the Heidens and collided with Jeremy. Like broken sticks they fell, Jeremy toppling onto Allison as Esther rolled between them and the terrorists.

Uneven streams of light bobbed and weaved around them as the staccato of gunfire echoed in the chambers of the Lord. The room filled with the cries of the wounded and dying, mingling their voices with the fearful screams of the living.

Esther untangled herself from the others. As she rose to a kneeling position, she saw Aziza's face suddenly caught in the probing glare of a thin stream of light. She too had stumbled during the first confusing seconds of the attack. Now she was on her knees, barely an arm's length from Esther, submachine gun in hand, her beautiful face frozen with fright. Aziza's eyes darted about desperately, seeking a way of salvation from this terrible day of judgment.

A split second later, Esther was outlined by one of the light pencils and a flash of recognition passed between them.

She had often heard that the events of people's lives flashed across their memories just before dying. But that was not what Esther saw. Instead, another drama raced through her mind at the speed of light, leaving every frame indelibly imprinted in her thoughts.

A beautiful young girl came skipping through the rock-strewn streets of a Middle-Eastern town, her freshly washed dress bobbing up and down at her knees. With bare, sandaled feet, she kicked a pink and blue ball against a high wall, then chased after it through the dirt and dust. The child's laughter was familiar, yet she knew she had never seen her. Esther watched her pirouette gaily, hands raised toward the sky. Suddenly a soldier stood in the street, pointing his gun at the girl.

"No," Esther cried, the call torn from the depths of her womb. "No!"

She heard the staccato melody of death.

She watched as the child stopped her dancing to look at the soldier. She glimpsed the dazed look of innocence lost, of bewilderment and dilemma.

The little child turned and looked at Esther.

Her eyes were full of sadness and pain.

Her lips formed two words.

"Help me."

Then her beautiful face exploded!

Esther felt the pain.

It ripped its way into her mind.

It slammed the breath from her body.

She reached for the face that was no longer there and as she did, she began falling... falling... into the darkness ... where she felt the pain no longer.

FORTY-ONE

MONDAY, 19 SEPTEMBER, 1950 LOCAL TIME
JERUSALEM, ISRAEL

John awoke with a start. Where was he?

Esther? Jessica? What?

He stared at the bare light bulb and gradually reentered reality. He looked across to the opposite bed where Edgar and Bob were snoring loudly. He turned his head the other way until he saw Gisele Eiderman. She was awake. She looked tired, but gave him a weak smile.

"We've got to stop meeting like this," she quipped.

John rolled over, letting his feet drop to the floor. He sat up, still embarrassed by the intimacy of their situation.

"I tried the floor, Gisele," he whispered. "It's hard."

"I know," she replied hastily. "I didn't mean anything by what I said. Just my attempt to lighten these moments with a little levity."

"I know," replied John. "Don't stop, whatever you do."

Edgar stirred, licked at dry lips, and opened his eyes.

"Bad breath alley over here, folks," he said. "And Bob snores a lot worse than Jill, that's for sure."

"Oh, yeah?" came Bob Thomas' voice from the far side.

"Well, the last few hours on this bed have given me one more reason why I married Donna and not a horse like you, Ed."

They chuckled quietly.

Each of them was sitting up now, except for Gisele. She had turned over on her side to face the others. Their banter sounded good to John. *Healthy, given their circumstances. Amazing what a few hours of sleep will do for one's perspective.*

John looked over at their two male captors. They were asleep.

His mind turned again to Jessica.

Where are you, sweetheart?

Thoughts of Esther and Jeremy made him depressed.

What is happening to them? Are they safe? Lord, please keep Your hand of protection over my family. Somehow, get us all through this mess and bring us together again.

He sat down on the floor facing the wall, and resumed the task he had broken off. The others watched with growing interest. With the same idea planted in their minds, they quietly checked the fixtures to which their chains were attached. After a bit, they shook their heads and directed their attention back to John. Silently, he twisted and pulled for another hour.

Outside the door, someone was talking in low tones. John twisted around until his back was against the wall fixture as Yazib and Pasha entered the room.

Pasha replaced the backpack on the table while Yazib walked over to where John was sitting.

"You like it down there, Reverend Cain?" Yazib smiled. "It does not look very comfortable to me."

"I'm not very comfortable, actually," John replied. "Would you like to remove these chains? That would go a long way toward making me feel more at home."

"Ah, yes, I am sure it would," Yazib responded agreeably. "All in good time, Reverend Cain. All in good time."

Pasha stood next to Yazib. John thought she had the coldest eyes of any human being he had ever known.

"Lean forward, Reverend Cain," Yazib commanded.

"What?"

"Lean forward. Quickly." He cuffed the side of John's head with his hand. John leaned forward, still in a sitting position. Yazib gave the fixture and chain a visual check, but did not try to reach in behind and pull on it. John was grateful. The device was looser as a result of his own pulling and twisting. But the small flat plate, lying flush against the wall, kept its weakening a secret.

TUESDAY, 20 SEPTEMBER, 0015 LOCAL TIME
JERUSALEM, ISRAEL

JOHN HAD NEVER SEEN THE MAN BEFORE. He looked to be about thirty years old, but he could not be sure. He was dressed in a rumpled white shirt and unpressed pants. Leather sandals were attached to his bare feet by straps. He had been in the room only a short time, whispering to Yazib, when Yazib took him by the arm and led him out the door. A messenger perhaps. But with what message? John wished that he knew. But he didn't. He didn't even know what time of day it was.

When Yazib returned, he was alone. He acted agitated and upset. He motioned to Pasha and they went back outside, leaving the door partially open. Since the others were outside on guard duty, it was the first time the prisoners had been left alone since their arrival. Yazib's and Pasha's muffled voices could be heard rising and falling. They sounded as though they could be arguing about something, but they spoke in Arabic and it was impossible for John and the others to tell for sure.

They looked at one another quizzically.

"What do you suppose is going on?" Bob asked.

"I wish I knew," John replied. "They are upset, so something is not going well."

"I wonder if that's good news for us or bad," mused Gisele, staring at the door.

Edgar glanced down at John, still sitting on the floor, his back against the side of the bed.

"How's it going down there?"

John smiled. He glanced at the door to reassure himself that their captors could not hear, then turned his attention to the fixture to which his chain was attached.

"Look."

He pulled the plate back about an inch from the wall. Behind it, Edgar could see that the crack in the cement had further deteriorated and the first threads of the eye were visible. It looked more like a large screw than a bolt. That was encouraging.

"How long do you suppose this thing is?" John asked.

"Who knows. A couple of inches? Probably more like four or five," Edgar answered.

"Unfortunately, I haven't anything to dig with other than my fingers."

"Maybe this will help," Gisele said. She began removing her belt.

"Thanks anyway, Gisele. If they catch me with that belt . . . well . . . "

"I'll take care of the belt, John. This is the part you need. The buckle just snaps off. See?" Gisele smiled as she held it up.

John took it from her. It was V-shaped. He turned it over in his hand, then pulled back the plate and inserted the buckle behind it. He began digging and scraping, using the buckle as a chisel while the others watched. John looked up and smiled.

"This is much better. It just might work, if I have enough time."

"Voices. Get rid of that belt," Edgar exclaimed, looking

over at Gisele. She pretended to be sleeping, while her hand worked it under the old mattress, just as their captors came through the doorway. Enough of a space around the eye screw had been dug so that John could push the buckle in behind the plate. Then he leaned back against it.

The three men and the cold-eyed woman they had come to know as Pasha stood near the doorway, looking at the prisoners.

"The news for you is bad," Yazib began. "The Great Satan and your infidel leaders have been unwilling to meet our demands. As a result, the city of Boston has been destroyed with a biological weapon! Hundreds of thousands are dead!"

John and the others stared at their captors incredulously.

"I don't believe you," John said, finally, breaking the silence.

Yazib stepped forward suddenly and kicked John in the ribs.

Again.

A third time!

John doubled over in pain, gasping for breath.

Edgar yelled, "Stop it!"

The two guards with guns lifted them to the ready position. Edgar sensed that everyone's nerves were on the edge and slowly sat back on the bed.

"You would not know the truth, even if it was about to destroy you," Yazib snarled angrily, his focus still on John. Twice more he lashed out savagely with his boot, catching John in the stomach and then across the side of his face. He lay doubled in a fetal position, trying desperately not to groan, not wanting to give Yazib the satisfaction of knowing just how much pain he was absorbing.

"And, for you, Reverend Cain, it is worse. Much worse."

Gasping for breath, John squinted up at Yazib who stood over him now, hands on his hips.

"Your army attempted to dislodge our team of Freedom

Fighters in California. We were given no alternative but to blow up the church. Our people gave their lives as soldiers of Allah. Your congregation is no longer, Reverend Cain. Because they rejected the cry of reason, the call of Allah, they have been doomed to spend eternity in hell!" Yazib paused, watching the impact of his words sink into the soul of the man doubled up on the floor. "I regret to inform you that your wife is among the dead!"

John shut the words out by pressing his eyelids tightly together. He worked to control the groan of anguish and defeat that fought to scream out from somewhere inside. He felt as though he would explode.

It was a moment he would never forget.

Never!

He wanted to kill!

In that same instant, without any warning, something else happened. Something defying real definition.

As John lay there on the floor, he felt . . . a *presence.* Something . . . no, *someone* had entered the room.

Who is it?

John had never experienced anything like it.

Maybe I've taken one too many hits on the head. What is going on? He was conscious of lying on the floor, twisting with pain. But the undeniable *presence* was there alongside him. Down on the floor.

And John knew something else.

He knew that *this mysterious presence was feeling his pain!*

John was not a man given to mystic flights of fantasy. That's why this seemed so incredible.

He knew what . . . no, *he knew who the Presence was!*

And he knew that he was dirty and bloody and beaten. But he was not broken!

He looked up just as Yazib spit in his face.

"Come." Yazib turned away from John's inert form, and

in Arabic said to the others, "I want to finalize our plans with the rest of you."

The others backed away from their prisoners and followed Yazib through the doorway.

Edgar, Bob, and Gisele were too overwhelmed for words.

They looked at one another, tears filling their eyes. Quickly they scrambled to help John from the floor. Bob's chain did not permit him to move that far, but Edgar and Gisele were able to reach him. They were silent, not knowing what to say, afraid even to look into John's face.

When they did, they were surprised.

John was trying to smile!

His lip was cut and swollen, but there was the sign of a twinkle in his eye. At least in the one that remained fully open. Edgar and Gisele looked at one another apprehensively. Had John finally gone over the edge? Had the beatings and the pressure made him snap?

"John, are you okay?" Edgar asked, concern outlining each word.

"I'm okay," John answered through gritted teeth, straining to resist taking a deep breath, knowing that if he did, he might pass out from the pain. "I could use a new rib or two, but I'm okay, thanks."

Gisele wiped at the blood oozing down his chin from the broken lip. John winced and mumbled, "I suppose I could use a face-lift too."

"You'll be okay," Gisele responded, but her voice sounded flat and unconvincing. "John, did you hear what that man said?"

"I heard him."

"I'm so very sorry..." her voice trailed off, tears spilling onto her cheeks.

"It's not true."

The others stared at John.

"It's not true. He's lying," he said again.

"How can you be so sure?" asked Bob. "Why would he say such things if they were not true?"

"It hurts to talk," John mumbled. "Can you understand me?"

They nodded.

"At first, I was like the rest of you," John explained. "Yazib caught me off guard. But then I watched him. And the others too. Did you notice how the others looked while he was telling us of their 'great victory'? Like the 'Niners had just lost the Super Bowl 54–0! If they've had such great success as terrorists in America, don't you think they'd show it in their faces?"

The others pondered and continued listening.

"My guess is that something has happened all right. But it's not to their liking. The main reason I don't think they're telling the truth, though, is hard to explain." John formed each word carefully. "Something happened while he was kicking me around. I felt something. There was a *Presence*— right here with me. I've never experienced anything like it before.

"For a while, I thought I might be dying and going to heaven. That's what it felt like. Then, the most incredible assurance came over me. There wasn't a voice, and there were no specifics. I don't honestly know how Esther and the people back home are faring. I don't even know where Jessica is or what she is doing."

A shadow of anxiety passed over his countenance and his voice wavered. He cleared his throat, and continued.

"All I can honestly say to you is that I have put them all in God's hands. I don't know any of the details, but the assurance that God is with each member of my family, and yours too, is very strong. That may not make any sense, given what we're facing here, but that's what's happening as I see it."

They were all leaning forward, studying his face as he struggled to talk to them. Edgar was the first to respond.

"Pastor, I know times have been hard for you these past couple of years. Jill and I have been prayin' every day for you and Esther and your kids. Even comin' over here on the plane, I felt this sudden need to pray for you. And I did too. Now, here we are in one really deep mess. But I want you to know somethin' 'bout how I feel.

"I been followin' you as my pastor for the last eleven years. I've seen others come and go in our church. But you've been a good shepherd to Jill and me. If she were here right now, she'd say the same. For what it's worth, I'm glad I'm here with you! Whatever happens, I want you to know that. This situation ain't your fault. There's no surprises with God. Remember? That's what you been tellin' us back home. So, He knew this was comin' down even before we left town.

"I say let's pray for strength and wisdom. And courage too. Didn't you tell us once that Martin Luther used to say, 'Pray as though everything depends on God, but work as though everything depends on you'? We're not the first Christians to be locked up in this city. We may not be the last. So let's do it. Let's pray as though it all depends on God, because it does. Then maybe He'll give us an opportunity to work as though getting out of here all depends on us!"

The others nodded in agreement and, chained to a wall underneath Jerusalem's Al Aqsa Mosque, they joined their hands and called on God.

After Edgar led in a brief, heartfelt prayer, John lowered his bruised, battered body to the floor. He sat facing the door, expecting their captors to return at any minute.

Meanwhile, he lifted the plate and, even though each move was painful, he worked Gisele's belt buckle further and further into the hole.

JERUSALEM POST, INTERNATIONAL EDITION

The Department of State issued a direct appeal to the Palestinian leaders of Harakat al-Muqawama al-Islamiyya [Hamas], urging them to use every means at their disposal to bring about the safe return of the American hostages believed to be held by extremists within their organization.

Twenty-five persons are believed to have been taken hostage by Arab terrorists who belong to the Palestinian Islamic Jihad, a small, right-wing fundamentalist group with roots in Hamas. The Americans were last seen boarding their tour bus at Ein Bokek. The bus was recovered late Saturday night near the Old City in Jerusalem.

Yesterday morning, the body of an elderly woman, possibly an American, was found in the parking lot at Nabi Musa. Authorities report that she was shot twice at close range. They are endeavoring to identify her at this time. It is unconfirmed whether or not she was a part of the missing group.

Security has been tightened at all borders and at Ben-Gurion International Airport. All military leaves have been cancelled. The IDF and other security forces have been placed on full alert. House-to-house searches continue. So far, no trace of the missing Americans has been found.

FORTY-TWO

The wail of sirens filled Baytown's city streets. Washington Avenue, normally filled with shoppers and delivery trucks, was blocked off by motorcycle police. Ambulances and patrol cars shuttled back and forth. Bright yellow fire department emergency vehicles raced by, warning lights flashing, air horns blaring, and sirens sounding their mournful lament.

People watched from the safety of store windows, or stood under awnings in the afternoon shade. Others sat in the outdoor patio at the Coffee Bean, drinking cappuccino. School had let out early. The subject on everyone's lips was of the Arab terrorists and the families being held hostage at Calvary Church and the terrible weekend events that had taken place in Boston.

Record school absenteeism had been noted at Baytown High, indicating the concern felt by parents for the safety of their children. School Principal Tom Hedgewick, who was known for his dry wit, commented at the emergency faculty meeting that the students were probably safer today than any other day, with as many police personnel as were in town.

A key factor leading to an early dismissal of classes, however, was concern for the seventeen students from Baytown High who were numbered among the hostages. The emotional upheaval among students who had turned up was high. Classwork concentration had proven, early on, to be impossible.

At nine o'clock, an assembly was called for the entire faculty and student body. When Mr. Hedgewick announced that school would be let out early, what normally would have been met with whoops of joy and stomping of feet was received in sober silence.

He went on to tell his audience that he was well aware of the legal ban on public prayer in school, but that he had decided to call the student body to prayer anyway. This announcement was met with an unexpected, spontaneous burst of applause. Mr. Hedgewick offered to excuse anybody who might be offended by something as radical as school prayers, giving them opportunity to leave. No one walked. Three students and two faculty members volunteered to lead in prayer. They were brief, to the point, and heartfelt. There were few dry eyes at their conclusion.

The same decision to dismiss early had been reached in the elementary and junior high schools scattered around Baytown. Parents were notified, buses ran early, and childcare programs went into operation.

Teens crowded into the parking lot at McDonalds, eating Big Macs, sharing fries, and downing large Cokes. A worried manager had called the police to alert them regarding this unexpected gathering of young people. In a few minutes, a motorcycle patrolman arrived. There were no problems, however, and after a while the patrolman asked for student leader volunteers to insure the orderliness of the gathering. They promised to call if problems arose with dope or weapons. About the same time, Mr. Hedgewick arrived, ordered a hamburger and a Coke, and settled into the middle of the crowd.

The patrolman left. A cheer went up from the students. Was it because he was leaving? Or because of what he represented in this unprecedented Baytown event? He chuckled to himself as he sped down the avenue and thought that he would never know for sure.

Now suddenly, at eleven forty-five in the morning, Washington Avenue was the place to be. According to radio reports, an FBI SWAT team had broken through to the hostages. There had been casualties, but the exact number was unknown. Someone reported that they had heard an explosion.

As if by magic, motorcycle officers swept down Washington Avenue and pealed off at each intersection, all the way to East Bay Hospital. EBH was the largest medical center in the area and it housed a trauma unit. Blood reserves had been bolstered. Medical personnel were in readiness at EBH as well as at neighboring medical centers. No one could guess the outcome of the event unfolding in their town. The possibility of hundreds dead or wounded was very real. They were determined to be ready.

High overhead, several television helicopters circled the city, capturing the drama and sending it live to their respective studios where images were flashed by satellite to millions of viewers watching at work or at home.

Three Baystar medical emergency helicopters lifted off the church parking lot. Twin Allison engines powered the white Messerschmitt air rescue units into the sky. Flight nurses worked over their patients, operating on-board cardiac monitors, oxygen and respirator equipment, oblivious to all else but the lives of the people who lay strapped onto the stretchers.

Next, two Army medical evacuation helicopters rose

above the mayhem, flying the most severely injured, in three-minute intervals, to EBH.

Police units and ambulances rolled back and forth between the church and the hospital. Then in less than thirty minutes, the street grew silent. Motorcycle officers could be seen talking to each other and conversing on their radios with the command center. After another ten minutes, they mounted their Harley Davidsons and roared up the street toward the church.

Someone remarked that the only thing missing was the rolling of movie credits.

All along the avenue, people stood in small groups, imagining what might possibly have happened inside Calvary Church during these last hours.

FORTY-THREE

The sanctuary erupted into deafening explosions, the rattle of gunfire and total darkness interrupted with brilliant flashes. All this was accentuated by frightening shouts and screams. It seemed to go on forever. In actuality, the attack lasted exactly forty-three seconds!

FROM HIS CRAMPED POSITION in the air-conditioning duct, Agent Hamdi carefully sighted his .308 high powered, silencer-equipped rifle on Akmed el Hussein.

"I have him, sir," he said softly into his radio phone.

"Hold it," came Hendrickson's reply.

Hamdi took note of the hand that held the detonator and considered, for a brief moment the possibility of shooting it out of the man's hand. He knew he could do it. But what if his shot set the detonator off? No. He could not take that chance. Besides, when he was finished, there would be only four targets for the entry teams to dispatch.

His concentration was nearly total now.

Suddenly, he felt shaken as the conversation below entered his consciousness. The woman was pleading with the terrorist leader. His hand wavered slightly as he listened. "Let these children live. . . . You will serve your purpose far better by taking my life."

He swore softly. *That woman, whoever she is, is bartering her life.*

He readjusted his aim.

Now he heard the entry team check-off taking place in his earpiece.

"Hamdi?"

"Ready, sir."

"All right. We'll do it just like we've rehearsed. Tell me the second he's down."

His heart was pounding. He took a deep breath.

Slowly he tightened his finger on the trigger.

A moment later, he said the words. "He's down!"

A boy's voice for a man's job.

"ALL TEAMS. Execute! Execute! Execute!"

Agent Corry slammed the master switch down on the electrical panel. The entire building was dropped into total darkness. His job was now half done.

HENDRICKSON FELT THE MOMENTUM of the men behind him. They struck the double doors with such force that the battering ram literally tore the left side door off its hinges while the right side splintered and sagged. The men rushed headlong into the darkness, stumbling over bodies that were scrambling to get out of the way.

Two flash-bangs were hurled into the center aisle. Hopefully, no one would be standing there at the moment. The sound was deafening and the flash bright enough to temporarily blind unprotected eyes. They would provide the edge of surprise that was needed.

"Down! Down! Down!"

Get everyone but the bad guys out of the line of fire! *Now!*

Flip on the laser light attached to each weapon. Hope the bad guys are still where they're supposed to be.

Search!

No! A civilian.

Search!

Yes! The agent behind Hendrickson fired at the same time someone shot from the left side.

The Arab disappeared.

Search!

Rapid fire on the right!

A cry. Someone got it. Hope it's a bad guy.

Search!

There he is, running to the left. He's shooting.

More screams!

More shouts!

Three lights seek him out simultaneously. More rapid fire. He's gone.

Search!

The woman! She's on her knees on the platform. There's a gun in her hand. She's firing!

A light from the left.

Hendrickson fired.

Shots from the left also.

In that same split second, someone else's hands reached into the light, toward the woman with the gun.

"Cease fire! Cease fire! Cease fire!"

THE STILLNESS WAS DEAFENING!

The laserlike lights continued their macabre dance, like

strobes at a rock concert gone out of control. But the raucous sounds of gunfire were silenced. It seemed as though the entire room held its collective breath.

Waiting.

At last, a child whimpered.

A moan was heard near the back of the sanctuary.

"Power on," Hendrickson spoke quietly into his radio mike.

Corry stood in the utility room with his flashlight trained on the master switch. As soon as he heard Hendrickson's voice, he lifted the switch.

Now he was finished.

He left the room on the run.

HENDRICKSON AND HIS MEN moved about slowly, surveying the chaos of the sanctuary. People came crawling out from under the pews where they had hidden for protection. They stared in utter amazement at the ominous looking men dressed in black, watching with a kind of reverent deference as SWAT team members checked the bodies of the people who, only moments before, had appeared to be irrevocably in control.

"Webber!" Hendrickson called to the Command Center.

"Yes?" came Webber's anxious voice.

"We're done. We're secure. We need medics."

"They're on the way."

A moment later, uniformed police and FBI personnel came running through the entrances. Medical teams hurried into the sanctuary to begin working with the civilian wounded, as well as the terrorists.

"How are we?" Webber asked, walking up to Hendrickson, who was standing in the center aisle, near the front.

"I think I have one man down, but alive. Johnson says the bad guy he's with is still alive. Barely. The rest are dead.

We've got some civilian casualties. I don't know yet how many." He hesitated. "There's a woman on the platform. When we took out the female terrorist, she came into the line of fire. I'm not sure about her."

"Medic!" It was was Dr. Orwell's voice. He was looking up over the back of a pew. "Over here quickly. We've got an irregular heartbeat. Bring some oxygen with you."

Hendrickson walked with Webber toward the platform. The shot of adrenaline that had peaked as he rammed his way through the door was finally beginning to subside. He watched the three medics on their knees, working with the civilian woman who had been caught in the line of fire. "Oh, no," groaned Webber, catching sight of her face.

Hendrickson looked over at him.

"You know her?"

"It's Mrs. Cain, the senior pastor's wife."

They lifted her onto the stretcher. An agent was ordering a Baystar helicopter to get ready for a run.

"What's her condition?" Webber asked the supervising medic.

"Barely alive. Hit in the head, the shoulder, and one went through her back and out her chest. Lost a lot of blood."

"Will she make it?"

The medic sighed and shrugged. "Who knows? Excuse me. I've got another situation here."

"What's with the other woman?" Webber asked, seeing several medics gathered around someone laying near the choir loft.

"She's pregnant. Her water broke. The kid is on the way. Looks like we're going to have to deliver right here!"

Webber looked at Hendrickson. They shook their heads.

"Life and death. I guess they're never far apart."

"What do you say we go get a drink?"

"Good idea."

"Hendrickson?"

"Yeah?"

"You and your boys did good."

"Thanks."

"You were right."

"What?"

"About Hamdi."

"Yeah. Well, he's a good kid."

"He sounds like a kid, doesn't he? I want to meet that guy before you leave, and shake his hand."

"Sure."

Near the doorway through which Hendrickson's team had entered, they sidestepped two firemen, busily getting another victim ready to be lifted onto a stretcher.

Webber put his hand on Hendrickson's shoulder as they strolled into the afternoon sun.

OUTSIDE, THE TWO MEN WALKED into the sights and sounds of parking lot pandemonium. The first Baystar helicopter was lifting off the lot. Another idled nearby, while a stretcher case was placed inside. A uniformed policeman shouted orders into a megaphone. Ambulances were lining up in the handicap zones. The blue van in which the terrorists had arrived was already marked off by yellow crime-scene tape. Two policemen stood guard.

Television crews were repositioning cameras around the patio steps. About fifty feet away, Webber saw Joe Randle talking with several reporters. *He did a good job with those people. I need to remember to tell White. He's a good man.*

"What can you tell us?"

"How is it in there?"

"Are all the terrorists dead?"

"How many civilian casualties?"

"Where did these people come from?"

"What did they hope to accomplish?"

Webber looked at Hendrickson.

"Think we can hold off on the drink for a bit? You and I had better give these newshounds some bones to chew on."

Hendrickson nodded.

"Ladies and gentlemen, if you'll be patient, we'll give you a statement in just a minute." Webber turned to Agent Corry who at that moment was walking past. "Corry, get Chief White and the mayor out here, will you? I think I saw them inside the building. If they ask why, tell them we're having a press conference. That'll get 'em out here."

"Yes sir," Corry answered.

"Excuse me a second," Webber said, looking over Hendrickson's shoulder at Joe Randle. "I want to be sure one other guy who deserves it gets a kudo."

CONNIE FARRER felt a little like a floating doll. Whatever the medics had given her was starting to work. They said it looked like a clean break, her left leg just below the knee. Her rib cage also needed to be X-rayed. They surmised that her injuries were not caused by the battering ram that had fallen on her. More likely they were the result of being stepped on as the SWAT team entered. She had been directly in their path with no time to get out of the way.

Connie clutched her cellular with both hands, resolved that nobody would take it from her. It was her first "touch-down pass" and she was determined to keep it on her shelf of memories. Five weeks at the station and a star in the biggest story she would probably ever cover. *What's more, I'm still alive to tell about it. Pretty good, huh? Thanks, God!*

She felt herself getting sleepy.

"I'm keeping this, okay?"

The fireman smiled.

"Lady, I don't care if you keep the offering plate. I heard

what you did with that thing. Pretty gutsy. You relax now, 'cause your job is over for today. The next stop for you is a nice clean bed and a room with a view at EBH."

Connie closed her eyes.

"It sounds glorious," she murmured. "I was there once when my mother had surgery and I always thought that the third-floor view of the hospital parking lot was especially enchanting."

She heard the men laugh as they lifted her from the floor.

FORTY-FOUR

Jeremy sat on the floor, his back against one of the choir pews. Allison's head was cradled against his chest and his arms encircled her protectively, though there was no longer a need to protect. Allison sobbed softly in his arms. He stared vacantly, watching as the medics worked on his mother.

Mrs. Orwell sat near them in the pew, her hand resting on Jeremy's shoulder, eyes moist with sadness as she took in the scene and lamented its hopelessness. She prayed silently.

Like a brushfire, a flood of pent-up emotion ran across the burned out field of Jeremy's mind. He could not stop rehearsing the events of the last few minutes.

Stark fear. They are going to kill us! No. Not all of us, only two. Who is this other couple? I don't even know them. She's pregnant. Now the Arab is demanding that Mom choose who is to die? How can she do that? It's impossible! But then this guy knows that, doesn't he? He's a devil! Wait. Mom ... what? She's offering to die in our place. No. I'll volunteer. But what about Allison? She'd volunteer too. She can't! I won't let her. Maybe the other guy . . .

What's happening . . . the Arab is falling . . . it's pitch black! Can't see anything. Voices yelling, "Down! Down! Down!" Someone falling against me, pushing me to the floor. Allison too. "Get down, Jeremy!" His mother's voice! A moment later, she rolled away and was lost in the darkness. I reached for her, but couldn't find her. Then, for one brief moment, I saw her outlined in the light. She was facing the Arab woman. It was . . .

Jeremy flinched involuntarily.

He'd never seen anybody die before. The Arab woman was dead before she hit the floor. He knew it. But his mother was a victim too. She'd thrown herself at him . . . and Allison, protecting them both with her own body. Now she looked as though she herself was drained of all life. *They say she's still alive. But she doesn't look it. O God, don't let her die. Please. Please. Please.*

They lifted Esther, backed off the platform, and headed up the aisle toward the exit. Jeremy pulled himself up to a kneeling position. Wordlessly, he looked at Mrs. Orwell, then at Allison who stood beside him now, still clinging to his hand. He got to his feet and stumbled after them.

"Wait, Jeremy," called Mrs. Orwell. "Allison and I will go with you."

They hurried up the aisle after the stretcher on which Esther's limp form was being carried to a waiting helicopter.

"She's my mother," Jeremy shouted. "Let me go with her."

The medic looked at him sympathetically.

"We can't take you, son. Not enough room. But ask that fellow over there." He pointed to Joe Randle. "He'll make sure you get there. East Bay Hospital."

The man pulled himself inside. "Okay. Let's go!"

Jeremy stood back, watching as the rescue helicopter

rose and banked away, heading across Baytown with its precious cargo.

Then he ran toward the man the medic had pointed out.

**1245 LOCAL TIME
WASHINGTON, D.C.**

"THAT'S THE BEST NEWS I've heard in weeks! Tell everyone that they have my deepest congratulations. I'm proud of all of you. Now you figure out *who*, and I'll determine *how* to honor your troops publicly and appropriately later."

"Thank you, Mr. President," replied the Attorney General. "I'll let them know your feelings."

"What's the word on casualties so far?"

"In Boston, two dead terrorists and we lost an agent. A member of the HRT unit we sent up there. We can't tell yet what problems the evacuation itself may have created. Dosha is still at large, but we think he's out of the area. Maybe the terrorist we captured will shed some light on that, but I doubt it. The mayor has been on the air most of the morning with the news. The city is settling down a bit, but it will be days before they're back to normal.

"Also, as you know, three hours ago one of our SWAT units cleared the church in California. Out there, we have four dead terrorists and one on the critical list, with less than a fifty percent chance of making it. One agent was wounded, but is in satisfactory condition. One civilian is in critical condition. Unfortunately, it may have been from 'friendly fire.' The pastor's wife. She took three hits. Her chances didn't look good at last report.

"Seven others were wounded by gunfire or from being injured in the initial attack. The television reporter with the cellular that you heard about has a broken leg and some banged-up ribs. Two elderly heart attack victims are in a local hospital in C.C.U. Their condition is still unknown.

And, of course, there was the one male civilian who was killed at the outset by the terrorists.

"All in all, I'm quite pleased to have contained this with what appears to be minimum loss. They tell me that it looks a little like a war zone inside the church. The networks are pooling a TV camera crew even as we speak, and we'll let them inside within the hour."

"Good work," affirmed the President warmly. "Now all we have to do is get those people home from Israel."

"That's out of our hands," the Attorney General responded quickly, grateful to be off the hook for this part of the crisis at least. "The CIA will keep in touch with the Mossad. We're ready to assist in any way we can, of course. No one seems certain as to what purposes they hope to achieve with the hostages over there. Maybe it's just a headline grabber. But they've definitely disappeared.

"This entire operation has been owned by a right-wing fundamentalist Muslim group calling themselves the Palestinian Islamic Jihad. They are a by-product of Hamas."

"Hamas," the President repeated. "I know a little about them, but refresh me."

"Hamas is an Arabic acronym that translates into the Islamic Resistance Movement. It's the more militant arm of the Muslim Brotherhood."

"Isn't the Brotherhood a kind of counterpoint to the PLO?"

"That's correct, sir. The CIA can probably give you more definitive stuff on this Jihad group, but I've been boning up a bit on it during the last couple of days. Bottom line is that the Jihad has made Palestine its central issue, and advocates armed struggle as its strategy for reform. Now that the PLO has been willing to negotiate for peace and for the creation of a Palestinian nation on the West Bank, this Jihad group is saying, 'Forget that. We want it all. Let the Jews go somewhere else.' "

"You mean they even want the portion that the UN ceded to Israel back in 1948?"

"Yes, sir. They want it all."

"Interesting. Well, the State Department is putting out a new travel warning for tourists headed for Israel, Jordan, and Egypt. We've already done the same for the rest of the Middle East," the President said. "Pretty soon, it may be safe for Americans only in the US and Canada."

"Hasn't been too safe this weekend, even in the US," she commented drily.

"I guess you're right. Stay in touch if anything further develops regarding this Dosha character. And congratulations again to all of you for a job well done."

"Thank you and good day, Mr. President."

FORTY-FIVE

"Why have you brought us here, Yazib?"

John leaned back against the cool, cement wall and squinted through eyes swollen half shut. He watched Yazib busy himself with the materials spread out on the table. Pasha sat on the edge of the far bed filing her nails, the assault rifle resting on the mattress beside her.

Yazib stepped back, his attention still focused on the table. The items had been moved around like chess pieces in a tournament. Everything seemed to have its special place. Slowly he turned around and faced the others in the room.

"Why have we brought you here, Reverend Cain?" he repeated. "You are here because you are going to help us."

"And how will we do that? John persisted. "We don't even know why you are here. How can you assume that we will help you, when we don't know what you intend to do?"

"Ah, you are a very curious person, Reverend Cain. And a very interesting one, I might add. I commend you for your courage. It is far greater than I would ever have expected. But like all other Americans and all your Jewish friends, you are fools. Forgive me if I offend you, but clearly that is what you are. You did not even realize that a war was in progress when you came to this land.

"You came on a lark. A religious pilgrimage. It is what you call a 'vacation.' However, what is only a lark for you is life and death for us. Our days and nights have been taken up for months in planning and training for this attack on the enemies of Allah. We have joined our souls with the souls of all the Mujahedin who have striven in the past to free Palestine. We are one with our forefathers who gave their lives for this land, ever since it was conquered by the companions of the Messenger until today.

"For you, this is a vacation. A religious odyssey. For us, it is the continuation of a long and dangerous war with the Jewish devils. It requires all our effort and dedication until the enemies of Islam are overcome and the victory of Allah descends!"

"But what purpose can we four possibly serve? And where have you taken the others who came here with me?"

"It will do no good for me to answer your last question. The four of you will not see your friends again until you meet in hell!" Yazib's eyes suddenly grew narrow and cold. "You want to know why you are here? I will tell you. You are here to blow up the Western Wall!"

John and the others stared at Yazib in disbelief, as he began pacing back and forth in front of them.

"Outside it is dark now. Pasha and I will be leaving you shortly to set in motion the final stage of our attack on Palestine's enemies. The items you see here on the table have been generously supplied by our good friends in Iran. These small containers are filled with a new and most powerful explosive. See?" He lifted one from the table and held it up.

"When we peel away the protective layer on the back, it permits the explosive to adhere to any surface that it touches. We will place each of these units on the Wall. As you can see, both the containers and this installation arm that we will use to place some of the explosives are of a color that blends in well with the Wall. It is possible that we may succeed in placing all six without being seen. When the explosives have been planted," he held up the ominous-looking black detonator, "Boom!"

John's heart sank.

"Surely you can't believe you will get away with something as crazy as this. And for what purpose? Even if you succeed, you'll touch off a wave of hatred and anger against the Muslim world that will never be stopped!" John exclaimed. "The Jews will retaliate by destroying the Dome of the Rock. They may even bomb Mecca. Then where will you be? You will spark a religious war with horrible consequences for your people."

Yazib smiled crookedly, enjoying his moment of self-assumed glory.

"Precisely. We must take the chance with the Dome. It may possibly be the price we pay to arouse our people, to shake some from their sleep and to inspire the overthrow of the occupiers of our land. But you are mistaken, Reverend Cain. Hatred and anger will flow like a river, it is true. However, it will not be directed toward the followers of Islam. It will be poured out instead upon the Great Satan, that dark and distant enemy of Islam, without which the State of Israel would have long since crumbled in weakness.

"You see, the destruction of the Jews' most sacred religious site will be the end result of a diabolical plot designed and carried out by Americans. Three men and a woman, to be exact!"

He paused, savoring the shocked looks on the faces of the hostages, and relishing the ingeniousness of the plan. He looked at his watch.

"Within the hour, the world will be informed that you were shot by IDF soldiers and Arab security guards, who vainly attempted to stop you from completing your wicked plan! You will be killed in the very act of destroying the Zionists' most unifying and holy symbol. Unfortunately, you will have succeeded in blowing up the Wall before you are stopped. What a tragedy. But at least your bodies will be found nearby and all the evidence for this terrible deed will confirm that it was carried out by Christian Jew-haters from America!"

Now John understood the reason the terrorists had changed into these uniforms. He had thought it was so they could avoid looking different from others on duty at Haram esh Sharif, if they were seen entering the compound. Instead, they were planning to kill their American prisoners before slipping away, melting into the confusion that would inevitably follow.

"When it is over, Reverend Cain, the Jews will find you with this detonator." Yazib held it up, turning it slowly in his hand. "And by the time you are discovered, it will have only your fingerprints. The prints of a right-wing Christian fanatic. A pastor of an American church, no less. Do you have any idea of the importance of this night? You should be honored. You will each play a significant role in our success. My only regret is that *you* will receive credit for this accomplishment instead of the Islamic Resistance Movement. But this is a small price to pay."

Yazib laughed, his eyes ablaze with excitement, as he turned back to the table.

"Come, Pasha. Let us gather our tools of warfare and be gone. Imad, you will come with us and remain in the shadows to watch for security personnel. We want no surprises until *we* say so, yes?"

Imad nodded soberly. He picked up the Galil leaning against the wall and began stuffing extra clips of ammunition into his pocket.

"Fathi, it is as we agreed earlier. You will stay with the

prisoners. As soon as Pasha and I are ready to set the charges, I will signal Imad. He will help you bring the prisoners to us at the Wall. If they refuse to cooperate, shoot them here and carry them outside. Understand?"

"I understand," said Fathi.

"Good. Now, Imad, help Fathi tape their mouths. And remember, the tape must be removed as soon as they are dead."

"Should we tie their hands?" asked Imad.

Yazib thought for a moment.

"Yes. Keep your knife ready, however. We will not have time to untie them later, so be prepared to cut them loose. Do not leave any rope behind. And if they try anything early on, just shoot them. You have the silencer on your weapon? Good. If you must kill them sooner, it will be of little consequence. No one will hear."

Yazib's back was turned to John and the others as he spoke.

"Reverend Cain, I am confident that you understand what is about to happen. Cooperate and you will live longer. Not much longer, I grant you, but a little while. And every minute of life is precious, don't you agree? Do not resist Allah's will, and you may rest assured that you will all die quickly. If you do not cooperate... I assure you, that you will each die an exceedingly slow and painful death... beginning with her!"

He looked over at Gisele.

Her eyes were full of apprehension, a sense of the inevitable rolling in upon her. Yazib smiled again. *She knows that she is going to die.*

Pasha moved around the corner of the table and paused in front of Gisele. She waited until the men had finished taping her mouth. Then she tied Gisele's wrists behind her back. With an air of calculated indifference, she shoved Gisele back on the bed and walked over to stand by Yazib.

The underground room grew still as Yazib picked up the backpack from the table. He had the air of a priest presiding over the elements of a Communion table. The table's surface was clear as he moved away. Nothing remained.

"Allah u Akbar," he said, passionately.

"Allah u Akbar," the others responded in unison.

"Good-bye to each of you, and especially to you, Reverend Cain," Yazib said, pausing at the door. "It has been a pleasure getting to know you. Come, Pasha. Our triumph is only moments away!"

The door closed behind them.

FATHI ADAHLAH MOVED over to the edge of the bed on which the terrorists had taken turns sleeping during these final hours to countdown. He looked at the two men on the bed. Their leader remained on the floor. He seemed to prefer that position, though it looked uncomfortable to Fathi.

He let his eyes wander across to where Gisele lay bound on the bed. *Very nice.* He had kept an eye on her from the beginning. *Too bad there is not more time. She could be a very enjoyable diversion!*

He turned the weapon over in his lap, checking it carefully, and wiping it down with a handkerchief pulled from his pocket. Additional clips were stacked on the bed. The light was not good where he sat, but it did not matter. He could see well enough for what was needed of him. Fathi was confident that they were all only minutes from their greatest victory.

That was when he heard choking noises coming from the group leader. He looked up and saw the man writhing on the cold floor, hands tied behind his back, the tape still over his mouth.

The black man was also making sounds, his eyes pleading with Fathi to do something.

He's choking, Fathi thought. *It would be funny if he died before I get to kill him. It doesn't really matter. In an hour, he'll be dead anyway. I wonder if he managed to take something.*

Unsheathing the Walther 7.65-millimeter PPK that he wore on his belt, Fathi walked over and stood between the two beds. The man was struggling to breath, the color on the back of his neck was turning a crimson red.

Fathi bent forward to get a better look.

JOHN WORKED DESPERATELY, but quietly. For hours, he had scraped with Gisele's belt buckle. He had been careful not to arouse suspicion, all the while wondering if he was getting anywhere, or if the effort was futile. Now the moment of truth was at hand. Time was running out.

He applied pressure to the chain. It remained firmly stuck.

Again.

No success.

A third time.

The sound of cement pieces falling to the floor echoed like cannon fire across the room!

At least, so it seemed to John. The chain had broken free. He was holding the eye hook in his hand!

He looked across to where Fathi was sitting. Apparently, he had heard nothing. He continued staring off into the distance. John exhaled a deep sigh of relief. Time to go into his act. It was nothing more than a desperate gamble. But there was no other way. He pushed the eye hook back into the wall.

He started coughing into the tape gag. Then John began making terrible choking sounds. He slid down to the floor, twisted around, and assumed a crouching position. Startled,

Edgar leaned over the edge of his bed to see what was the matter.

John motioned toward the wall with his head.

Instantly, Edgar realized what he was doing.

Edgar turned back toward Fathi and did his best with pleading noises, and urgent looks to get Fathi to come closer.

AT FIRST, he feared the man wasn't going to get up. Edgar's eyes pleaded with their captor as the sounds of choking continued between the two beds. Slowly, the terrorist got up and ambled over to see what could be the problem.

Edgar waited. He had not forgotten the lessons learned in the ring as a young man. *Timing is everything.* The Arab bent forward to get a better look at the man whose back was to him, bent over and agonizing with something caught in his throat.

John shifted his weight to his left foot. out of the corner of his eye, he could see Edgar's hand at the side of the bed, warning him to wait . . . wait . . . now!

He spun around on his pivot foot, swinging the chain with all his might! At the same moment, Edgar's foot flashed out and struck the barrel of the handgun. John felt the heat of bullets spewing around him, like molten lava, from the mouth of a volcano. Edgar kicked desperately again, this time kicking the weapon out of Fathi's hand as John continued his awkward twirling dance.

The chain coiled once around Fathi's neck and face, and then halfway again until the wall plate and hook smashed against his nose and mouth. John yanked hard on the chain, pulling him forward, stepping out of the way as the man fell to the floor. Fathi tried to get up, just as John and Edgar rammed him forward into the cement wall. He fell back to the floor, unconscious.

Both men were perspiring as they turned their backs to each other and began working on the ropes. The knots were tied too well. John bent backward over Fathi's inert form and managed to pull his combat knife from its sheath. As he held the blade out behind his back, Edgar worked the rope on his wrists back and forth along the knife's edge.

All at once, success! He was free!

Quickly, he took the knife and cut loose John's wrists.

Fathi began to stir.

Edgar picked up the Walther.

"You move, mister, and you are dead!" Edgar's voice was cold with pent-up fury.

Fathi froze in a kneeling position while John rummaged through his pockets, dumping the contents of each on the floor. He took Fathi's combat knife and tucked it under his own belt.

"I hope he's got the keys," Bob said anxiously.

"He does," John replied, his hands moving from one pocket to the next. "He has to. He was supposed to take us outside. Ah, here they are."

John pulled the small key ring from Fathi's side pocket. He tried first one, then another. The third key did the trick, opening the ankle brace that had kept him chained to the wall since their arrival. Quickly, John moved to the others and released their fetters as well.

Bob walked over to where Fathi had been sitting a moment before, picked up the remainder of the tape, and wrapped it around Fathi's face and mouth.

"Take off your shirt," ordered John.

Fathi looked at him questioningly, apprehension etched into the lines in his young face.

"Your shirt. Take it off!"

Slowly, his eyes never leaving John's, Fathi removed his shirt. John took it and then slipped the man's leg into Edgar's ankle brace and locked it. The last of the tape was used to bind Fathi's hands tightly behind his back.

The four of them stared at each another with looks of disbelief.

"Good job, John," Bob exclaimed. "This is incredible. I can't believe that we're free."

" 'Free' is a relative term," Edgar said philosophically. "We are a long way from 'free.' Take it from a brother who knows."

"Edgar's right. Are you ready for what we have to do?"

"Do we have a choice?" asked Bob.

Both Edgar and John shook their heads. Gisele said nothing, her eyes still on the man who, until a few minutes ago, had been designated as her executioner.

"We all go home. Or we all stay. It's as simple as that," John answered. "If we can capture the others and make them talk, maybe they'll tell us where the rest of our group is located. We may even get to them before they finish putting those charges in place."

John took the Walther from Edgar.

Bob cradled the automatic weapon in his arms. "I trained on one like this when I was in the army," he said.

"Ever kill anybody?" asked Edgar.

"No," was the quiet response. "But after what these bozos have put us through, I think I'm ready."

Carefully, they opened the door. It was dark, but on the far side the exit leading to the staircase and the courtyard had been left open.

"Chances are pretty good that this Imad character isn't far from that door, so be careful," John whispered. "Come on. Let's go."

A light, cool breeze embraced their faces as they moved stealthily out of Al Aqsa, up the stairway, and out under the starry Jerusalem night

FORTY-SIX

0145 LOCAL TIME
JERUSALEM, ISRAEL

Yazib and Pasha moved through the long shadows with catlike silence. They darted past El-Kas where Muslims wash before prayers, making their way along the stone esplanade, swiftly, quietly, ever watching and listening for security personnel. They stayed close to the trees, although, for the moment, they were not concerned about Jews. They would not be on the Mount, especially at night. Despite the rancor and hatred shown them from their implacable foes, the Jews still offered respect for these favored shrines of Islam.

They walked out into the open now, casually and confidently, toward the Western Wall. That was when an Arab policeman, standing across the way, saw the two of them walking. He put out his cigarette. Smoking in this area would be interpreted by the devout as desecrating the holy shrines. He started toward them. At last he recognized their Israeli uniforms, and stared at their brazenness with an open mouth.

As they drew near, both Israeli soldiers smiled and saluted in greeting.

JOHN LED THE OTHERS up the stairwell, and they began making their way along the edge of the building. To their right, the magnificent Dome of the Rock stood out against the night.

Popular Arab tradition held the original purpose of this grand mosque to be the commemoration of Mohammed's ascension to heaven. This had always amused John because he knew that like so many Middle East contradictions, a more recent structure known as Qubbat el-Miraj, the Dome of the Ascension, existed nearby. There was a more cynical theory about Ommayad Khalif Abdul Malik ibn Marwan's motivation in constructing the Dome during the years 688–691, suggesting that it was built to overshadow the Christian churches in the vicinity which were attracting many Arab converts. Whatever had been the builder's motivation, it was indeed an impressive structure.

Daily prayers were over hours ago, so no one was about. Tall evergreens lining the great esplanade pushed upward into the night sky. The wide stone porch of the Temple stretched out in front of them.

Just then, John saw Imad crouched down in the shadow of the El Aqsa Mosque. It looked as though he was cradling his weapon and gazing off in the distance, toward the Wall.

John gave a hand signal, motioning Edgar to circle around and come along the edge of the El-Kas fountain. "Stay in the shadows," he warned.

A moment later, they saw Edgar advancing steadily past the far edge of the fountain. Imad saw him at the same instant. He tensed, total concentration focused on the figure coming toward him. He lifted his gun and pointed, then lowered it again, apparently uncertain as to what he should do.

The decision was made for him.

Bob slipped along the building toward the crouching figure. Suddenly Imad turned. He heard something behind him.

It was too late!

The stock of the confiscated automatic weapon jarred Imad's head and neck. He dropped to the ground with a groan. A handkerchief was quickly stuffed into his mouth and tied with one of the pieces of cloth torn from Fathi's shirt. With two more strips, they bound his feet and hands, leaving him unconscious in the shadows.

A rapid search of his pockets turned up nothing of significance. Cigarettes. A Swiss army knife. Matches. A pocket flashlight. Some ammunition clips.

John turned the flashlight over in his hand.

"Bob, you stay here. At some point, one of those two out there is going to either signal or come back and tell this guy to bring us out and kill us. If they come back, do what you have to do. You understand what I mean?"

Bob nodded grimly.

"If one of them comes back, you've got no choice. My guess is, though, they'll signal. That's probably what this flashlight is for. Answer back with the same signal you receive. If it's supposed to be anything other than that, we're dead anyway, so don't worry about it. Edgar, get his gun and the clips and let's go."

The three of them stopped at the edge of the open esplanade. There was no cover here. John peered across the way, trying to spot the remaining two terrorists. Finally, he saw them off to the right, almost invisible in the shadows nearest the Western Wall.

The Western Wall!

It was the holiest shrine of the Jewish world, revered as the last relic of the last Temple. John had been there on numerous occasions and had felt its awesome power. The Western Wall is all that remains of the retaining wall built by Herod around the second Temple in 20 B.C. Ninety years later when Titus overran the city, he spared this part of the Temple Wall with its huge blocks, in order to show future generations the greatness of Rome that had been able to destroy the rest of the building.

From Byzantine times forward, Jews were allowed to come here to honor the anniversary of the Temple's destruction and to lament the dispersion of their people. Standing before the face of this high Wall, they wept and prayed. It was because of this tradition that it became known as the Wailing Wall. This practice continued for centuries until 1948–1967, when Jews were forbidden access to the Wall by the Jordanians.

Then came the Six Day War. When it was over, the city had been liberated, and overnight the Western Wall became a place for national rejoicing and worship. Tonight, the unspeakable was scheduled to happen. The Wall was destined for destruction!

John studied the two shadowy figures standing less than fifty feet away from where he stood, hidden in the darkness with the others. Could these Arab young people, filled with their hatred and bitterness, really pull it off? They believed that they could. And John agreed. There was a better than fifty-fifty chance that they just might do it.

Explosives from Iran!

John assumed they would be powerful enough to do the deed. Worse yet would be the conflagration of pent-up fury that would follow. The fallout from tonight's action would be fearsome. Somehow these people had to be stopped!

The trio said nothing as they took stock of the lower, eastern side of the Wall. John was able to easily discern its upper outline from the floodlights directed toward the opposite side. He maneuvered further into the shadow of one of the tallest pine trees and then stopped abruptly, staring into the darkness.

An Arab policeman was sitting quietly, leaning back against the tree just beyond where John was crouched.

He was looking straight at them!

Why doesn't he say something? Surely he sees us.

But the policeman did not move.

Slowly, the trio edged closer. John grimaced when he saw that the man was not watching them at all. He was propped up in a sitting position against the tree.

The front of his shirt was sticky with blood.

His throat had been cut!

John looked across the open space between them and the Wall.

Where are these killers now?

YAZIB PLACED THE THREE CONTAINERS in Pasha's hand. A light breeze swirled from west to east. The night was cooling rapidly and her hands were cold. He felt the familiar stirrings as they touched. This was a woman he could love. He had little doubt of that. He wondered how she felt about him. He was certain that she was attracted to him, but their time together had been spent in such extraordinary circumstances that he couldn't know if it was really love.

Perhaps, when this is all over...

"I am ready, Yazib."

The sound of her voice drew him back to the moment at hand.

"You will be all right?"

"Yes," she said, placing the containers in the pack, before throwing it over her shoulders. Pasha reached for the Galil assault rifle she had leaned against the Wall, removed the safety, and looked up at Yazib.

"Remember," he said, "from the time you lift your hand and signal, you have five minutes. Two minutes to take out the guards and the next three to place the explosives and get away. If you take longer..."

Yazib shrugged.

"I understand. I will not be late."

Yazib withdrew a pencil flashlight from his pocket and turned in the direction of Al Aqsa. Three quick flashes. The signal to Imad. He waited. No response. Where was he? Had something happened? Surely he can see the signal from there. Apprehension began to form. He flashed again.

There! Three quick flashes out of the darkness.

Yazib breathed easier. He turned to Pasha. "Make your way carefully. Just before you reach the Gate, wait for two minutes. By then, Fathi and Imad should have had time to bring out the prisoners. Make certain that I can see your hand signal. From that moment, it will be exactly five minutes, and the charges will be detonated. Run, join the soldiers when they rush toward the Gate. Then, slip away. You remember the address where we will meet?"

She nodded. "It is well into my memory."

"You must be there by three o'clock."

She nodded again, understanding that if she or any of the others failed to arrive by that time, they were on their own. The likelihood of their escape would be greatly diminished if they missed getting into the escape route.

"Once we have regrouped and no longer need the 'insurance,' the remaining hostages will be disposed of and we can declare our mission to be a success. Unfortunately, if the news we have heard is correct, it will not be so great a success as we had hoped for, on a worldwide scale, but still a success nonetheless."

Pasha smiled coolly, then touched his check with her hand. "It is all the more reason that we must succeed with this part of the plan."

"Ilael liqa, Pasha." *See you later.*

"Hazz sae'id," she whispered. *Good luck.*

JOHN TENSED AS HE SAW the small flashes of light coming from the direction of the Wall. He watched for a response from Bob.

Nothing.

He glanced over at Edgar, then back to where Bob was supposed to be waiting.

The signal was repeated from the Wall.

There! Three flashes in response.

Now John watched to see what would happen. He heard someone release a breath, only to realize that the sound was of his own making. Was it the right response? There was no sudden movement to indicate otherwise. Nothing out of the ordinary. It must have been what they were looking for.

John, Edgar, and Gisele continued their vigil, remaining deep in the shadows, squatting alongside the dead policeman. John guessed they were at least fifty feet from the two terrorists. Yazib and Pasha were lost for the moment in the shadows, but John knew they were there.

What are they up to? How are we going to get to them or past them to tip off the authorities?

Movement in the shadows.

A dark figure could be seen moving along the Wall toward the Morollo Gate. The other half of the team hoisted up to the top of the Wall, quickly dropping down and out of sight from anyone on ground level. But not before John could make out the person's physical features.

Yazib!

"It's happening. Either they get away with this devilish plan or it's up to us to stop them. What shall we do?"

John looked at Edgar.

"I say *we* finish what they started!" The old prizefighter's glare sent the message. He had heard the bell ring and he was ready to fight!

Gisele looked anxious. She swallowed once and gave the others a weak smile. "I'm with you guys."

John's eyes returned to the Wall. "I'll take Yazib. Gisele, you come with me. Edgar, go after the woman. "Here, Gisele. Take this and use it if you have to." He thrust the Walther into her hands.

"But I don't know anything about handguns," she protested. "You take it."

"No. I'll need both hands to get on top of the Wall." John was not certain he could use the gun anyway. He had never killed before. "I've got this knife. That will have to do. Here. The safety is off now, so if you pull the trigger, it will fire. If one of them comes at you, shoot. I mean it!"

Gisele nodded lamely, careful to make sure her fingers were nowhere near the trigger.

"Now, let's go do what we have to do," John ordered, and he began moving cautiously toward the Wall.

PASHA LOOKED BACK into the darkness along the wall, lifted her hand, and then dropped it. She walked out of the shadows toward the Morollo Gate. As expected, she saw that the heavy wooden gate was locked. With practiced agility, Pasha scaled the wall next to the gate and peered over the edge to the other side. Two soldiers were standing guard. They looked up as she stood, surprised to see an Israeli soldier staring down at them from atop the Wall. A woman, no less, dressed in olive Class Alephs complete with sergeant's stripes, and carrying the standard Galil assault rifle at her side.

They had barely recovered from their surprise when the soldier nearest to the Gate noticed the silencer attached to her weapon. Definitely *not* standard issue. But he was too late.

Her weapon spit death at both soldiers. They fell onto the pathway. Pasha lowered herself from her perch above the Gate. Stepping over the dead soldiers, she raced down the path. Glancing at her watch, she saw that she was fifteen seconds behind schedule. Now she was at the bottom of the short path. From here on there was no more cover. Pasha ran out into the open toward the floodlit Wall.

Looking up, she saw Yazib at the center of the Wall, lowering the second explosive charge into place.

No alarm yet. Amazing. Anyone who looks this way can see us.

She tore the protective strip away from the adhesive base and placed the first charge as high as she could reach on the right-hand side, the small southern section reserved for women. Then she ran around and came to the center of the Wall.

Pasha checked her watch.

Forty seconds.

Glancing up again, she saw the telescopic arm being retrieved directly above her. Standing on her tiptoes, she pressed the second package against the Wall. Her heart was beating now with crescendo force as she ran toward the barrier in front of Wilson's Arch, at the north of the exposed portion of the Wall.

Twenty-five seconds!

She shifted the rifle to her left hand and reached for the last explosive package. As she did, she saw a soldier running toward her. He called out in Hebrew, "Khaki! Khaki!" For a second, she hesitated, then reached up and pressed the final package into place.

The first soldier was joined by another now and they hurried toward her, yelling and shouting. She waved as if to say that everything was fine. They continued running toward her. She started walking in their direction, waving her hand. She could see one of the soldiers speaking into a radio pack as they came closer. When they were about thirty feet away, the woman in the sergeant's uniform leveled her weapon and fired. Both men went down.

Just then, a third man appeared, off to her left as she faced away from the Wall.

"Stop," he shouted, in English.

I've got to get away from here. This place will explode any second now.

"Drop your gun, Pasha," the man said. She looked up. The man was black. And he had a weapon pointed at her. *Impossible. Is it the American? It is. Something has gone wrong!*

She turned and fired wildly!

Pasha felt the searing pain, a split second before she heard the gunfire.

One!

Two!

Three slugs drove her backward onto the huge stone esplanade! The gun fell out of her hand and she landed on her back. Her hands went to her abdomen and breast. They became sticky with warm blood. She looked up. Two figures, directly above her, were struggling with one another on top of the high Wall!

JOHN RAN ACROSS the open space with Gisele following behind. They breathed a sigh of relief when they reached the shadows of the Wall. They had not been seen. John looked up. The Wall looked higher than it had—much too high.

How do I get up there? he asked himself, knowing that Yazib had done so only a short while earlier. *Never mind.*

"Gisele," he whispered. "It's too high. You'll have to help me. Give me a boost."

Gisele gave him an "are you kidding" kind of look. Gingerly, she put the Walther down on a flat stone. Then she squatted and cupped her hands together.

"Lift with your legs, not your back. Okay? We've only got one chance!"

She nodded and John could see her steel herself for the

thrust. He put his foot in her hands, and whispered the countdown.

"One, two, three!"

John launched himself with all the energy he could muster. Gisele's lift, fueled by the moment's adrenaline, made the difference. He hit the upper edge with his stomach, feet dangling. He pushed himself the rest of the way over and landed with a force that knocked the wind out of him.

Yazib was at the opposite end, his back turned away, working the telescopic rod with both hands.

Keep moving!

Scrambling to his feet, John ran toward Yazib. At the same time, he heard shouts below. He was suddenly possessed by the feeling of walking a tightrope. The height! Oh, how he hated high places!

Yazib looked up and saw him coming. He dropped the rod over the side and turned toward John. He blinked unbelievingly, his concentration momentarily broken. His hand swept across the top of the Wall, feeling for his weapon, but he had turned away from it rather than toward it. With the other hand, he felt for the detonator that he had placed beside his gun. Yazib started to stand just as John fell on top of him.

Below, in the place where worshipers were slated to gather in a few hours to pray for the peace of Jerusalem, gunfire erupted!

Grunting with the physical force of the attack, the two men wrestled back and forth along the top of the wide Wall. Yazib knocked John backward. He fell between Yazib and the gun. *Where is the detonator?*

Yazib rushed him, his foot catching him in the rib cage. John felt the searing pain as the blow smashed against his earlier injury. He grasped for Yazib's ankle and twisted it sharply. He heard a crack and a cry of pain as Yazib pitched over him, stretching out in a desperate attempt to get at the gun. John yanked on his leg and pulled him back. Then he rolled around and came to his knees.

The detonator.

There it was!

Near the low edge of the top of the Wall. He looked at Yazib. He had seen it too and was lunging for it. John threw himself on top of him, beating him with his fists, twisting his face around to the side. He fought with a fury he had never felt before. Then he saw Yazib's hand reach out and fold around the detonator.

With his last ounce of energy and adrenaline, John pounded Yazib's hand with his foot. He heard the cry of pain. John kicked again, this time his foot catching the detonator, causing it to slide away from both men. It came to a stop at the center of the Wall, near the western edge.

With the force of a hammer, Yazib knocked the wind out of John again. Relentlessly he pounded John's face and stomach and ribs. He worked on him like a man gone mad. Perhaps he had. Suddenly, he was off of John and standing over him with the gun in his hands. A gun exactly like the one John had given to Edgar. Only this Walther 7.65-millimeter PPK took on cannonlike proportions as John stared into the business end of the barrel.

"You! I don't know how you got loose. But you have become a liability, Reverend Cain. You are no longer an asset. You've come near to ruining our grand cause. However, I shall now complete this task in the name of Allah, and we shall die together."

Yazib backed away, edging over to the detonator. He bent to pick it up, his eyes never leaving John.

With the gun in one hand and the detonator in the other, he stood up. His fingers ran across the surface of the black box, searching for the button. Where was it? He glanced down and saw that it had been turned upside down in the melee. The button was underneath.

In the precise moment that he glanced away, John slipped the knife from his belt.

Yazib sensed his movement and looked up. As he did, the detonator slipped in his hand. Instinctively he tried to keep it from dropping, causing the gun to waver slightly.

John threw the knife.

He had never thrown a knife before.

It flew past Yazib, disappearing harmlessly over the Wall. But it came close enough to cause him to step back and dodge away from its arc.

As he did, Yazib stepped on a loose rock and stumbled backward toward the floodlights. He fought to regain his balance. For an instant, he hung there, looking at John. Then the detonator fell from his hand and teetered on the edge of the Wall. John lunged for it and scooped it in with his hand.

Yazib's gun hand was high above his head now as he desperately tried to stop the inevitable.

His left foot lifted slowly into the air.

His face contorted in disbelief as he went over the edge.

A long, hollow scream signaled the end as he fell, twisting into the forecourt, landing face down with life-crushing force, inches away from Pasha's eyes.

Eyes frozen open in death!

From on top of the Western Wall, John could hear the sirens. Another burst of gunfire from somewhere. Yelling. The sound of trucks. Cars. The pounding of feet.

Then darkness settled in over him.

▼▼▼

The Islamic Resistance Movement [firmly] believes that the land of Palestine is an Islamic Waaf [Trust] upon all Muslim generations till the day of Resurrection. It is not right to give it up nor any part of it.
Those who are on the land have the rights to the land's benefits only, and this trust is permanent as long as the heavens and the earth shall last. Any action taken in contradiction to the Islamic Shari'a concerning Palestine is unacceptable action, to be taken back by its claimants.

— *from the* Hamas Charter, *Article Eleven*

Glory to Allah who did take His servant for a Journey by night from the Sacred Mosque to the Farthest Mosque, whose precincts We did Bless — in order that We might Show him some of Our Signs: for He is the One Who heareth and seeth [all things].

— The Holy Quran, *Sura 17:al-Isra':1*

But on Mount Zion will be deliverance; it will be holy, and the house of Jacob will possess its inheritance.

— The Bible, *Obadiah 17*

▲▲▲

FORTY-SEVEN

The first rays of early morning sunlight crept into the room, bathing the sterile white walls with a warm glow. He swiveled his head in both directions, becoming aware of the soft pillow and the clean white sheet over his body. A bottle filled with some sort of clear liquid dripped its mysterious substance intravenously into his arm. Across the room, a mirror and sink. Beyond the window, there was only sky. Blue sky. Nothing else. In front of the window, a small table with wheels. And a vase with bright-colored flowers.

He forced himself up on his elbows and attempted to shift to the side of the bed. Pain shot through his body. With an involuntary groan, he fell back onto the pillow.

"Hello, cowboy." The voice was low, but musical and a bit sexy with its heavy accent. He rolled his head to the right. She was very attractive, standing there in her nurse's uniform. Black hair. Skin, a deep bronze. Dark eyes. How did she get in here?

"Where am I?"

"You are a guest of the Hadassa Hospital. I am your

hostess. Well, actually, I am your nurse. My name is Katya. How are you feeling?"

"Great, so long as I don't move, breathe, or talk."

She laughed.

"You have not lost your sense of humor."

"How did I get here? I don't remember."

"An ambulance brought you here several hours ago. You are a celebrity, Reverend Cain. I understand that you are Israel's hero."

"Hero?" John tried to grasp what she was saying.

"You and your friends. You saved the Wall. You risked your lives for our people. More than that, you have kept us once again from the 'mother of all wars,' as our old friend in Iraq loves to call it."

John forced himself to think. It all came back quickly. The hijacking of the tour bus. The climb over the ancient Wall. The secret room beneath Al Aqsa. Overwhelming the man called Fathi. The dead policeman. The fight on top of the Wall. Yazib falling . . .

"My friends?" John leaned forward, grimacing in pain as he did.

"Please, Reverend Cain, try to remain still. You have several broken ribs and a fractured collar bone. Your friends are all well and asleep in their own rooms here in the hospital."

"All of them?"

"Yes. Two men and a woman. You all appear to have been through a great deal."

"What time is it?"

She looked at her watch. "Five minutes past six in the morning."

"Katya, has any word come of my daughter or the others in my group?"

"I'm sorry. I do not know," Katya replied, smiling brightly. "You must rest now. The doctor will be in shortly. I believe the authorities are also outside, waiting for you to awaken and fill in the details of your adventure."

John reached over and grasped the nurse's hand. "Please, will you have someone check regarding my family and the church in America? I was told by our captors that . . . that my wife . . . had been killed. I need to know!"

Katya's eyes darkened with sadness. "I will ask for you, Reverend Cain. Perhaps the others will have some word. I will pray for you that this is not true. I only know what is to be read in the papers."

"The papers? It is in the newspapers over here?"

"Of course. And on television. But lie back and rest for now. I will go find Dr. Kamen."

Katya exited quickly and John settled back to stare at the ceiling, his mind whirling with bits and pieces. Fragments. Nothing seemed to connect. Only scraps of thought caught in a cyclone of timelessness.

The door opened.

She stalked into the room. She was short and heavyset, and had the weathered face of a woman in her late fifties, one who had seen it all and was no longer impressed. Her eyes were deep brown, her hair cut close, salt and pepper. The salt appeared to be winning out.

"How do you do, Reverend Cain? I am Dr. Yudit Kamen. I have been assigned to see to it that you get well, starting immediately!" She smiled, a crooked, toothy smile. "You will cooperate, of course, yes?"

"Of course." John forced a smile.

For the next few minutes, the doctor poked and pinched and prodded the full length of John's body.

"You are sore, yes?" she said, after an extended silence.

"Only from my head to my feet," John answered honestly.

At last, seeming to be content that she had done her job, she came close to the head of the bed. "First of all, from what I understand, you can thank God that you are alive. Three broken ribs. We already have them taped and you will heal. One fractured collarbone. We'll position your arm in a sling for a couple of weeks. You will heal. Multiple bruises and a slight concussion. Again, Reverend Cain, you will heal. That is not an opinion. It is an order! Understand?"

John could not help smiling. The word that came to mind was "biddy." Yet in spite of her irascible ways, Dr. Kamen exuded a warmth and a professionalism that could not be denied.

"I understand. And my friends?"

"Bruises, minor injuries, nothing major. Looks like they had a cakewalk compared to you. Or else they are much quicker on their feet. Don't worry. They are resting and they are well. And to hear them tell it, you are the reason that they are alive."

"No," he assured her, staring up at the ceiling. "I am not the reason. The God of Abraham, Isaac, and Jacob is the reason we are alive."

He looked over at Dr. Kamen. Her eyes were glistening. She reached out and gripped his hand, patting his arm with a tenderness that embarrassed them both.

Just then the door opened and a man in uniform, together with two others in plainclothes, stepped into the room.

"I will leave you for now," said Dr. Kamen, standing back. She turned to the three strangers. "Don't be too long with my patient. He needs some rest, not government interrogation."

"No, wait," said one of the men. She stopped near the door.

"Reverend Cain," began the man in the blue sport jacket and gray polo shirt, standing by John's bed. "My name is Noel Kupperman. This is Peter Dintz and Colonel David Ribbut. Colonel Ribbut is with the IDF. Peter and I are with Mossad. You are familiar with these organizations?"

John nodded.

"Reverend Cain, you have our deepest thanks for what you and your friends have done. If it were not for your heroic efforts, this day might well be the first day of an all-out war. You have saved the most sacred symbol of our nation. More importantly, you saved her soul!"

The others stared at him, apparently needing to size up this unknown preacher from America, whose name was now on everyone's lips in Israel.

John tried to think of an appropriate reply. None came to mind, so he said nothing. He was about to inquire regarding Esther, Jeremy, and Jessica, when Kupperman continued.

"Now I must ask of you another favor still. I have just spoken to my headquarters by telephone. We have a most unusual situation that has developed in the last few hours." He turned to Dr. Kamen. "We must take Reverend Cain with us immediately. He is needed in the city."

"Absolutely not!" Dr. Kamen retorted indignantly, both hands planted firmly on her ample hips. "This man is injured. He needs rest. He should not be moved for several days. No. I will not hear of such a thing!"

Kupperman took the doctor by the arm and led her to the far side of the room. With his back to John, the two of them conversed quietly but heatedly in Hebrew, and with abundant hand gestures. Abruptly, the doctor threw open the door and left the room, turning long enough to give Kupperman her most withering glare. Kupperman walked back to the bed.

"The doctor is making preparations for you to go with us now. I sincerely believe you would agree with this decision if all the facts were before you. But the simple truth is, we cannot accomplish what must be done without you. Please do not ask questions. Just relax and let us make you as comfortable as possible. We will travel together in an ambulance. Dr. Kamen will join us."

Kupperman turned and left the room.

The other two men stood looking at John, saying nothing. He stared back. Inside, a gnawing apprehension began to mount.

THE AMBULANCE RIDE took about half an hour, even with the police escort. Dr. Kamen, along with Kupperman and the colonel, rode in back with John. The other man sat in front with the driver. There was little small talk. Dr. Kamen inquired as to whether he was in any discomfort. He was, but he said no. After about fifteen minutes, she asked if he would like some pain medication. He declined. He wanted to be alert for whatever was ahead.

When the ambulance finally stopped, John could hear excited voices outside, some in Arabic, some in Hebrew. The door opened and two men prepared to remove the stretcher.

"Hold it!" John said emphatically.

They stopped, everyone looking at him.

"I'm not going unless I walk."

"Reverend Cain," protested Dr. Kamen. "You are still going through a period of shock trauma in your body. I'm afraid I must insist..."

"And *I'm* afraid *I* must insist," responded John. "Wherever we are and whatever we are doing, I intend to be standing when it happens!"

A slight smile broke across the colonel's face. He said nothing.

Everyone waited for someone to take charge.

"Help this man up!" commanded Dr. Kamen.

"Thank you, doctor." John sighed as they helped him out of the ambulance and stood him on his feet. He was surprised at how weak he felt. The pain in his rib cage was sharp and his head felt like it could easily drop off. *Maybe this was not such a good idea.*

"I may need to lean on somebody, but let's go."

He took a first hesitant step. Then he looked up and scrutinized the surroundings.

"What are we doing here?"

John recognized the alleyway in which they were standing. He had walked through here many times before.

"You know where we are?"

"Of course. This leads to Gordon's Calvary."

"That is correct. So let us walk slowly, Reverend Cain, for your health." They began making their way along the alley. Curious Arab children and teenagers followed the party, some trying to sell their first customer of the day a postcard or a cheap wooden camel. The police stopped short of the entrance to Gordon's Calvary, quickly forming a wedge, and began moving onlookers away.

"A very strange thing has happened during the night," Kupperman said, as they neared the end of the alley. "As you know, this is a religious site operated by a Christian mission organization. Early today, when the first employee arrived, she heard singing coming from inside. The door was still locked, so she did not know what to make of it. She ran down the road and got a policeman. Together they went into the garden and, well, here we are. Let's go in and see for ourselves."

Inside, the store looked familiar to John. Books and pamphlets lined simple wooden racks. Religious trinkets and Holy Land pictures were displayed as well. Merchandise was tastefully presented. However, beyond this room, through the far door, was one of his favorite places in all of Israel. The woman behind the counter smiled but said nothing as they walked by.

"Good morning, gentlemen." A well-groomed man came around one of the book displays. He was probably in his sixties, balding, with brown and gray-flecked hair.

"And you must be Reverend Cain." He spoke it not as a

question, but as a matter of fact, a crisp British accent aug-
menting the resonant tones in his bass voice. "My name is
Carson. Gerald Carson. I oversee the mission. I must admit
that I do not normally get up this early, but when our staff
member called, I hurried right over. I'm pleased to meet
you. Your deeds are already filling the airways and the
newspapers."

John was beginning to weary of hearing the same com-
mendations repeated over and over, but he nodded politely
and tried to smile. He was growing irritated, however, with
the feeling that total strangers appeared to know more about
what was going on than he did.

"All right. Why are we here?" John's voice showed an
edge of impatience.

"Come with me." Carson shook John's hand, then led
the way through the far door, talking over his shoulder as
they walked. "When my staff member first arrived, she
heard singing from inside. The place was still locked from
the evening before. It has to be kept very secure in this
neighborhood. And so she went to find a policeman. When
they walked into the garden..."

Mr. Carson led them outside.

Birds sang. Flower blossoms along the pathway glistened with the dewdrops of early morning. It was an oasis
nestled in the heart of a bustling city. Only the roar of buses
leaving the nearby station on their first run of the day reminded John and the others that there were thousands of
people coming and going all around them.

"... this is what they found."

John stopped and stared in astonishment.

He could not believe his eyes!

Patricia Hansen, Mary Callahan, and Jerry and Susan
Cloud sat directly in front of him, on a stone bench. Nick
and Patricia Micceli were next to Harold Eiderman, and Jill
Anderson was on the low wall nearby.

Shad Coleman, Adele Smith, the Mitchels, and Greg and Debbie Sommers had formed a circle on the small stone patio. Ruth Taylor, Donna Thomas, the Watsons, and Dan Wilson were standing in front of the entrance leading into the open tomb, believed by many to be the place where Jesus was buried and from which He rose on the third day.

"Thank God! You are here. I can't believe it! You are all here! It's incredible. But how on earth did you get to this place?"

Jill and Ruth ran up to him, wordless concern etched in their faces as they stared at their pastor, bruised, bandaged, and obviously in much pain. It was Harold Eiderman who asked the question on everyone's lips.

"Are the others . . . ?" he halted in mid-sentence, unable to continue.

"They are all fine," John said, breaking into a smile. "And they don't look nearly as bad as I do. They are resting at Hadassah Medical Center."

A cheer went up and people began hugging and pounding and laughing and crying, all at the same time. They rushed up to John then, wanting to touch and hug him. He held up his free hand.

"There's nothing more I want to do than hug and kiss everyone of you! I still can't believe you're all here. It is just too wonderful. But take it easy, okay? Most of me is sore right now, and with the drugs that the good doctor here has pumped into me, I'm not sure where the safe-to-hug places are."

Everyone laughed, though their eyes were filled with concern.

"Can we sit down for a few minutes? I want to know exactly how all of you managed to get *here*, of all places. What has happened since I saw you last?"

"Actually, we are also very interested in that question being answered," added Kupperman from Mossad. "The policeman who found you says the door was locked when he arrived. Did someone give you a key? Our belief was that you were being held around the city in different places. Were we wrong in that assumption?"

The group grew silent now, looking at each other, apparently uncertain as to who should be the spokesman. Finally, Nick Micceli stepped forward.

"Well, John, as you know, the terrorists initially separated ten of us out of the group that first night. Once we left the bus, we were taken across what looked to be farm terraces, and then through an old cemetery. We walked along a path until coming to an opening in a huge rock. That was when the flashlights and candles came out, and they led us inside.

"I remember a dark hole on the right side of the opening. I couldn't tell how far down it went, but it looked deep. Once inside, we began climbing up through an underground room of stone steps. Eventually, we saw where an avalanche had closed the stairs off from wherever they used to go. I don't think anyone had been there for a long time. There were two small, cavelike rooms off to one side. They put us in these rooms and chained us to the walls. All the while, our mouths were kept taped and our hands bound. Then they left us in the darkness.

"Because it was so dark, we sort of lost track of days and nights. They had taken our watches and valuables. None of us have any passports. They are all gone. At that point, we were just grateful to be alive. We could hear our guards outside and occasionally caught a glimpse of flashlights or candles. Twice they brought us something to eat, which we accepted as a hopeful sign. We decided that you don't bother feeding someone you are going to kill right away."

"If you were gagged, how did you eat?" asked the colonel.

"They removed the tape to permit us to eat. Two of them always stayed until we were finished. Then they retaped our mouths. We decided that maybe we were close to civilization and they didn't want to take a chance that we might yell for help. We prayed a lot for one another . . . and for the rest of you!

"Then sometime last night, two men came. They didn't say a word at first. They just entered the rooms and began unlocking our leg chains. When we were all free, they ordered us to follow them, but to be quiet.

"When we walked out, we saw that the regular guards were there all right, but they were sleeping. We couldn't figure what was going on, but we followed the men anyway. I thought they must be relocating us to a new hiding place. We went down the same steps we had walked up earlier and, as nearly as I can tell, retraced our path to the same highway where we were taken off the bus. When we got there, two vans were waiting."

"Did the vans have markings? Did you notice the license plates?" asked Kupperman.

"No markings. They were what I would call 'army green.' Wouldn't you say, Dan?"

Dan Watson nodded affirmatively.

"I didn't have a chance to look at license plates. Did anyone?"

People shook their heads.

"All right," Kupperman said, obviously disappointed. "Please go on."

"That is really all there is," Nick continued. "We were driven here in the vans. The men got out, unlocked the door to this place, and led us out here into the garden. They told us we should wait. They said that the others would be coming, and when we were all together, we should wait here until a woman arrived. When she came, we were to ask for our pastor by name. They gave us the feeling that you were well known here, John. Then they advised us not to talk to anyone else or go anywhere until you arrived. So, here we are."

A hush fell over the group. Only the sounds of birds and the noise of the nearby city awakening to a new day broke the reverie. No one seemed to know what to say or do next. John was still trying to absorb what he had just heard when Larry Mitchel spoke up.

"We had more or less the same experience," said Larry, looking around at the group. "We were taken off the bus here in the city and stuffed into old automobiles. Then they took us to rooms in pairs or in threes. We were tied or chained, whatever seemed to be handiest. The place where I stayed had no windows. We had our gags removed only once for food. So some of us are kind of hungry, now that we think about it."

There was a shuffling of feet and smiles on faces over Larry's last comment.

"I assure you, my friends, we will provide you with the best breakfast you have ever enjoyed," smiled Kupperman. "An American breakfast. At least as American as we can make it in the land of lox and bagels. But tell me, who freed you?"

"We've been discussing this among ourselves since arriving here in the garden. We all showed up at different times," said Nick. "Our group was the first, and we were brought here by the two men I mentioned. I thought, initially, that they were Arabs. Dark hair, dark eyes, bronzed skin. Could have been twenty-five or thirty years old. They spoke perfect English. No identifiable accent. Later, we decided they might have been Jews. To be real honest though, we don't have a clue."

"We came next," Donna Thomas spoke up. "A man with brown hair and a blond woman. She looked almost Scandinavian. I remember wondering what she could possibly be doing here."

"For us, it was a man with red hair," said another.

"Red hair? Did these people give you any indication as to

who they were or where they came from?" asked Colonel Ribbut.

"No. We asked, but they wouldn't say."

"Where were your guards?"

"Sleeping. Like Nick said his guards were doing."

"Was this true for all of you?" asked the colonel incredulously.

Heads nodded everywhere.

"This is amazing," commented Peter Dintz, who up to that point had made no comment, content with scribbling notes on a small writing pad. "I've never heard of anything like this!"

Again there was a lull in the conversation.

Finally, the silence was broken by John.

"I have," he said, a quiet, almost reverential tone in his voice.

The others looked at him.

"Actually, I *have* heard of something like this happening before," he continued, as he moved to sit down on the edge of the low garden wall. "In fact, it happened right here in Jerusalem."

"I don't quite follow you, Reverend Cain," said Kupperman, a questioning look on his face. "I've never heard of anything remotely like this happening in our country and I've lived here all my life."

John smiled.

"I suppose not. But it did. There's a record of it in the New Testament Acts of the Apostles, chapter 12. One of Jesus' disciples was named Peter. He'd been thrown into prison by Herod and the church was praying earnestly for him. The night before his trial, while he was sleeping between two soldiers and bound by chains, with sentries at the prison door, someone entered his room.

"This person awakened him, ordered him to get dressed and follow him out. At first, Peter thought he was dreaming.

He did not believe it was really happening. Then, when he found himself outside, he realized that an angel of the Lord had delivered him from prison. He went to a house where he knew friends would be present. They were so surprised they could hardly believe their eyes when they saw him, even though they had been praying for him all night."

"Reverend Cain," said Colonel Ribbut, chuckling in protest, "are you trying to tell us that 'angels' did all this?"

"Colonel, I'm not *trying* to tell you anything. Perhaps when your investigation is complete, you will find some more logical answer to the events of this night. However, I sincerely doubt it. Did anyone in the IDF or Mossad have a clue as to where these people were being held?"

The three men were silent. Dr. Kamen was watching John intently.

John looked around. "I need to say this to all of you. A kind of 'confession,' I guess. In recent months, I have been wondering whether or not God was really there. Every member of my family has been under unbelievable stress and pressure. Since Jenny's death, our prayers all seemed to hit the ceiling and bounce back unanswered. It has been the most difficult period in my life. And it's not over yet. I don't know what the situation is back home. I don't know if Esther and Jeremy are safe. And . . . I don't know where Jessica is!"

John cleared his throat as he forced back the emotions that lay just beneath the surface.

"But I have to say that seeing all of you here this morning, safe and recounting the miracles of the past night, has certainly blown away the shadows of doubt in my heart. Until another answer can be proven, I'm going on record as believing that the God of Israel and His Son, Jesus, sent the angels of heaven to take care of us all."

"Reverend Cain," Kupperman interrupted. "My sincerest apologies. In the confusion of all these events, we have committed the gravest of errors. I thought you had already been informed about your family. According to reports we have received from your country, Mrs. Cain is in serious, but stable condition in the hospital. She received gunshot wounds when your FBI stormed the church building in which she was being held hostage. You have a son also. He is well and uninjured. Please forgive us for not giving you this information sooner."

John felt his knees weaken. He took a deep breath and kept his eyes on the stone pavement in front of him. *Wounded. My Esther, wounded by gunfire!*

"You are certain she is out of danger?"

"That is the report we have received," Kupperman assured him. "Her condition is serious, but stable. As for your daughter, Jessica, I am sorry to say there is no news."

John closed his eyes and leaned back. He felt someone's hand touch his shoulder. He opened them again. It was Kupperman.

"We have everyone in Israel looking for her," he declared. "I am confident we will find her soon.

"It was only this morning that we became aware that she had been left behind. Your friends at the hospital told us when you were brought in. Our best reasoning is that she has been kidnapped by the same group that took you hostage.

"We have questioned the hotel personnel. However, one of them is missing. A desk clerk. He was last seen on the afternoon your bus left the hotel. Another clerk remembers a young girl coming to the desk and asking for assistance. She informed them that she had been left behind.

"The missing clerk told the girl that he would contact you as soon as you arrived at your next destination. He even provided her a room in which to rest until you came for her. About a half hour later, he told the other desk clerk that he had an errand to run. It is the last anyone has seen of either of them. We believe that this man is a member of the PIJ, the group that took you prisoner."

John stared for a long moment at the open doorway leading into the empty tomb. With a sigh, he stood to his feet.

"Let's join in a circle and thank God for bringing us together again, shall we? We have so much for which to be grateful." John looked over at Gerald Carson, who had been quietly observing these most unique of all events to ever occur in his garden. "We're on your turf this morning, my brother. Pardon us for barging in like this, but on behalf of everyone here, thank you for receiving us with such graciousness. Would you mind leading us in prayer? The God of Israel has been mighty good to all of us."

Mr. Carson beamed.

There in the garden, near the empty tomb, Jew and Gentile alike joined hands, offering up thanksgiving and praise to the Lord for His mysterious and wonderful works, and asking the Lord to watch over Jessica Cain.

The next four days passed quickly.

Imad Safti and Fathi Adahlah were taken into custody to await trial. Yazib Dudori and Pasha Bashera were acknowledged for their crimes, and their remains sent to Gaza for burial.

Evelyn Unruh's remains were transported to Tel Aviv and prepared for the flight home.

Gisele Eiderman, Edgar Anderson, and Bob Thomas were released from the hospital and reunited with their spouses. All of the hostages underwent thorough physical examinations at Hadassah, and were given clean bills of health. Telephone calls were made to reassure anxious family members at home.

John spoke with Jeremy. The report sounded worse than Kupperman had relayed. Esther was not being permitted any visitors other than Jeremy. Doctors were encouraged by her progress, but indicated that she was still not completely out of danger. Her eyes had opened once and it seemed as though she was aware of her surroundings. Then she slipped back into a comalike sleep. Her physicians were hopeful that this would change for the better in the next twenty-four to forty-eight hours. All vital signs were strong.

At first, John was torn between rushing home to be at Esther's bedside, and remaining in Israel to search for Jessica. *No one should have to make such a choice. What shall I do, Lord?* After talking with Jeremy, John decided to remain with the group until Saturday. In the meantime, he was determined to turn over every rock in Israel to find Jessica.

All of the Americans were interrogated at IDF and Mossad Headquarters. There were repeated interviews with the Israel Television Network, CNN, and numerous other radio, television, and newspaper reporters. *Time* and *Newsweek* prepared cover stories for their next editions.

The Israeli government provided chauffeured limousines, each with professional guides, to enable the group to visit the sites they had missed in and around Jerusalem. Armed security was always present. At first it was uncomfortable, but soon the Americans adapted and actually enjoyed finishing out the balance of their interrupted excursion. And this left John free to look for Jessica.

After several hours spent with Kupperman and other law enforcement personnel, however, it was becoming apparent to John that looking for Jessica was like trying to find a particular shooting star out in the heavens somewhere. It was not impossible. But to be successful, one needed to know what to do, where to look, and how to properly use all available resources.

It quickly became evident to John that he was unable to do this. He was a foreigner in a strange land, the victim of circumstances he did not fully comprehend. He fretted. He pounded desks. He apologized. His moods ran the gamut from hopefulness to utter despair. By Thursday, he was becoming resigned to the possibility that he might have to go home without her.

Late Thursday, the Knesset, Israel's parliament, met in special session to acknowledge the nation's gratitude to "the Americans who risked their lives in order to preserve the Western Wall, Israel's most holy site, and who, by their actions, restrained forces that might otherwise have drawn our nation into a grave military conflict with its neighbors." One hundred eighteen of the one hundred twenty members of the Knesset were present. All honored the Americans with a standing ovation. Some were later overheard to say that it was the first time Israel's parliament had ever been united on anything.

The special session was followed by a tour of the Knesset and a state dinner in the great hall where on other occasions leaders of the free world had dined, including an historic evening hosted by Golda Meir to honor her special guest, Anwar Sadat.

At last, weary and drained, John and his intrepid travelers were at Lod airport. It seemed to John that at least a year had passed since they had begun their Israel odyssey through this same port of entry.

Security was tight. Packages and suitcases were rummaged through in typical Israeli fashion. A large crowd of well-wishers had gathered in order to catch a glimpse of the Americans as they departed. Officials from both Jerusalem and Tel Aviv were present, though John was never quite sure who they were or what they represented. Media people followed them as far as security would allow.

John looked around, wishing he could say good-bye to David. He had sent David's wife flowers and a letter of condolence. Returning here would never be the same. He would miss his Jewish friend.

And Jessica!

He choked back his emotions at the thought of leaving the country without her. But he took solace in the realization that he could be back in a matter of hours. He knew that a grateful nation was leaving nothing undone in its efforts to recover the missing twelve-year-old daughter of their country's latest hero.

He had made the decision. He needed to be with Esther.

At last, the boarding call came.

John did not look back.

SAN FRANCISCO'S INTERNATIONAL AIRPORT was overrun with media and news personnel. The captain had been notified of the situation in advance of their arrival. After discussing it with John during the flight over, he radioed ahead to ask that someone take charge of preparing for a brief press conference. Airline personnel on the ground proceeded to make arrangements.

John and his group were taken off the plane even before first-class travelers were permitted to exit. The fact of their presence on board had quickly circulated among the passengers. For the most part, however, they had been left to themselves. Now, as they walked past others who politely remained seated, people reached out to touch them and offer congratulations. Spontaneous applause filled the cabin as John and his group waved good-bye.

The reunion of tour participants with family members took place in the V.I.P. lounge. When he entered, John saw Jeremy standing off to one side. They walked toward each other without a word, until they stood inches apart. Then they stopped, their faces struggling with emotion, both remembering the way they had parted two weeks earlier.

"I love you, Dad."

"I love you too, son!"

They threw their arms around each another in the biggest bear hug either of them could remember!

After a few minutes, John called for the group's attention. "Let's go, gang, and get this over with. The sooner we do, the sooner we get to go home. Next year in Jerusalem!"

A chorus of groans greeted the familiar old saying.

"Tonight in our own beds!"

Cheers and hoots filled the room in response.

Gradually, each person pulled away from their family members and formed up behind John in the way that had become so familiar during these past days.

"We're ready, pastor," a voice called from the back. "We'll follow you anywhere!"

"I think we just did!" another voice yelled back.

The rest laughed as John started through the door.

A cheer went up as John Cain emerged from the room, followed by the group that had set off, unnoticed, from this same location a couple of weeks earlier. Bulbs flashed. Cameras whirred. Questions were shouted. For the next twenty minutes, their faces and stories were carried across the nation on every major television network.

JOHN'S IMMEDIATE ASSESSMENT was that the man had a "good face." The lines spoke well of life experience. There was sadness in the eyes, but a twinkle too. And the lines around his mouth suggested that laughter lurked behind the timely concern that was now a part of his countenance. Here was a man who had touched life's sadness without being fatally wounded by it.

When they stepped off the elevator, the man's eyes were on Jeremy. He started forward, then hesitated, as though embarrassed at his intrusion.

"Dad, this is the man I told you about on the way home. Mr. Brainard, this is my father."

They shook hands, smiling at each other.

"I feel like an intruder, Reverend Cain," Grandpa said, stepping back, still sizing up this man whose face had become a familiar fixture in newspapers and on television during the past week. "But when I left to come out here, you were still missing and I just had to come. I know it sounds strange, but I felt that God wanted me to be here with your family for some reason. So I came."

John studied him for a moment, then reached out and and gave him a hug. When they stepped back each man's eyes glistened with emotion.

"I'm thankful that you came, Mr. Brainard."

"Call me Jim. Actually, most everybody calls me Grandpa, so take your pick."

"Okay, Jim. And my name is John."

"Thank you, John, and now I want to let you go. Your wife has been through as much as you have. I understand she's sleeping, but I'll bet she'll be glad to wake up and see your face!"

"Thanks. Stay here and I'll be back."

"I'll be here. In a convoluted kind of way, we have been together in this thing, even though we've never met before. I'm looking forward to getting better acquainted."

"So am I."

"I'll stay here with Grandpa," Jeremy offered.

"No, son, you go with your dad. This is a time when you should all be together."

They parted, John and Jeremy starting down the hall. Grandpa Brainard went back to his chair, and began thumbing through the sports pages to check on how his Red Sox were doing.

A NURSE OPENED THE DOOR to room 212 and then stood to one side. John stepped past her, with Jeremy following close behind. The sunlight streaming through the large, picture window reminded him of another hospital room, half a world away. Deja vu.

He walked to her bedside and stood quietly. A white

sheet covered her, gently following the contours of her slender form. Her eyes were closed. Her hair fell loosely across the pillow, accenting the pale face and lips visible above the sheet. Carefully, as though fearful that she might break, John reached out to touch her hand.

The nurse came around to the other side of the bed and bent close to Esther's ear.

"Mrs. Cain."

Esther stirred.

"Mrs. Cain. You have a very special visitor."

Esther's eyes fluttered. At first, she seemed unable to focus, and her eyes closed again. Then, all at once, eyes still closed, her face softened with awareness.

"John. O John, darling. You're home!"

Her eyes opened again, this time rimmed with moisture.

"Hi, sweetheart."

Esther moved her hand toward him, touching his cheek as he bent to kiss her lips.

"I love you, John."

"I love you too."

"I thought . . . for a while there, I thought I might never see you again."

John tenderly kissed her hand. A tear from his own eyes splashed on her wrist.

"Hi, Mom," Jeremy stood at the foot of the bed. "How are you feeling today?"

"O Jeremy, hi. Better now, that's for sure. Your dad is home!" Esther looked back at John. "You *are* home!"

Her face suddenly became serious. "Is there any word on Jessica?"

All the way home, flying across the Atlantic and the North American continent, John had wondered how much Esther knew of Jessica's situation. It was one of the first questions he asked Jeremy on the way home from the airport.

The story was in all the newspapers, Jeremy informed him, and on television too. The doctors had decided it would be best for her to be informed, once it was known that John and the others had been rescued. They waited until Friday, when she finally awoke from the deep sleep into which she had slipped on Monday. Then, with Jeremy present in the room, they had told her. Her response had been one of surprising inner strength, given her history of depression. Jeremy said that the doctors were very pleased.

"Everyone in Israel is looking for her," John replied, watching to see how she handled the news.

Her eyes closed and a tear squeezed past these entrances to her heart. When they opened again, she smiled up at John.

"I know God is watching out for her, darling."

Her fingers wrapped around John's hand.

John could not respond for fear of breaking up.

"Honey," she said, "try not to worry. I'm glad she was with you. Somehow God is going to be glorified in all this. Who can tell? If she had been here with us, she might have been killed."

John hadn't thought about that possibility before.

Jeremy sat in a chair on the opposite side of the bed.

John stroked Esther's hand, his eyes never leaving her face.

"I'm a different woman than when I saw you last," Esther said.

John certainly could not disagree. From all he had read and heard, there was no doubt that she was a heroine. And a look of serenity had replaced the tight lines that he remembered were there before he had gone away. His last sight of her leaving the airport, that haunting look of emptiness, had lurked in his memory every day until now.

"God has truly touched me. Like you, I've been to the edge and looked over. And now, I'm not afraid anymore. I'm not afraid of death. I'm not afraid of life either. I know that

God has to have some purpose in all of this, though I can't begin to understand what it might be. I've had to resign myself to His will.

"While we were being held there in the church, I didn't know what to do. I so desperately needed you to be there. When I realized they had taken you hostage too, I almost went crazy. There was only one thing that I had in my power. One thing they could not take away. Prayer.

"I began to pray, John. I had to place you and Jessica and Jeremy into God's hands. And myself and the rest of our people who were trapped there. Whatever was going to be, I knew that I could not control it. I could only trust God. There was nothing else.

"Darling, I don't think I can find the words to tell you what that act of surrender did for me. Later perhaps. Oh, I've lots to tell you about what has happened. Right now, though, I want to hear you tell me everything you've been through. Don't leave out a single detail! O John, I love you so!"

John gazed into Esther's eyes, trying to fathom the depths of her transformation. She was definitely a different woman.

It was not false bravado.

It felt genuine.

Gently, he took her in his arms and kissed her again.

JEREMY HAD NOT FILLED his father in with the personal crises through which he and his mother had lived, leading up to that fateful Sunday. He had thought about it on the way to the airport, and decided that would come later, if and when his mother chose to share it.

For now, watching the bedside reunion of his mother and father, it felt as though it was enough just to be together again.

Really together.

FORTY-NINE

It was eight o'clock, but Calvary Church was already packed to the doors. Normally it was the service with the smallest attendance of the day. Not this Sunday. Today people wanted to come early, to be there when Pastor John Cain returned to his flock.

Newspeople were in abundance, not a few of them comparing notes on the length of time since last they had been in an actual church service. Individual cameras had been checked with ushers, over the protests of news photographers, local gawkers, and tourists from out of town, all hoping to capture on film the residue of the previous weekend's hostage saga.

An arrangement with NBC, ABC, CBS, and CNN had resulted in a pool of equipment and crew, to provide for the nation this first gathering of a congregation following their unnerving experience at the hands of foreign terrorists.

Connie Farrer sat at one end of the third row from the front. Ushers had encouraged her to sit on the front pew so that her leg splint would have more room. She declined, still feeling self-conscious as a result of the notoriety she had experienced during the past few days. Jody Ansel sat next to her and beyond Jody, Mr. and Mrs. Tom Bernstein. Both Connie and Tom had notepads in their laps.

Always the reporters, thought Jody, smiling to herself.

Later in the evening, Tom was hosting a KFOR news special recapping the hostage events here in Baytown. It would be Channel 4's seven-thirty news lead-in, followed by an hour-long, prime-time NBC special called "September Strike!"

On the front row, side section, Jeremy and Allison sat together with John Cain and Allison's parents. Jeremy had asked Phil Heiden to join them. Sherri and their baby, Esther Suzanne, were at home this morning, watching on television. Many around them were curious as to the identity of the white-haired gentleman sitting next to John. No one seemed to know. Both John's and Esther's parents had flown to the Bay Area to be with their children and grandchildren. They sat in the row directly behind John and Jeremy. Jim Copeland, Sherri Heiden's father, was also present and sitting next to Phil. His wife, Suzanne, had stayed at home with Sherri and her new granddaughter.

Elizabeth Ralsten and her son, Geoff, were sitting next to Esther's parents. When they first arrived, they had slipped unobtrusively into seats near the back of the sanctuary. When someone mentioned to John that they were present, he asked Jeremy to go back and bring them forward to sit with their family. It was important to John to honor this woman and to publicly convey, both to her and to the other members of Calvary Church, that no ill will remained over Ken's and Geoff's actions. Ken had elected to stay at home, still too embarrassed over what he had done in his desperate need for self-preservation. John knew he would need to reach out to Ken very soon and help him begin the healing process.

Thelma Lunder and her daughter, Lucy, whose husband and father had been laid to rest on Tuesday afternoon, sat quietly in the pew beside Mrs. Orwell. Most of those returning from Israel with John had already experienced enough media mania to last them for a lifetime. They had opted for a later service, giving them the chance to sleep in. Edgar and Jill Anderson were there, however, just across the aisle from their pastor, still serving as silent spiritual bodyguards for this man they loved like a son.

At exactly eight o'clock, Terri White stepped to the pulpit and invited the congregation to stand. The choir entered from the rear doors, processing steadily down both center aisles and singing,

A mighty fortress is our God,
A bulwark never failing.

As the words echoed across the bullet-pocked sanctuary, the congregation spontaneously joined in the familiar words,

Our helper He amid the flood
of mortal ills prevailing.
For still our ancient foe
doth seek to work us woe —
His craft and power are great,
and, armed with cruel hate,
On earth is not His equal!

There were no dry eyes, not even among the most jaded newsmen.

The congregation was led in prayer by Edgar Anderson. In his simple, direct style, the former prizefighter gave thanks to God for His faithfulness. He asked the Lord to put His arms around Thelma and Lucy Lunder and Evelyn Unruh's family in these days of their sorrow. He asked the Lord to bring "our little Jessica" home quickly and safely. He prayed for the people of Arab descent, especially those who were suffering the present animosity of the world community, as a result of the actions of their radical Islamic brothers. He concluded by asking God to bring peace to Jerusalem.

As the people listened to this black man pray with such warmth and compassion, eyes moistened again; and those whose churchgoing experiences were rare, were surprised and a little embarrassed over the feeling level at which they found themselves responding.

People applauded when Phil Heiden stepped to the platform and told of the birth of their first child. They laughed and applauded again as he pointed out the exact location on the platform where his daughter had been born.

The network television program director shook his head in disbelief when Phil told the congregation that with Pastor Cain's encouragement, the church board had determined that today's offering would go to help those of Arab descent living in the Bay area, Christian or Muslim, who were jobless or faced with some other genuine human need.

To ensure against public criticism, he indicated that the offering would be counted by an independent group of Christian, Jewish, and Palestinian community leaders from the area, and deposited in a special fund to be administered independently from Calvary Church. Phil encouraged the community at large to join the members of Calvary Church by contributing to the fund in a symbolic act of reconciliation, Christian love, and goodwill.

Even the most cynical of these present began reaching into their pockets as the offering plates were passed. Tears were wiped again as the soloist sang,

> When peace, like a river attendeth my way,
> When sorrows like sea billows roll,
> Whatever my lot, Thou hast taught me to say,
> "It is well, it is well with my soul."

Then, as was his normal practice, without introduction

John Cain stepped to the platform and looked across the pulpit at the people who were gathered there before him. His arm remained immobile in its sling. The bruises on his face and neck were clearly visible, though the swelling around his eyes was almost gone.

As he opened his Bible, the congregation rose in unison and began a thunderous applause. Embarrassed, he looked down, gripping the pulpit, attempting to gather his emotions together. Then he held up a hand to quiet the people. The applause continued. Tears ran freely in a release of pent-up love, relief, and gratefulness to God for what He had done.

When the crowd finally quieted, they were still standing as Dr. Orwell walked up to where John stood and put his arm around his shoulder.

"Pastor," he said simply, "I think you can see that I speak for us all when I say, 'It's good to have you home.' I love you, John, as do we all. You've led us to our Lord and taught us how He would have us live, week after week, for the last twelve years. Last Sunday, I guess we all wondered if we would ever see each other again. It's much too early to sort out all the purposes that God may have had in mind in this. But I'll say it again, John, it's good to have you home!"

A chorus of "Amens," and "That's right," and "Welcome home, John," followed Dr. Orwell's heartfelt words.

More applause.

Then slowly, the people began to sit down.

"IT HAS BEEN an emotional roller coaster here this morning as the congregation welcomes its shepherd home," the announcer said softly to the live audience gathered around television sets in homes and in bars across America. "I don't know when I've ever felt anything quite like this before. At least not in a religious service. Let's go back to the sanctuary now and listen as Pastor John Cain speaks to his flock."

"THESE ARE THE WORDS of Jesus to all who would hear Him today," John began. "You will find them in the New Testament, in chapter six of Luke. I can think of nothing else this morning that is more important for us to hear.

" 'Love your enemies, do good to those who hate you, bless those who curse you, pray for those who mistreat you ... if anyone takes what belongs to you, do not demand it back. Do to others as you would have them do to you. If you love those who love you, what credit is that to you? Be merciful, just as your Father is merciful. Do not judge, and you will not be judged. Do not condemn, and you will not be condemned. Forgive, and you will be forgiven.' "

John paused and looked up from the Bible he held in his hand. Every eye was riveted on him, sensing his pain. Waiting.

He closed his Bible and laid it on the pulpit. With his hand, he made a sweeping gesture across the room.

"This is a sanctuary," he began, "a place dedicated to the worship of God. Last Sunday, for most of you who gathered here at the nine-thirty service, it began as a refuge from the grind, a sacred site where perspective could be regained and hope rekindled.

"But it was suddenly turned into a place where predators hunted without rules. What we consider precious they treated as profane. Cowardice and death took charge for a while, but heroism and honor won out. The bullet holes in the furniture and walls can be repaired. This carpet, stained with the blood of both victims and vanquished, can be replaced. Visitors will one day join us in worship and never know of the carnage that was here, unless we tell them.

"But you will remember," John said. "You *must* remember! Not so that you can hate, but so that you can love again."

John paused and let these words sink in. Then he continued. "I know what it feels like to want to kill." His voice became soft, his eyes sad. "On Jerusalem's Western Wall, I experienced feelings I had never known before. I was determined to kill. There was no other answer to my situation. Nor to yours here in this room. The brave men who set you free last Monday, and those who put their lives on the line for the city of Boston, had no other choice but to kill, so that you might live.

"But for a moment, I was truly frightened. Not because of the fearful circumstances. No. I was frightened because I actually *wanted* to kill. It burned like a fever in my body. I was angry at what had happened to all of the people for whom I felt such responsibility in Israel. I was angry at what I had heard was happening to you here at home and to the people of Boston. I wanted to hurt someone. Hurt them the way they had hurt those whom I loved."

The people listened attentively. They understood the way their pastor had felt. They were back in the worship service of the past Sunday and once more felt the fear. The anger. The disbelief. And for some, the desire to kill.

"Today, however, I am a different man than when you last heard me speak from this pulpit. I am forever changed. I understand, as never before, that we cannot remain isolated and insulated from the rest of the world. Ordinary people like you and me are affected by the extraordinary circumstances of our time.

"I can no longer see a rock thrown or a peacekeeping soldier die without being moved. I cannot look at those who hunger without doing something to help feed them. I cannot see the faces of missing children on milk cartons without praying for them. I cannot let the rest of the world go to hell morally, physically, or spiritually, and say, 'It's not my problem. There's nothing I can do.' It is a problem that belongs to us all, and we must all do something about it!

"I am still learning what it means to love my enemy. I thought I used to know. That's when my 'enemy' was someone who disagreed with me or treated me spitefully in the church. That was another life. Now, I've discovered I am unable to resist passively. Not when innocent people are endangered and killed. I'm sorry. I wish I could turn the other cheek more effectively, but as yet, I cannot. There is one thing that is true, however. I *am* learning not to hate.

"The psalmist wrote, 'O Israel, put your hope in the Lord, for with the Lord is unfailing love and with Him is full redemption.' Let me urge you, dear friends, to discover the 'unfailing love' and the 'full redemption' of our great God."

John continued speaking quietly, yet every word was clear and distinct. The resonant tones in his voice struck chords of response in the hearts of his listeners. He commended the people for their courage. He told them of Esther's progress in the hospital. He consoled the Lunder and Unruh families and promised to visit all those who had been wounded or who were still in the hospital after last Sunday's incident.

He acknowledged Jim Brainard, told of the crucial role he had played in Boston and of the "leading of the Lord" that brought this Roman Catholic layman to the side of the Cain family.

Then he asked them to keep Jessica in their prayers. This was the only time he acknowledged the presence of the television cameras.

"Wherever you are in the world, if you know of Jessica's whereabouts, I ask you to contact me so that we can make plans for her safe return home. And, Jessica, if through some miracle, you are watching . . . " John paused and drew a deep breath. The cameras panned to the audience, to faces wet with tears. "Remember, Jessica, your mother and dad love you with all our hearts, and God loves you even more."

The camera pulled in until John's face filled the screen.

"Look at that," the program director breathed softly.

John was smiling!

EPILOGUE

The night was cool, with just the slightest touch of a breeze. Stars stood out like tiny torchlights against the black sky, and the half moon attested irrevocably to the presence of the big dipper, suspended there in the heavens, above their heads.

John and Esther, wrapped cozily in long, white pool robes, leaned back into the patio chairs. Her hand reached out to his. He smiled and covered it with his own.

His arm sling had been discarded two weeks earlier. The dark bruises on his face were mostly reddish now, some completely gone. A small scar remained visible under his right eye, a reminder of the traumatic events of more than a month ago.

On this quiet evening in late October, low garden lights cast their inviting glow, blending lacy shadows in among the flowers and trees around the pool. The pool lit like this was still a favorite scene for John.

He glanced again at Esther.

She was looking up into the night sky, smiling.

"What's the smile about, darling?"

Esther didn't move or shift her gaze.

"See that moon? And those stars? When I see them, I feel as though we are close to her. Somewhere, this very night, our little girl has been looking up at that same moon and those same stars."

John squeezed her hand. She turned toward him, her eyes bright.

"I know she is alive, John. I just know it!"

"I believe it too, darling. I don't understand how or why the Lord permitted this to happen. Of all the people not to make it safely home from Israel, it had to be the eldest and the youngest. I can't see any purpose in it. I'm afraid for her. But I know she is alive. I can't tell you how, but I know it."

They looked up at the stars.

"Remember me telling you about stumbling into Amsterdam's red-light district with Jessica?" Both of them laughed. "She was determined to pray for that one particular girl."

"For a little girl, she does have a great heart for people," Esther agreed.

"What I didn't think to mention to you before is that the next morning, Jessica and I went to Anne Frank's house. I wanted her to see it. It was like I had this great need to take her. At the time, I thought it was just to give her a better perspective on the Dutch people than she had gotten the night before. Now I'm not so sure."

"What do you mean?"

"She's been taken prisoner, that is for certain. For all we know, she may be held somewhere all by herself." John halted, clearing his voice as it broke with emotion. "Sometimes, I can hardly stand the idea of her being there without us."

"I know. A year ago, this would have destroyed me," said Esther, pensively.

"Now, I think perhaps God led me to take Jessica to

Anne Frank's hiding place. I wish you could have seen her. She was so taken by it all, not fearful in any way, just deeply moved. Maybe, when she thinks about Anne Frank, that little girl's episode will help her take courage."

"You may be right. I've been drawn to the Apostle Paul's words these past few days, 'And we know that in all things God works for the good of those who love Him.' Maybe that experience will help her."

Esther went on. "The other words of Paul that have been like a personal promise to me since this all came about are these. 'And the peace of God, which transcends all understanding, will guard your hearts and your minds in Christ Jesus.' When I look at our circumstances, part of me feels as though I have been torn apart. And yet, this entire experience has given me strength that I've never known before. And amazing as it seems, I'm more at peace than I have been in months.

"When I think about Jessica, which is most of the time, I have the feeling that she may be in danger, but that she is alive." She paused, reaching out to grip John's hand. "O John, what are we going to do? How will we ever find her?"

"I don't know. I honestly don't know. But as soon as we get any word as to her whereabouts, I will go after her."

"I'm going too!"

"We'll see about that when the time comes. Right now, you've got to get over your wounds completely."

Esther stood and began untying the belt around her robe.

"What are you doing?"

"While you were gone, I had a very special time in prayer with the Lord. In it, He let me see how much He loved our Jenny. And how much He loves us all. I have truly been in a healing mode ever since. The most deadly wound that I've been carrying all this time . . . well . . . the Lord has brought total healing. But there's one thing that I used to do that I've not done since Jenny died."

John sat perfectly still, watching and listening.

"For so long, I was not able to forgive myself. I felt so responsible for her death. I had no joy and there were no tears. Everything was locked up and I couldn't get it out. You remember how we used to come out here and enjoy our yard and the pool ... I loved swimming with you and the children. But I lost all that when Jenny died. I couldn't bear even to come out here. And from inside the house, I used to watch you standing here at the edge of the pool. I felt your terrible pain, my darling, and my guilt just became greater."

"I'm sorry," John said, reaching his hand toward her. "I've never blamed you. It was a horrible accident, that is all. It was no more your fault than mine. It just happened, and only God knows why."

"I know, love. I knew it intellectually a long time ago. It was my heart that could not accept what had happened. Can you forgive me for the way that I've been these past months?"

"Of course, I can. I do. And will you forgive me for not being as sensitive as I should have been concerning where you were in all this? I was too wrapped up in my own hurt. I failed to be there for you."

Esther smiled.

"You are forgiven. I put all that away weeks ago. But it is part of the healing process to be able to talk like this. Thank you, dear."

"For what?"

"For coming home, safe and sound. For being my husband. My best friend. My lover."

She dropped the robe into the chair and walked to the edge of the pool.

"Be careful," John cautioned. "The bullet wounds have barely had time to heal."

She turned to face him and held her hands out, away from her body. Her hair was already growing back over the shallow head wound. In the low garden lights, he could see the other small scars, mute testimony to her narrow escape. She smiled. Then without a word, she turned back to the water.

When she dove, hardly a ripple broke the surface.

John watched as she swam, slowly and easily to the far end. Then, turning toward him, she started back.

So graceful. So relaxed and beautiful. Like a gazelle.

John laid his robe on the chair and stepped in to meet her.

They stood in the water, inches apart, eyes on each other.

"She is October's child, you know," Esther said softly.

"What?"

"Jessica. Her birthday is July 23. That makes her October's child."

John looked at her for a moment, puzzled, then slowly nodded and smiled with understanding.

Their lips touched.

Hand in hand, they walked up the pool steps and out of the water and dried off in their robes.

Tenderly, they embraced under the half moon and the Big Dipper and the starry heavens.

Then they went inside.

Where is she?
What has happened to
October's Child?

Jessica was positive that her eyes were open.

So why couldn't she see anything?

She shut them again, felt her eyelids press tightly together, then opened once more, just to be sure.

I must be in bed.

No. It was too hard.

Did I fall out of bed onto the floor?

Her head throbbed with each pounding heartbeat, forcing a wince of pain.

She lay perfectly still, trying to gather her surroundings into her senses, straining to see something.

Anything.

But, there was nothing.

No light in the window.

No stars in the sky.

Only the darkness.

And, the voices.

At first they were nothing more than a quiet murmur. Jessica could not make out what was being said. She closed her eyes again, pushing everything out of her mind. Her head was swirling. She felt groggy.

Still, the voices remained. Low. Distant. Unintelligible. Their words seemed strangely ... foreign!

Maybe Daddy's watching television in the other room.

As she listened, they grew louder. It sounded like an argument. Though she could not understand what they were saying, Jessica was able to recognize the language.

They're talking in Arabic.

But, how do I know. . . ?

Slowly, the mental cobwebs melted into the darkness and memories began flooding in.

The bus.

The tour group had left their hotel in the bus.

Without me!

Her thoughts were jumbled, running together in a kaleidoscope of nondefinable patterns, as she tried to grasp that slippery, incomprehensible fact. It did not make any sense.

Why? How could they have failed to see that I was not in the bus? I always sit in the front seat. The one nearest the door.

All at once, fear tore through her stomach, clawing and flaying at her insides. Jessica tried sitting up, but, for some reason, she couldn't.

What's the matter with me? Why can't I get up? If only I could see . . .

Questions.

They danced randomly across her mind, like pirouetting ballerinas, then scattered abruptly and disappeared, as though whisked away by some invisible magician's hand.

That's when the realization hit her!

She couldn't move because she was bound from head to foot. Packaged for delivery. Wrapped with tape like an Egyptian mummy!

Now, totally stricken with fear that rose inside her like a giant ocean wave, Jessica shut her eyes and cried out for help. A moment later, the wave of fear that had been building, came crashing down inside her brain. She heard only muffled sounds. No words traveled beyond her lips. Tape covered her mouth too, barricading her cry against its escape.

Just then, a motor started up.

A door slammed.

Seconds later, she could feel herself moving. It dawned on her. She was not in a room at all, but rather in some sort of vehicle.

Is this a truck? Maybe that's why the air is so stale.

She bounced helplessly with each bump or pothole in the

road as the vehicle lumbered along, gathering speed as it went.

Panic pierced her brain.

Fright played the bogeyman in the darkness.

Who are these people? Where are they taking me? What are they going to do to me? Daddy! Where are you?

But Daddy did not answer.

Jessica's unprotected head banged painfully against the truck bed as the roar of the engine, the scraping of gears, and the sounds of wheels on pavement filled her mind with such terror that she began convulsing involuntarily. Instinctively, she fought back the bile that threatened to erupt from her stomach, realizing, as she did, that she could choke to death if she didn't get control.

Concentrate. For goodness sake, don't throw up!

Jessica closed her eyes tightly. Slowly, the panic receded. She breathed deeply through her nose. Again. Again. She felt her hammering heart.

O God. How can this be happening?

The nightmarish horror of her predicament came rushing in with sickening force. Her worst fears were being realized. She had always been careful never to get into compromising or dangerous situations. Yet, in spite of this, here it was.

I want to go home. Daddy, where are you? Mom, oh, please, help me?

In this darkness on wheels, so far from the home she desperately wished for, Jessica's youthful ebullience and enthusiasm for adventure disappeared. It was history. Instead, consuming terror stalked through her mind like a character from the late-night horror movie she had stayed up to watch with her friends at Doris' slumber party last summer. Reality suddenly became more terrible than any monster that had ever lived beneath her bed, waiting to carry her off into the night.

Tears broke free, running unchecked into her hair and ears, as the silent screams of all the world's missing children fought to escape her lips.

Twelve-year-old Jessica Cain knew she was being kidnapped.

John and Esther leave no stone unturned in their effort to find Jessica before it is too late. But, in the end, it is up to the young seventh-grader from California, now a prisoner in a foreboding land, to gather the courage to resist those who would barter her for politics and power.

By chance, Jessica overhears a man with a scar on his cheek tell those gathered in the next room that she is to be offered for ransom and then killed. She is frightened even more as she listens to the description of a secret terrorist plot that will strike at the heart of America.

She desperately wants to tell someone who can help. But, who can she trust and who would believe her anyway? After all, she is only a child.

Caught in a web of international intrigue, she awaits her opportunity to dash for freedom. And, while she waits, she is faced with the mysteries and contradictions of both Islam and Christianity. Faith and practice are matters close to Jessica's young heart. But, staying alive may force her to break the rules.

Thus, the hunters and the hunted begin a deadly game against overwhelming odds. It is a game of hide and seek that twists and turns from Israel's ancient countryside to the veiled land of Iran, from the Suez Canal to the battle-scarred mountains of once proud Yugoslavia.

Jessica desperately struggles against forces bent on destroying both her and the world that is her future. Her courage and daring lead her into a labyrinth of danger, as the dark shadow of a master terrorist looms ever closer.

Marwan Dosha becomes her nemesis, a man obsessed with a diabolical mission of revenge and assassination that threatens to bring the world to the brink of utter chaos and destruction.

He knows that she knows his secret.

Now, he must stop her from telling it to anyone.

Left with nothing but a child's simple faith and untested ingenuity that is fueled with a desperate desire to survive, Jessica Cain fights back in the only way she knows how.

She must hide. She must run. And, whatever else, she must stay out of reach of the man with the scar on his cheek.

Watch for
October's Child
Coming in Summer 1995